STRAW
HOUSE

WOOD
HOUSE

BRICK
HOUSE

BLOW

STRAW HOUSE
WOOD HOUSE
BRICK HOUSE
BLOW

DANIEL NAYERI

ILLUSTRATED BY
JAMES WEINBERG

CANDLEWICK PRESS

Copyright © 2011 by Daniel Nayeri
Illustrations copyright © 2011 by James Weinberg

First edition 2011

Library of Congress Cataloging-in-Publication Data

Nayeri, Daniel.
Straw house, Wood house, Brick house, Blow / Daniel Nayeri. —1st ed.
p.   cm.
Summary: A collection of four novellas in different genres, including a western about a farmer who grows living toys and a rancher who grows half-living people; a science fiction story of the near-future in which the world is as easy to manipulate as the Internet; a crime story in which every wish comes true and only the Imaginary Crimes Unit can stop them; and a comedic love story in which Death describes himself as a charismatic hero.
ISBN 978-0-7636-5526-6
[1. West (U.S.)—Fiction. 2. Science fiction. 3. Mystery and detective stories—Fiction. 4. Love—Fiction. 5. Short stories.]   I. Title.
PZ7.N225Str 2011
[Fic]—dc22   2011013675

11 12 13 14 15 16 MVP 10 9 8 7 6 5 4 3 2 1

Printed in York, PA, U.S.A.

This book was typeset in Melior.
The illustrations were created digitally and with ink.

Candlewick Press
99 Dover Street
Somerville, Massachusetts 02144

visit us at www.candlewick.com

To Alexandra:
you shine

CONTENTS

TOY FARM

He had built his whole house out of straw.
Can you believe it? I mean who in his right
mind would build a house of straw?
— **Big Bad Wolf, *The True Story of the 3 Little Pigs!***
Jon Scieszka

THE SUN WAS faithful again that morning, rising above the farm with a shine so fresh it tasted like gazpacho. The birds sat in the trees, ignorant of the wickedness of grown men, and sang a fluty trill. When their song ended, the tape rewound and they sang it again.

The daisies in the window boxes opened their petals and spun like pinwheels. From way out behind the red barn, a tardy rooster—in need of a winding—eventually called out a salutation. The wooden cuckoo owls in the eaves of the barn, rattled out of sleep, exhaled their hoots like complaints. A poor real-life bee had wandered somehow onto the farm and confused itself. It bumped its rear end into the painted smiley faces of the toy flowers. With delicate plastic petals, they enfolded the bee as real flowers would, but it was little consolation for no pollen. That morning the whole farmhouse seemed to yawn and whine as it sat on the high-tide hill.

On the nearby porch, a sleeping Pup began to stir. When he took notice of the irritated bee, he switched on and bounded toward the window box. Pup ran a few excited circles. He went: *bark bark bark* and then did a backflip. Then *bark bark bark* again and another backflip. The bumblebee flew away with a noticeable wobble. Pup chased after it, toward where the farmer walked in the early dawn light.

As Pup bounced across the planted furrows, he seemed to forget about the intruder. The dewy mounds of dirt were shaking off sleep, wiggling like wet dogs and shivering in the breeze. Pup stuffed his nose into one of the mounds. Its brown bud poked out of the soil, probably the makings of an ear. Pup trembled with the desire to dig it up, but he knew the farmer wouldn't allow it. Several rows down, a stubby black stalk was the jumper of the season, already grown out a full two inches. Pup ran over to investigate and barked for the farmer to come see. The plastic tube widened as it rose and from above looked hollow. Under it ran a long set of bumps below the surface — equidistant cars of a train.

As the shadow of the farmer walked across the furrow, back to the house, the stalk made a muffled *toot-toot* from its underground locomotive. And the black caboose puffed its first little cloud.

Never in need of winding, the dawn had grown into day. Pup ran to the fence at the edge of the rows, where a scarecrow leaned back on a post with his arms splayed out, his head drooping below his shoulders. He wore a straw hat, the shape of a tepee with a wide languid brim, and his nose looked like the beak of an old woodpecker: long, sharp, then suddenly bent. His pants were cut off at the ankles and frayed into loose hay.

Sunny was young in the face. His neck was kneaded and long, as though he'd been choked to death. Pup hunkered down at his foot and barked as loud as he could. Sunny was his partner. When Sunny shifted his weight from one bare foot to the other, Pup thought they were both moving. He darted out ten yards, realized Sunny hadn't followed, and scampered back to Sunny's feet. Finally, with a snort, Sunny jerked his head up. Pup barked. They could hear the scuffles and bleats in the barn, the animals ready to be fed and let out. Pup barked again. "I know," said Sunny. "I know. Shut up."

Sunny squinted at the sun. He'd overslept again. He heard the defiant caw of a crow, perched on the fence a few posts down, but didn't care enough to shoo it away. The farmer had already disappeared into the house. Sunny lifted his sleeve up to his mouth and pulled out a piece of straw to chew on. At his feet, he saw a tin cup full of coffee. Dot must have left it for him before starting her chores. Sunny was new to coffee and still preferred it with five tablespoons of sugar and so much cream it was the color of straw. Sunny picked it up and took a sip. It looked placid and lukewarm.

Somehow, the stale nature of his drink seemed purposeful to Sunny, as though Dot was nagging him for sleeping too much. Sunny threw the rest of the drink onto the ground and set the cup on top of the fence post.

As soon as Pup settled back down, Sunny pushed off from his fence post and walked toward the pasture, on the other side of the farmhouse. From what he could tell, it was a beautiful morning, with beautiful feelings everywhere. The whole world was waking up toyful and bright, with a growing feeling that everything was going everybody's way. Sunny looked down at Pup squirreling along ahead of him. He tried to spit at Pup's head—nothing came out. He said, "Aw, hell," because he didn't much like everybody, and he didn't like their way.

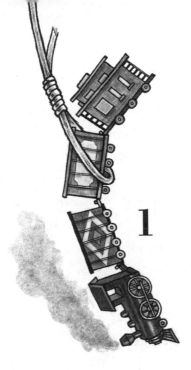

1

THE FARM ITSELF wasn't much but a couple buildings on the wide country plain. About two days' canter to town, half day at a panicked ride. Behind the plains was a bluff and behind that a shadow of a mountain, but no one knew anybody who'd been that far.

The farm sat by itself, some trees and a creek to the immediate west, and hills and hills and hills the rest. The farmhouse sat atop a rise, with its porch like a bowl haircut. In front of it was the empty hundred-yard pasture, cordoned off by the split-rail fence and the dirt road beyond that. On the other side of the road was the first outcrop of trees, then the creek. The red barn with the chicken coop behind it sat to one side of the farmhouse, the vegetable garden to the other. And behind the house, in the east where the sun was sure to hit first, were the rows. The rows were precious. Nobody went there but the farmer, who walked them in the early light. And Sunny.

Of course, the plains were empty, so nobody was really around to trespass the rows. But if they did, Sunny was there to scare them off. And Pup was there to back him up.

After they crossed the empty pasture and arrived at the split-rail fence, Sunny threw a rock at the ornery crow that'd followed them, and Pup conserved energy by sitting stock-still like a show dog. He had a way of yammering that sounded like a cicada, then he'd suddenly remember to save some for later and go into standby. He used to be Boy's dog, since they'd come up in the same harvest, but Boy had left him on outside once and Pup had nearly run himself to death. Sunny had found him the next morning fallen over in the pasture, lying on his side and kicking his feet in tired spasms. So Pup learned from that day to keep still. Plus he never left Sunny and steered clear of Boy.

Pup had a proprietary notion about Sunny's right foot, and as soon as Sunny took up his position on the fence, Pup took up his on the foot. Soon Sunny could hear the low hum and rattle of Pup in sleep mode. The soft part of Pup's warm belly lay across the straw bundle, and his appendages splayed out in all four directions. Sunny knew the belly was warm because that was where the battery went, under the shaggy fabric. Sunny shifted his weight to his left foot, then slowly lifted Pup with his right. The little dog's paws drew in as his body rose from the dirt, like a banana peel picked up from the middle. His head dangled to one side, his tongue the other. Sunny held him in the air awhile, but Pup didn't stir other than the belly breaths and a few distant yips to ward off bad dreams. Sunny eased his foot back down. Pup's legs spread out again into a furry starfish.

A whistling breeze swept through the straw in Sunny's shirt. A bristling wheeze. The last scratches of winter seemed content to stir dust in an empty pasture, chill one young man and his sleeping dog, then draw against the sun and die. The tall grass seemed to wave good-bye.

"Hey, Sunny!" said the farmer's daughter. "You gonna let those poor animals outta the barn or what?" She stood on the porch steps, shouting across the hundred-yard pasture. Her hair was auburn, tied in a ponytail. Her eyes were the color of fresh basil. "Or you just gonna mill around all day?" she added.

"No," said Sunny.

"What?" said the farmer's daughter. Sunny often mumbled when he spoke to her.

"I said, no, Dot, I ain't gonna mill around all day." They called her Dot, short for daughter.

"Good," shouted Dot. "I know you're givin' up your foot in the noble pursuit of a nappin' dog and all, but I could use your help."

Her low opinion of his usefulness rankled Sunny. He ground the straw in his mouth into a thousand hairs. He brought a shirtsleeve up to his mouth and pulled out another piece. As he did, he peered down the road. The previous evening, Sunny had spotted a stranger, now still just a speck on the horizon. But soon he'd walk by on the road, bringing news of town. Sunny turned back to the farmer's daughter. She was tapping her foot on the porch step. "I'm waiting for that stranger," he said.

Dot crossed her arms. "And you can't do both?"

Sunny shook his head no.

"Oh, I get it," said Dot. "You're gonna protect us."

"Somebody's gotta do it," said Sunny.

"And somebody's gotta let the stock out."

Sunny smiled. "Guess that'd be you."

Dot marched across the pasture, toward the red barn, all the while glaring at Sunny.

Fifteen minutes later, she stamped back across the pasture, toward her vegetable garden. She didn't look at Sunny. "Aw, hell," said Sunny, under his breath.

As she disappeared over the crest of the hill, she shouted, "Told you so."

Sunny already hated the stranger, who had a hobble and was taking forever. The man would have been tall if he stood up straight, maybe even two rakes high. His torso was normal, but he had legs like a stilt man at a fair, with as much meat to them as regular legs, only stretched like saltwater taffy.

To walk, the stranger had to jut out his knee to the side and extend one long leg forward. Then he'd swing his body over the extended leg, pivot out to the side, and extend the next leg forward. As a result, he winced constantly at the hyperextension of his knees as he bobbed up and down along his stride. He wore trousers up to his underarms, a plaid shirt, and a mangy corduroy cap. His arms weren't particularly long, considering his lower portion's proportions, and his goatee was equal parts black and white.

About thirty yards off, the stranger looked up and caught Sunny peering at him. He raised his hand in the air. Sunny looked down at his feet and kept his arms crossed. Pup woofed from their side of the fence, did a couple backflips, then hid behind Sunny.

When the stranger finally shambled up the road, Sunny kept silent and picked at the straw in his sleeve. Then he crossed his arms and tilted his hat, like a sleepy gunslinger, in the hopes of look-ing burly.

"Hola, chacho," said the lanky old man, stretching his lower back and grimacing.

"I ain't a chacho. Where you come from?" asked Sunny, without turning.

"Mami and Papi, like everyone else," said the stranger. "All of us chachos, yeah?"

Sunny couldn't tell if the man was making fun of him or being careless the way old men are of young men's pride. The stranger chuckled as he reached in his pocket and pulled out an orange. The stranger had thick jagged fingernails, the color of fossils, with cracks in them like old bars of soap. As they talked, the old man staked the orange on a forefinger and spun it in both directions across the nails of his other hand. His mangled claw stripped the orange peel like a lathe.

"I suggest you ride on through," said Sunny. He didn't care about news anymore. He just wanted the stranger gone.

"Are you the only farm around here?" asked the old man. He began scraping the orange clean of the veins and skin.

"We can protect ourselves," said Sunny.

"Easy, chacho," said the stranger, tossing an orange segment to Pup. "I look for work."

Sunny snorted. Pup licked at the fruit with a woolen tongue, then swallowed it whole.

Field hands didn't come around much. People in town usually told 'em not to ask Sunny 'cause he always said no, and there wasn't much else this direction. Sunny looked the man up and down. The stranger straightened himself for inspection, wiped a hand over his goatee.

Sunny wondered for a second what it'd be like to live all those years with legs like split rails.

"What can you do that I can't do better, old man? Besides mounting a velocipede."

"Being old is something," said the stranger. He didn't seem irritated, which irritated Sunny.

"Yeah, it's something, all right," said Sunny.

"My name is El Sobrino del Mago," said the man with a little bow. He lifted his corduroy cap and some dust wafted out.

"I don't care," said Sunny.

"You call me Sobrino for short."

"Or nothin'."

"Mago mean 'magician.'" From Sobrino's mouth, it came out "majeecian."

"You deaf?"

"No."

"Then shut up. I said I don't wanna call you nothin'," said Sunny.

Sobrino took a gangly step back to get a different look at the young man as he put the last orange wedge in his mouth. Some liquid sluiced into his goatee, escaping through the toothless gaps in his mouth. Sobrino's teeth weren't in any better shape than his fingernails. In the silence of their stares, Pup did another backflip.

"You are rude to me, no?" said Sobrino. He sucked through his teeth at a piece of pulp. It made a rattler's hiss.

"I can be any way I please, stranger," said Sunny. Something metallic in Sunny's sleeve caught the light and glinted at the old man. "You're trespassing," added Sunny.

"Ah, not yet," said Sobrino, pointing at the fence.

"The deed extends to the oak," said Sunny, nodding at the tree on the far side of the dirt road. Sobrino looked over his shoulder at the tree, then back at Sunny, then down at his hand. Sunny had pulled a throwing dart from his sleeve and held it like a knife. The metal arrow was as sharp as a surgeon's needle, with a blue and red flight at the base.

Sobrino put his hands in his trouser pockets and glanced up the deserted road he'd come by. Then he said, "No."

Sunny leaned forward, in case he misheard, and in case he needed to jump the fence.

"No, the farm don't end there, or no, you ain't leavin'?"

"No, you cannot be however you please," said Sobrino.

"'Cause I'll chop you down, you hobo-lookin' Paul-el-Bunyan."

"For asking to work?"

"For being cute."

"No one has called me cute before."

"Don't be cute. I ain't your taco amigo."

The old man turned his head and looked at Sunny with one eye, then turned and looked with the other. Sunny tensed, because he was barely eighteen years old, and he'd never been in a real fight.

Sobrino suddenly sprang forward. Sunny stumbled backward over Pup, who let out a pitiful yelp. Sunny righted himself and thrust the dart in front of him like a knife. Sobrino was leaning over the fence now, imposing himself into Sunny's space. Sunny's hand shook. "Shut up!" he screamed, even though Sobrino hadn't said anything.

Finally, Sobrino leaned back again and bared a muddy grin. Sunny couldn't decide whether the man's smile was alarming because he was dishonest or because he was old and ugly. Pup was afraid. He rolled over and showed his belly. The old man nodded at the dart Sunny was holding and said, "That? I got ten of that." He scraped one hand across the fence post. The pine ribboned under his nails.

Sunny switched the dart to his other hand. He said, "You ain't welcome here."

"I should be," said Sobrino. "Is your house?"

"It's the farmer's," said Sunny, "but I'm the right hand, Sunny."

"Aha . . . Sony." The way he said it, it rhymed with phony. "Sony the sheriff of the farm."

"You could say that," said Sunny, still gripping the dart and shifting from toe to toe.

"I do say that, Sony the sheriff. 'Cause I going to like you, Sony. You and me will be, what you call it? Amigos rancheros."

"Why?" said Sunny.

"You are the only sheriff."

"Me and the farmer's daughter."

"Is she like you?"

"Like me? Like what? Mean and whatnot?"

"No, like you, a straw man," said Sobrino.

"Why, you got a lighter or something?" said Sunny. He stepped well out of reach, in case the old man had something to burn him with.

Sobrino showed his dirty palms. "Easy, easy, chacho."

Sunny put his outmatched dart back into his sleeve and put a piece of straw in his mouth in the same motion. He ground on it like a fingernail, then got another one. He was embarrassed for having yelled "shut up" before. Sunny turned to walk back up the pasture toward the farmhouse. He said over his shoulder, "If the farmer's daughter ain't got work, you gotta leave."

Sobrino hollered after him, "No problem, boss. I pick the best peaches, from high up, yeah?"

Sunny rounded the hill toward the vegetable garden, where the farmer's daughter was working. He spat hard and said, "Aw, hell," under his breath.

2

THE VEGETABLE GARDEN wasn't more than a dozen acres, bordered by alfalfa from some years back that kept coming up every year on its own ambition. The farmer's daughter worked it alone, with Sunny helping out during picking season. Wasn't one of those industrial outfits, like the thousand-acre corn kingdoms you heard about in town.

Leeks and cabbages. Tomatoes and garlic. Squash and cauliflower. Almost in that order. The farmer's daughter could grow anything, just about. People in town said she was gifted from the ground up, her with eyes the color of fresh basil.

She'd kept them in turnips and beets all winter, which Sunny and the toys didn't have much use for, but they used the crops to barter for batteries, spare lightbulbs, and touch-up paint. They always ran out of cherry red when the RC fire trucks came up in the summer and drove around crazy in the gravel.

Sunny stepped through the alfalfa onto the freshly tilled soil. His foot sank into the cool dirt, which he didn't feel but knew was cool because it was moist. Pup struggled to climb over the furrows and yapped for Sunny to wait up. Sunny reached down and scooped him up.

In the middle of the garden, the farmer's daughter was leaning under the hood of a green tractor. Sunny knew there was nothing under the hood but an empty compartment, even though the whole thing was the same size as a real tractor. Boy was sitting in the driver's seat, pressing the big round "On" button with both hands. He was dressed, like always, in the full dress uniform of a military cadet. The undershirt was painted on, but the rest of his clothes were inter-changeable. The brass buttons on his cuffs, epaulets, breast pockets, and down his chest made up a substantial part of him.

The tractor's body was one big green molded piece of plastic, but the big tires in the back were real rubber. The front tires turned on their axle as a single unit. The dash was just the big red "On" button and a black steering wheel. On the back of the tractor, there was a ring about the size of a Hula-Hoop.

"I hate this tractor," the farmer's daughter said as Sunny approached. "You hear me, tractor? I hate your pull-'n'-play guts. You damn ten-token bargain-bin carnival prize."

Boy laughed and put all his weight into pushing the button. He didn't weigh much, but he was the right size of a six-year-old. "It can't hear you like I can," said Boy. "It's just a tractor."

The farmer's daughter tried to slam the hood down, but it had one of those magnetic latches in the front, where you push down to make it pop up. So it came up. She slammed it again. It still didn't catch. She reached up and put a loose strand of hair behind her ear. Her other hand was on her hip.

"I'm gonna melt this thing and put it in the attic, Sunny."

Boy mewled at the mention of the attic. He sat back in the tractor and moved his wrists in circles. If ever anyone mentioned the chest of cast-off toys in the barn attic, he'd rotate his wrists and roll his fingers like he was playing piano. To have so many points of articulation, working ones, showed he was high quality, and he wasn't broken. He had a fine white military hat, and the black bill had chipped a little, but he wasn't no broken tractor.

"Farmer wouldn't like that," said Sunny as he dropped Pup on the ground.

"Tell him to grow 'em with engines, then."

"Springs loose?"

"No."

"Got you this far."

"Two lines in two hours."

Sunny watched her walk to the back of the tractor and grab the big ring. The front hood was still open like a hungry, hungry hippo. Sunny walked over to see if the latch had snapped where she'd slammed on it.

"Met that drifter I told ya about," said Sunny.

"Is he just traveling through?"

"You could say that," said Sunny. He wasn't in a hurry to tell her about the standoff. He saw that the latch was busted, with the magnetic head snapped clean off.

"He still around?"

"Yep."

"Well, which is it? He staying or leaving?"

"He's looking for work."

The farmer's daughter yanked on the ring and propped one boot up on the tractor to get a better foothold. Sunny pulled out his dart, then untied the piece of twine he used as a belt. He pulled the twine over a notched part of the metal arrow and yanked to make two pieces. He threaded the smaller piece of twine through the latch on the tractor. He brought down the hood and tied it off tight. The farmer's daughter growled as she yanked hard on the ring. Neither paid attention to Boy, who was leaning over the back of the tractor, saying, "Pull it to the left, Dot."

Sunny tied the larger piece of twine back around his waist.

"We don't have any work," said Dot.

"I told him," said Sunny.

"What'd he say?"

"He wondered if I was the farmer. I said no. He said ask the farmer."

"What'd you say?"

"Said I'd ask you."

"We don't have work."

"Pull it to the right," said Boy.

"Come help me with this," said the farmer's daughter.

Sunny went around to the back of the tractor. Pup left the bulb he had been digging up.

"He's real old," said Sunny. "Called me chacho. Said I'm a kind of sheriff."

"Just turned eighteen and already a sheriff," said Dot. She wasn't much older, thought Sunny, for all that. Dot said, "But old don't mean kind. What if he's an outlaw? What if he's wanted, like me?"

The two of them grabbed the big ring and pulled. It spooled out on a few feet of string, making a whirring noise from inside the tractor. Then the line caught and the string retracted back. The tractor lurched forward a yard. Boy fell into the seat and laughed.

"Like you?" said Sunny, as they grabbed the ring and got purchase once again.

"Didn't you know, Sheriff? I'm wanted in five counties."

"You an outlaw?"

"Nah," said the farmer's daughter, smiling. "Just good-looking."

The two of them pulled again, this time jerking past the caught-up section. The whirring lifted to a higher pitch as the wheel inside the tractor spun. As the ring reeled back, the tractor hopped forward, this time falling into a steady gear and driving on. Dot clapped her hands, then knocked Sunny on the shoulder.

"Thanks, Sheriff."

"Gets wound around itself sometimes."

Sunny considered telling her that the old stranger had come armed. The farmer's daughter trotted up to the moving tractor, jumped on the step, and leaned over Boy to straighten the course. Sunny grabbed Pup and walked alongside. She set Boy on top of the hood and reclaimed her seat. She said, "You know, they got a hangin' judge in town. Ain't even bothered to take down the scaffold since he came."

"Brought his own hangman, too?"

"Nah, does it himself, they say. Likes the feel of it. That wish-bone sound they make."

Sunny spat some straw, then picked at his tongue for a few remaining threads.

"They say he pounds his gavel, then takes off his robe and puts on a hood, hangs folks right then and there."

"Judges from the gallows," said Sunny.

"The saloon next door."

Sunny had spent some time with a hangin' judge before the farmer had found him. He hadn't been much bigger than Boy at the time. Dot knew it, too. When they got to the end of the line, the farmer's daughter turned the steering wheel to head back the other way, and Sunny kept walking on toward the farmhouse. When she saw he was going, the farmer's daughter shouted over the whine of the tractor and Boy's excited whooping, "If he's an outlaw, ain't no better time to leave town."

Sunny raised a hand in the air to say he'd heard. He hadn't told her that the old man backed him down, made him fall on his heels, and then tried to teach him about hospitality. He also didn't mention that Sobrino was armed with ten fingernails that a hangin' judge would have considered visible admissions of being up to no good.

It was nearly late afternoon, and he hadn't checked on the billy goats. They might have eaten each other's tin horns by now. Sunny plodded up the hill toward the farmhouse. He stopped on the side, under the shadow of the eaves, to take a drink of water from the hose. His back ached as he bent to turn the faucet. His back always ached. It was the way he slept. He turned the knob all the way and looked around for the end of the hose. A few seconds passed. A few feet away, an orange mortar shell bobbed up from the grass. It shook, then sent an arc of water in every direction. Pup barked and started running circles around it, trying at once to dodge the water and still get wet.

"Aw, hell," said Sunny. He twisted the sprinkler bomb off of the hose as though he was popping open a soda bottle. He tossed the globe to Pup and drank from the hose. The water soaked into him, drew his cords taut, and made his limbs feel weighty. He poured some water at the foot of the hollyhocks growing up the side of the house. Inside their purple blooms were baby doll shoes.

Sunny decided it was a sheriff's business to shield the women and children from fear. He walked across the front of the house, along the porch. To his right, all the way across the empty pasture, he could feel Sobrino watching him. Pup had to sprint to keep up. Sunny wasn't afraid of the stranger's weapons; he just didn't want the old man to feel like he'd taught Sunny a lesson. The inhospitable thing to do was ignore the beggar till he shuffled off. The ornery crow sent up a chattering call from out by the woods behind the pasture. It had found something, but what, Sunny didn't care to know.

3

THAT NIGHT, THOUGH Sunny listened for it, the coyotes didn't sing a prairie dirge. A dreary purge. He sat on the unlit porch of the farmhouse, dueling a lazy cricket's hum with the creaks of his rocking chair. He couldn't play a harmonica, since his lips were always as dry as a threshing floor, but he would have. His straw hat hung on a post from a purple plastic screw. A buttery smell wafted from the rows in the back of the house—a mix of rich soil and Play-Doh.

Pup had long since fallen asleep at Sunny's feet. The moon looked like a fingernail had punctured an eggplant. Instead of moving on, Sobrino had set up camp on the far side of the oak, just beyond the property line, as a sign of respect maybe. The way he'd leaned over the fence as though it was nothing, Sunny wondered if camping beside the tree wasn't a joke. Like carving up the fence.

The only light, sparing the feeble glaze of the moon, was Sobrino's campfire. Sunny could see it across the pasture. It was a glittery wink, a hundred yards away at the end of a black tunnel, ready to burn him down. Even if he soaked his limbs, a fire that bright could eat Sunny down to the buttons.

Sunny'd spent the early evening rounding up the livestock, untangling a kite from an apple tree, and tightening the bands on a collapsible pony so it wouldn't collapse all the time. He'd found ants in the gum-ball machine and gum balls in the ant farm. One of the gum balls was actually a dinosaur sponge capsule. Sunny considered pouring water on it and smothering a few ants to teach them a lesson. Then he couldn't figure what that lesson was exactly. He took the gum-ball machine out to the barn and set it on a crossbeam above a horse stall. He'd find a home for it later.

When he thought he heard the scratching of three blind windup mice from the barn, Sunny figured he'd better find a home for the gum balls first thing in the morning, before any real mice got to them. For now, Sunny had just battened everything down, as if a tornado was fixing to rip across the plain. The cotton-wool sheep wanted to graze in the pasture, but Sunny wouldn't let them get that near the stranger.

Sunny lifted his sleeve to his mouth and pulled out a long piece of straw. He bit off the end and spat it out the side of his mouth. The night was cold. The cricket stopped humming for fear he'd give away his position. Sunny drew his feet in and sat up straight. He squinted and saw half an outline of the stranger in the distance, sitting by the flames with a stick in his hand. He was poking the fire, sending up sparks like poison mist into the air. A kettle of black coffee sat in the red coals. It was too far away to hear the crackling of the fire as it gnawed the wood, but Sunny could imagine the sound.

Sunny wiggled his exposed toes. He wondered what it would feel like to put leather boots on them and prop them up near a fire.

He didn't even own a pair of boots. There'd never been a need. Boots were for fighting: kicks and protection from getting stomped on. Now Sunny wished for some. The farm was too far from town to run for help, and farther still from anybody you'd call a neighbor. Out there, it was any kind of law you negotiated for. You could do whatever it was someone else wasn't stopping you from doing. If you were big enough, you could steal a whole farm.

The creaking of Sunny's chair seemed too loud in the new dark hour. The silence was a language of the trees. They had waited all day for everyone else to shut up.

Sunny got up quietly so Pup wouldn't hear and grabbed his hat. He stepped clear of the loose porch steps straight onto the grass. It was darkest in the gulf between the farmhouse and the campfire, but Sunny didn't need the light. He walked just a few yards in front of the porch, still on the crest of the hill, where a six-foot post had been pounded into the ground and nailed with one perpendicular beam. It stuck up like a piece of fencing someone had forgotten to build on or take down.

Sunny knew exactly where the stake was. He yawned as he walked up to his bedpost. He leaned back on it as though it was the side of the barn, shifted a little, letting the post adjoin the groove of his back. He fixed his hat so it'd cover his eyes, crossed his arms, and put a foot up on the pole.

He could just see the fire through the mesh of his hat.

Sunny breathed a heavy sigh and settled in for the night. He fell into an unwilling sleep and dreamed that coyotes were sneaking down from the buttes to steal one of his velveteen rabbits.

When the crow called out a murderous cackle, Sunny snorted awake, but the last hour of the night was dewy and still. The camp-fire had been put out. As he closed his eyes again, Sunny heard a raspy sound, like the old stranger sucking pulp from his teeth.

4

THE ORNERY CROW stepped left then right on the oak branch, watching Sunny, who stood in the pasture with his head down and his hat over his eyes. The bird's plumes were so black they were purple. It raised its throat and called three times in succession, but Sunny didn't move. He still leaned against his bedpost, with one foot up and his arms folded. The crow thrust its belly out over the empty space and opened its wings. It flew over the dirt road, the split-rail fence, and the hundred-yard pasture, and landed on Sunny's shoulder.

The morning light had already climbed up over the farmhouse and spilled out onto the pasture. The farmer had walked the rows and gone inside already. The bird clamped tight on its perch, but Sunny didn't stir. His muscles were like coiled ropes, taut but giving. The crow bobbed his head. Sunny had no particular smell, leastways not like carrion would in his position.

The crow decided to explore. It stuck its beak into Sunny's ear and pulled out a bit of straw. A hand came up, lethargic with sleep, and scratched unconsciously at the itch. The crow flew up out of reach and landed back on Sunny's shoulder when his hand fell.

The crow gripped Sunny's shoulder and plunged its whole head into his ear canal. It rummaged for some time. Finally the flapping of its wings knocked Sunny's hat off his head.

Sunny didn't wake, but Pup caught sight of the straw hat blowing across the pasture and came running. The crow didn't hear Pup's yips and backflips, because its head was dug so deep in Sunny's skull. Other dogs might have pulled back their ears while their hackles came up. Pup just squatted in his one position and yapped the only round tone he knew over and over.

The crow didn't even notice when Sunny roused and wiped his nose with his sleeve. He wondered where his hat had gotten off to. Pup bounced at his feet to get his attention.

"What is it?" said Sunny.

Pup tried to backflip in such a way as to point at the bird growing out of Sunny's head.

"What? I ain't a carny show. Git."

Sunny started to lean over, to see what was wrong with Pup, but the crow felt the swaying of his perch and began batting its wings at the side of Sunny's head. Before Sunny could grab more than a handful of feathers, the crow pried its head loose and fluttered off, cawing its cusses back toward them. Pup ceased his conniption once the bird flew off. Sunny patted his ear to survey the damage.

He'd be fine, but he'd overslept. He'd stayed up to keep an eye on the stranger—Sunny looked over to Sobrino's camp but didn't see the old man anywhere. The wind was already blowing away the ashes of his fire. The fescue grass was bent where he'd slept. "Aw, hell," said Sunny.

At his foot was another cup of coffee with sugar and cream—and the crow had added a mess of straw floating on top. Sunny kicked over the cup. He spotted his hat in the far corner of the pasture, blown up against the fence. It slapped the rails intermittently, like a loose screen door. Pup sat as still as possible on a wagging tail, panting with a stupid-looking grin.

"Heaven and hell," said Sunny. On his way toward the fence, Sunny swung his foot out and knocked Pup onto his back. Pup rolled over one and a half times and rushed back up alongside Sunny.

Sunny squeezed his temples to juice the sleep out. He could hear the pull string of the tractor whirring all the way in the garden. He picked up his hat and dusted it as he walked to the back of the barn. The chickens would be nervous in the coop. Usually, he'd have had them out hours ago.

Sunny opened the coop and pulled out each hen, gently holding its aluminum body with both hands so it wouldn't dent. Instead of feet, they had one yellow wheel nestled under them, with a gripped surface like a print roller. He dragged each hen across the ground so the wheel could build up enough energy for the day. Then he pulled each hen back toward him, putting two fingers hard on the wheel so it wouldn't spin out as he lifted the hen off the ground. He repeated the step till the pressure seemed to tighten the chicken's breast and its drowsy warbles became hungry clucks.

As Sunny released the wound-up hens, Pup greeted them with a lick. Then they'd wheel around in curious circles, looking for chicken feed they might have missed from the previous day. A few of them had dented a wing as they stirred in the coop all night, and Sunny had to soothe these while he worked the aluminum with his thumbs. The uneasy hens burbled inside their gullets, afraid of any pain, even the healing kind.

Sunny'd been repairing the chickens since they'd been grown in the rows. One of them he'd really had to fix up after he'd found it nearly flat on the gravel road. Only difference to it afterward was that it looked like a piece of paper, balled up and smoothed out again.

After he'd wound the last hen, Sunny stood up and scattered seed in the dirt lot between the coop and the back of the barn. The hens swirled around one another, rocking on their wheels to peck seeds, then spinning on to search for more.

Each had a keen sense of the others in the manic tangle, or else they'd bump, crumple the aluminum where they'd hit, and fall off their axes. So they kept some miraculous clearance but whizzed around together out of a flocking instinct. Any one of them by itself was light and inconsequential, almost lost without the garbled lot of all of them together.

All the gaggling awakened the whittled rooster from its comatose sleep. It rolled on its track atop the chicken coop and coughed out a morning call, heedless of its uselessness at noon.

In the silence that followed, Sunny heard a scraping sound from inside the barn, punctuated by taps. Pup heard it too. Sunny remembered the gum-ball machine he'd stowed above the stalls. He scattered the last handful of seed and walked to the barn door. If the old man had trespassed onto their land, Sunny would have to fight him.

The front half of the barn was a wide-open hangar with three ten-foot bay doors, and the back half was made up of two rows of animal stalls. The second floor was the attic, with the chest for toys broken beyond what you could repair or love despite. The only access up was a pull-down staircase in the main bay that was always kept shut. Even Sunny spooked himself sometimes thinking about the bone yard above his head while he worked.

When Sunny opened the back door of the barn, a wedge of light cut into the space. The barn was hushed in a way it never was. The animals had gotten out the front bay door, which he could see was ajar. The feed troughs had been kicked over, but no animals had stopped to get at the spilled novelty foods.

Pup got himself worked up as he hustled from stall to stall. He sniffed at the troughs, yapped at them, did a backflip, and then sniffed them again.

Sunny followed the scratching sound to the last stall. He'd put the gum-ball machine on the crossbeam above it, but it was gone now. Maybe it had toppled backward, thought Sunny. He opened the stall door.

A stick horse leaned into the back wall, its face pressed into the corner. It had scraped down the straw bedding to the packed dirt floor and was still going, with frantic and exhausted hops on its one leg, like it was trying to get a good hold and push itself through the wall. The tapping sound was its left eye, a black button clacking against the side of the barn.

Sunny looked down at his own feet. The scattered remains of three blind mice filled the stick horse's stall, a gory mess of springs, gears, and whiskers. Sunny lurched backward, falling against the facing stall. The windup keys on their backs had been ripped out and lay useless in the shape of wishbones. The mice had been cracked open like crab shells and looked almost inside-out.

At Sunny's shock, the stick horse awoke from its stupor, then threw itself even harder at the wall. Pup came running, then skidded to a stop and slowly backed away.

Sunny opened his mouth to say, "Aw, hell," but he clapped his hand over his mouth to catch a sob coming out instead.

He came down to his knees and picked up a tiny spoke and a gray felt ear. He whispered, "Shhh, baby, shhh," to the stick horse as he started to gather the mutilated parts of the mice. Little by little the horse stilled itself out of its panic.

Sunny would need a rag to sop up the oil that'd spilled from the bellies of the mice. It had already soaked through the straw into the dirt, but it wouldn't be decent to leave it. Sunny had a rag he'd used to stain the bookshelves in the main bay. He was about to go get it when it appeared next to his ear and he heard over his shoulder, "Take it, chacho."

5

SUNNY STOOD UP. He didn't take his eyes off Sobrino.

"This is no good," said the old man, shaking his head. "I am sorry."

"You're sorry?" whispered Sunny. He stepped out of the stall. He didn't want the old man looking at the mice, didn't want him able to admire his own handiwork.

Sobrino backed up. He looked confused, like he wasn't sure he'd said what he meant to in a language he wasn't quite family with. He said, "Sorry for you, yes. I am sorry for what is happened."

Sunny took another step toward Sobrino. "I believed you the first time."

"Oh," said Sobrino. "Good." He stood up straight and patted his trousers. He was so tall he could look over the crossbeams. He could have reached up and plucked a whole gum-ball machine from its resting place.

"You're real sorry," said Sunny, picking up a rake that was leaning on a stall door.

"Sí," said Sobrino, eyeing the rake.

"Yeah, I see."

Sunny swung the rake overhead as hard as he could, like it was a pickax. It would have forked into the old man's skull if Sobrino hadn't leaped backward, pushing off with his elongated legs like a springboard. The old man flew twenty feet and landed on his back between the first and second stalls. The impact knocked the air out of his lungs. He grimaced and put a hand on his lower back while Sunny dashed forward, swinging the rake. He shouted like a war chief, flailing and weeping as he swiped at the old man on the ground.

Sobrino struggled to push himself up, into a crab walk. He scurried on all fours, with his belly facing the ceiling, dodging Sunny's rake just as if he was a daddy longlegs.

Using his fingernails to get a grip, he wrapped his stilted legs around posts. Like a spider, he crawled up the stalls and over the crossbeams. All the while Sunny chased him, punching the rake into the wood and screaming cuss.

Sobrino leaped into the main bay and disappeared over the tops of the bookshelves Sunny had been building. Sunny charged after him, overturning three of the unfinished shelves. Then finally, Sobrino reappeared on the side wall, scrambling toward the bay door. Sunny dropped a few darts into his hand from up his sleeve and hurled them. One dart flew end over end, hit the wall backward, and fell to the floor. The next one flew straight and stabbed into the wall, just behind Sobrino's heel. Sunny finally aimed with the third one and pinned Sobrino's shoe to the side of the barn. Sobrino didn't notice. He scurried toward the door, but his foot stayed pegged to the wall and yanked him backward. Sobrino fell to the dirt.

As Sobrino hung upside down, prying his foot loose, Sunny came running up with the rake for his kill shot. Just in time, the old man slipped his foot out of the shoe and turned around to block the handle of Sunny's rake, but not before the tines cut three neat lines into his shoulder.

Sobrino groaned. He grabbed Sunny's hand and squeezed it till Sunny heard his knuckles clack into each other like marbles. Sunny cried out and tried to wrest free, but he couldn't. And he couldn't figure how the haggard old man with pockmarks all over him could have a grip like a noose.

It surprised him that there was a kind of strength that came with muscles and a kind that came with living a long time.

Sobrino bent over to stare the kid right in the eye. He forced Sunny to extend his arm and hold the rake out sideways. Sunny tried not to wince. Both of them breathed hard. Sobrino dragged the sharp nails of his other hand over the rake as though he was playing a piano riff across the handle. It fell to pieces like a chopped carrot.

Sunny stopped struggling, and Sobrino finally let him loose.

Sunny rubbed his knuckles. Sobrino pressed his shoulder where the rake had grazed him. The cuts didn't bleed, maybe because the old man didn't have any blood to spare. He looked like the sun had shriveled him up into jerky, made him tawny and kinda mangled already. Sunny couldn't imagine a country of men like him, picking oranges from the top boughs and singing songs only they could understand. He figured Sobrino must have been a stranger every place he'd been.

The back door of the barn slammed open. Pup leaped out from the corner he'd been hiding in, and ran for shelter under Sunny's leg. They heard the stick horse stamp into the wall, thrash a few times, and then fall down.

The farmer's daughter rushed in, followed by Boy and a trail of windup chickens. They came running toward the main bay but stopped short when Dot saw the mice in the last stall. Boy stopped and stared. Slowly, he raised a hand and gripped the back of Dot's pant leg.

The gaggling chickens wheeled around hysterically, gabbing at each other. Some of them were racing so fast that they ran out a whole day's worth of winding and fell over in a terrified faint. Others ran headlong into the first wall, or foot, or chicken they came across. They crunched like soda cans and sent up dust where their wheels ground little ditches in the dirt floor.

"What happened?" said Boy.

"He killed them," said Sunny, lathering up for more fight.

"Why?" said Sobrino. "Why I kill them?"

"'Cause you're old and you're weird," said Sunny.

"Maybe a cat did it," said Boy, trying to make sense of the ugly sight.

"A cat can't bend metal like that, Boy," said the farmer's daughter.

"A metal cat," said Sobrino.

"We ain't grown a toy cat in years," said the farmer's daughter. "They're too complicated."

Sobrino glanced at Boy and the seam line that ran along the crown of his head, cadet's hat included, and down each cheek. The brads were either flesh colored or uniform red and looked like mosquito bites or various other bumps little boys acquire in the woods. The farmer's daughter put a protective hand on Boy's shoulder. Sobrino looked into her eyes the color of fresh basil and recognized something in them from a long time ago. "Your name is Dot," he said.

"I ain't got a name," said the farmer's daughter, running a hand up to put a stray hair behind her ear.

Sobrino chuckled and it sounded like *eh-eh-eh.* "The farmer's daughter, that is your name," he said.

"That too, I guess," said Dot.

"How'd you know her name?" said Sunny. He stepped closer, wagging another dart.

"How you know my name?" said Sobrino.

"You told me."

"That's right. Sobrino del Mago, at your service, no mouse killer. Majeecian. Farmer friend and nice to mice."

"When'd I tell you my name?" said Dot.

Sobrino went *eh-eh-eh* but didn't answer Dot's question.

He leaned over, very slow, and pulled up one of the bookshelves. He took a broken piece of a shelf and put it on the woodworking bench. "I help, yes?"

"No," said Sunny. "You leave. Or I cut you open."

Sobrino tried to chuckle, but it died in his throat, like suddenly it embarrassed him to beg for their welcome. His sheepish smile did nothing but showcase his rotten teeth. Everyone stood around looking at each other. Then Dot said, "He ain't the murderer, Sunny."

"Don't matter. Maybe he's *a* murderer."

"That's a dumb way of thinking."

"You're dumb," said Sunny. Immediately, he felt silly for it. He put the hand holding the dart down to his side.

"Dumb, dumb," said Boy, absently kicking up straw.

The farmer's daughter patted Boy forward so he'd go stand by Sunny, away from the stall. She helped the stick horse up and let it go hopping out of the barn to run out its fear. Then she took off a boot and started gathering the body parts in it.

Sunny looked at the one booted foot and the one pistachio sock sticking out of the stall where the farmer's daughter kneeled on all fours to pick up the mess. Dot ushered the mice into the warm boot. Sunny felt guilty for taking advantage of the intimate moment to gawk at her.

Dot stood up and back into the main bay, cradling the boot with both arms. Sunny, Boy, and Sobrino stepped aside as she reached for the pull-down staircase. She climbed into the attic. Pup followed her up to the foot of the stairs and then caught a smell from up there he didn't like. Sunny, Boy, and Sobrino stood in a semicircle, looking up at the floorboards, which were spaced just enough apart to see Dot's shadow moving above. The singular footfall of Dot's lone boot walked above their heads. The toy chest creaked open, followed by sounds that may have been Dot crying for her friends before she buried them.

Sunny paid his respects as best he could, hoping the mice'd be comforted somehow by his silence. Sobrino had covered his face with grimy hands and was speaking muffled words without so much meaning as rhythm, like a canticle no toy would ever know. Even the hens were wheeling around quietly.

When Dot came down from the attic, her green eyes were red and her red hair seemed brown, as if she'd wilted a little. She picked Pup off the floor and let him lick her cheeks. Then she walked out and turned toward the vegetable garden.

Boy started to run after her, but Sunny put a hand on his head and held him in place. "She don't need help today. You can make yourself useful around here."

Sobrino didn't talk for the rest of the morning, smart enough to know it'd only start a fight. Sunny opened the barn doors wide and let the light evaporate the dew inside the main bay. He and Sobrino picked up pieces of the bookshelves and cleared the workbench for repairs. Boy talked to himself, having a volcano adventure, poking into every stall for magma pits and narrating as he went. He never saw any toys that had fallen into the pit and died, but he was mindful that he might and assured himself that it'd be okay if he did, 'cause of lava being so hot it'd melt you quick and painless.

The pall of the morning stretched over into the afternoon. The chickens wouldn't circle farther than five feet from Sunny, clucking to tell each other how speechless they were over the whole ordeal.

Something continued to rustle in the attic, like the rattling stones of a graveyard shifting to find beds for those that were new.

When they'd finished picking up the busted planks, it became apparent that Sunny's library was a bramble of piss-poor workmanship. Corners weren't butted up to each other, baseboards were uneven, and he'd beveled edges for no reason at angles that didn't match. Sobrino couldn't help but grin when he saw some finishing work Sunny had done on one shelf. It looked like he'd tried to carve an undersea pattern with turtles and kelp. He said, "You carve this?"

"Yeah," said Sunny. "This is gonna be Dot's library."

"She like, what you say, squeeds?"

"Huh?"

Sobrino pointed to the tentacle shapes. "Arms like branches— squeed."

Sunny said, "Those are grapevines."

Sobrino had never heard of ocean grapes. "This is a tortle."

"That's a daisy."

Sobrino said, "Oh," then sputtered, opened his mouth, and laughed. Sunny couldn't figure how a man with teeth like Sobrino's could bring himself to laugh at the sorry state of anything else.

"You can leave now," said Sunny. He turned to the workbench and picked up a few tools. When he couldn't think of anything else to do with them, he put them back down. Sobrino quieted himself down to a chuckle. *"Eh-eh-eh,* leave." Then he pointed at a turtle foot and exclaimed, "Leaves!" He had to hold his stomach as he burst out laughing again. This time Sunny whirled around and dropped a couple darts from his sleeve between his fingers, ready to let them fly. Sobrino put a palm out. "Wokay, chacho. Just the carving is fonny. Like the chickans do it."

The old man turned his attention back to the botched carving. He leaned down low to get a good look and dug his fingernail into the wood. The jagged nail seemed like it could break off at any second. But instead of breaking, his fingernail cut into the wood, easier than if he were painting each stroke. The white pine curled under his fingernail as if it was white chocolate.

Sunny half expected to come around and see a scrub of claw marks cross-hatching over his work. But the old man had rescued the floral pattern, and the squids were now ivy, as they were supposed to be. The tortle daisy could have fooled a bumblebee. And under it sat a little turtle, real as a picture, wearing a magician's cap.

Boy giggled at a crow, its wings carved deep with black shade, perched on a tall stalk of corn, looking out defiantly and never flying off. "You carve tons better than Sunny," he said, squeezing himself between the legs of the two men to look. "Don't you think so, Sunny? Tons better. And he doesn't cuss so much while he's doing it." Sunny took a side step toward Sobrino to block Boy's vision, but Boy wouldn't be silenced. "Did you see the turtle, Sunny? He's smiling at you. And the wood didn't split. And he didn't cut himself, or get splinters behind his ear somehow, or kick Pup ten feet into the air." Pup yapped from whatever corner he was sniffing to affirm the claim.

Sobrino leaned down and lifted Boy by his underarms. Boy made an automated *wheeee!* The old man said, "Look up there, chacho," and he sat the kid up on a crossbeam.

Sunny looked at the old man. The old man was looking at him, so he looked down. He gripped some straw with his bare toes. He said, "You running from the hangin' judge?"

"He's no good," said Sobrino.

"No good for you."

"For anybody."

Sobrino grimaced as he kneeled near a bookshelf. He gestured for Sunny to lift a shelf while he fixed the pegs that held it in place. "I asked you a question," said Sunny, lifting the board.

"I just look for work," said Sobrino.

"What does a 'majeecian' do, huh? You a magic outlaw?"

Sobrino set the pegs right and took the board back from Sunny. He motioned for Sunny to lean down.

"What?" said Sunny, bending close.

"Shhh, chacho, shhh." said Sobrino. Then in the hush he placed the shelf on its right pegs, set it straight, and whispered, "Majeek."

Sunny straightened up. From the rafters Boy said, "Ooooh, there's a gum ball up here." A lone red gum ball sat on the beam above the stick horse's stall, all the way across the barn. Boy started crawling toward it. As far as Sunny could tell, there wasn't any other sign of the gum-ball machine. He'd search the fence line for droppings later on—maybe a bobcat had carried it away in frustration after the mice had proven meatless. Sunny brought his sleeve up to his mouth and grated on a mouthful of straw. Then he lifted the next shelf and let Sobrino get back to work.

Boy reached the gum, popped it in his mouth, and started blowing bubbles. In all the farm, only Boy had a feature like that. He laughed and kicked his legs out. Pup stood below him on the ground, flipping around and sharing in the excitement.

"If he hung you," Sunny told Sobrino, "you'd have just stood up through the trapdoor anyhow. The gallows ain't that tall."

"How do you know?" said Sobrino, struggling with a peg broken off in its socket.

"Used to be a gallows dummy. What they call an effigy. They'd hang me to make sure the knot's right and the lever's workin'."

Sobrino poked a nail into the socket to pry the peg loose. He said, "You live 'cause the farmer took you?"

"And 'cause straw don't choke, no matter how hard you string it up."

The peg unwedged, and Sobrino stood up. He put both his hands on Sunny's shoulders. "See, chacho," he said. "I am tall, and you can breathe. And this"—he showed the broken peg. "This—"

Sunny interrupted him. "I know, *majeek, majeek.* It all came to rights."

Sobrino squeezed Sunny's shoulders to get him to look up.

"No," he said. "This is broken forever. It's dead."

Sobrino tossed the broken peg over his shoulder. Three hens rushed to peck at it, soon as it landed, and ended up crunching each other's beaks.

Across the barn, Boy kicked his legs in indiscriminate joy, then lost balance, fell backward off the crossbeam, and crashed to the straw floor of the stall. There was a pause, a settling of dust—then a squealed *wheee!*

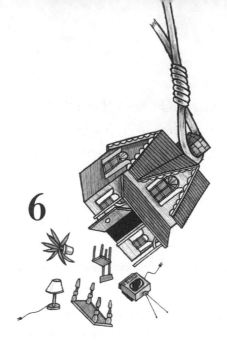

6

NIGHT WAS ALL around them. The farmer's daughter played
a somber tune on a rainbow xylophone that chimed like a funeral
in a tiny cathedral. She sat on the porch in the rocking chair next to
Sunny. Many of the toys had gathered in the yard, looking up at the
two of them on the porch, maybe waiting for some kind of eulogy
that wasn't coming. The light of a dozen glow-in-the-dark blobs set
on the railing cast a radioactive tint on the assembly. A light-up peg
board sat on a stool with the words "4ever in r hearts" arranged in a
multicolor pattern.

Sunny held a red clock-face toy with a big arrow in the middle
pointing at pictures of farm animals. He pulled the handle. "The
chickens say: *cluck cluck cluck!*"

A couple hens burst into wailing clucks. The arrow spun around
on the clock face. Sunny looked stupefied with exhaustion, but it
made the toys gathered in the yard feel better, vocalizing their
mourning for the ones that were otherwise noiseless. He pulled the
handle again. "The mice say: *squeak squeak squeak!*"

The toys in the yard rattled in the wind. A pinwheel buffeted before toppling over. A rubber ball maundered down the hill. A tricycle just lay there on its side, and the screen doors of a dollhouse slammed an irregular salute.

Sunny'd given Pup his whole dinner of sausage and beans, and now the dog was sleeping on his side by Sunny's feet, snoring unevenly. The farmer's daughter had come back from the garden dried out, like a whole layer of bark needed scraping off. She was bouncing the head of the mallet on the green bar of the xylophone in long yawning notes, and she said, "The farmer ain't gonna come out here, if that's what you're thinking."

Sunny looked at her, then at the toys scattered around the porch steps. "I wasn't thinking it."

"They are."

"They're just saying good-bye."

"No," said the farmer's daughter, "they're waiting for an explanation."

"Easy," said Sunny, putting the clock-face toy aside and bringing his sleeve back for a pull of straw. "The old man did it."

"That isn't what I meant, but you're an ijit for thinking it after he held your hand all day in that barn."

The sound of Sunny's shoulders cocking back in irritation was the same sound as shucking an ear of corn. The way Sunny saw it, being old was just another way of saying you'd done a lot of bad things.

"It's true," said Sunny.

"It ain't true."

Dot bounced the wooden handle of the mallet on each color of the xylophone to hear the ugly clack of each one, making a tallying din. Dallying tin. She said, "I think he's a giant."

"You think?" said Sunny.

"Not like a blue-ribbon pumpkin," said Dot. "They got these stories about giants in the mountains. Magicians."

"I seen his magic," said Sunny. "They got better tricks in Town Hall."

"Magicians used to be giants."

"He ain't either."

"Would you let me talk? If you can hurl a huge rock down a mountain, you can make it rain boulders. Can you do that?"

"That ain't magic."

"That's magic," said Dot. "If you can do that, you done magic the rest of us can't."

Sunny looked out at the blackness, past his post, over the pasture to where Sobrino was camped. The old man hadn't lit a fire out of respect—or to keep Sunny from watching him all night. He could have been towering just outside the light of the porch, or lumbering toward the barn. Sunny squinted but couldn't make out a thing.

"Yeah, well. I can juggle," he said.

"Good for you," she said.

"So now he's shriveled up."

"Yeah," she said without looking up, tired out with him being so cocksure.

"He can't be older than the farmer," she thought aloud.

Sunny smirked. "You're the one mad the farmer ain't out here. I just assume he don't care."

All he seemed to care for was coddling a bunch of baby toys out in the rows. Sunny could hear Dot draw her breath. "That's different," she said.

"Y'all are supposed to be his kids; it ain't different," said Sunny.

Dot played the next note like a book you slam by accident. She almost threw the mallet but stopped herself. A mad tear watered her cheek. Sunny was equal parts ashamed of being an ingrate and proud of his own commitment to truth telling. Dot composed herself, pruning the one tear from her cheek, and said, "You're a real sonofabitch, Sunny."

Sunny picked a fleck of straw from the tip of his tongue and said, "And you're a farmer's daughter."

"You don't even know he talks like you're his own, too. You don't know 'cause you're busy pickin' on a poor dying Mexican who's just trying to find labor enough to buy an orange. Farmer should've made you a field hand after saving you from bein' a judge's sandbag. Instead you think you're a sheriff now, you dumb runt."

Sunny took the whole straw from his mouth and rolled it around his finger. He didn't look anywhere but straight at the porch railing. When she was finished, he got up to leave.

Pup lifted a drowsy head. Dot and Sunny heard a noise for the second time, coming from the barn, this time a shambling sound.

Sunny froze. The farmer's daughter sprang up, holding the mallet like a hammer. The sound was urgent and substantial, like something as big as a bull. It rustled around the bookshelves in the main bay, looking for something.

Dot whispered, "The stick horse."

Sunny put a finger in the air. "Shhh."

They heard a few steps, a spell of silence—then a snap of wood and rubber like a flinging catapult. Some frantic skitters, then just one or two. Then nothing.

In the breathless pause, the ornery crow made a laughing caw from Sunny's bedpost. The farmer's daughter ventured, "Sounded like a mousetrap."

Sunny grinned. "Big enough to pin a mechanical bull. Made it this afternoon."

"You made it?"

"Me and Sobrino."

"If he helped you make a trap, why would you still think he's the thief?"

"All I said was he's a suspect."

"That's not all you said."

Dot sighed at the thought of all that conversation wasted. It seemed Sunny didn't want to be right; he just wanted to be confident.

She grabbed the light-up peg board to go investigate. Sunny shook his head no.

He whispered, "Could be more than one."

"What if he runs off?"

"Naw," said Sunny. "If his back ain't clean broke, he's got a headache he ain't gettin' up from."

Dot seemed to weigh an option on each eyebrow. She hoped one trap would scare off whatever thief or gang of thieves there was in the barn. Or else for a few hours till sunrise, the strangers would have run of the place.

"Do you have more traps?" she asked.

"No," said Sunny.

"I'll get the toys inside," she said.

Sunny nodded and stepped off the porch into the night. For the moment, he felt unafraid. He was sure he'd turned an outsize stranger into a slobbering carcass. Maybe old Sobrino couldn't help himself, perverted as he was by all those years stewing in the world. Or it could have been some other bad man. Either way, Sunny had protected the farm. The farmer could hide all he wanted in the house; Sunny didn't need him. All he needed was a corner to back into and a dart in his hand, and the whole daggum world could come looking for a fight. Sunny would oblige.

He swaggered into the front yard toward his bedpost overlooking the pasture. When he could make out the figure of the brazen crow perching on his post, he squared up beak to beak with the bird. Both of them stretched their necks. Sunny smiled and whispered with a magical waggle of his fingers, "Shazam."

7

THE LOCKING BAR of the oversize rat trap hadn't bitten clean through the body of a man. It had come down on a left shoulder and pushed till the legs went down into splits. The body was pinned in the weird angular gesture, like an unstrung marionette. The arms looked like bent spokes.

In Sunny's line of work, there was an appreciation for the art of scaring people off your land. He and Sobrino stood side by side, looking down at the mangled stranger. There wasn't any blood, though it had cuts. It didn't wear clothes, aside from a pair of jean shorts. Its fingers were curled up and turning brown. Next to the trap was a stick. A cloth horse's head lay nearby. The straw stuffing had been ripped out.

"Is no living," said Sobrino. It sounded like *leaving*.

Sunny glanced over his shoulder. "Got that right," he said, crossing his arms. "He ain't goin' nowhere."

"No," said Sobrino, striding in front of him and putting his gnarled hands on the lock bar embedded in the stranger's collarbone. "Is no alive."

The farmer had already walked along the rows in the early dawn light, but short of the upstart caboose, the crops were still too timid to sprout. Sunny hadn't gone to meet him.

Sunny took a step back as Sobrino lifted the mousetrap bar. The body slumped over and gave off a smell like old cabbage. "Jeez, I know, quit jostling it," said Sunny, gagging a little.

The farmer's daughter appeared in the bay door and said, "He ain't sayin' it's dead. He's sayin it wasn't ever alive to begin with."

"Sí," said Sobrino, then added, "Yes, exacto."

Even Sunny, who was usually blindsided by other people's feelings, could hear the prickles in her voice. She went straight toward the body, smacking her shoulder into Sunny's back as she passed. "You used the stick horse as bait," she said, kneeling to pick up the head.

"Just a fake one, Dot," said Sunny. "We couldn't well use cheese."

"It doesn't matter. What if he'd seen it? You know how scared he'd be?"

She swept up the stick and the scattered straw as quick as she could. "Come on, now," she said, which was what she said when she really expected better of somebody.

"Who?" said Sunny. "The farmer? The horse? I tied it off by the chicken coop; the sheep too. They weren't here to see anything—"

"See what?" asked Boy, who was standing in the doorway rubbing his eyes.

Dot froze with the fake stick horse in her arms. With one giant stride, Sobrino scooped her up to his chest level and did a full round, like a dandy two-step. When he put her down, not three seconds later, everything in her arms was gone.

Dot looked down at her empty arms, then up at the giant. He winked and showed his empty palms with the after-flourish of a disappearing act.

The farmer's daughter turned to Boy and said, "Nothing."

"Go on," said Sunny, but by then Boy had seen the body. "Wow, is that a toy?"

"No," said Sunny, and stepped in his line of sight. Boy dodged around to peer at the body. Its head hung limp, like the bones had gone soft.

"Does he like to play with toys?" asked Boy.

"No," said Dot, interrupting Boy. "If you see one, you run and get us, you hear?"

Boy was too mesmerized to nod. Sunny didn't like to baby anybody. He said, "Boy, that guy's dead."

"No living," corrected Sobrino.

"It was never alive," corrected Dot.

"How do you know that?" said Sunny.

"It's a homunculus," said Dot.

There was a silence, and Boy said, "They don't play with toys?"

Sunny had only heard of such a thing as a homunculus. He whispered to the farmer's daughter, "You sayin' he's a plant?"

She nodded.

"Aw, hell," said Sunny as he went over to the body, which was starting to wrinkle like a fallen leaf. Sunny could see inside a cut on its shoulder. The meat was dense like a squash. Its face was generically male and smooth, without dimples or pocks. On the side of its neck, Sunny could see a burn mark, like a cattle brand.

Sobrino picked Boy from the ground. He made the gleeful auto-response and then went back to his pensive scowl. "Why don't they play, Sobrino?" Boy found it useful to his thinking to pull on Sobrino's goatee.

"When a man is hanged," said Sobrino, "under him it grows a little plant. When you take and grow the plant, it's a man or woman."

"You can grow people like toys?"

"Sure you can," said a voice from over by the stalls. At the same time, a yapping Pup came tearing in from the back door, tumbling over his own front feet, toward Sunny. The message was to be afraid.

At the sight of the figure that appeared after Pup, the homunculus in the trap jerked a few times, trying to stand at attention.

"You can grow 'em nice and big, and then tell 'em to do anythin' you please," said the man.

He was wearing denim jeans and a denim jacket. He was more round than tall, with sweat stains at his armpits and across the paunch under his belt. His neck looked like a custard, and his nose was bulbous and red with burst capillaries. He had gin blossoms on his cheeks, and his lips were black with the permanent tattoo of chaw.

"Who're you?" said Sunny, squaring his shoulders, ready to protect the farmer's daughter.

"Who'm ah?" said the man, chomping at the same time on a mix of chewing gum and chewing tobacco. "Why, I'm the owna o' that homunculus you so savagely tore up. It's mah property."

He made a portly bow. "The Growin' Man, at y'all's service."

"You're on our property now, mister," said Sunny. "And your dummy killed some friends of ours."

A mocking laugh gurgled out the Growin' Man's throat. "An' now you've killed mine."

"It wasn't alive," said Boy, volunteering his new fact.

"Certainly not like you." The Growin' Man grinned, licking his black lips at the marvelous sight of such a creation as Boy. His tongue was dyed green and blue with candy.

"It was half alive," said the Growin' Man.

"Half alive ain't life—it's just moving," said Dot.

The Growin' Man sat back on his haunches and stuck a paw in his jacket pocket. "Well, wouldn't you know it," he said. He made a *chup-chup* noise when he chewed, like the sound of pulling your boot out of slop.

Dot wouldn't look the man in the eye. The rancher leered at her as though her discomfort were delicious.

He pulled his hand out of his jacket and produced a handful of gum balls. Their colors had leaked all over his sweaty palm.

"Where'd you get those?" said Sunny, stepping forward.

The Growin' Man pushed the gum balls into his maw. He smacked and said, "A darlin' little machine I found."

"You're a thief."

"How do you know?" said the man, laughing. Then he added, "Maybe they broke themselves by runnin' under mah boot. Toys will be toys, after all."

The Growin' Man puckered his stained lips and whistled. From the back door, another figure emerged, lurching, as if at the rancher's command. The creature was human, mostly. Its arms hung at its side like overladen branches. Its legs were hairless but coarse, like tree trunks shucked of their bark. Dot was startled.

Sunny leaped toward the figure and swung both his arms. A row of darts bloomed out along the newcomer's bare chest. The homunculus groaned and stumbled backward a few steps. It struggled to stay upright but kept coming.

"No!" Dot shouted. Boy buried his face into Sobrino's neck. Pup added to the noise.

The homunculus swung its arm at Sunny. It had the same powerful languor of a steer and about as much language. Sunny ducked and jammed a couple more darts into its underarm. Then he hopped back. He snapped his wrists, and two more darts dropped down from his sleeves. It was a showboat thing to do. He acted like a bullfighter, punching into the senseless creature, while he stared down the Growin' Man to show it wasn't very taxing. Then he flung the darts and hit the homunculus dead center of its heart. It took a few more steps and dropped to the ground.

"Bull's-eye," said the Growin' Man, and clapped. Then he put his hand in his pocket. Sunny heaved his chest out, more for a bucked-up effect than to catch his breath. "But as long as the hangin' judge is in town, I got a full herd."

Sunny charged forward. He wanted to push a dart up through the folds of the man's throat like a sewing needle. But as he came rearing up, the Growin' Man pulled a lighter out of his pocket and flipped it open. The tiny flame was barely enough to brand a neck with, but Sunny panicked at the sight of it. Like a cat on a greased counter, he fell backward at the Growin' Man's feet. Then he scratched at the ground to get purchase going the other way.

The Growin' Man chupped his lips in open delight over Sunny's fright. Sunny scrambled back behind the farmer's daughter, clutching her shoulder and gaping at the lighter's flame. The Growin' Man snapped the lighter shut, but it was all he needed to burn fear into the side of Sunny's neck, saying he was owned property.

The Growin' Man looked the farmer's daughter up and down, admiring every piece of her. He gave a solicitous nod to Sobrino, then turned to go, leaving his new homunculus to dry up along with the other one.

From where Sunny was standing, he could see the creature he'd dropped. Its green eyes, the color of fresh basil, were starting to go brown. As he left the barn, the Growin' Man said, "I'll be out back, settin' up camp. Real pretty eyes she's got, eh, Sunny?"

Sunny took his hand off Dot's shoulder.

8

SUNNY STAMPED ACROSS the pasture with his sleeve up to his teeth, gnawing the straw like he was grinding cud. He spat the pulp and every once in a while hollered out, "Cotton . . . Aw, hell, cotton!"

The Growin' Man's camp had taken over the chicken coop, along with the entire dirt lot behind the red barn. All the livestock had scattered before the homuncular gang could dismember them like the three mice. The chickens, senseless, a few of them headless, still had wits enough to wheel around the barn to the farmhouse. They huddled under the porch, cooing to each other till the farmer's daughter arrived to listen to their grief. By midday more and more toys had tucked themselves into the porch, as though it were the hem of a mother's skirt. Dot, a true farmer's daughter, wasn't much for dresses or sympathizing and chose instead to settle the children down, then get back to work. But a few of the anxious toys were babies, just plucked from the rows last season. It would have been a sin to leave them alone, so Dot kept the three windup chicks, a rubber duckling, and a couple field mice shivering in her shirt pockets. She went out to the barn to search for any toys hiding in the hay bales, and Sunny went into the pasture, looking for the livestock. Neither of them had an answer for the Growin' Man's invasion, but if they lost the livestock, then there wasn't any point to it anyhow.

Sunny kicked at the tall grass, missing Pup by a few inches. Pup was weaving in and out of his stride, leaping up to see above the grass line. He'd sniff and point with his muzzle in a different direction every ten feet, doing a cartoon impression of a hunting dog. The noonday sun was so bright, it made the boiling air drone in his ears and everything else sound far off. Sunny'd heard a long time ago of days so hot, the haystacks would spontaneously combust—moisture packed inside them would just roil up and catch fire.

Sunny tried not to think of himself as a pressure-packed straw house, bubbling inside with tears he wasn't pansy enough to spill.

Sometime in the previous night, the stick horse must have snapped its halter as the Growin' Man's gang approached. It had scrambled all the way past the fence into the edge of the woods. Sunny found it first, hopping up and down at the trunk of the old oak next to Sobrino's camp. It might have figured a homunculus couldn't climb trees—apparently neither could stick horses.

Sunny held it for a while, whispering his apologies for tying the creature in the exact wrong spot. He knew the horse wanted to hear that the fright was over, but he couldn't bring himself to say it. It'd be coddling and likely untrue. Instead, he led the horse through a hole in the fence, across the hundred-yard pasture, to the front porch. Pup ran behind with his own encouraging yaps. As they passed the post on the crest of the hill, the ornery crow squawked; it seemed for no reason other than to startle the stick horse. Then it ruffled its neck feathers, cocky as a wrangler that just roped a bronco. The stick horse clopped up to Sunny's rocking chair and fell down beside it in exhaustion.

Sunny wiped his forehead with a handkerchief he'd found in a magic set and headed back to round up the electric sheep. He hollered, "Cotton!" as he straddled the split-rail fence and crossed the dirt road. They were trained as best you can train sheep to come running at the sound of "Cotton." Which is to say, not at all.

Sunny stepped well clear of where Sobrino had lit the fire. The crow had swept down from the post, followed the line of the earth, and rose up in time to clear the fence. It scooped into an apple tree right behind Sunny, to see what he was up to and to hurl insults at his backside. Sunny paid him little mind. If he wanted to, he could skewer the bird with a dart, and maybe he would, after he'd penned up the last of the livestock.

Sunny ducked into a crab-apple glade. From here, obscured by tree branches, the fence line was a brown perforated music staff. The crow cussed at him, and Pup yelled back. Of all the toys, Sunny hated the sheep. Fool creatures, clouds of senseless cotton balls, filthier than folks would guess. Even the hens rolled away from them—annoyed and afraid of getting caught in their mindless grazing.

*   *   *

A sheep sees grass, and it eats grass. Figuring whether it was walking itself off a gorge or getting itself lost in a thicket was a little too taxing on its motor. Sunny imagined they'd trundled away from the Growin' Man's gang, bleating their terror, then stopped somewhere in the woods when they'd forgotten what they were bleating about. They looked down, saw grass, and hell if they could contribute a lonely cent to their own salvation.

Sunny'd have to grab each one before it ran off, truss it up or flip the "Off" switch, and put it over his shoulder. No other way to get each mutton-headed one back to its own farm. Sunny grumbled, "Aw, hell," just thinking about it.

The crow shrieked again, Pup flipped, and a frightened ewe called out a slightly digitized bleat. Sunny jerked toward the sound. Over by a sapling grove, he could make out a grown man from behind, shirtless, with discolored spots along his back like the bruises on a banana. It was holding the sheep upside down in the air, shaking it as though it was one of the pigs. Instead of nickels, the sheep was frantically dropping pellets.

Sunny hunkered down and sprinted toward the man, keeping upwind and out of sight. He dropped a dart into his palm. It had a gold runner with silver glitter. He dropped a raven-colored dart into his other hand. Sunny crossed the fifty yards of ground without a noise, snuck up behind the homunculus, and punched one dart down into the right shoulder and stuck the other one up through the right elbow. The homunculus bellowed, but before it could drop the sheep, Sunny sprang to its left and put another two darts into the shoulder and elbow joints. With its arms stapled in the locked-out position, the homunculus could only whirl around stiffly. Sunny leaped sideways and kept behind it, but only for so long as it took to drop a dart into each hand and stab them together through the plant's neck. As he did so, he leaned forward and spoke in its ear. "You ain't like her. You're nothing but dead wood and timber."

The homunculus broke at the knees and toppled sideways. Sunny spat and reached up to bite another piece of straw.

The ewe stared up at the sky, kicking its legs and fully expecting to start walking at any minute. Sunny picked it up, but it was struggling so hard to get away that he finally had to reach under its belly and flip the switch. Its low hum subsided, and the sheep's head slumped.

On the way back, Sunny looked up in the apple tree, but the crow had flown off. The fence, obscured by intermittent branches, looked like the stitches on a leather drum, holding the farm and the whole world together.

Without warning, a spring rain started up, despite a mostly clear sky. Sunny let the droplets shower him, as well as the sheep on his shoulders. It was good growing rain, to make the crops hearty. The late-season planting would probably sprout by that very evening.

Back when he was a hanging dummy, the rain would soak into his stuffing and make him heavy. His body would dangle, a wet lumpy sack, stretching his neck like taffy. But those were days he didn't remember very well, like a childhood someone else told him about. Those were the days before the farmer had taken him off the scaffold and put life in his limbs. Now the rain was refreshing, plus it made Dot happy.

*   *   *

Sunny was smiling by the time he entered the barn, everything damp and safe from kindling. His patience had been rewarded. And even though the farmer was yet to show his face, the kind rain was all the protection Sunny needed—or thought he needed—to go behind the barn and face the Growin' Man's fire. He set the ewe down in a stall and nodded to Dot and Sobrino, who stood by the back door.

The farmer's daughter said, "Got one?"

Sunny flipped the switch under the sheep's belly and said, "This and the horse. Out on the porch." The sheep took one look around and started to scuttle with held-over panic until Sunny pushed its head down. It saw a pile of alfalfa, lost the thought, and started eating. Sunny walked out and shut the stall.

"Sunny. Sunny!" said Boy. He was dangling his legs from the crossbeam, looking down on Dot and Sobrino's work. "Did you see me when you came in? I was up here, Sunny. Did you see?"

"No, I didn't see you, buddy."

"Sobrino put me up here. Sunny. Sunny."

Sunny was watching Sobrino lift a plank up to the back door while the farmer's daughter hammered in nails. "What're you doin'?" he said.

"Have to bar it up," said Dot. "They're on the other side."

"Well, what good is that gonna do? They can just walk around."

"Well, then, they can walk around. This door ain't open to 'em."

"Found one in the orchard already," grumbled Sunny to no one in particular.

Sobrino lifted another plank, and Dot hammered even harder.

"We're scared!" said Boy, bouncing.

"Seems like it," said Sunny. "He's got us good."

Dot wheeled around and pointed her hammer at him. "You finished cleaning your mess yet? 'Cause you got sheep halfway to town."

"That ain't my fault," said Sunny.

"Oh, ain't nothin' Sunny's fault. If you only had a brain, right . . . Sheriff?"

Sobrino kept busy pushing the nails into the plank with his thumb. Boy shouted, "Tell the farmer; they can't harm us!"

"Why didn't you tell us?" said Sunny, staring her in her basil eyes.

"I don't know him, if that's what you're askin'. The farmer found me in town and grew me up."

"Why aren't you like them?" said Sunny.

"Why aren't you?" said Dot.

"They're grown men; we're grown boys!" shouted Boy. He was fixing to topple off the crossbeam. If Sunny had asked her again why she hadn't told him, Sunny knew she'd have said 'cause he wouldn't have understood, the implication being that he wasn't old enough to understand.

Sunny looked over her shoulder at the barred back door. It was a coward thing to do, by Sunny's estimation, surrendering the chicken coop. He decided the whole lot of 'em was scared witless. Down to the one-legged horse, they were past hysterics, shivering in woolly-brained fear. They were hoping the farmer would show up and save them. Sobrino turned to look at him—an expression like realizing sheep won't ever be shepherds. Sunny saw nothing but a broken old Mexican.

*   *   *

If it weren't for Sunny, they'd've all just let the rancher squat wherever he pleased. In fact, if it wasn't for Sunny, thought Sunny, the Growin' Man would be sitting on the farmer's porch right now, with his gang running around lawless, busting up the toys for whatever pleasure they got out of it.

Every gunslinger understood the principle. Any man who ever met another on the range, with nothing around to keep 'em civilized. They'd decide the law between themselves, with their two guns. And whoever was alive would be right. Whoever was right could have the can of baked beans.

The other one could well die or hobble to town for somebody else to hold up the law on his behalf for his remaining days. Sunny knew that's all a lawman did, really: win fights no one else could. Sunny squeezed his fists till they crinkled.

He walked out of the barn. If either Sobrino or Dot said anything, he didn't hear it. He dropped a dart into his hand and turned toward the chicken coop.

9

PUP CAME BARRELING around the corner of the barn. When he reached Sunny, he was running so hard he went ten feet farther. Then he turned around, scrambled back to Sunny, and trotted beside him toward the chicken coop. He walked with his chest out, like a police dog. Sunny swung one foot out to push Pup away. Pup was lifted into the air, then landed and kept walking alongside his partner. This wasn't no time to squabble with your deputy. Sunny stopped. Pup took a few more steps, stopped, then scampered back. "You ain't coming along," said Sunny. Pup wagged his tail. He was excited about coming along.

Sunny shook his head no. Pup opened his mouth and let his tongue hang. "They'll take you apart. Go on, git."

Pup yapped again and backflipped.

"Sorry, Pup," Sunny said. "I know you mean well." Then he booted the dog ten feet into a grass bed.

Sunny cussed at himself and put a sleeve up to his mouth. He dragged out a piece of straw and tried to rev himself up again. The encouraging rain had already passed over. There wasn't even a straggling cloud to remember it by. He looked up at the infinite flare and had to shield his eyes.

He said, "Aw, hell," and walked on toward the coop. When he turned the corner onto the dirt lot, it looked more like a mining camp. The Growin' Man was standing with his back to him, watching a homunculus digging in the dirt at his feet. Two others were pulling out the side walls of the chicken coop and propping up the roof on stilts to make a lean-to. One of them had ears like a cat, the other a snout. "Saw you comin' a mile off," said the Growin' Man. He turned around, hands in his denim jacket, bubble-gum chaw dribbling down his chins.

"Then you saw me chop down your boy," said Sunny. He felt the rainwater coursing through his in-between spaces. The Growin' Man chuckled at the idea. "A tree falls in tha woods, and not a real person there to hear it."

The homunculus fidgeting in the dirt behind him stood up. Its eyes were open, or rather its eyelids had been pruned so they never shut. They were Dot's color, but five sizes bigger from constant use. That's how come they'd seen him coming. Sunny glanced again at the builders with the inhuman snout and ears. They'd been grafted on from an early age. Sunny imagined that one could hear a wolf walking on snow and the other could smell the blood inside a human heart.

The Growin' Man made a *chup-chup* sound, a self-satisfied

smacking. "You can breed 'em into any which size and shape. Tie a branch to they fo'heads, and they'll spit up cherries."

"My dog can smell, too," said Sunny.

"Can't make 'em quite like you, though. With feelin's an' such. Like how scared you ah, that's sweetah than a nectarine."

The Growin' Man licked his lips. He put a hand in his pocket. The same one he'd pulled the lighter from last time. Sunny took a step back. The Growin' Man pulled his hand out. Sunny flinched. The Growin' Man grinned and opened his hand to show a fistful of birdseed. He mused, "Thought I'd help you feed those hens'a yours," and tossed some in the dirt.

"Then you stole the wrong seed," said Sunny. "Those aren't for the birds. They *are* the birds. Left from the late planting. Give it." The Growin' Man shut his fist around the remaining seeds and shoved them back in his pocket.

"You can't grow 'em, anyway," said Sunny. "You don't know how."

"But ah will," said the Growin' Man. "Tell me, how come the farmah chose you of all those hangin' dummies to bring to life? You special? He feed you somethin' to make you walk and talk, and tell him how stupid he is?"

Sunny cleared his throat and declared, "You're all trespassing our land. This is your last warning."

The Growin' Man was tickled. "A warnin'," he said. "Well, ain't that a decent jestchah." Then he laughed and stepped aside. Behind him, where the wide-eyed homunculus had been working, was one of the sheep, its innards scattered from its belly. Sunny recoiled. The dirt was muddy with spilled oil.

"A warnin' seems real kind of you, Sheriff," the Growin' Man said, pacing. "A real do-right thing to do. Is that what you always aw? A do-right man?" Then he leaned toward Sunny, close enough to kiss him if he wanted, and whispered, "No, course not. You're nuthin' but do-right straw."

Sunny couldn't take his eyes off the gutted sheep. He squeezed his ducts with a thumb and forefinger to keep from crying. The pig-faced homunculus caught the briny scent and sniffed at the air.

The Growin' Man spread his arms as he expounded on his thoughts. "Ah imagine you're feelin' guilty, with this heah clock-work sheep remindin' you that you aw yo'self a killah of mah peculiah brand of livestock."

That wasn't what Sunny was feeling.

"But ah would alleviate any of yo moral compunctions by informin' you that my unfortunate herd heah is not quite alive, just *half* alive, so you go on feelin' superior an' whatnot to a degenerate such as mahself. For these toys of yours are very much living creations, an' ah intend to dissect as many as ah I need to figure out why."

"You're the only killer here," Sunny said.

"Don't be hasty now, son. They're still toys. You're still just straw. Whatever that farmah has done, it's cured you of bein' inanimate, tha's all."

Sunny wanted to cut every one of them down. He glared at the obese rancher, talking down to him for not being flesh, something better than a half-alive homunculus but not human either. The Growin' Man just wanted better toys. He wanted them to imagine their own ways of hurting people. And he seemed to think that if he could give his cattle brains, then they wouldn't be so mindless.

Sunny nodded at the electric sheep. "You can't eat it," said Sunny, although he knew full well the Growin' Man didn't intend to. "It ain't meat. It ain't real."

"Then, why do you care?" said the Growin' Man. He came so close that Sunny could smell the hot candy odor from his mouth. He was himself an overgrowth of flesh. "You ain't real eithah, Sunny boy. You 'fraid ah won't eat you when ah'm done?"

He made that *chup-chup* sound, like he had mint jelly on the roof of his mouth. Sunny wouldn't be able to hold off any longer. He was breathing like he'd run from clear on the other side of the vegetable garden. He looked at the sheep one last time and clenched the dart in his hand. He couldn't do anything but leave it to them. For now, he'd have to run off, as though he was the thief. He'd have to tie off this part of the farm and gather all the toys to the porch before the men could get ahold of any more.

As he turned, Sunny swung his arm. The dart nailed the hand of the cat-eared man into the roof of the chicken coop. The homunculus made a vacant groan and unstuck its hand. Sunny walked off. The Growin' Man chuckled and blew a bubble with gum and chaw.

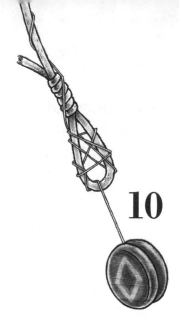

10

THE LATE-AFTERNOON rain had mustered the rows and brought them strong into the growing season. The jumpy caboose was aboveground, almost up to its rails. On either side of it, a pogo stick and tasseled baton presented tall stalks. Out by the LEGO bushes in the far corner of the field, an entire dollhouse was coming up, wild from last season. Even the late planting was stirring under the mounds of dirt.

Sunny leaned on the fence with his arms out on the perpendicular beam, not particularly looking over the rows. His hands dangled at the wrist. His head was rolled forward like a turnip. His nose seemed to be propping it up against his chest. Pup lay at his feet, whimpering, and licking between Sunny's toes in hope of cheering him up.

The farmer's daughter walked up to the rows from the back of the farmhouse with a glass pitcher. Sunny didn't budge the entire time. Dot came up behind him and said, "Made you my melonade. First watermelon of the year."

Sunny's head jerked up. He sniffed and looked around. "Huh?"

"Melonade," repeated the farmer's daughter.

"Oh, yeah." Sunny took a cup. He poured some on Pup's head and held the rest. Pup sprang up and started licking at his own floppy ears.

"They're coming up nice," said the farmer's daughter.

"Mmm," said Sunny.

The gradient spheres of twilight made everything look twice-baked, the color of rust and dusk. Dust and rusk. The braggart crow hooped once around the field and landed on the handle of an extendo-claw near the dollhouse. It spat a defiant caw, then lifted one leg and put it down, mocking them.

"You're gonna have to stake the vines pretty soon," said the farmer's daughter. The crayons were hanging heavy and low to the ground, in bushes on the western edge of the rows, where they'd rot if they weren't propped up.

Sunny said, "Yeah." They'd need time to ripen into their full colors.

Sunny took another drink. It seemed like she was waiting for Sunny to come up with a plan to kick out the Growin' Man. Dot poured some in her palm and kneeled down to let Pup lap it up.

"So what's it like, being a plant?" said Sunny.

The farmer's daughter looked up at him, but he was staring out over the rows. She said, "Prolly feels the same as anyone else. Used to be just alchemists that'd grow us. They'd sneak under the gallows at night like grave robbers and dig up the sprouts. Then they'd try to figure out how to shove their dead lovers' spirits into our husks."

"And here I figured you didn't have the farmer's eyes was all."

"I got a lot more than eyes from him."

The farmer's daughter scratched Pup behind the ears. He thumped his foot in the dirt. The crow called out to make sure everyone was watching. "Look, Sunny, I shouldn't have said what I said. About the sheep being your mess . . ." she trailed off.

Sunny said, "Why idn't he out here, Dot?" The farmer's daughter stood up, wiping her wet hand on the back of her jeans.

"How should I know?"

"You and me, we're each a homunculus to him—"

"That's a lie," said Dot.

"We're only half alive, like the Growin' Man says."

"Shut up, Sunny."

"We ain't nothing but stuff."

Dot poured some melonade on Sunny's feet. It shut him up for a minute.

"The only reason I have to hate the farmer is he stuck me with you and letting you think you're sheriff. Jeez almighty, I come to apologize for callin' you an ijit, but I guess I was right the first time."

Sunny noticed the rows nearest to them, the final birdseed plantings of the season, sprouting the very tips of their beaks. He said, "Then, we're no better than the toys."

"What made you ever think we were better than the toys?" said Dot. "They're alive, too. And we all got purposes. I'm a daughter. You protect the rows. What else you want?"

Sunny wanted something in common with Dot, whatever it was. Something as general as life—as being a son and a daughter, a man and a woman—instead of a bag of straw and a beautiful tree.

One beak popped out of the ground and shook off the dirt—

a cardboard head and white balsa-wood wings. The bird flapped a few times, sending black soil into the air, till finally its legless body unmoored itself from the ground and launched into the air. It flew toward the setting sun, as if racing to catch the thing before it dove under the horizon. The farmer would be out in the early dawn of the next morning, humming a deep eternal love song as he walked among the rows.

But by then the birds of the season would have gone. Sunny wondered where they'd fly to before their wings finally gave out from the strain, never being able to perch. Or if a spring rain would soak and flatten them against the earth, turning them to half-decomposed paste. Like seasonal flowers, the birds were a disposable fancy.

"Hey, Dot," said Sunny, wondering for the first time what the farmer did that the Growin' Man wanted to know so badly. He guessed it had to do with planting birds every season, even knowing they were temporary creatures, almost broken from the very start. "What do you want to be when you grow up?"

The farmer's daughter watched a second and third paper bird struggle out of the dirt and into the air. One of them clipped a wing and wobbled as it flew. Then she said, "Taller."

Sunny stood with his back on the fence, letting the last of the light warm his face, while the farmer's daughter leaned forward from the other side, with her elbows resting on the crossbeam. Soon it would be dark and the farm would be an unsafe place, with mindless men roaming around, tearing up helpless creatures in the vain hope of bettering themselves.

But for the time being, Sunny and Dot stared out onto the rows as tens then hundreds of white paper birds nuzzled their way out of the dirt and took flight toward futures not one of them could compre-hend. Several birds grazed right past the ornery crow, and more kept sprouting right below its perch. At first it cackled at them, unwilling to give up the roost, then finally took to the air. It swept right over Sunny's head and belted a huffy call.

Pup shook all over with excitement, his tail wagging his entire bottom half, but he remained where he was in an attempt to be a good dog. He looked up at Sunny. Sunny nodded, gave him a little nudge with his foot, and said, "Go on, git."

Pup tore out from the post, down the plow line of the middle row, barking as he shot toward the last sliver of the sun. An exclama-tion of birds, like white confetti, burst into the sky, and, featherless, they fluttered toward singular and short purposes.

Dot patted Sunny on the shoulder and walked back toward the farmhouse with the pitcher of melonade. She was Sunny's friend.

11

THE FARMER'S DAUGHTER stepped into the firelight of
Sobrino's camp and said, "Would ya like somethin' to drink?"

Sobrino extended his tin cup to her. "Gracias," he said.

There weren't more than a few twigs in Sobrino's fire—out of
courtesy, Dot suspected. Or maybe so as not to draw attention from
the Growin' Man's gang. It surprised her how many toys huddled
next to him, finding shelter in the cricks of his knees or nestled
under his arms. A plush lion was sitting as close to the fire as its
frizzy mane allowed and kept its tail touching Sobrino's hip at all
times. The old man watched a row of penguins climb up the toes
of his left foot and slide down the arch, only to march around and
climb up again.

"Is dangerous, no? To come here?" said Sobrino, whirling a finger
at the dark around them. The moon, like the farmer, was absent, and
the stars looked like evening primroses, blooming in haphazard
yellow clusters.

"I can take care of myself," said Dot, pouring a cup for herself and planting herself on the other side of the fire. "I ain't no delicate flower."

Sobrino giggled, a soft *eh-eh-eh*. "Maybe a thorny flower, a cactoos."

"A prickly pear."

"Una rosa."

"Maybe if I put my hair up."

The both of them took a sip. Dot spotted a movement behind Sobrino. It was one of the baby sheep. A few of them were still wandering around from one patch of grass to another, on Sobrino's side of the dirt road, unaware that even the reckless squirrels were trembling on the farmhouse porch.

"This one saw a dried-up man in the woods and ran here," said Sobrino. "I would bring to you tomorrow." He'd tied the lamb to the old oak with a yo-yo. The lamb was nibbling on the fescue surrounding the base of the tree, any ordeal with dead men long forgotten. "Thank you," said the farmer's daughter. Sobrino went *eh-eh-eh*. It was a language Dot didn't know, so it sounded stupid to her ears.

They let silence sit with them for a while. There wasn't any more melonade to offer. The fire had done its deed and called the wandering toys. Now it was ready to flicker out.

Without the lonesome nocturnes of the wood owls to the prairie, the farm was breathless. There seemed to be more rustling than most nights. Every tree sounded like a willow.

The old giant constantly shifted his position to stretch his joints. He pushed deep into the palm of one hand with his thumb, then squeezed his swollen knuckles one by one. When he pushed back his shoulders and swung his head in a circular motion, the bones in his neck and collar made a sound like a cannonball rolling down a staircase. His skin looked overstretched, like his whole body was scar tissue. Dot wondered if he really was one of those giants from the mountains, hurling boulders over his head during lightning storms, howling at his strength. As a young man, he could have dashed chunks of the earth big enough to be called the world's teeth.

Dot said, "You could help us. You could run them off the farm."

Sobrino looked up at her and shook his head no.

"How come? It'd be magic, wouldn't it? You're a magician, ain't you?"

"Sí," said the old man, "But is no easy. He wants your—" He was having trouble thinking of the word, so he pointed at his chest.

"He wants to know how Sunny and the toys and me turned out like we did. How come the farmer's toys are more human than all those men."

Sobrino nodded.

"Hell, even I don't know," said Dot. "He sings over us, then goes inside. He don't even use fertilizer."

Sobrino squinted at the fire and ran a dirty thumb and forefinger over his goatee. He seemed to have expressions for situations Sunny and Dot hadn't even lived through. He might have been an emotional giant as well, with feelings drawn out so long they twisted up into cords and soaked in sad and joyful brine till they'd smoothed and hardened at the same time.

"Sony is scared, yeah. A showdown is coming for the chacho. Scared he is not man enough, so he waits. Maybe he becomes a man tomorrow. Then he can fight." Sobrino made a gun with his long index finger and shot.

The farmer's daughter looked into the dying fire and remembered Sunny's flinch at the Growin' Man's lighter. All Sunny knew about being a man was what he'd learned watching a bull run headfirst into a red barn. He still thought the highest law was to leave everybody well enough alone. "He don't stand a chance," said Dot, and got up. "I know it's his job now, or he's taken it on himself, but jeez, he ain't got a fool's shot at doin' it right."

Sobrino nodded. "Too scared," he said.

"Yeah," said Dot, "or too young or there's too many of 'em. Too somethin'."

She left the pitcher for Sobrino, wiped the dirt from her jeans, and climbed over the split-rail fence, back toward the house. As she crossed the hundred-yard pasture, she heard a rustling sound out on the periphery. If one of them pieces of chattel approached her, she'd tear it apart.

Sunny hunkered down in the tall grass of the pasture, trying to keep out of her sight till she walked past where he'd been watching from. He felt a new kind of ache, worse even than being hung by a rope. Dot had never been a friend to him. He headed back around the pasture the long way, over the hill, and behind the house.

The babies in the rows were all asleep. It seemed even the grown men had shame enough to leave them be. Sunny avoided the thought that the rows were exactly the Growin' Man's purpose and that he'd be coming for them soon enough. The plant men had squatted in the chicken coop way back behind the barn, walked down past the dirt road into the sapling orchard, and even crawled around the barn a little. But none of them had approached the farmhouse, the vegetable garden, or the rows. Not just yet. Sunny couldn't turn a blind eye to that.

He stood over the rows for the rest of the night, only failing his guard at the early dawn when he fell asleep. He woke up only in time to catch the farmer's last shadow pass by. "Wait!" shouted Sunny, but the farmer couldn't hear him. The farmhouse's screen door was already shut.

In the morning, Sunny didn't find any new toys broken by the Growin' Man's gang. He left Dot alone to her work in the vegetable garden. Boy counted all the toys and fit them onto the congested porch. So much of the farm had been battened down that soon it'd be a regular war machine. Soon there'd be no reason to avoid a fight—even one that everybody thought they'd lose.

By midafternoon Sunny had finished his chores. He walked to the barn and opened the doors of the main bay wide. He let Pup chase the chickens in circles out front, to run their spools down for the day. Ever since they'd shuttered up the barn, it had dampened like a sweaty bandage. The homunculus that had been caught by the trap left behind the smell of moldy pumpkins.

The first sunlight that swept into the barn lifted a cloud of fibers, flax, and dust. It swirled out of the bay doors and let in sweet air you couldn't see.

A whispering sound seemed to crawl into Sunny's ears from above in the attic. Maybe the toy grave was rattling to demand the remains of the sheep, which were still scattered at the foot of the rancher's lean-to for all anyone knew. Or maybe it was nothing, just a draft between the floorboards. Sunny didn't pay it any attention.

Sunny didn't have any chores left but to go fight a man. Instead, he picked up a few loose planks of wood in the main bay and began a new bookshelf. The sun set once again.

Sunny had been a hanged man—or an effigy of one, anyhow—and no stranger to suffocating. He missed the feeling of dangling alone from a broken neck and the feeling that nobody knew his troubles, nobody could ever quite understand. But now, for all its isolation, for all the miles between town and the farm, Sunny couldn't think of a single place to be alone. The farm felt more like a day care sometimes, with so many feeble hearts to care for—a man would nearly drown in stuff and people to have relationships with.

Being on display for being lonely was what Sunny liked so much about the job of a sheriff. The point was having society and then choosing to reject it—but not running off so fast it couldn't chase after.

In short, when he considered what a man ought to be, Sunny thought of a lone gunman of the law. And when he thought of a woman, he thought of Dot.

"But you never know what to do, 'cause farmer no tell you nothing, eh?" said Sobrino.

Sunny turned around from the shelf he had been staining. Sobrino stood in the barn door, prodding the baby sheep he'd found the day before with his foot so it would amble inside.

"Old man, you didn't read my thoughts," Sunny said as he

dunked the rag in the wood stain and dragged it across a shelf. "Don't pretend you read my thoughts."

The old magician put his hands up in surrender but made the *eh-eh-eh* sound like he was impressed with himself all the same. The stain pooled in places where Sunny had pushed too hard on the soaked rag, like the dark splotches of sun pocks on Sobrino's hands.

Sunny worked up a mean thing to say for when the giant made fun of the bookshelves again. But nothing came. Sunny glanced over. Sobrino had tied up the sheep and grabbed a cloth from the bench. He was staining the tops of the bookshelves where Sunny couldn't reach. He mouthed the word *majeek.*

It occurred to Sunny that if he'd stained the wood before constructing the shelves, he wouldn't need a stilt performer to reach the tops. He thought of Sobrino helping him a few days back, probably biting his tongue to keep from saying the same thing. "Whatever," said Sunny.

"¿Que, chacho?" said Sobrino, gliding the moist cloth over the shelf in even strokes.

"Nuthin', shut up."

"I no say nothing."

"Whatever. I ain't yer chacho."

"Wokay," said Sobrino. After a minute Sunny hurled the soppy rag across the barn and hit the grazing sheep square in the side of the head. It made a delayed baying sound and fell over. A brown splatter stained its cotton wool.

"Aw, hell," Sunny said. Wood stain dripped from every shelf. "Why didn't you tell me to stain the planks before nailing 'em together?"

Sobrino didn't turn around from his work, but Sunny could tell he was grinning, just by the way his head bobbed. Sunny couldn't say anything or he'd look stupid. He couldn't just ask if Sobrino and Dot were having lots of secret meetings and talking behind his back. It'd seem like he didn't know already.

Pup heard something outside and stopped chasing the hens. He bolted through the bay doors to meet what was coming. Sunny whipped around. He twitched at the wrists, and two darts dropped in between his fingers. Pup came running back into the barn, then ricocheted out again. The farmer's daughter walked in a moment later with Pup ahead of her and Boy following behind. Sunny quickly returned the darts to his sleeve.

She was holding a tractor's pull-'n'-play ring. The pull string was frayed at the end. Her basil eyes had been crying.

"They disassembled the whole thing," she said. She waved the ring as bloody proof. "I went to put some tools away, and when I walked back to the vegetable garden, I didn't even see it at first it was so scattered."

Sobrino set his cloth down and put his hands into his trouser pockets. "The whole thing," she said, "chair to chassis. Stupid man, stupid, stupid gang can't even tell the tractor was already broken." She wagged the drawstring at Sunny like an accusation or, worse, an appeal. "And I found it, and it was torn apart, Sunny. Even the one-piece molds."

The farmer's daughter let the plastic hoop fall to her side. She trembled. Boy stood behind her with his whole hand in his mouth. They both looked at Sunny, expecting something. Sobrino looked at him, too.

Sunny pulled a clipped piece of straw from his sleeve so he wouldn't have to say anything. He looked down at his bare feet and dyed hands, then up at Dot and Pup and Boy and Sobrino. The hens had even paused to look. If the homuncular gang had trespassed onto the vegetable garden, then the rows would be next. He flexed his jaw. They'd need a new tractor.

Sunny exhaled. It came out in the shape of "Aw, hell," and he marched past them out the barn and around it to the back lot.

He approached the back of the barn, grumbling cuss and stuffing his fingers into fists several times. He turned the corner and saw the Growin' Man lounging in the chicken coop with his hands behind his back and a homunculus standing beside him, holding one of the hens upside down by its wheel.

The Growin' Man said, "Heard you comin' a mile—"

Sunny punched the dead calm homunculus in the face and grabbed the hen. Then he leaned down into the prone rancher's face and spat, "Here's what you heard: You and me dance in the pasture at noon tomorrow. Then I spill you open like that gum-ball machine, yeah?"

The Growin' Man chupped and blew a bubble in Sunny's face. "Ah'm gonna let 'em eat yo pretty little straw heart," he said.

Sunny straightened up and looked at the homunculus. It rubbed its cheek, not because it could feel anything in it, but because it puppeted what living things did. Sunny clobbered the homunculus again, across the other cheek, and left, holding the mortified chicken.

12

SUNNY DIDN'T GO back to the main bay to work on the bookshelves. He wanted something he was good at. When he passed the front of the barn, he dropped the hen. It went unicycling back into the tangle of chickens, which resembled nothing more than a dust devil made of prairie junk.

"Sunny!" Boy shouted.

But Sunny kept going.

"Sunny?" Dot called after him. Pup came running to tag along. His yap made Sunny look over his shoulder. This time Pup saw the kick coming. In the same motion that Sunny wheeled around to kick the oncoming dog, Pup rounded off his path into a U-turn. Sunny's sweeping foot just whiffed past Pup's ear. It flapped like a curtain in the wind. Pup scrambled back to the barn. Sunny nearly lost his footing, swinging around so hard. He cussed at himself and stumbled on.

"Did you win?" asked Boy, a disastrous question to put to any lawman, because if you had to ask, the answer would always be no.

Back in the barn, Sobrino didn't say anything as he fixed the stain job Sunny had botched. He made a soft teakettle noise between his teeth, themselves stained every shade of brown, and soothed the brambling chickens. Pup let Sunny be and resigned himself to Boy's equally heedless company. Dot pulled down the staircase to the attic and carried up the tractor's ring.

To Sunny, the farmhouse porch looked like a merry-go-round come unglued and left piled up with its constituent parts. Fearful toys were gathered into a cavalcade of stuff that couldn't take care of itself.

As he passed by, all the toys leaned in his direction. Sunny tried to ignore the shivering of a miniature tambourine in their midst. He stopped at his post and looked down the hill to the hundred-yard pasture. Tall grass swayed like a rattler's tail. Good chance he'd be lying in that grass the next day.

He pulled out pieces of straw from his sleeve and let them drop. He rubbed a few stalks between his thumb and forefinger. The owl and the crow were screaming at each other in the oak tree on the far side of the split-rail fence. The remains of Sobrino's campfire kept Sunny from going over there to escape the pasture and the visions of himself in a standoff with a man he couldn't quite look in the eye. Even the black embers of a cold pit sent frenzy through his stuffing. A lone spark, drifting like a bee, could send him up in a wicker blaze. He slumped over so far as he leaned on his post that his body made the shape of an *S*.

A windup monkey with a pair of cymbals made a series of warning clangs on the porch. Sunny looked up from ripping at his sleeves. On the western horizon, a few silhouettes shambled toward the farm. He could tell what they were, even way off in the distance. Like him, the homunculi were effigies, stand-ins for real living folks. They would walk through the night and arrive by the end of the next day. Endless numbers of them could be coming—insensate meat missing whatever it was that would have made them flesh.

Sunny tried to tighten his jaw, started to say, "Aw, hell," in a detached, resilient sort of way. But his quavering chin kept harassing the notion. Sunny sniffed hard and ran toward the back of the house, across the rows, toward the vegetable garden.

Sunny found the first piece of the tractor at the stretch of alfalfa that extended across the entire width of the vegetable garden. He blinked at it and pushed a toe cautiously against it, but it didn't move. It was a piece of green plastic, basic tractor green, probably from the fender. He surveyed the garden where Dot's affinity had produced crops, every one of them worthy of the state fair. In town they said she had green thumbs.

Sunny bent down and poked the plastic. Its sides were perforated where the homunculus had grabbed it with both hands and ripped off chunks. Sunny imagined the creature getting to the center of the tractor and finding nothing and thrashing at it in some savage frustration—one that made it search in as unlikely a place as farm equipment in the first place.

It was a fact that the homunculi weren't afraid of anything because they didn't care for anything. But as Sunny picked up the first piece

of the lacerated plastic, he realized they also were marked by something else. It was wanting that held them upright. They felt just
enough to miss whatever it was they were missing. And with the
Growin' Man promising they'd find it here, they were free to try
every darn thing to fulfill themselves, even eating the dashboard of
a tractor—hoping it could be the heart of them—and letting loose a
primal yawp when it cut them going down.

Sunny cradled the fender and stepped through the alfalfa patch
onto soil the machine had plowed just a few days previous. The
scattered remains were like disparate flushes of color a kid might
scrawl on an otherwise orderly drawing. With the last bit of daylight, Sunny scavenged around the vegetable garden for broken parts
to bury up in the attic.

The ornery crow followed him with short hops from one shrub
to another, and a few times when it thought Sunny had stopped
listening, it flew onto his hat. By the sound of its cackles, it seemed
to get satisfaction out of Sunny's ineffective swatting. By the day's
end, Sunny didn't notice it, other than a slight quiver of his ear.
Maybe Sunny even got to thinking he deserved it.

The farm was denim blue in the dusk by the time Sunny hauled a
little red wagon, piled high with tractor parts, across the porch. He
stopped at the foot of his bedpost. A white paper bird was lying
in the dirt. One wing had torn off in the crash. The other flapped
to stave off stillness. Sunny kneeled down. The bird was using up
the last of its life trying to flutter off. Sunny picked it up. When he
turned to place the bird on the wagon, he saw the crow perched on
top of the tractor parts, as proud as a cattle king.

Sunny cussed and flung a dart at the crow, clipping one of its wings as it flew away. The crow squawked and arced behind the farmhouse to find better company.

As Sunny crossed in front of the porch, the toys didn't pay any attention. He staggered with his head down, like a beast of burden, pulling a yoke so heavy and leaning so far forward that his nose nearly plowed a furrow in the dirt. The farmer's daughter must have been soothing the hens to sleep or taking the old man's counsel over his. Sunny considered regretting a few things.

It was full dark. The clouds were roughhousing the moon. The Growin' Man would own the place if he won. He had had no need to go sneaking around the night before. Even if he lost, his full gang would arrive by the next day, and they would overrun the farm.

Sunny opened the barn door. Inside, the library almost shimmered. It looked like the old man had laid the entire coat of wood stain, evened out the first one, and then gone over it with a finishing lacquer. Where the shelves had teetered or stood crooked, they now stood level. In as much time as it would have taken Sunny to sand a few shelves, Sobrino had carved a vernal wood into each sideboard with his craggy fingernails. Along the top was a bas-relief of wild-flowers in a field, something Sunny couldn't have done no matter how long he spent. Magic, thought Sunny. There was a bookend the shape of a tortle.

Every picture book on the farm had been gathered and shelved. Dot must have brought them. Must have put her hand to her heart when she saw it all finished. As he thought of missing that moment, the grin on Sunny's face fell through a trapdoor. If Sobrino had just left it alone, maybe Sunny's woodwork wouldn't have seemed so childish. Sunny stared at Dot's gift, then finally shrugged, said, "Hell," and went back to get the tractor parts. He tossed them into the attic without setting foot on the landing. As he replaced the pull-down staircase, Dot showed up with her hair all around her shoulders and said, "Hey, Sunny! Did you see what Sobrino—?"

Sunny shouldered past her before she could finish. He grumbled, "Whatever," so she'd know she could've been saying anything and it wouldn't have mattered to him.

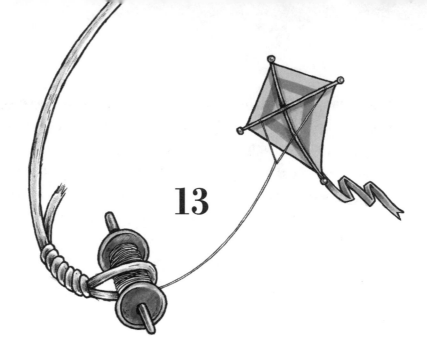

13

I<small>F</small> Y<small>OU</small> G<small>OT</small> to thinking about it, you might think the sun was trying to be obnoxious, rising up every day like it was poking you on the shoulder over and over again with the promise that whether you were sick of 'em or not, you had another day coming. Out by the rows, Sunny opened one eye and licked at the sour film around his mouth. His head hurt from sleeping too long in the heat. Neither Pup nor the carrion crow was around.

Almost every toy was now coming up in mint condition. The caboose was entirely grown, puffing clouds as it drove between imaginary stations, clambering along the rows, and making high-pitched toots for every whistle-stop connection.

All the crops stirred a little in the breeze. A yellow kite was only tethered by its buried spool. A pair of purple teacups rattled on their saucers. Even the mulch of rhinestones and jacks were unscuffed and newborn to the world. The farmer had come and gone already. And though Sunny thought he could recall the medley of the farmer's tune from his sleep, he thought the next time he heard it, he'd tell the farmer to keep his precious humming to himself.

Sunny had missed the early dawn light by a good margin. In fact, when he got his legs under him, he realized there was no shade to speak of. It was midday. He'd overslept. Dot had left another tin cup of coffee with sugar and cream at his feet. He craned his long neck, but he couldn't hear the animals baying in the barn. She must have done his chores again. He dragged a hand across his face to wake himself and muffled the sound of "Aw, hell," which he repeated as he started running to the pasture on the other side of the farmhouse.

There wasn't any time to comfort the hens. He glanced over at the porch as he sprinted past. All the toys were gone.

Sunny had imagined himself the clink-step gunslinger, leaning on his post, maybe even dozing under the brim of his hat, a long piece of straw dangling between his teeth. The Growin' Man would have come into the pasture and seen the law waiting for him. Instead, Sunny was barefoot and out of breath when he reached the men in the yard. The Growin' Man's hands rested on his gut. Only one homunculus stood on either side of him, aimless. A bee zoomed from one to the other, pollinating their hair.

The farmer's daughter and Sobrino stood way off to the side, between the gang and the farmhouse. Dot held a long-handled shovel. Sunny tried to gulp his breaths and avoided putting his hands on his knees so he wouldn't seem weak.

The Growin' Man said, "Take yo' time, son. Wouldn't want but a fair draw between us." He chupped his blue and black lips as though he'd told a good one. They stood fifteen yards apart. Dot hollered from over to the side, "We penned up the toys in the house, Sunny. Don't worry about anything."

Sobrino added, "Ayo, Sheriff."

The Growin' Man looked over at the girl and snorted. Sunny held his side and paced a small circle. He considered a quick draw right then to get the jump, maybe put the man down with a single shot. Slowly, so no one would notice, he lowered a dart into his hand.

"You aren't thinkin' of gunnin' me down like a bandit, aw you, Sheriff?" The Growin' Man nodded at Sunny's concealed palm. Then he mused, "Or maybe you're cold-blooded is all. Fascinating."

Sunny tried to speak in a lower tone than was his naturally. "You can still leave on your own, stranger. We don't want your kind here."

The Growin' Man's jowls rolled as he laughed. He said, "Oh, but ah want yo' kind, Sunny . . . which, ah suppose, is the exact nature of our cross-purposes." He removed his metal lighter from his denim jacket and flipped it open. A flame licked at the sky. He flipped it shut.

Sunny wasn't stepping back this time. His fingers twitched. If he let a dart fly, he could probably—he got the image of the Growin' Man taking ten, twelve darts in his blubber without slowing his charge. Sunny could windmill his arms and send a Gatling's worth of darts, and the man would still close the distance.

Sunny shifted his weight and adjusted his grip on the dart. The Growin' Man chupped his lips and said, "You're wonderin' if you can plug me with enough darts to stop my pushin' this here flame into yo' chest. Well . . ." He didn't finish the sentiment, letting it drift into the space between them. A storm wind blew steadily now. The tall grass slapped at their thighs.

"They do what you want," said Sunny. "Why do you want to make 'em human?"

The crow shrieked as it circled above their heads. The Growin' Man said, "You ought to know. So they'll take things without my havin' to tell 'em. They'll gossip as easy as drinkin' watah. Be cruel and lie for their own ambitions. Maybe I'll teach 'em to be afraid, like you ah right now."

The Growin' Man licked his blue and black lips as he toyed with the lighter. The sudden whorl of air around them gave Sunny hope for rain.

"We don't do that," said Sunny.

"Yes, you do," said the Growin' Man, "but ah love that you say you don't. That's precious."

Sunny noticed the Growin' Man's eyes glance in the direction of the barn several times, without him meaning to, it seemed.

Sunny said, "Aw, hell," and shouted to the farmer's daughter, "Dot, where are Boy and Pup?"

The farmer's daughter stammered before saying, "Hiding out in the barn. Why does it matter—?"

The Growin' Man sneered wide and showed his mouth full of gum balls and chaw. Then he whispered the words, "But you're too late."

A dozen homunculi groaned as they climbed over the split-rail fence. They'd walked all night without rest. They marched across the hundred-yard pasture. Sunny took off at a dead run toward the barn. "Hold 'em back!" he shouted at Dot as he passed. The Growin' Man lumbered after Sunny. One homunculus staggered toward the farmer's daughter, the other toward Sobrino. As Sunny sprinted to the barn, he heard Dot grunt as she swung the shovel. A gong and a wooden groan.

As Dot and Sobrino met the wave of trespassers, Dot sidestepped a lunging tackle, put two fingers to her lips, and whistled. The screen door of the farmhouse opened, and every able toy poured into the front yard. The tangle of hens consumed one grown man. The stick horse had made its mind up to be brave and stampeded down the hill with short hops. Even the baby train came to help. It made a nuisance of itself driving in circles underfoot. It caused one man to fall backward over an oblivious sheep grazing in the middle of the fight.

When he reached the barn, Sunny could hear frantic scratching coming from the attic like he'd never heard before. He ran through the library under a wailing cry of "Sunny!" and came to a sudden stop. Boy sat on a crossbeam, tears running down his rivets. A homunculus stood on its tiptoes and reached up, but it was unable to grab Boy's foot. The barred back door stood wide open. A second homunculus kneeled on the ground, pulling out the wires from Pup's disassembled belly.

Only Pup's tail was moving. It jerked a little every time the homunculus touched a wire, as if the dog had gone into shock. "Stop," Sunny whispered. For some reason, he didn't want to disturb Pup with unnecessary noise. But the homunculus had one absurd purpose, to find the wire marked *life.* "Stop, stop!" Sunny screamed.

He held the dart in his hand like a dagger and ran at the two grown men. As he passed the one standing on tiptoes, Sunny made one sweeping motion. He jammed the dart through one ankle and into the other. Then he lifted the skewer as he ran, upending the creature.

He gained speed and barreled into the man kneeling over Pup. The two somersaulted over each other. When they stopped, the homunculus was on its back, Sunny on top. He stabbed it all over with another dart. The homunculus tried to sit up and reach for Pup, but Sunny shoved it back down.

Even after the homunculus stopped moving, Sunny kept on. He was poking air holes into a potato, crying as he did. Bits of plant sprayed at his face as he jammed the dart down again and again. His begrieved lowing was the word "Stop, stop, stop" ground up with gagging and tears and strain.

Behind Sunny, the first creature sat up. It reached down and pulled out the dart that pinned its ankles together. It limped toward Sunny. Boy shouted, "Sunny!" But Sunny was heaving too loud to hear. The homunculus stumbled the last few steps and tripped toward Sunny. But in the last second, Sunny spun around as the homunculus fell and punched the dart upward into the creature's heart. He held the man up. He said, "It was love, you idiot, in that damn song. There wadn't anything else." Then he let the homunculus drop onto the mulched remains of the other.

Sunny ran over and fell on all fours next to Pup's separated parts. The sounds from the attic were like a graveyard coming to life. Before Sunny could say he was sorry, the Growin' Man stepped into the barn. "Ah saw *you* kick that po dawg," he said, "twice."

Sunny wiped his face with his shirt and sniffed hard. The Growin' Man walked toward him. He had the lighter open.

· 95 ·

The rancher saw his dead cattle and said, "Those dumb things. Sometimes they're only good fo kindlin'." Then he tilted as he charged, holding the flame out like a knife.

Sunny swung his arms across his body, and two darts buried themselves in the man's gut. The Growin' Man didn't even seem to notice them as he thrust the lighter at Sunny's face. Sunny dove to the side and rushed behind the rancher, retreating to the main bay for more space. The rancher put the lighter to the browning limbs of the two creatures on the ground. They blazed into a bonfire.

Sobrino and the farmer's daughter came in the back way. Dot's shovel was broken. Sobrino had a tear in his corduroys, and blood was seeping out. Dot stepped around the fire and gathered Pup. She stuffed the smallest pieces into her shirt pockets. Sobrino reached up and grabbed Boy from the rafters. Only he, with his stilt legs, could have reached, thought Sunny as he circled a bookshelf to keep clear of the Growin' Man's advance.

Above them a thunderclap was either the storm outside or the toy chest in the attic falling on its side. The Growin' Man lunged at Sunny, lighter blazing. Sunny hopped backward and landed two darts into the fat man's extended arm. The Growin' Man yowled and dropped the lighter.

"Sunny!" Dot shouted from the stalls.

The bonfire had spread to the piles of feed in the stalls. The mounds in the corners went up like crashing waves into the side walls. The posts were started to singe. Dot cradled Pup in her arms. Sobrino pressed Boy's face into his collar. "Go!" shouted Sunny. "Get them out."

The Growin' Man yanked the darts out of his arm and picked up his lighter. He moseyed over to a stack of hay bales and held the flame up to a corner. Sunny felt animal panic inside him as the bales turned into a column of fire. The Growin' Man said, "Yo' farmah friend should be hanged for givin' you all those lovely feelings and nothing to do with 'em."

The burning column of hay dropped coals onto the nearest bookshelf. The picture books caught immediately — each of them a Roman candle. "Me, I'd give you purpose. I'd brand you all pretty and fine, an' herd you, make you feel needed on this big ol' farm."

Everything burned. The bookshelves made aisles of fire. The crossbeams crackled. The paint on the stalls had started to peel off. Sunny wheeled around, afraid of every direction. A spark fell on his ear, and he howled, clawing at it. The rancher walked toward Sunny with the lighter. "Ah'll even let you plant a few rows fo' me," he said. "We could both be farmahs."

With fire all around him, Sunny wrangled a single clear thought from out of his fear. He glanced up. As the Growin' Man approached, Sunny threw a hail of darts, staking each of the rancher's boots to the ground. The Growin' Man tried to lift his foot but found he couldn't. Sunny reached up and grabbed the pull string for the attic stairs.

"Wait," said the Growin' Man. Sunny yanked the cord. The Growin' Man saw nothing but a heap of debris and broken toys, including parts to make a working tractor, a sensible sheep, and three mice with something close to 20/20 vision. The mountainous procession poured over the Growin' Man. A part of the barn roof made a yawning sound, then collapsed into the attic loft. Sunny had no place to go.

* * *

Outside in the dirt lot near the chicken coop, Sobrino rushed to put Pup back together before it was too late, the wall of flames towering over them. Dot watched him work. She turned to see if Sunny was coming out. Boy stood over Sobrino, shouting, "Pup. Get back together, Pup!"

The little dog mewled as Sobrino's long dirty fingers reached into his plastic belly and pulled out two sides of a frayed wire. The old man twisted it back together. Pup jerked fully to life and kicked all his legs trying to scramble away. Sobrino's hold was firm. He lifted the dog back into Dot's arms. Pup smelled her and settled down.

"Thanks," said Dot. The supports of the barn had crumbled. It seemed to rock back and forth, then the top half folded into the frame. Sparks billowed into the black wall cloud covering up the noonday sun. The entire sky looked like smoke.

"Maybe it'll rain," said Boy.

"No," said Sobrino.

The farmer's daughter squatted down and turned Boy's shoulders to face her. She brought his chin up and said, "You're metal, Boy. You could run in there and save him. You're old enough."

Boy shook his head. "I'm only tin," he said, showing her his hands.

"I know it's a lot to ask, Boy, but Sunny's in there." Dot looked like she might bolt toward the burning barn herself. Boy was summoning tears to help make his case.

"I'm not a real soldier," he said. "I could die."

"Boy!" said the farmer's daughter. "You're a daggum—"

Sobrino's hand on her shoulder kept her from finishing her sentence—"toy." The old giant leaned down. "Tranquilo," he whispered.

Tranquilo meant nothing to the farmer's daughter. She hugged Sobrino's waist, her arms reaching all the way around and back to her own shoulders. She said, "He could go." Sobrino's cotton shirt smelled like mold.

He said the same word again. "Half alive is still something," he added. "Something" sounded like *soam-tink,* and it meant "precious."

Dot pulled away from Sobrino and stared straight up toward his face. He smiled. His teeth were marbled like thick-cut bacon. He leaned over and whispered to her, "Sobrino del Mago, nice to mice, Pa to straw, can do majeek, *eh-eh-eh.*" He was strange, surely, but he was no longer a stranger. He turned and ran into the burning barn. A droplet of rain hit Dot in the face, and another pinged off Boy's metal hat. It had come too late to console anybody.

Sobrino took two long strides, coiled like a spring, and dove into a gap in the flames. He flew. He crossed the charcoal grill of the horse stalls sideways like a rocket, then rolled and came up standing in the main bay. Sunny was curled up in a ball on the charred ground. At any second the attic would fall and crush him. He was sur-rounded by burning shelves. They swayed and threatened to topple. Cindered pages floundered through the air on clipped wings. Sunny clenched his eyes and whispered to himself the only thing he could remember, the song the farmer sang to him in the early dawn light.

A lit ember landed on Sunny's neck and seared through. Sunny squealed and scratched at it like a wild animal. He scraped out the burning straw and shook his hand. He looked up, his face covered in soot. All he could see was Sobrino's filthy hand reaching down to him.

In the muddy lot, Dot and Boy and Pup keened in the rainstorm. The side of the barn was a massive curtain of fire. Without warning, it tore into smoldering planks. The whole structure collapsed. The barn had burst. Sunny's body was flung out. His hat and one leg caught fire as he flew through the flames. He landed hard on a shoulder. Dot ran to him as Sunny squirmed in a puddle and rolled around in the mud. Then Dot helped him to his feet.

Sobrino had hurled him like a villain from a saloon. But the fire had buried the old giant with the attic toys and the Growin' Man as well. Sunny put his whole weight on Dot's shoulder. He weighed practically nothing. What had happened in the red barn was unbearable.

He quit believing good men were good killers. Her eyes were still the color of fresh basil.

OUR
LADY
OF
VILLAINS

So the three little wolves built themselves an extremely strong house. It was the strongest, securest house one could possibly imagine. They felt absolutely safe.
— The Three Little Wolves and the Big Bad Pig
Eugene Trivizas

Baby's gonna be all right,
'Cause ain't nobody
Gonna tell her what to do.
  —Isaiah 5:20
    WIKI TRANSLATION
    OCTOBER 2062

Woe unto them
That call evil good
And good evil.
      —Isaiah 5:20

FOR IMMEDIATE RELEASE

The Shalom Corporation™ Announces "ReCreation Day™"!

Dear RL Tel Aviv Users:

Shalom from Shalom Corp™!

As you may have seen on the network servers, the global timeline for what some experts are calling "the most significant event in human empowerment" has been moved up to this quarter of the fiscal year!

In only three days, ReCreation Day™ promises a better world for everyone. A new heaven and a new earth.

And the best part is, you don't have to do anything! No sign-up, no membership fees, no firmware download! Installation of new air is an included feature for all Shalom Corporation™ users!

As we strive to provide the highest quality of customer service, we would like to address a few concerns you may have about the incident a few villains have dubbed the "Tel Aviv Uprising." . . .

"The Book Log of Janey"

WE ARE ALL waiting on a villain named Boomer. I don't know why Boomer (he? she?) goes by a handle. Villains usually go by their real names. It's a symbol that we don't live on the networks.

Some people think villains are TPT (trailer-park trash, blech), but we're not. We're not. They think we think we're too good for tech. But we use plenty of stuff. Father Canseco grows hydroponic onions and jalapeños and uses a nitro-pac to seal them. And Sister Tanaki teaches me old English with a handheld Wiktionary.

We just don't go online is the only thing. The people in the city treat us like "villain" means crazy means dirty. Father Canseco says we don't want to be like them because heroes come up with the stories they want to tell about themselves. Sister Tanaki says nobody should be allowed to tell their own story. Not if you want the true parts.

Nali used to hide a music player with a smart chip, to stream SxyGrrl's songs from the networks. I used to listen, too. But that is not something I want to remember anymore. She pretty much unfriended me 'cause I didn't want to go with her to the protests. Today she came back from them with a bandage wrapped around her head. A circle of blood had stained through the gauze, and Sister Tanaki . . . freaked? frogged? wigged out. (I still have trouble with the slang of the old language. Sister Tanaki says I'm only "classroom fluent," but since I've never been in a classroom, I'll take that as a comfortable.)

Father Canseco heard Sister Tanaki wailing and rushed down from the observatory to help. It seems Nali was caught in the Portland Uprising.

Of course, Sister Tanaki disapproved. Of course. She did that thing when someone breathes hard through the nose—snort. She snorted her disapproving thought. (How do you say WTF in old English? It takes soooo many words.)

Sister Tanaki runs around the lighthouse saying, "Ach! Ach!" when she disapproves of something (everything). Nali and I call her Sister Aki. She is a very little woman.

She said, "Ach!" when she saw Nali's blood, and scuttered into the supply locker for heals. Father Canseco doesn't like us using heals 'cause the drinks are just nano-bots in sugar water, he says. Sister Tanaki brought a bottle, anyway, but Nali refused. She wants a scar, so she can tell people she was there, when they protested ReCreation Day. I guess it makes her hardcore.

Father Canseco cursed the Hello Corp police, but Nali said they didn't attack her. They even had mobile camera units filming them as they brought bottles of water to the protesters. It was actually another villain who pushed Nali down when he tried to run away. The corporation guards helped her up. She says one of them was very cute. He put on the bandage as they drove to the police station.

Father Canseco cursed again (under his breathing?). Nali seems to like Hello Corporation now.

FOR IMMEDIATE RELEASE

Dear Real-Life Oklahoma City Users:

Howdy from Howdy Corp™!

As you know, the "Oklahoma City Uprising" was a completely isolated incident, caused by a few disgruntled villains who irrationally oppose ReCreation Day™ and human progress.

As you can see at *this link,* Howdy Corp™ security removed the mob as politely as possible from the private property. Incidentally, the financial damage caused to each taxpayer (after counting all insurance claims, bystander lawsuits against the city, and police wages) amounted to $16.34 per person. The sum has already been deducted from your online accounts.

Sadly, the villains didn't even have a good reason for opposing ReCreation Day™ and incurring the outrageous expenses they caused.

ReCreation Day™ has been tested by all of the world's safety and security agencies. After a barrage of scientific tests, ten out of ten experts agree with statistical certainty: the event will NOT relapse your cancer.

ReCreation Day™ is nothing but the expansion of our NoFi (Nano-Fidelity) hotspots, the final marriage of real life and second life. Howdy Corp™'s beloved People all over the world have enjoyed our NoFi rooms in cafés and shopping malls for the past decade. When the air of these rooms is saturated with our patented nano-machines, it is as though a whole new life begins. You can visit Paris with our synesthesia tours, and our nano-bots will simulate every aspect of the country, down to the smells of baking baguettes, the uneven cobblestone streets, and the sounds of the Seine as it flows through the city. Our nano-bots can even reconstitute a fine French cheese on a molecular level for you to taste. And the tours are only the beginning.

In the NoFi hotspots, you become your own avatar. The hero of your own story. Imagine living in the networks. Would you like to buy a new shirt? Easy. Call up a rack of Urban Outerwear's casual clothing, and it will appear right there in your bedroom. The nano-machines sync with the store's online catalog and weave each shirt instantaneously. Pick the one you like and put it on. The cost is simply deducted from your accounts, which will appear on your display, suspended in the nano-enriched air in front of you. Our hotspots allow you to have any meal, any car, any entertainment your credit limit will allow.

Our global silos have been steadily releasing nano-machines into the earth's atmosphere for the past ten years. In fact, many users have already noticed the health benefits of breathing nano-enriched air.

ReCreation Day™ is the moment when all the machines are uplinked and the entire world becomes a NoFi hotspot. As has been widely reported, all leveling information, social profiles, handles, and gamertags will be retained. Now you can walk to work as your level-60 Mage, and nano-tangible orcs may ambush you on the train. You use your MP to cast a fire spell—deadly to the orcs but completely harmless to fellow commuters.

The nano-miracle event will also neutralize all the current air pollution and radioactive fallout within days (offer is subject to delays over certain locations, including Oklahoma City).

"The Book Log of Janey"

I DON'T UNDERSTAND how the nano-machines work. They are just tiny machines. How do they create physical things? Where do they get the raw materials?

Do they do little miracles??

Nali is sleeping now. She stayed up all night in jail, talking to the other protesters. Father Canseco thinks she's been brainwashed by the corporation. He has been whispering with Sister Tanaki about cortical scanning devices (CSDs). We need one to see if they programmed Nali or implanted a chip. She said she likes Hello Corp because they were nice to her. She's my BF. I was nice to her 2.

Father Canseco was like, "This is exactly what ReCreation Day is all about."

And Sister Tanaki was like, "Ach!" as she cut the Hershey bars for dinner. She prefers them raw, on Rice Krispies patties. Sushi is Nali's favorite, too.

Sister T was OD upset, and Father Canseco was like, "Nano-machines are small enough to pass through the blood-brain barrier. In the NoFi rooms, they are literally sending waves of uplinked machinery through your body. They can program some to stay in your head and control your thoughts."

Sister Tanaki's hand shook, and she had to put down the sashimi knife. Father Canseco was all, "They could have forced Nali and the protesters into a hotspot. How can we ever know?"

"We will never even see the machines," said Sister Tanaki, low voice.

"This 'ReCreation Day,'" he spit out, "would turn even the air against us."

"We could never hide." Sister Tanaki, crying.

FOR IMMEDIATE RELEASE

Ni Hao from Ni Hao Corp™!

Here at the corporation, we believe in full disclosure. The villains in the "Beijing Uprising" did bring up one point on the network message boards, which we will address:

Jimmy-Ling said:

> *"The Ni Hao Corporation will eat our brains the second all their nano-tyranny-machines go online! They call us 'villains' b/c we're against NoFi. Well then, I'm a villain. I use my real name, not some handle I made up to present myself as a* **[expletive redacted by Ni Hao Corp]***! I'm a villain because I'm tired of eating 'nano-enriched protein bars.' I'm a villain because I hate the Ni Hao Corporation and their level-whatever president, 'Calam!ty Shine.' What kind of handle is that?!* **[Expletive redacted]***. And mostly, I'm a villain 'cause I don't want to be a 'hero' . . . and if I disappear the day after ReCreation Day, then you'll know why. Or you won't, because the Ni Hao Corporation won't let you."*

Our very own president, C4L4m!Ty_$h!in3 — President Cal, answered Jimmy-Ling, assuring him that our *privacy policy* would never allow half the crimes he suggests we would commit.

In fact, what Jimmy doesn't understand is that after ReCreation Day™ (launching this quarter of the fiscal year), he could use the NoFi atmosphere to be completely free. He could fly wherever he chose, at regular taxi-fare prices, by asking the nano-machines to create an invisible platform under his feet. (Of course, the machines would not cross international boundaries—that would be illegal—and hopefully Jimmy has a job that pays better than slandering Ni Hao Corp™ on the networks all day. :)

Links are also provided for the rest of the thread on Jimmy's post. Feel free to express your own opinion.

And remember, you're all heroes to us.

Forum

[+] [Browse >>]   [Post >>]   [Search >>]

All   Reviews   Rules   General

312 [General] **"No to RC–Day!!"**   2062–03–11   **Jimmy–Ling**   312

1 Jimmy–Ling said: "No to RC–Day!!"   [...] [expand]

2 Cal said: [...] [expand]

3 Jenny Cho said: [...] [expand]

4 SxyWench69 said: [...] [expand]

. . .

289   ChickenConPollo said: Yo, was madz hot of Cal 2 post. Bizzy but wrote in n–e–way. Ni Hao rox.

@Jenny Cho y r u defending him? Villains r BOR–ING! get a life instead of hating everything. Its peopel lyke u who held everything back in all history. Im glad villains r a pathetic couple LOSERS an not majority.

@SxyWench69 ur hot. Got more pix?

WE ALL LIVE in a lighthouse 'cause ships don't need them any-more. The old oil rigs are the new shoreline. Nali & me sleep inside the light room at the top so we can look out the windows. Nali used to hide the music player under her bedroll. We would hide under the bedroll and listen to SxyGrrl.

Our real fathers (not like Father Canseco) were both out of the country when they closed the borders. Our moms both died (weird: I just noticed BF stands for best friend and bird flu).

Uh-oh.

Just now, Nali came downstairs with her music player. Sister Tanaki saw it first. *Ach!* Father Canseco looked up from his book.

Nali is pretending not to notice. She is opening the pantry and getting a Funyuns salad.

"What are you doing?" said Father Canseco just now.

"Huh?" Nali says. She's pulling out one earbud. "I couldn't hear you."

(He's upset.) "I said what are you doing?"

Nali has her back to us. "I'm getting food."

"I see that," says FC. "Is that player online?"

"Hel-lo, how else could it livestream?" said Nali, sarcastic+1.

Father Canseco is putting down his book on Saint Martha.

Obvs, Nali wants to be a hero now. They always seem :). Villains are always :(. At least Father Canseco seems that way. Maybe vil-lains in other places aren't so down on themselves.

I'm more like :|

I guess that makes me a boring little villain.

A River of Raunch

Customer Review (★☆☆☆)

by **Colson "TuneCritix" Pruitt**

May 12—Call me an old crank. A repressed nostalgic grouse. A Luddite. A villain even. Call me whatever you like, but I still think SxyGrrl is the worst thing to happen to the music industry since Hello Corporation patented the guitar.

So sleazy is her website I thought she was an actress. And is it just me, or does she most resemble a buttered squirrel? Her music (ha!) is nothing but tasteless moaning and a synthesizer, but who'm I to judge? I'm an ancient 37, still writing in old English, and she's had five of the last ten chart toppers, including the unintentionally tragic "Life, Money, Sexcetera," and the mildly disturbing "Luv Slap."

Is that what passes for sexy these days? Excuse me, sxy?

And now comes the next iteration of this poor girl's self-inflicted abuse. Her newest project has her constantly livestreaming on the networks . . . nothing new so far . . . and singing (is that what it's called?) impromptu concerts for the tone-deaf fans logged in. It's a subscription to mediocrity. Not a livestream, but a live river of raunchy lyrics, pulsating gyrations, and superficial commentary.

In other words, Hello Corporation is genius.

Now every Sxy.Chik, Elvish-Sxy, and SxySosheMajor can gorge herself on the minute-by-minute sexploits of a prepubescent digital idol who technically doesn't even exist outside the 3D-imaging department of Hello Corp and whatever cut-scenes the marketing teams come up with.

And forgive the rant here, but can we please come up with a society wherein every woman DOESN'T choose to define herself as sxy and sxy alone? Are they coming up with these handles themselves??

Of course, I will lose the inevitable flame war in the comments section. So I'll leave aside any pearlish references to Pygmalion. I will say, however, to dull the knives you fangirls (fangrrrls) are sharpening, that I did subscribe to the livefeed in order to write this article. I even went to a NoFi room for the club nite and danced. Heck, I even joined her on the sxy shopping spree when she sang to her new shoes.

I did all that. Call me a villain, but I'd rather listen to two monkeys fighting over a jackhammer.

"The Book Log of Janey"

FATHER CANSECO IS waiting for Boomer because Boomer might have a CSD to use on Nali. But Nali can't wait for Boomer, because Father Canseco has finished writing his book (the wood kind), and he promised months ago that she could go to deliver it.

After what just happened, I'm not sure he'll let her.

We never used to get mail, so we don't know all the snailmen. But recently Father Canseco got a bunch of letters from Father Clay in Washington State. And then he worked on his book even more.

Sister Tanaki used to tell me my dad was a snailman. But I think that was only so I wouldn't hate him for not finding me. The snailmen travel in old oil cars, without smart chips, so no one can track them. It's dangerous and slow (*snail* rhymes with *mail,* but it used to mean slow).

I could go to Washington in ten minutes on the gauss rail. Or I could just nano-conference in a NoFi room; it's the same as being there. But snailmen go there themselves to deliver paper letters for the villains.

They roam wherever they can, so if you want your return mail, you either pay them a ton to come back or just send somebody with them and have them come back alone. It's not so dangerous for us, because Father Canseco isn't that conservative. He lets us come back on the trams or airbuses. But Tyler (hotz!!!!), the boy who comes for Father Clay's mail, he has to ride a bicycle for six days! Off-road!! Without a Taser!!! (Off-road b/c of the border guards.) (No Tase cuz Father Clay is super strict.)

Boomer is supposed to be the best one of all. The last snailman who came by said B actually delivered from NJ to San Diego once. And B isn't afraid of Mexico.

I just heard Sister Tanaki dropping a tray of food.

Father Canseco got the door. Nali is still in the bathroom (won't come out since the fight over the music player). I think Boomer's here. Finally.

ChickenConPollo: Yo U round?

ChickenConPollo: yo!

ChickenConPollo: :*(. . . That's u with a black eye, son.

[ChickenConPollo logged off 20:45]

PolloConChicken: hey!!!!!!!!!!!1111111oneONE

JeebuzKilla: WHAT?!

PolloConChicken: y didn't u spk?

JeebuzKilla: I wuz w/ a XX. Wut?

PolloConChicken: U? N a XX? Pls . . . A real one?

JeebuzKilla: STFU. She's cool.

PolloConChicken: After Re-Day, u can pay to have a digi-girl hang on yer arm.

JeebuzKilla: hologram?

PolloConChicken: no. Real.

JeebuzKilla: all u could afford would b a holo-gramma.

PolloConChicken: hyuk hyuk. U wanna quest or wut? This's sposed 2 b a group project.

JeebuzKilla: "Cave of Algebra" . . . blech. Gonna fail that class. Wait, u have 2 handles?

PolloConChicken: Yep.

[PolloConChicken logged off 20:58]

ChickenConPollo: Yep.

JeebuzKilla: HC don like that.

ChickenConPollo: Yeh well, H Corp can kiss my **[redacted by Hello Corporation. Hello there . . .   :)]**.

JeebuzKilla: Whoa. Did u c that? Wut does "redacted" mean?

ChickenConPollo: I aint afraid of Cal. He dont even deathmatch anymore.

. . .

ChickenConPollo: C wut?

JeebuzKilla: Nuthin. g2g

ChickenConPollo: Wut bout homewerk?

ChickenConPollo: Hello?

[JeebuzKilla logged off 21:09]

"The Book Log of Janey"

WHEN I SAW him, I thought Boomer had gotten cancer as an adult. I hear if you get it late in life, it could kill you or the fever with it could make you act like Boomer (who twitched like the flag at the top of the lighthouse).

Turns out Boomer was a he. His skin was the color of a scab. His scabs (lots) were as black as his hair. His hair was a tangled Afro, like a burnt-out star cluster.

He scratched at his arms. Father Canseco asked if he'd like to come inside and sit down, and he was like, "I got fleas, Mr. Canseco."

FC was like, "It doesn't matter to us. I'm a father." But Boomer stayed in the entryway and said, "No, you aren't."

I didn't like him until Father Canseco stepped aside and Sister Tanaki brought the Spamburgers from the kitchen. He put his hands up, shields at maximum, disgusted×5. Sister pushed the tray up to his face, "Eatuh."

"Go ahead," said Father Canseco. "It's enriched with minerals that kill the fleas."

"I know," said Boomer. He pushed the tray back at Sister Tanaki. "Excuse me, lady."

"Eatuh²," said Sister Tanaki.

Apparently Boomer only eats organic food, stuff he finds in the farms. That's where he got the fleas. And the malaria is probably what makes him so skinny (plus organic food's hard to find).

And I thought I was a freak. . . .

Sister Tanaki ran back to the kitchen and returned with a can of stewed tomatoes, but Boomer said that was nano-fortified, too. She said, "Ach!" and Boomer thought she was cursing him. He pulled in his chin (retracted?) and said, "Stay away from me, crazy. What kinds of villain are you people?"

"Well, now, son—" said FC.

Nali came downstairs.

"Rather have fleas," said Boomer. "And you," he said to Sister T. "You been to a NoFi room. I can smell the nanos all over you."

Sister Tanaki was like ORLY?!? But it was true—she visits with her family in Nagano sometimes—so the *Ach!* died in her mouth (retr-Ach!-ted :).

She stalked off, muttering. I guess our little church of villainy is really softcore. Esp compared to Father Clay. Nali jumped off the stairs into the entryway and said, "Hi! I'm going with you for the return mail."

Boomer didn't seem to smell the nanos on her. He just seemed annoyed by how loud she talked. Nali said, "I've been to the rooms, too, but it's cool 'cause we're not that conservative, and actually I'm kind of into it. I think Calam!ty Shine is a total genius if you think about it. I mean, most people already think so, but villains are soooo old school. Blech. Anyway, I have a music player for the trip. Do you have an adapter? Doesn't matter, I guess, 'cause it has pretty good speakers. I've got all of SxyGrrl's livestreams. . . ."

Nali leaned into him 'cause she doesn't get *personal space*. Boomer staggered back till he hit a wall. Nali followed with her hands flailing and diarrhea of the mouth.

Also, what is "old school" supposed to mean? Like, we're

boring or something? Never mind. She can say whatever she wants. Whatevs. NBD.

Boomer stumbled backward into Father Canseco and jumped. He reminds me of a mangy cat.

FC did his "I'm nervous but I don't want *you* to be nervous" laugh. But Boomer was immune to that spell. FC said, "[Laugh, laugh] Now we can be friends."

"Just 'cause you have my fleas doesn't make us friends," said Boomer. He pressed into the corner of the entryway. Father Canseco exhaled. He looked at the ground, the couch, the lamp. I knew he was looking for a book to read, which he does when he's sad/tired.

He said, "Well, we've mixed blood, anyway. Jane, why don't you get ready to leave with Boomer while I get our mail."

(Oh, suxor).

Nali goes: "WTF! Backwards Day?"

what we iz now

by: **MC Flescher, feat. SxyGrrl**

from: **Yo Corp Records**

Yo, where you at NYC?
No, really, where you at?
This MC Flescher
Comin at ya in 2062
In No-Fidelity
Cuz that's how we iz . . .

[enta tha beat]

Now errybody be eatin dat gobbuh-ment cheese
They killed tha bees and felled tha trees
No one's gonna say, "This is too much grease!
Do you have anything all-natural pleez?"

Can the nano-machines
Bring back tha streams?
Bring back tha dreams?

Can't drink tha water, so we drink Hi-C
And all mah whiz smell like Mista Pibbs

Now rich girls say they like da fizz
All I miss is mah mamma's grits
The FDA is nuthin but fibs
And D.O.A. he own da biz
Every Hello, Hi, and Hola is his

But I ain't afraid of no gobbuh-ment list
Cuz I iz what I iz

Hey, SxyGrrl, can u gimme a kiss?

[SxyGrrl]
Whoa oh uh-oh
I'm a NoFi grrrrrrl.

Thas just how we iz now
Don't ask me how
Don't ask me now

[SxyGrrl]
Whoa oh uh-oh
R u my NoFi boi?

"The Book Log of Janey"

NALI WENT RAMPAGE on overdrive when Father Canseco said I was the one going with Boomer. Majorly OTT.

And Sister Tanaki said something like fifty-five *Ach!*'s 'cause I help her with housework and she's pretty obvs that she doesn't like Nali's 'tude these days.

For a millisecond I was all *woot*. Boomer's weird, but getting to leave Portland? Hecks, yeah. But then Nali took the blue pill and everybody flipped out. Father Canseco got upset, and he's been nervy about mailing the book, anyway. Sister Tanaki was still boiling that Boomer wouldn't eat her famous Spamburgers. Nali crapped a whole live cow. And I kept inserting, "It's okay, I can go next time," when I wanted to say, "Got my toothbrush right here. Ciao ciao, fokes."

Father Canseco put the book down on a table so he could argue better (he uses his hands like most people use verbs). The paper pages of his book were bound by string and leather, like this one I'm writing on. But he wasn't writing a book log like me. I think it was a history. Anyway, Boomer grabbed it in the melee and walked out.

Father Canseco didn't notice. He was all defending himself to Nali 'cause she said he was her personal hero (a pretty cheap shot IMHO). When FC noticed the book was gone, he twirled in place looking for it, and his neck practically spun the other direction. He's old as Bilbo, so Nali shutted up, 'cause little old people shouldn't move so fast. FC did the speed-run out the door and grabbed Boomer by the arm outside. Nali, Sister Tanaki, and me all ran to the doorway to listen.

Boomer yanked his arm back and said, "Don't touch me, ever."

Father Canseco started to say "son" but caught himself. Instead he said, "S'okay, it's okay. I'm sorry I touched you."

"This is the package, idn't it?" said Boomer.

"Yes, it is," said FC. "It's incredibly important that it reach Father Clay before ReCreation Day."

(That's only three days away.)

Boomer had his back against the car. Father Canseco is like a billion years old, and still Boomer looked more frail.

"Okay," said Boomer, twitch, "let me get going, then."

"Right," said FC. He glanced back at the house. He said, "Right, yes, well, I was also hoping you had a cortical scanning device in your trunk."

"Why?" said Boomer.

"It scans the brain."

"I know what it does. Why do you want it?"

Father Canseco lowered his voice, and Sister Tanaki leaned forward and whispered, "Ach!" 'cause she couldn't hear. I've always had pretty good hearing skills, tho. FC said, "Our youngest, Nali. We think she might have been brainwashed by the Hello Corporation."

I couldn't tell if Nali could hear. She was behind me, with her hand on my shoulder trying to pull ahead.

Boomer scratched at his forearm. Looked at us through the crack in the doorway. Nodded at me. I think. Then he said, "The one all up in my chili?"

Father Canseco nodded yes.

Boomer turned and tossed the book in the open window of his car. He walked around to the driver's side.

"I don't have a scanner," he said, "but I can tell you nobody's been washing any brains of anybody's. They're all as dirty as they ever were."

"But she was caught up in the Portland Uprising," said Father Canseco.

Then Boomer said the part that made me make the gasp that made Sister Tanaki startle like a cat and made Father Canseco realize we were hiding behind the door and made Nali shout, "I knew it! Villains are sooo unorganized!"

He said, "Portland? I thought the uprising was in Seattle."

Search Results: **"Calam!ty Shine"—Virus**

A mythic Internet virus, first thought to be discovered in 2031, though there is no evidence that it even exists. Known as "the world beater," the **Calam!ty Shine (Cal) virus** is believed to be, by many cultures, so embedded into the networks that it is essentially what people have always called the "ghost in the machine."[1]

History

In 2045, Mavis Radits, a systematics engineer at the World Bank, discovered what she thought was a glitch that seemed to have siphoned tiny amounts of money from every electronic bank account since the very beginning of the World Wide Web. By doing so, it had become the single largest controller of global money markets. It had not hoarded the stolen funds, simply redirected them under millions of digital holding companies, eating entire economies at a time. Cal had become the market. "It was a beautiful and deliberate flaw. As elegant a design as a single-cell organism. A tiny freckle printed into the very DNA of the Internet. Then I looked closer. It was quite malignant."[2]

Though Ms. Radits immediately reported the sighting to Interpol and the UN Security Council, the Cal virus was never officially discovered. (Doubtful claims have been made by numerous Internet personalities, but no proof has been provided.)

Authorities claim the Cal virus is a myth. Fan sites call it "the perfect strand of code" and "the god code." Whoever could control it would be literally the king of the net—controlling all currency.

Speculation escalated again when the Shalom Corporation™ (aka Salaam Corporation™, Hello Corp™, Ni Hao Corporation of the People™, etc.) introduced its newest president in 2050—a man also named Calam!ty Shine.

No one knows which came first: the man or the virus.

References

1 Ron Lamney, "The Shade Replied," JussDaFax.com.
2 "Interview with Mavis Radits," BingoBoingo.net.

Man named Cal   (Go)

Search Results: **"Calam!ty Shine"** — **Person (born ?–present)**

The president of Hello Corp™ (known by other names depending on the country — an example of **chameleon marketing**).

History

Largely unknown. No records of his schooling can be found. Many fan sites claim this to be his greatest feat, erasing all previous web presence — ReCreating™ himself as a first miracle.

Cal first appeared on the world stage after the press release announcing him as the new president of the largest corporation in the world. No reason was given for the surprise appointment. Vice President Murphy, the front runner for the job, filed her resignation three days later. Some believe the Calam!ty Shine virus had simply funded a complete shareholder buyout. Speculation swirled around the disappearance of the entire board of trustees a few days prior to the announcement, but Hello Corp™ provided a full accounting of the board members at a press conference later that month. Each of the members of the board chose to retire to luxury after vetting the new president and coming to the conclusion that he was, in fact, the greatest president any corporation (or governing body) could hope for. [last edited by: Sign–In Corp PR Div.]

Cal was an immediate superstar with the most searches of his name on the networks.

Cal is the current reigning champion of the Street Fighter tournament. A level-90 lich king. And holds the records in speed runs for over fifty retro titles.

Associates

Cal only quests on the networks with a mysterious figure labeled **Baku_The_DreamEater**. He is a part of no clans and has defeated all the group campaigns by himself.

In RL, he was recently spotted at various NoFi clubs with the digital idol **SxyGrrl** (where she could take her nano-tangible form). In June 2060, a paparazzo by the name of Donnie Machinko claimed to have photos of Baku leaving the back of a club in which Cal had been spotted. Hello Corp™ News Division won the auction for the photos, paying a reported 2 billion. Machinko has since disappeared.

Search Results: **"Baku_The_DreamEater"** — **Person/Thing**

[Entry deleted]

"The Book Log of Janey"

I'M SITTING IN Boomer's lime-green car—a VW Bug, shaped like a snail (perfect for a snailman). It runs on petroleum and leaves a streak of Bug sludge wherever it goes. I put my knees on the dashboard so I could write this, and Boomer said, "This ain't your lair."

I said, "These aren't your knees."

He seemed to like that.

I think he's glad I came instead of Nali. After she ran inside and slammed the door, I hugged Father Canseco. He told me to be good, and I told him he was a great dad (even if he isn't a real one). I felt bad, 'cause he might think I only said it because he let me go. I'll be back in four days.

Bookmark: I'll tell him again after a while, so he knows it's just a regular feeling.

The road from Portland to Walla Walla is brand-new. Too bad we're not on it. The path we're on is paved like a bone garden. We can't go very fast, or we might hit a ditch and puncture the Bug belly. The trees give us cover from the checkpoints on the main roads.

Boomer won't let me play SxyGrrl, and the Bug doesn't have a real music player, anyway. It uses compact discs.

He doesn't talk very much. And when he does, it's to himself. Like when he goes, "Transmission sounds scratchy . . ."

And I said, "What's transmission?"

And he said, "Issat an apple tree? Crab apples? Naw, can't be." (I didn't say anything.)

He acts like he's alone. Maybe all the people he takes for the return mail are mean to him. Or maybe he knows they only need him to get someplace. Fare-weather friends.

One time I tried to answer him, awkwurd. It went:

> Boomer: Should stop and eat.
>
> Me: Sister Tanaki packed some Slim Jims if you want.
>
> Boomer: [snaps out of it] Wha?
>
> Me: You just said lunch, and I just—
>
> Boomer: What is that smell?
>
> Me: I just said, Slim Jims.
>
> Boomer: [stops the Bug] Get out of my car.

I thought he was gonna drive off and leave me, but he just hates the smell of food (says he can smell preservatives). I sat on a rock and ate lunch (Pepsi, a couple of SJs). He opened the Bug and poured water into a tank. Then he leaned against the hood and ate a couple of raw carrots. They drooped in sad frowns and still had dirt all over them. He even ate the greens at the ends. I tried to show him all the fortified nutrients in my soda, but he laughed. It has more protein than a whole bucket of chicken. I don't think he understands chemistry.

I said, "I've never been to a NoFi room before. Can you smell any nano-machines on me?"

He was picking at a flea tangled up in his hair. "No." He snickered like he'd heard a joke.

I said, "But I thought nano-machines were everywhere. Wouldn't that mean you smell them all the time?"

Boomer's left eye shivered. He scratched his forearm like maybe a nano-machine was biting it. "Yeah, they're in the air we breathe. But they won't be *on* till ReCreation."

"So you're saying you can only smell machines that are turned on?"

He got back into the car, and I followed. Then he said, "Naw, I'm saying I can't smell them at all."

"How'd you know about Sister Tanaki?"

"I say that to everybody," he said, starting the car (engine is 10× louder than electrics). "Their reaction usually tells me plenty."

He looked at the plastic bottle of soda in my hand and said, "You should throw that in the bushes. Your remission might give out."

It was one-time-use plastic, so I tossed it out the window. Nobody wants cancer twice. It's supposed to be worse the older you are—like chicken pox.

We drove for another two hours, and I didn't say a word. Boomer talked to himself about farms we passed and crops he could steal, about a rock that threw off his alignment (?), and about how he used to be a kid in Trinidad, with no parents, so he made money by making deliveries. I think that last part was to me, but I stayed quiet and listened. If Boomer becomes my friend, he'll be a very different kind from Nali.

After his story I said, "Hey, Boomer?"

The dirt road was dark, and it was too dangerous for headlights, because we were close to the Washington State line. Boomer was squinting at the glass, and it was raining. "Hmm?"

I said, "Do you have an avatar online?"

"Nmm-mmm," he said, which was a no.

"Then why do you go by a handle? What's your real name?"

The rain sounded like a keyboard. He said, "Boomer *is* my real name."

"Your mom actually named you Boomer?"

"I told you, I didn't have no mom. It's just what they called me."

That was about ten minutes ago. I pulled out my book and starting blogging so I wouldn't forget. The rain has gotten even harder. Boomer told himself we'd pull over soon to sleep. I'm glad he's not a hero. But he doesn't seem like one of us either.

I hope Father Canseco is all right with only Nali and Sister Tanaki. If I were home, I'd be taking him a glass of mint tea right now. He'd be writing in his book. But the book's finished now, and in the backseat of this car. So I guess FC isn't where he usually would be either.

"Did you do it?"

> "He was exactly where he should be / From what I could see, up in the tree / He was starting to work on book number three."

"That one doesn't matter. Did you get access to the house?"

> "I did get in / to do the sin / you could have heard a stabbing pin."

"What? Quit talking like that. Did you do it or not?"

> "He was luckless."

"Good."

> "Not loveless, but certainly lifeless."

"*Yes* or *no* answers or I'll kill you, Baku."

> "Yes."

"You went to the villain's house?"

> "No."

"Then, what was it?"

> "... hrrm ..."

"Oh, jeez. You don't have to say *yes* or *no*."

> "Lighthouse."

"Okay, fine, you went to the villain's *lighthouse*. You know what, just tell it to me in detail, *without* the poetry."

"It was a dark and stormy night—black and white. The snailman and the girl had already driven away. I found a way inside by crawling through an open window. I could smell the old lady sleeping—her tasty, tasty, tasty dreams of countries she has never seen.

I kept creeping.

The villain Canseco was in his room—his doom. Leaning over a fresh-bound book; my fangs they shook. Here was a man, made up almost entirely of his dream.

He didn't even scream.

A musty rug. A dusty lamp. A live old man. One of these things was not like the others.

When I leaned over the working man and drank the whispers in his ear, he scribbled nonsense on the page and made the slightest gasp. I was the asp, and he was Adam. He slumped and fell sideways dead."

"Soooooo all that was to say Father Canseco's dead. And the package is already on its way to EXACTLY the place I told you not to let it go."

"Yes."

"You know what you are, Baku? You are BOR-ing. That's what you are. I shudder at my own boredness. Now get the book and kill whoever's with it and write your crap poetry on your own time."

"Yes, Cal."

"Yes, Cal—you beast of borecraft. I'm hanging up."

MAJOR PIECE OF INFO: the uprisings yesterday weren't just in Portland or Seattle. They're everywhere. That means villains aren't so freakish (or at least there are more of us :).

We stopped at a weigh station to figure that out. Boomer parked something like five miles in the woods, and we hiked so no one would see the Bug. There are cameras everywhere and more satellites than stars, but who's going to watch all of it? If you want someone specific, they have face-recognition software for that, but to watch a billion reality shows = too much work.

For a guy whose body is as crooked as an extra-crunchy Cheeto, Boomer can walk srsly fast. His knees make clicky sounds. Before we crossed the edge of the parking lot, he stopped and handed me earbuds. He put another headset on himself. They were so old, people would think we were homeless. But at least they wouldn't think we were villains. My stomach made a drum roll when I saw the restaurant signs. Boomer must have heard it and said, "You have your own money?"

"I have an account," I said. "We're not *total* noobs."

"If anyone asks," he said, "you're my daughter, and we hitchhikin'."

I said, "If anyone asks, I'll tell them to mind their own business."

When we got inside, it was full of screaming kids, all of them trying to get inside the NoFi rooms to quest. The ones who had already come out were swinging their arms like they were still sword fighting. Some went to the PC stations and kept questing, without the nano-immersion.

Parents were trying to get the kids to eat their fries and pizza before they went into the rooms, but the kids preferred to eat the in-game food—not only makes you full, but refills hit points. And it comes with ale or grog or mead. Course, the in-game food is crazy expensive DLC (that's "downloadable content"—in case Sister Tanaki ever reads this. Hi, ST! Quit reading my blog ;).

Boomer said, "I got someone to see," and walked over to the McDonald's playland. The toys in there looked mad old (like a busted springy chair shaped like a duck and a pit full of plastic balls). Nobody was in there but a few drifters.

I got a few lunch bars and a mocha latte. The NoFi rooms have two sets of doors. You walk into the first set, and the doors shut behind you—like an air lock in the space station. If you're going into the room, the air gets saturated with uplinked nano-machines (some of the kids say it tickles their lungs at first, but the parents say they're just imagining things). When you leave the room, the nano-machines get sucked out. They're so small, they flow right through your chest. Then the second set of doors open. After ReCreation Day, they won't need those doors anymore. They won't even need the rooms anymore. And these kids will bankrupt their parents' accounts in no time.

Boomer sat down next to me and said, "Buddy of mine just told me he heard of riots as far out as Buenos Aires."

I said, "What's Buenos Aires?"

"City someplace far," said Boomer.

"So they're all over the world?" I said a little too loudly.

B shushed me and covered by saying, "Yeah, cities are all over the world."

I always thought Nali and I would have to fight over hot Tyler to be the last villain couple on the planet. I just figured we were a few weird families who liked building their own compost heaps. But the way Boomer talks about us, and the way Father Canseco was so paranoid about ReC Day, makes it sound like it's a whole secret society or something. They can't talk over the networks. Do the snailmen travel all over the world for villains? Wouldn't that make them villains, too? I wish I could ask Father Canseco. Boomer whispered to me, "Lot of people following Saint Martha these days." (Martha = patron saint of villains). The local news called us an evil survivalist cult. Maybe we're really a whole religion.

He just went to the gift shop to buy antibacterial lotion, and then we'll leave . . .

. . . weird. The monitor on one of the NoFi rooms just ran a banner that pointed at me and said: *Jane Doe, you've got mail.*

Parents are all murmuring and looking at me. It used my real name instead of a handle, so now they know I'm a villain. I may as well take these scratchy earbuds out. I should go see what it is. Boomer will kill me when he gets back—

Now it says: *From S. Tanaki.*

Everybody's staring. How does it even know I'm here? Do they have scanners at truck stops? Why would Sister Tanaki use a NoFi room to send a message?

I should go. . . . .

NoFi™ ROOM INTERFACE

Please wait while the air lock is sealed and gently filled with our patented nano-machines. . . .

Air-lock saturation complete. Please enter. . . .

Welcome to the Hello Corp™ Nano-Fidelity Chamber. Gosh, that's a mouthful.

> **Login:**
> **Password:**
> **Are you a new user?**

You chose: **New user.** Scanning retina for ID. . . .

Hello, **Jane Doe!** We have Urgent mail for you. But first, please fill out the brief questionnaire so that we can serve you better. What is your social security number?

I'm sorry, I don't recognize that input. What is your social security number?

I'm sorry, I don't recognize that input. Hmm, looks like our keyboard or audio sensors may be malfunctioning. No problem, the cortical scanning software of our nano-machines is a safe and easy way for us to read all the necessary information that will help us serve you better. Please note that nano-machines will now flow past the blood-brain barrier in order to complete the scan.

I'm sorry, the air lock will not open until the cortical scan is complete. Please stand still.

This scan was authorized within the User Agreement you signed when entering the air lock. Please do not think about any traumatic or stressful memories — such as car accidents, chemotherapy, or wild bears — as that can result in harmful brain-wave interaction with the nano-machines.

Scanning complete.

Hi, **Janey.** As a free trial, please enjoy the configuration of your favorite place, **Father Canseco's study,** at no charge to your account. Livestreaming location. . . .

Wait, **Janey.** Before you exit, would you like to hear your message from user **S. Tanaki?**

You said: **"Fine, fine, just hurry,"** meaning the affirmative. Accessing five-sensory messaging now. . . .

> *"Ach! Janey, Janey! Listen to me. Father Canseco dead. Dead.*
>
> *His heart just stop and he fell. But he leave you a message.*
>
> *Here, take it. I'm sorry. Really sorry."*

End message. Log out? Would you like a printout of the object transmitted by **S. Tanaki** to take with you? Printing now. Deducting cost from accounts. . . .

And remember, after ReCreation Day™, you'll be able to access our nano-services from anywhere. Only three days away.

Thank you for joining us. At Hello Corp™, a Good-bye is never forever.

Good-bye.

"The Blog of Janey"

. . . ALL IT SAYS is: "J—Find &" (the line scrawls out unfinished).

What does that mean? Find and what?

He's dead. I even saw it after the room turned into his study. It even smelled like it (molded books, warm Snapple). He looked asleep. He wasn't my dad or anything, but still. He found me in the compost heap when I was a baby, so he is my dad. Edit. Was my dad.

I ran out of the nano-room and fell. When I woke up, Boomer was carrying me, running through the woods to the Bug. I cried into his shirt. I think he sang me a song.

ChickenConPollo: yo, candy pants, did u c tha vid?

JeebuzKilla: don't call me that.

ChickenConPollo: DID. U. C. THA. VID?

JeebuzKilla: WTF stop shouting. No I didn't c whatev vid ur talkin bout.

ChickenConPollo: I can't talk to u till u have. Here *[link]*.

. . .

JeebuzKilla: LOLz

ChickenConPollo: u saw it????

JeebuzKilla: yeh. Chick walks out of a NoFi and faints like a donkey.

ChickenConPollo: I thought she was cute. But I mean at the end, the thing comin out.

JeebuzKilla: naw, she's busted.

JeebuzKilla: who the homeless dude who picked her up?

ChickenConPollo: whatev she's prolly eleven. No, at the end. Looked like a hunchback.

JeebuzKilla: I didn't c it.

ChickenConPollo: how could u not c it?! Little Asian
    chick walks out, falls. Black dude picks her up
    and leaves. Then a mad ugly hunchback limps
    out the NoFi room and follows.

    JeebuzKilla: didn't c it.

ChickenConPollo: u blind?! Thing had fangs.

    JeebuzKilla: nope.

ChickenConPollo: watch it again. It was Baku.

    JeebuzKilla: Baku_The_DreamEater? BS

ChickenConPollo: ur a candy pants.

    JeebuzKilla: ur mom is a candy pants.

ChickenConPollo: UR mom is a candy pants.

                    . . .

    JeebuzKilla: hey, I just clicked on the link again and
    the vid's gone.

SOMETHING IS CHASING US. Boomer won't talk about it. I think he thinks I'm still covered in nano-machines or that I was chipped with spyware or that the satellites are tracking us. He's mad that I went into the room.

The nanos can't leave with you (right?). I told him about the air lock that kills the nanos before you leave, and he just grunted, "I know 'bout the air lock," which I thought made my point. B kept driving in the dark, in case they were tracking us some other way. I didn't put my knees up on the dashboard this time. If I make him really mad, he might kick me out, and I'd have nobody. Sister Tanaki and Nali are probably burying FC right now. The lighthouse isn't safe anymore, but then it probably never was. I guess it doesn't matter if ReCreation Day happens or not—heroes can kill villains whenever they want, anyway.

I could hear Boomer scratching his fleas. He must have the map memorized 'cause it's almost black without headlights and no moon. The stars look like pixels in a broken monitor, and there are so many, I can almost see what I'm writing. There are 100 billion stars in the night sky. 100 trillion is how much Hello Corp is worth.

But if all the air is filled with offline nano-machines already, then there are 100 quintillion nanos in the atmosphere (and rising). They used to call them astronomical numbers, then economical numbers, but soon they won't call them anything. The numbers will be as invisible as air—nano-air (O_2 2.0).

I'm still glitched on the note Father Canseco sent me. Find &.
Find what? And then what?

Boomer doesn't know, either. He's squinting at the windshield. I opened my mouth to ask him something, and he went, "Shhh," without even seeing me. Then I tried to ask how he knew I was gonna ask something, and he said, "Shhh, not yet."

I looked behind us. The back of the Bug was piled with old boxes, tarps, a tool box, etc. Through the window I could barely see a hunched-over figure sprinting toward us. It looked like a fantasy monster, like Troll Boss chasing up through a quest. (It was limping but moving super fast.)

I turned back around. I said, "There's something—" and Boomer said, "Shhh."

We ramped a fallen tree trunk a little later—my knees cranked into the dash, but I didn't say anything. The underside of the Bug made a crunch sound like a recycler, Boomer cursed under his breath, and I said, "Shhh" (ha!). He glared at me and shook his head, like I was hopeless, but he then he smiled for a nano-second. :)

For dinner B had half a lettuce and some cashews (I offered him some of my canned ravioli, but he said no. Looks crazy malnourished). The road became level, and the woods thinned out. It become national farmland. B sped up, and I think we lost the thing behind us.

I opened my window—the air smelled like dish soap, but cold and new. The tree leaves rustled like that noise e-books make when you turn the page.

I wonder how loud squirrels are. In the vids (or animes), they make that nibbly sound, but you can turn the volume as loud as you want. Maybe in RL they're really quiet.

I said, "Hey, Boomer? Is it all right if I talk now?"

And he said, "What kind of question is that?"

And I said, "Are there any squirrels around here?"

And he said, "Squirrels? They had sense enough to go extinct a long time ago. Just that nobody knows 'cause nobody tells them."

(I guess FC didn't know about it or he would have told us. He was probably too busy with villainy to pass messages about squirrels. Or maybe he knew Nali & I wanted to be veterinarians.)

I said, "What about owls?"

"Those are zoo animals," he said.

I thought, *Maybe this is like when rats run off a sinking ship, & maybe the whole world really could use a ReCreation Day, & maybe heroes are actually the good guys.*

We came out of the woods and into the farmland. Clouds covered the stars, but the ears of corn gave off enough light for me to keep writing. I said, "Hey, Boomer? Do you think the animals know something we don't?"

And he looked at me like *srsly?* He chuckled and looked at me again. Then he said, "Girl, please. They know damn near everything we don't."

E, listen, I've been thinking about this, and I have to say it: You got a real problem with your seasonal menu. Now, before you start texting mean-spirited stuff at me, hear me out.

Last season you went super ethnic with the Ecuadorian *manteca* (lard?!), and your abuela's pork-belly recipe, and what was that— the yucca salad with the chorizo oil. And you're slamming that on top of the permanent pan-European menu you've got—people are deciding between fried fish 'n' chips and a salad that's drizzled with sausage fat. I mean, really? What makes you think those "Ladies Who Lunch," who send back friggin' tuna tartare for being undercooked, would want a damn salad with meat gristle on it? This ain't Ecuador, Edwin. Your menu may as well have a huge middle finger pointing at the patrons.

And pastry was just confused. I went back there one time and saw Allison thickening flan with cornstarch (seriously, keep her on the Ducasse book).

Listen, I'm not knocking your food. But things are changing. You know that, E. We had one of those briny little soup sippers come out for a consultation at our place, and he said it's all about "chameleon marketing" now. Like how Hello Corp is Hola Corp in Ecuador and Bonjour Corp in France or whatever.

You just make your menus out of those silicone sheets with the digital ink inside, and then this guy's company sets up a little machine thing on the front door that figures out who is coming in based on their cell-phone signal. Once they know who it is, they have all kinds of marketing crap they figured out already, so the menus display whatever the people are probably gonna like.

I know what you're gonna say. This doesn't make you a short-order cook.

The beauty is you keep the menu you want. But instead of galbi, it's called "Teriyaki Steak" for some rock star who comes in and "Lightly Seared Japanese Medallions" for an uppity old banker's wife. Genius, right?

You feed people whatever *you* want. You call it whatever *they* want.

I'm telling you, I heard this crap about Hello Corp, made me wanna turn into a villain. He said chameleon marketing is what solved that whole Middle East thing and what McDonald's has been using for years (I always wondered why my menu said "Burger King" burger).

Anyway, I can give you this guy's e-mail. You'll wanna filet the little dweeb the first ten minutes, but with all this "nano-enriched" junk food costing jack crap and being good for you or whatever . . . it is what it is. You gotta do what you gotta do.

Let me know.

P.S. Had maple asparagus gravy on a baked sweet potato at Char-Char's place. Unbelievable.

RE-CREATION DAY COULD be anytime now. At a station we saw another press release saying it'll be a "surprise launch," with lots of teaser trailers. Basically, you can buy a package and sign up for a creation theme, and wherever you are at the moment the nano-machines uplink, right there, stuff will happen. Like extinct animals will run up to you, or pirates will show up in your pool, or your car will get upgraded to a Ferrari (big $$$).

Oh, and Boomer thinks all the villains will die from mysterious causes two seconds after the uplink.

Around lunchtime we finally got to Walla Walla, "brought to you by the WahWah convenience stores." Portland is sponsored by HGH Athletics (they call it Sportland).

We had to stop at a WahWah (which is where we saw the press release). I wanted to send a message to Sister Tanaki—"How r u? Nali still actin wyurd?"

Boomer wouldn't let me.

He's been much nicer to me since I fell down and that thing chased us. He let me play music to fall asleep. At the WahWah, I stayed in the Bug because there were cams all over the place.

I leaned back in my seat so no one would see me and stared up at a streetlamp. There were scratches on the lamp's glass cover— partial lines and stuff. I was just looking at it, and when I turned my head and closed one eye, the marks looked exactly like an amperand: &. I sat up and angled my neck. It wasn't an accident. Like if it was dark and the light was on, it would catch all the scratches at the right angle and shine the & on the pavement next to the Bug.

I opened the door and leaned out. The door cast a shadow on the ground, and the sun was reflecting off the lamp, so you could barely see it in the daytime, but there it was: &.

O. M. G.

I had no idea what it meant.

When Boomer came back with a Hershey bar, I showed him the sign. He said, "Yeah."

I said, "You knew about it?"

"They're all over the place."

I went, "Fwhaa?!"

Then he pointed out another one, scratched on the air pump across the station. "Why didn't you tell me?" I said.

"I'm no babysitter," said Boomer.

I went autofire on the questions (an old Nali attack) till finally he gave up.

"I just know, all right? Quit askin' so many friggin' questions."

"What does it mean?"

"I dunno. I just seen it before. I met Father Clay's kid here."

"Tyler?" (Me very interested).

"Yeah, him. Clay's more strict than Canseco was. They meet snailmen by the *and* signs and drive them to a hideout."

"So it's just a meeting spot?"

"Far as I know."

I think if Boomer had a pet, it'd be the Suxor dinosaur (and he'd feed it fun and good times).

Meanwhile, the load time on the meet-up was 56K—we waited for Tyler to show up forevs. And then after filling up his water bottle from the hose by the bathrooms, Boomer came back and said, "Idn't like the goon to be so late."

"He's not a goon," I said, "and he could beat you up, I bet."

"Everybody thinks that." He shrugged.

That's prolly how Boomer's survived so long by himself. Everybody sees him sulking around the truck stops and gas stations, scratching at his fleas and the allergic reactions to organic food—nobody thinks such a loser would be asked to protect mail. I don't think he's a loser. He just seems like the *last* person I'd ask for help.

I started getting worried when it got dark and Tyler still hadn't shown up.

It's dark now. B says Tyler is prolly dead, but that's a mean loser thing to say.

[Real-Life News]

"Binkley C here, your celebrity correspondent for *RL News*, reporting from the city of Walla Walla.

"The light of the Tastee-Freez glows a little dimmer tonight, as police and medical crews work overtime to clean up a horrific sight of grisly murder and spilled sno-cones. The motive is still unclear, but one thing is certain—judging from the promos on the Net, SxyGrrl *was* spotted at this very Tastee-Freez, wearing some fierce Galliano tights and our own summertime must-have, rainbow sandals. The body of a teenage boy was found this evening, with no outward signs of injury, except for several scratches behind his left ear.

"The victim did not have any ID, and a facial recognition scan revealed that he had never appeared on any reality TV shows. Police believe this could be a villain-on-villain crime and point to the recent local disturbance in the population as evidence that the small sect of villains in Walla Walla may be dangerous.

"Wait, what's that? It seems we have a witness on the scene. We're crossing the police tape to get an exclusive interview . . . Ma'am? Ma'am? Tell us what you saw."

> "I saw'll it! It was sumkinda monster had big hunched-over look to him and limped and claws and errything it said rhymed."

"Ma'am, are you saying it spoke in rhyme?"

"Sure did. Iambic pentameter if'n I ain't mistaken."

"It was the monster that killed this boy?"

"Sucked his brains out his ear! It was horrible. Boy kept saying, 'Oh love, oh love.'"

"That's sad. Do you think the little goon meant to say 'Olov,' referring to the mysterious inscription found all over the city, which police believe refers to an underground rebel leader and villain sympathizer?"

"A wha?"

"Ma'am, I notice you're wearing a ratty housecoat; how would you like a makeover in our next segment?"

"A which?"

"Never mind."

"Found his wallet, too. It said Tyler."

"That's great, ma'am. Perhaps we'll never know what happened here at the Tastee-Freez, a celeb hotspot. And perhaps the police will finally bring light to the shadowy figure known as Olov. But no matter what, these questions remain: What monster prowls the streets of Walla Walla? Who *is* Olov? And what is SxyGrrl wearing to Club 47 tonight? Tune in after the break for the answer to at least *one* of these mysteries. Till then, you've been hangin' with me, Binkley C . . .

". . . Are we out? Did you get that look on her face? Uh-mazing. I smell an Emmy. The Olov connection alone is worth a million hits."

"The Blog of Janey"

I SHOULD MAKE a list of everything that happened so I don't forget: 1. Tyler was killed and Boomer thought a monster named Olov did it. 2. We found a bar with the & sign above the door. 3. Boomer got into a fight (turns out *no*body can beat him up). 4. We met Father Clay (I missed Father Canseco even more). 5. We met Olov (and found out about Africa, crazy).

Okay, I should go back now.

I was watching Boomer sleep, 'cause I kept dreaming about FC and didn't want to close my eyes anymore. (Maybe I'm all noidal, but if I close my eyes and sit quietly, I *feel* the nanos all over me. I know, impossible, but I do. Even inside my eyelids. It feels like I've been to the beach too long or like I've put on too much makeup and my pores are full. It doesn't tickle. It feels like dried sweat.)

Boomer slept holding a claw hammer to protect us. (What could it do against a smartgun with tracer rounds?) He swatted at the air and mumbled things about a girl named Celia. His eyes jerked around under the lids and flipped open before I could hear or see anything. He pulled the lever next to his backrest and sat all the way up. Then I heard the first siren of the cop cars speeding GTA-style toward us. He said, "We gotta go."

That's how number 1 happened. I googled around in the glove compartment for Boomer's phone. It had the CNN report out about Tyler—some info bimbo.

So that was number 1. I said that already. Ugh. I wonder if this is all my fault. If Olov is the name of that hero from our chase sequence in the woods, then maybe he killed FC. And if he's chasing us now, he probably killed Tyler 'cause of me.

Wish Father Canseco had finished his sentence. Find &. Okay, found it. Now what?

(I am aware that *current* me knows who Olov is, since I'm past number 5 already, but I'm staying true to the moment. Otherwise the timeline would get effed. Also, this must be why someone would just pay for a nano-reenactment of anything they want to record. Eeg, look at me, I'm bannering for Hello Corp.)

Numbers 2 and 3 are pretty much one big one. We drove past the Tastee-Freez and saw all the flashing lights and an ambulance. I cried into Boomer's shoulder. I must have said "Why?" or "It's not fair" while I was sobbing, 'cause he goes, "Cry all you need to, Janey, but don't go telling yourself it wasn't fair. It's always fairest. And if it ain't, it's in your favor," which is maybe true, but still (glad I didn't say FML).

We found a disgusting old bar with the & sign carved into the stucco, above the door frame. It didn't necessarily mean anything, but B got out and walked around the back. The one-story building looked deserted from the outside (the only window was blacked out and had iron bars).

Boomer came back around and said, "It ain't a hero HQ. Doesn't even have satellite." (Apparently some places lure villains, and then they go all melee and beat the frag out of them — and it barely makes the RL news feed.)

Boomer was all, "Stay in the car."

I got out of the car. "I can help," I said.

"Last time, you got yourself tagged on a million vids and almost punctuated by that killer gimp."

"You are such a lag."

He stopped short of the greasy-looking door and said, "You alive? That package still en route? Yeah? You welcome, then."

I walked toward the door. "I don't care. I'm coming, anyway." He was filling up on the rage gauge. (He kept snapping his index finger against his middle finger—back and forth. It made an angry *flick flick flick.*)

"I can't hit you," he said finally, "and I can't just as well leave you to die by your own fool thinking, so . . ."

"Why not?" I said. It was probably stupid to ask why someone isn't willing to kill you, but I wanted to know. It's not like he was going to get more money from FC.

He goes, "'Cause I ain't no hero, that's why." He opened the door for me. I prolly should have taken the victory and STFU, but instead I curtsied and said, "Why, thank you, villainous Mr. B."

He rolled his eyes and mumbled, "Butthead."

Inside, the air was gelatinous. A pack of rogues was in a corner running a pirate server and drinking from vases. Scattered poets sat alone and stared deep into their monitors. At the bar sat a line of trucker dudes ordering by the pint (any one of them could have been the tank on a raiding party). Behind the bar, two hotz babez wore cowboy boots and made the frappuccinos.

So, basic espresso bar.

"Hey, sweet cheeks," grunted one trucker coming out of the bathroom (still not zipped up, BTW). "'Nother round of macchiatos, half-caf, no foam, with a finger of soy milk—and make it triple quick, yeah?" Then he pointed a thumb at her (like he was holding a remote) and went, "Bloop, Bloop, BLOOP!" like it was fast-forward.

The other truckers chuckled. In fact, on second look, they were all the same trucker. The company must have found the best one and cloned a ton of them. One had a scar across his chin, and another hadn't cut his hair in a while (the ugmo with his fly out had a barb-wire tattoo on his forearm), but they pretty much all wore the same jeans and cutoff red flannel shirts (all with a patch: "Property of 10-4 Good Buddy Corporation").

Boomer went up to the bar and leaned on his elbows. He raised his voice and said, "Looking for somebody by the name of Olov." The trucker closest to us cocked an eyebrow (but didn't say anything). The rogues snickered (but they were always doing that). The barista browsed over and said, "What'll you have?"

"Looking for Olov," repeated B.

"We don't serve that," said the girl.

"He ain't a drink."

"Then why're you asking me?"

"I'm asking if you've seen someone around here by that name."

"I see lots of people."

"I'm asking about just one guy."

She nodded at the truckers. "There are *lots* of just that one guy." (She was trolling for a flame war, obvs.) Boomer paused.

"So you're saying you and Olov never friend-requested."

She put a hand on her hip, went *tsk*, and said, "I'm saying we don't serve villains."

I jumped in before B could reach over and strangle the little skank and said, "Do you serve hot cocoa?"

I'm a sweet little girl who just wants a tasty treat. So she did a 180 and grabbed a pouch full of "nano-certified" cocoa flavoring.

Boomer shook his head and breathed out. He looked at the trucker next to him and said, "What about you? You know Olov?"

The trucker looked up from his cappuccino with foam in his 'stache. He goes, "Well, if it's your seat, then why isn't your name on it?"

Weird, right? I was all WTF, at the time, but B explained it to me later. Basically, the trucker wasn't answering Boomer's question (obvs) 'cause he was imagining a different scenario. You know, that scene where the hero sits at a bar and a villain comes up behind him and says, "You're in my seat," and then a bar fight breaks out? In this case, B didn't even have to say what the villain says, 'cause the trucker was imagining pretty hard that he was the hero, and heroes always need good reasons to get into bar fights. Heroes watch a *lot* of movies.

So B said, "You want a reason, I'll give you a reason." He grabbed the porcelain teapot behind the counter and shattered it over the trucker's head. Dude went game over on the floor.

The other clones of the trucker all stood up from their seats and said, "Ay!" But then they all waited for B to say some kind of villain thing like "I'm gonna kill you" and then telegraph a punch for ten seconds so the hero can counter. It was crazy to look at them all there in a line, all thinking *they* were the star of the show. How can *everybody* be a hero? But that meant Boomer had the jump on them 'cause Boomer didn't fight like the vids or the games.

Actually, Boomer didn't fight like *anybody*. His "pounce" was more of a gangly seizure, but mega-fast, and hit like a meteor spell. Boomer grabbed the first guy by the shirt and pushed him backward into the next guy. The two of them into the third guy. B pushed them all into the wall. They fell in a heap. And then Boomer went ani-mal. Morph sequence was half a second. It wasn't awesome, like a werewolf. It was ugly, like a crazy person shrieking and growling. He thrashed at the truckers, clawing with his hands and ripping any-thing he could with his teeth. A couple of times he scratched at his own face. Every movement was totally random. Zero logic, just a raging 99-hit hyper combo. Jumping on one guy, biting his shin, then howling, then trying to yank another guy's arm off.

If the truckers grabbed him, he squealed like a pig and flailed till they let go. They were all like @_@ confused. The main trucker who came out of the bathroom (windows still open on his laptop, if you know what I mean) pulled out a Taser, but B put his hand right on the electric prongs and ripped it away. He jumped at the trucker's face and gnashed and spat and whaled on him. The other truckers ran out of the bar, and when the captain could pry himself away (shirt completely tattered), he ran off, too.

Boomer stood in the middle of the espresso bar, soaked and pant-ing. Single *most* embarrassing thing I've ever seen. But he won, so I don't really know what that says about anything.

That was 2 and 3 basically.

I keep expecting Boomer to be a certain way, but he's just soooo *disappointing*. (Examples: "He'll be nice to me," but he isn't. "He'll save me from the monster," but he lets Tyler get killed. "He'll protect me from heroes," but he practically craps his pants and acts like he has rabies.) I guess he's not the villain every little girl dreams about. (Not exactly, anyway.)

I have to go to bed now.

Atlantic Yearly E-zine

[A back issue from 2045]

Interview with Dr. Shuler von Piffle-Paff

Atlantic Yearly: Tell us, Doctor, a little about your background.

> **Dr. Piffle-Paff:** I was born in Geneva—well, to be honest a little outside of Bern, but my mother was in a motorcar on the way to Geneva. In that sense, I wasn't *positioned*, astrophysically speaking, until we reached our destination, and I perceived the sky. The first vision of the cosmos, understanding our relative location to all things "other"—this is when we are all born, yes?

AY: Yes, of course. And now some background in your field of study . . .

> **PP:** Oh. *Oh.* Ha-ha. I see I missed the point, didn't I?

AY: That's all right, Doctor.

> **PP:** This exact situation right here. The *mis*reading, is very much what I am fascinated with.

AY: I don't understand.

> **PP:** Precisely.

AY: What is that exactly?

> **PP:** Not exactly, *precisely.*

AY: Doctor, I'm completely lost.

PP: For example, one party has delivered a communicative piece of data—we can call this the apple. You have given me an apple. But through misreading, misunderstanding, I see what you have given me as a quince.

AY: A quince. The green fruit?

PP: Exactly.

AY: Or is it *precisely*?

PP: No, it's exactly.

AY: Oh.

PP: But this is the point, do you see? Either you have given me a quince and are wrong in thinking it is an apple. Or I have been given an apple and misperceive a quince.

AY: How can you tell which of us is wrong?

PP: Aha! But you cannot. *And,* AND, there is a third option. If you will remember, these fruits were symbols. They stood for communication. SO, perhaps you HAD an apple, but through *imprecise* language, you gave me a quince!

AY: It turned into a quince?

PP: Exactly and precisely. By virtue of imprecision (or is it vice?). And this has even greater value, since many scholars believe the quince is, in fact, the forbidden fruit of Judeo-Christianity: the "apple" with which the serpent tempted Eve.

. . .

AY: The quince was re-created by human literature.

PP: Very good. Yes.

AY: But you're a nano-biologist, yes?

PP: Nano-physicist.

AY: How do you feel about the Hello Corporation's new
NoFi initiative?

PP: By Hello Corporation, I assume you mean Guten Tag
Corporation.

AY: The one owned by Calam!ty Shine.

PP: Ah, yes. Calam!ty Shine. I think the concept of nano-
atmosphere is fascinating. Presumably, it could allow us
to "recode" our material world.

AY: Could you give an example?

PP: Certainly. Imagine a world where you live in a small
studio apartment, furnished with a bed, a lamp, and not
much else.

AY: Done.

PP: You have a computer with various media—books,
films, music, et cetera. But how did you get this media?

AY: Download.

PP: Well, now imagine simply "downloading" your bed,
the lamp, even the computer itself.

AY: You're saying the nano-machines would build whatever I wanted.

PP: Whatever you could *afford*. But more than that. It would "livestream" these objects. Meaning as soon as you wake up in the morning and walk into the bathroom to shower, the nano-machines could break down the matter in your room and "fax" it to someplace else. Perhaps to a reporter like yourself, in a similar studio across the globe, where it is nighttime and she needs to sleep.

AY: So it could recycle molecules?

PP: Remarkable, yes?

AY: Couldn't that put an end to the global food and resource shortage?

PP: It *could*. But this would require the upper class to give up, say, a decorative vase full of flowers in order for a child to eat.

AY: You don't think it would happen.

PP: Our shipping system these days is not so terrible. Yet we send too little. And the corrupt agencies of many poor countries leave the food rotting on the docks. You only gave me half your apple, and I did not eat it.

AY: I see your point. You don't seem very excited by the possibility of a "ReCreation Day," as Cal called it recently.

PP: Well, that would be decades away, still. I would be long gone.

AY: But nevertheless.

> PP: Nevertheless, the trouble with nano-fax is the
> material cost. For example, what if both you and the
> journalist across the globe wished to sleep at the exact
> same time? An afternoon nap perhaps. Who would
> get the bed? Of course, this is a silly example, because
> there is plenty of organic matter to make two beds.
> But suppose this on a larger scale. Nano-machines are
> miraculous, but they cannot actually create new matter.
> No technology can truly build something out of nothing;
> there are only so many atoms to go around. What if one
> country were to use them all? Would this erase a moun-
> tain range someplace else? Would it recycle the clothes
> off of someone's back? These are terrifying, even sci-fi,
> implications.

AY: So you're saying the whole world would get
eaten up?

> PP: Oh, no, no. Nothing like that. Atoms are recyclable,
> after all. Once the machines have the materials, they can
> use and reuse them, passing them back and forth. It's
> only the initial cost I am worried about. How much will
> the machines need? And where will it come from? We
> need just enough to realize everyone's desires, a worry-
> ing prospect, no?

AY: Hello Corp says they will first draw from junkyards
and post-industrial parkland.

PP: Enough to fuel a hundred nano-chambers perhaps, but an entire nano-atmosphere?

AY: Speaking of which, the first NoFi rooms are coming soon, I hear.

PP: Yes, I suppose we shall see a small sampling of our new earth.

AY: Thank you for your time, Doctor.

PP: You are very adorable. I would like to refer you to my grandson.

AY: Is he a physicist, too?

PP: Oh, no, no, no. He is quite serious.

AFTER BOOMER WENT berserker barrage on the trucker clones, I grabbed him by the elbow and we logged out of the bar asap. His eyes were darting around like a screensaver. I pulled him to the Bug. It was locked. I turned around and said, "Gimme the keys," but he was scratching his forearms.

"Boomer, the keys."

Nothing. He was *tewtilly* primitive.

I thought, *I've been riding with an animal. He could have killed me.* As I reached into his jacket, I tried to avoid touching the fabric. Must have been infested with lice and fleas.

Then we both heard, "What do you want with Olov?" B whipped around and snarled, but didn't attack. An old man was standing behind us. He didn't have any enhancements. His clothes looked like fiber (jeans, boots, tucked-in shirt, white hair and beard, old-man belly). He was either a villain or a bum.

"Father Clay," said Boomer.

"Oh, you finally found your words," I said to B.

"Boomer," said Father Clay, unclenching his fists (I only noticed then that the father was on DefCon 5). "I didn't recognize you."

"I cleaned up," said B. "Had to bring the kid with me."

(I was like: You *cleaned up* and you look like this?!)

"I thought someone had stolen your Bug," said Father Clay.

"Nah."

"I suppose you heard about Tyler," said Father Clay. His Santa beard quivered a little.

"Yeah, I heard about it. We have some kind of monster after us.

On foot, but he's fast." Father Clay looked up from the pavement. "A what?"

"A monster," I said. "They got a shot of it in a vid." I offered him B's phone, but he stepped back.

"Thank you, young lady, but I'm all right."

"He's a proper villain," said Boomer.

(I forgot. Father Canseco wasn't strict with Nali & me. He believed in moderation.) "Sorry," I muttered.

"You must be Janey," he said. "Father Canseco told me you'd be coming."

All I could think to say was, "He's dead now."

"Yes," said FC . . . Father Clay. His lips disappeared under his beard. (I wish I didn't have to call him FC.)

FC2 said, "I can take you to Olov."

"How?" I asked. "He's harder to track than the Cal virus."

"No," he said, opening the car door and getting into the driver's side, "she isn't."

"Have you killed them yet?"

      "Not quite, but they're in sight."

"I hate you. You are the *worst* cold-blooded death dealer
I've ever seen, Baku. I'll take care of this myself. You're
too boring."

      "I did kill a villain, Tyler was his name. / Faked the
      news, and gave Olov all the blame."

"Yeah, great. I took a nap a few hours ago. Nobody
cares."

"The Book Log of Janey"

FATHER CLAY DROVE US, Boomer and I crammed in the passenger side. I was in the middle, the armrest jammed into my kidney, trying not to touch either man (especially Father Clay). Boomer crumpled himself up like a Coke can so I could have most of the space.

FC2 made us cover our eyes with blindfolds. I guess Tyler would have helped usually and done the knots tighter, 'cause I pushed mine up a little and sat back, and I could see everything.

Outside of Walla Walla was a beautiful billboard forest. (I've never seen so much real wood paper.) Some were just the size of real-estate signs and old campaign ads for city-council nominees. Others had thick trunks, covered in a bark made of flyers and post-cards stapled on top of each other. At the top were massive banners with sleek designs for stuff I'd never even heard of. Some of the colors had faded, and some of the edges were torn. In fact, the whole forest was slowly decaying.

I don't understand how people can say we should get rid of them. I would make this place like a museum, and I'd get people to come and see it—this is where banner ads and pop-ups came from.

When we stopped, I pretended to squint as I pulled off my blind-fold. Boomer got out and stretched his legs. It was just a blank field. Tall green-yellow grass for all 360. The only clickable thing was a water well. It was about as tall as me, with a cone-shaped wood top.

FC2 trundled (big belly bouncing) behind the well and grabbed a camo-color tarp. B helped him cover the Bug. Now it looked like a big green pimple, but I guess unmanned Hello Corp police planes wouldn't know any better. The well had a flip hinge like an old laptop. Father Clay opened it.

"All right, get in," said B.

And I'm like: R u talkin 2 me? (Not gonna lie, I thought they wanted to kill me and throw my body down the well.) B must have noticed, 'cause he said, "There's a ladder."

"Of course there's a ladder," I said. "I mean, what, it's not like you guys were gonna kill me and throw my body down a well."

I climbed down the ladder. After a few feet, the narrow well widened around me. Boomer and FC2 followed me down. The ladder finally ended at a narrow platform, about the size of the landing in our lighthouse tower. And just like our house, it had a spiral staircase going down, but this one was made of stones. Real fire candles sat in little notches cut into the rock wall, lighting the way. The landing was grated metal. Through the grates, I could see the top of a huge bell. I was like, holy poops.

I wasn't in a well. I was in a steeple.

Below me was the bell tower, and below that was a whole cathedral. The villains had sunk the entire church into the ground, all the way up to the top of the tower. No way any heroes could find it. It's like natural cloaking. *This must be what chameleons are like,* I thought.

We climbed down past the iron bell, all the way to the steeple floor. It was a dark room, the size of a large closet, with nothing but the bell rope (they prolly never pull it). "How did you bury a whole church?" I asked.

"With the most advanced technology in the world," said FC2, "our hands."

I felt him squeeze past me to open the door. It was sealed tight. I heard him grunt, but then . . .

Tracking shot: Two rows of columns holding up the ceiling of a massive sanctuary. Wood pews. Marble floor. Wagon-wheel chandeliers holding long burning candles. The windows were colored glass, reinforced from behind with sheet metal so the dirt wouldn't crash in. Everything had jagged edges and was embedded with dust.

(Zero tech. Not even electricity. Like, straight from the DOS ages.)

Father Clay breathed in the air (cold & moldy). "Welcome to the Cathedral of the Blessed Saint Martha, Our Lady of Villains."

The altar at the front of the church was an oak countertop with potted plants and a few ancient appliances with their tangled wires. Behind the counter was a marble statue of Martha. She had short hair, tilted her head sideways, and looked straight at the camera. Her eyes squinted when she smiled.

Her apron had a flower print. Her elbows pivoted off her hips, each hand out. One was holding a pair of gardening gloves, the other an old glue gun.

Father Clay pointed out the knife handle sticking out of her apron pocket. "It symbolizes our lady's anti-tech DIY nature and also refers to the episode in her life when the heroes imprisoned her on trumped-up charges for helping a young man with his finances."

"She was in jail?" said Boomer.

"Every saint must suffer," said FC2, then added, "Persecution by prosecution," with a ;).

Even baby villains (goons) know about Martha's incarceration.

They had to play reruns of her teachings every morning at 11:30 Eastern, 10:30 Central.

Next to the statue was a pile of zines. I pointed at them, and FC2 said, "We have the largest collection of Our Lady's magazines . . . even several of the double-sided Halloween editions."

(I asked B later. "Magazines" is just zines in old English. Don't know what "maga" means . . . maybe wood paper. So this blog is a magablog . . . ? Mega-blog is mo like it, kapow! JK JK. hehe. :P)

B kept looking at the bell tower like he expected the monstro to come barreling down and kill all of us. When I thought about Baku, I realized that the steeple was the only entrance and exit.

FC2 showed us around, even the compost heap they had dug outside one of the windows. Boomer didn't care. (I wonder if all the snailmen are so distant . . . like NPCs . . . non-playable characters or whatever's between heroes and villains.)

He interrupted FC2 and said, "No disrispeck, Pops. But you said we'd come down here and meet Olov. If he ain't that thing that's chasing us, then let us know and we can log out."

FC2 LOLed & B was like 0_o.

"I'm sorry, Boomer. I thought I was being clear. *This* is Olov." He was still pointing at Martha . . . I had to think about it for a second. I was like, <loading . . . loading . . . loading . . . >, and then, Ohhh! Our. Lady. Of. Villains. OLOV.

I said, "Wait. So Olov doesn't exist?"

"Of course she exists," said FC2.

"Not like in our hearts," said B. "In real life. Real enough to kill Tyler."

FC2 cast *befuddle* on himself. Or at least on his face. He seemed to think Olov, Martha, whatevs, was as real as real life. But then, I guess heroes think the second life on the networks is just as real as RL. Maybe old-school SL is whatever you believe in your heart. Weird.

FC2 said, "Well, no, she's no longer with us physically."

"So she didn't kill Tyler," I said.

"Oh, no, of course not," said Father Clay. "Villains use the name Olov as a code, to meet one another. But Hello Corp spams the networks with negative press. They tell people he's some kind of mysterious evil leader."

"So the monster killed Tyler *and* Father Canseco," I said. I was standing near the altar, next to Olov's sensible shoes, shaking. On a nearby communion table was a goblet of mulled wine and a plate of cran-raisin scones. I was thinking about Father Canseco. No wonder he was an outsider; he even had a digital ink newspaper (I didn't even know about Olov). Or maybe he tried to tell us, and Nali and I didn't care—I dunno. If I'd listened, maybe I'd know what "Find &" meant, too.

B and FC2 chatted about ReCreation Day and the uprisings. FC2 made a gaggy noise that sounded like a stifled laugh when he talked about the arrested villains. He tugged at his beard every time he did it, so you could see if he was :) or not. Even I got suspicious. I only shook his hand a couple of times, but FC2 used to talk super slow, like he was thinking about every word. And his eyes used to be calm.

Boomer was scratching at his forearms, and his blinking was set to autofire. I could tell he was tewtilly noidal (prolly code orange), but FC2 thought it was just Boomer being Boomer.

For example:

> B goes: "Do you think Cal will kill the villains when the nano-machines uplink?"
>
> FC2: [gag! cough cough] "He certainly could, couldn't he? Let's hope he has mercy. Heh-heh" [beard tug].
>
> Boomer: [squint, blink, blink, squint]
>
> Father Clay: "Do you know if the other villains are doing anything about it? Do they have a plan to revolt, or is Father Canseco's book the only information they have?"
>
> Boomer: [suspicious grunt, blink, blink, blink]

Totes shady. Father Clay was an arch villain. Why was he asking such stupid questions?

The convo was very nonsmooth. Boomer is always quiet, but this time he was on guard mode. FC2 gag-laughed over the silence. It was creepy and kinda heroic.

I was still by the communion table, staring at my feet. The wood floors of the church had a layer of dust. You could see everywhere we had walked, like snow tracks. I made shapes with my toe. After a while I noticed that I had drawn three &s. Then I remembered (suddenly), not about Father Canseco's message, but that the floor *shouldn't* have been dusty. The place was old, yeah, but Father Clay had a huge rogues gallery of like twenty villains. He said they were all locked up from the uprising or looking after Tyler's body, but that was all recent. Lots of feet should have shuffled across the floor every day.

I bent down, like I was tying my shoe, to look. I didn't discover anything, 'cause dust is just dust. But whatever, it wouldn't have been there in a space that twenty-one people lived in.

Boomer asked FC2, "Do you know anything about the monster chasing us?"

And FC2 was like, "It's probably Baku_The_DreamEater. He's no Cal, but they quest together. I hear his attack is eating brain parts by sucking them through the ear."

"And they die?"

"If he wants. Or he eats just their dreams, and they get a glassy look to them and walk around cocktail parties saying, 'Hello, what do you do for a living? . . . Hello, what do you do for a living?'" (O. M. G. the seventh circle of Facebook.)

Boomer said, "You mean, those are his attacks in the network games, right?"

"Hmm?" said FC2.

"He can't just suck brains in real life. He only does that in the video games, on the networks, yeah?"

"Oh," said FC2 (gaggy). "Well, he could do it in real life with nano-machines, when they uplink I mean, after ReCreation Day."

"Right," said B.

"Right," said FC2.

"But that hasn't happened yet," said B.

"Right, right," said FC2.

That's when I saw it (I was still kneeling to "tie my shoe"). On the leg of the communion table, next to the statue of Olov—a & carved into the wood. And then, on the cuffs of Olov's homemade pants, a row of embroidered &s.

Suddenly, the switch flipped. There was something wrong, and I knew it. And I knew what to do. And *finally*, I knew what "Find &" meant.

To my loyal readers, I'd like to announce that my first chapbook, *Meditations on the Color Heartbreak,* written under my pen name, Danny Blacksad, will be released in PDF in two weeks. Please pre-order a copy *here.* Like all my fellow wordsmiths, I'm hoping to publish with a wood house as well. More on that later.

For now, feast your spirits on this little treat I found with the Goodai Mate Corporation cache-search engine. An unpublished draft of a Collins poem, from the turn of the century.

It's a little "on the nose," as they say, but accurate, no? My mom collects these things called pagers. And yeah, sux about the fish.

My favorite image—"ocean of oil rigs"—is so . . . naive. He never even considered wind turbines. We haven't had an ocean of oil rigs since '47 . . .

Consummations

Someday the industrial wasteland will seem beautiful to us.
Postcards of urban sprawl will say, My darling, I wish you
were here.
As with brownstones and old barns, we will tour our children
through the factories and their fallout creeks like Gorgon's hair.
The warehouse district of Baltimore will be a cultural heritage

site, its girders cantilevered across the polluted harbor—
what an engineering marvel. How practical we have been.

In the future a plastic and rubber vacuum will decorate our
porches as a churn of the postmodern age, recycling dust
into filters and filters into trash bags, trash bags into garbage
trucks—which scuba divers use now for a reef system.
They are their own fish.

Someday our nature will become as Nature.
Past the overgrowth you will discover a bald landscape like a
tidy cap on the earth's once-bushy scalp.
The machines that build Magic Markers, all those plastic wrap-
pings you need scissors to pry, the wire that came with your
first cell phone—each will have an item number and two or
three bidders at the auction houses.
They will say of us, Wow,
They really lived as if every day was the last.
We will have eaten our shame.
Post-consumption quaintness.
An ocean of oil rigs.

Someday we will have flipped all the valences.
Eat your Twinkie.
Don't throw out the garbage.
Will you look at that sunset? Can you believe they used to put
orange juice in these?

I JUMPED UP from not tying my shoes. B scowled at me, but I def preferred it to Father Clay smiling at me like, "What is it, little darling? <cough> I'mgonnakillyou <cough cough>."

I said, "Uh, Father Clay, do you, um, know what ampersands mean?"

His eyes looked like a game of *Pong.* He said, "Heh-heh, what an odd question. They mean *and,* I suppose."

I said, "Yeah, but, what does it mean to us villains? Father Canseco said we should 'Find ampersand.' "

"It must be a sentence fragment," stammered FC2.

"I thought that too at first," I said, "but then Boomer showed me that you guys use the symbol to mark friendly bars and stuff."

"Oh. OH! Right, *that* ampersand. Of course, we use it to mark friendly bars and safehouses."

"I just said that," I said, "but what does the symbol *mean*? It has to stand for something."

He didn't know. I could tell. I didn't even know until I saw Martha's pants. The font was stretchy so I could make out the code. Or I didn't even know it was a code until I @_@.

The & has two loops, connected by a long line, and ends with a sideways arrow.

An O. An L. Another O. And a V.

Our Lady of Villains

Olov

&

"Find Olov."

Thx, FC.

Boomer was ready to turn into a shrieking rage criminal, but if I was right about our situation, that would have been a kill screen for us. FC2 was pretending everything was normal. I said, "You know what? I bet Father Canseco explained it in his package."

FC2 was like: !

"You have it with you?"

"I'll go get it," I said, and jogged to the back of the sanctuary, to the bell tower.

"You must be tired," said FC2, "I can—"

"It's cool. I got it," I said as I yanked on the stuck door.

I ran up the bell-tower steps and climbed out of the top into the grassy field. The sun was in sleep mode. The air was lukewarm. I breathed it in, and it tasted like stale water.

The scene wasn't full of stuff, just me, the church steeple, B's car with the tarp over it, a few clouds, and the moon. Still, it felt like the blades of grass were anti-aliasing. And when the wind blew through them, I could see a little slowdown. I got that weird feeling that behind me was nothing but an empty black screen.

I stopped by the steeple. Then I whipped around as fast as I could. I could swear each cloud in the sky was popping in just out-side my vision. I could almost catch up to it—the grass field extend-ing into the blackness as I spun, and withdrawing from the other direction, like there was only 180 degrees of grass field to go around.

I kneeled down by the steeple and pushed the grass aside. The exposed stones of the steeple were weathered, but if you looked close, every fifth one was weathered the same way, as if it was texture-mapped. I scooted around to check another side. w00t. There it was, etched in the brick:

NOFI CHAMBER 256-62931

PROPERTY OF HELLO CORPORATION

The entire church was a NoFi chamber (creating a nano-reconstruction of the church). Who even knows where the real one was? The steeple and the bell tower must have been the air lock (no wonder the door was hard to open).

I pushed on all the bricks to find the concealed panic button, but nothing. Then I heard, "What are you doing?"

I screamed and fell back.

I scrambled to my feet.

I said, "Nothing! I'm not doing anything."

FC2 climbed out of the steeple. He said, "It didn't look like nothing."

"I dropped something." (In my head I was like, OMG.OMG. OMG.)

"What did you drop?" he asked. He made an emoticon I'd never seen, like the frame rate dropped in the middle of a grin, so it jerked into a sneer.

"What did I drop?"

He walked toward me slowly. I backed away.

"Mmm-hmm."

"I dropped a, um, hair clip."

"Oh, I see. You dropped a hair clip. And you were looking for it by the base of the chamber."

"Yep," I said.

"I mean, steeple."

"Right, that's what I meant, too."

My back hit Boomer's car. Father Clay stood over me. He said, "Do you know anything about the Cal virus, Jane?"

I bobbled my head, meaning yes and no.

"It's perfect. Like ultima perfect. It took the whole Internet and overpowered one part by eating another part. Like a tapeworm. Do you have any idea how smart you'd have to be to write something like that?"

Me: [no]

"You'd have to be brilliant. Only Cal himself could do it. He made the god code."

Me: [okay]

I was bent backward over the hood of the car. FC2's breath smelled like Mountain Dew. "Do you think you could trick somebody that smart, Jane?"

Me: [no]

"You're right."

Then he straightened up, and I stopped holding my breath. His eyes closed as he smiled and said, "Just thought I'd come up to see if you needed a hand. Poor girl, you must be exhausted from the trip." (Like nothing happened.)

I said, "I'm fine. Boomer can help."

"Oh, no," said FC2. "He's getting adjusted inside."

When he strutted back to the steeple, his old-man limp was gone. He said, "Come in whenever you like. And bring the book."

As soon as he went back down, I crawled under the tarp and got into the car. (Total freak-out. Hands shaking. Everything.)

I don't know how long I've been here. I don't know what's happening to Boomer. I don't know who this Father Clay 2.0 is or what happened to the original. I don't know what Father Canseco would want me to do. I don't even know where I am. Gawd, I *hate* not knowing so much.

I *do* know they want FC's book and that they don't know anything about mine. I'm writing all this now, in case when I go in after B . . . if I don't come out and they destroy FC's book . . . then someone will find this one.

I wish I had somebody.

I even miss Nali and Sister Tanaki.

I hope Boomer is all right.

TO: FATHER CLAY

As always, my brother, I greet you with all my villainous heart and hope that you and your beloved minions are secure in the love of Olov—not tempted by the vain pleasures of a second life, a life of your own making.

I am sending this book with my precious adopted daughter, Jane, who as you know is dearest to me. When her parents left her to me, she was premature and has kept her small size even as she has become a woman in front of my eyes. What's more, she is not pretty. Not by the world's standard, anyway. Not "sxxy," as they call it. But I think it's this "flaw" in her that has been her greatest blessing. Instead of the world being attracted to her, she is attracted to the world. In short, she is curious in a way beautiful people need never be.

What Cal offers people like Jane is a chance at ReCreation, but ReCreation into what? Taller, prettier, sxxier? I do not want my daughter constantly escaping into a wish that she be someone else.

These poor disconsolate customers. These poor people who are crafting their own stories out of self-love, and the desire to be better, and best. I ask you, brother, are these heroes heroes?

I think this trip will show her the one fundamental truth that separates Olov and Cal.

We cannot, any of us, be the hero of our own story.

This is why Cal calls us villains, and why we accept the name. But as you know, he is no longer content to marginalize us. I am now convinced that ReCreation Day will be a worldwide massacre.

Enclosed with this letter are my transcripts of the interview with an arch-villain, Rood. I warn you, it is jarring. The information he imparts about his journey from Africa, the atrocities he suffered at the hands of Hello Corp, and the secrets they have managed to keep because of the media hegemony will cause a global uprising ten times the size of the recent events.

Rood is a good man. He is still in hiding. I am afraid to write his location in case this letter is found. For now, his spirits are constant. But when I first met him, Brother, I will admit that I wept to see him. He had only just disembarked from the cargo ship on which he had stowed away from Gibraltar. His body was scarred nearly beyond recognition, a tangle of bones. It was not starvation, Brother Clay. I could suffer the idea of starvation. It was the nano-fax, nano-recycling, whatever hideous lie they have devised to call it.

Rood was a sub-Saharan, of the kind we have long washed ourselves of any responsibility. The history he relates of the past ten years is nothing short of alien. When the NoFi chambers went online a decade ago, few of us associated it with the closing of national borders (for fear of outbreaks, they said!). The Africans began noticing changes in their environment only when the shadow of Kilimanjaro began to alter. Can you believe it? The mountain itself was being shaved. As the NoFi chambers increased, more and more organic matter was necessary to compose whatever random hero fantasy was playing in each NoFi room in the first-world nations. (How else could the chambers afford to build entire elfin forests, if the trees were not first uprooted from Africa?)

As Rood tells it, the experience was sudden. The nano-revolution here was a nano-holocaust there. Entire stretches of the savanna, Jeeps and corrugated metal, lakes and their vast population of creatures, were all dismantled by the machines and reconstituted as cartoonish swords and stadiums and fashion catalogs.

They are carving up the whole of Africa, Brother Clay, an entire continent mined for its constituent parts.

Rood led his family in the mass exodus to Gibraltar—his family like the Jews fleeing plagued Egypt. Day after day, the mountains were leveled into molehills. The plant life was first drained of chloroform, blanching trees into gray stalks, and then vaporized as filler material.

You can foresee the nightmarish conclusion, I am sure. The NoFi chambers don't simply build inert objects. They re-create for us, with God's own dirt, new men and new women (sometimes orcs and sometimes lovers).

As they walked across the continent, the people of Rood's village survived as scavengers of the lowest order. Some hoarded food and water, but there was no place to hide it. Food stores would vanish, sometimes overnight. Rood's daughter scoured the dry riverbeds every day, only to find a few tiny fish, fallen along the cracked earth. Madness was the only recourse, under the growing fear that one day *people* would begin to disappear.

Like any true heroes, the machines came for the children first. They were taken in a manner Rood could never defend. From his arms, from his grasp, his daughter was dissolved into vapor. This, it turned out, was a blessing. She was young and small, and all of her was necessary at once. Rood's son, a broad and solid young man, was taken in pieces. In the end, his wife could suffer no more and finished the job of the nano-machines for them with the sharpened bark of a baobab tree. In what can only be called a satanic irony, the machines took the bark first.

In those days of the journey, only Rood remained, staggering through a vast dying wilderness, crazed with grief. He was able to find and kill a starved lion. By wearing the dead creature as he traveled, he was able to divert whatever nanos floated unseen around him, hunting for bio-organic cells to fulfill some child's purchase a continent away. The nanos scraped from the lion's meat before the man's. He describes with a tragic smirk that he is the only person to be saved, because God "fed" him to the lion.

In the final leg, Rood describes a post-industrial parkland more barren than any desert. His protective coat was eventually itself eaten, and soon the nano-machines began to dissect him—imperceptibly at first. A mild itch, then a raw stinging. Before Rood made it to the ship, the machines had cut notches of his hide. His cheeks are pocked, his neck perforated. I could not look at the gouges in his stomach but once. All fat has been butchered off the lean meats. Since finding us, he has begun to heal, of course, but is scarred terribly.

Brother Clay, we must tell the world that Africa is extinct. Are we not all heroes for having missed it?

As per our discussions, you know what to do with this book. It contains all of Rood's evidence. When you have taken care of spreading the information, please send word back through Jane. I trust and hope the very best for you.

Oh love of Olov,
Roderick Canseco

P.S. Jane will be a great help to you, but please also chaperone her with Tyler (a father worries).

"The BL of J"

WOW. GOTTA B quick. This is totes F'd up. How can nanos mine
Africa? Issat possible?

Have 2 tell B.

FC2 def a hero, maybe Cal?

Is B OK if FC2 = Cal?

FC <3ed me sooo much. :'(

G2G, spread info on Net.

Rly scared.

I ————————

The tarp over the car got ripped off just now. Sunlight blinded me
(didn't even know it was daytime). I screamed until I heard, "It's
me," in B's voice.

He made it out, but his face is scarred like Rood. His forearms are
eaten away.

I just told him, "B, I think Father Clay is Cal. He's gonna kills us."

And he said, "Shhh, I know." He made me put my seat belt on
and asked if I was hurt by the machines. He wouldn't say anything
else.

Now we're driving. I don't know where we're going, but we're
getting away from here. I wish we knew what FC2 1.0 was gonna do
with the book. Boomer's boosting through the billboard forest now.
Wait, something's wrong . . .

PolloConChicken: yo, candy pants. Answer quick I got sumfin hecka cool

. . .

PolloConChicken: YO!! you on er wut?

JeebuzKilla: I'm not answering till u stop callin me *candy pants*.

PolloConChicken: R U effing kidding me?

JeebuzKilla: no. I'm tired of everyone being mean on the net.

PolloConChicken: u think if I stop calling you candy pants (even though this is the *most* candy pants request evah), then the whole net will be nice?

JeebuzKilla: it has to start somewhere.

PolloConChicken: LMAO

. . .

PolloConChicken: hello?

[Message could not be sent to "JeebuzKilla"]
[Friend request sent to "JeebuzKilla"]
[Friend request accepted]

PolloConChicken: I can't believe U unfriended me!

JeebuzKilla: friends don't call each other names.

PolloConChicken: *Oh. Em. Gee.* fine, fine, I'll stop calling you candy pants.

JeebuzKilla: thank you.

PolloConChicken: now, dear friend, can U *pleez* click this link?

JeebuzKilla: sure thing, buddy.

An old Volkswagen Bug is weaving through a billboard forest. Ads are flying by in a blur. The car is speeding in one general direction, but it never seems to reach anything. The billboards keep cycling past in an endless loop.

The landscape begins to slow down, but the car's tires are still spinning at full speed. It wasn't the car that was moving, but the landscape around it. The car is fully stopped with its tires racing.

A girl sticks her head out the window. The billboards disappear and the landscape terraforms into a grass field and a water well. The car idles next to a tarp.

An old man approaches the stationary car. As he walks, his limp becomes a swagger. His face morphs from an balding old man with a beard to a young blond man with a sneer—facial scan confirmed—young man is Calam!ty Shine, online celebrity, president of Log-In Corporation.

JeebuzKilla: this is crazy, wut is this?

PolloConChicken: shhh. It's livestream from Walla Walla.

JeebuzKilla: you hacked this?

PolloConChicken: no it was open. Random satellite nobody cares.

JeebuzKilla: The picture's kinda fuzzy

PolloConChicken: Just listen to the blind people software then. Hold on.

[Zooming . . .]

"What do we do? He's coming. Boomer, he's coming."

The girl is panicked. The driver, Boomer, puts the car in reverse, but it doesn't move. Cal says, "You don't get it yet, Boomer? The whole place changing under you?"

The girl shouts, "You already uplinked the nano-machines."

"Good girl, Janey. You're right."

"We gonna stop your 'ReCreation Day,'" says Boomer.

Cal shrugs. "What a juggernoob. You think we'd risk a day-in-date disaster on the biggest tech leap in human history just so people can feel comfortable with a new idea? We uplinked *years* ago. There's nothing for you to stop."

A monster appears from behind the water well and jumps twenty-five yards into the air—a hurling goblin king. It lands in front of the car, punches down into the engine, and shatters the windshield. Janey screams. The car bounces like a seesaw.

"Hello, Baku," says Cal.

"I eat dreams and drink screams," says Baku in a prerecorded rhythm.

Boomer and Janey scramble to open the doors as the front of the car swirls into a powder around Baku's arm. He makes a throaty gurgle, like a snake swallowing a frog. When the hunchback pulls his arm out of the engine, there is no engine to speak of, just a gaping hole.

Cal says, "Did I mention we get superpowers?"

"It's not a cheat code or a god mode," says Baku.

"Yeah, we've just been leveling up longer than you," says Cal.

Boomer gets out of the car and slams the door. "You gonna spit out my car," he says, and marches toward the monster. Baku rises onto his haunches, in a ready position, but Boomer doesn't wait for any bell or battle prompt. He grabs Baku by the fangs and pries his mouth open. Baku tries to yank away. He shakes his head like a bull, but Boomer spreads Baku's jaw until a <crack> and then a <clack>. A last tremor roils through the monster. Then Baku slumps to the ground with a permanent yawn, his tongue formless and obsolete.

"Guess that's Game Over for Baku," says Cal. With his hands he mimics a little explosion and makes the sound effect.

"Quit playing and give us back the engine," says Boomer.

Baku's body plays a dismayed sound file, then turns gray and begins to crumble. The particles drift with the wind. Boomer looks at Cal. "So you just recycle them?"

Cal nods. "Just like the press releases promised."

Janey is standing next to the car. She's holding two books. "What if people want to bury their family? You treat them like compost?"

"Oh, Baku wasn't a person," says Cal. "It was software. My co-op quest partner. Sweet AI, though, right? I mean, we do treat *people* like that, but I'm just saying Baku wasn't one of them." He puts his hands in his pockets and rocks back and forth on his heels.

Janey mouths something to Boomer . . . cross-referencing facial recognition software . . . confirmed . . . she says, "I've got a plan." Boomer runs around the broken car and grabs Janey. They run to the well. She is holding two paper books.

"Where're you going?" says Cal. "I could just stop your hearts if I want."

"But that would be boring," says Janey.

"No, it could be cool," says Cal.

"Then why didn't you do it in the sanctuary," says Boomer, "insteada letting the machines eat me up?"

"Oh, 'cause that was cool, too."

Boomer doesn't respond to Cal as he flips open the top of the well. Janey and Boomer climb in. Cal sighs. "Fine," he says, and follows. "But you're starting to bore me."

> JeebuzKilla: BWAAHH! Is there a camera inside?

> PolloConChicken: maybe ;)

> JeebuzKilla: RLY? Put it on! We're missing stuff!!!!

> PolloConChicken: Aren't you even interested in trying to transfer our profiles to the ReCreated accounts? We'd B superheroes.

> JeebuzKilla: we can't can we?

> PolloConChicken: No, I already tried. BUT MAYBE, maybe I DID find a cam by jeeniusly patching into the well (which is a NoFi chamber) and streamin the security tape. :)

> JeebuzKilla: Wut?! Did you or didn't you?

> PolloConChicken: If I did, who'd b tha man?

> JeebuzKilla: ugh. YOU. you'd b tha man. All right?

PolloConChicken: and who'd be tha candy pants?

JeebuzKilla: whatver. I would. >ur l4m3rz<

PolloConChicken: you'd b wut?

JeebuzKilla: I'd b the candy pants!!

PolloConChicken: Wow, I didn't know that about u.
Les just watch the vid.

Janey and Boomer run into the sanctuary toward the statue of Saint Martha. Janey breathes heavily and holds the books to her chest. Boomer looks around the building.

"Shouldn't have come in here. We're trapped," says Boomer.

"No, this will work. It's not like we can run, anyway."

A noise from the bell tower. Cal walks down the steps. "I wish you guys wouldn't retreat so much. It's kind of a letdown."

Janey runs down the middle aisle of the cathedral. Boomer tries the side windows, looking for air vents. They are shut tight. He curses and searches the wings. A noise from the statue of Olov. Janey spins around. The marble breaks and Baku_The_DreamEater hatches from inside it. The monster chomps its teeth. Cal enters the sanctuary and says, "Guess he used a continue. Sorry to wreck that sweet frag you had, B, but, you know, can't kill a hero."

Baku jumps down from the altar and stalks toward Janey. Cal approaches saying, "Janey, Janey, Janey. You are in a whole multiverse of trouble. You have the two greatest heroes of all time, and they're willing to kill you for the book you're holding. And the only teammate you have is an accountless old-world fleabag who doesn't even know how to play the game. Choose your own adventure, Janey. What do you think?"

"I think you murdered a whole continent of human beings."

"Oh, come ON! I'll build it back once the nano-machines start mining outer planets."

"What about the people?"

"They're done. But were you friends with any of 'em?"

Baku prowls forward. Janey has her back to the hero reborn. All three of them hear a shriek. Boomer stampedes at Baku, who turns just in time to get rammed in the side. They tumble into a pew and roll. Boomer gnaws at Baku's neck, breaking fingers that try to push him away. As they roll, the space around them changes. Baku must have a main line to the NoFi chamber and is trying to win an advantage. Boomer snarls. Even Baku looks disgusted. Boomer isn't programmed to act wild. He is the opposite of programmed. Baku kicks him off. As Boomer stumbles backward, a wooden pillar leans slightly to catch him. Boomer grunts. A newly formed spike on the pillar has impaled his shoulder. Baku jumps up and sinks his fangs into Boomer's arm, right below the wooden spike. Boomer shrieks in pain.

Cal says, "Give me the book. Or eventually one of my Bakus will kill your animal friend."

Janey runs sideways down a row of pews. "Come and get it, hero," she says. "This evidence will ruin you, and your little company, too."

Cal follows her down a parallel pew. "Oh, come on. You can't be serious. My company doesn't have anything to do with this."

"It's an evil conglomerate."

"Enh! Wrong! Boring answer," says Cal. He follows Janey out of the sanctuary, into the vestibule at the bottom of the bell tower. "First of all, evil conglomerates are cliché. Hello Corp is, like, one of the Ten Most Desirable companies to work for. We have great insurance packages."

Janey backs away from Cal's reach by climbing the stairs to the bell tower. "For you, maybe."

"For everyone who works for me."

"And kills everyone else."

In the sanctuary, Boomer gouges Baku's eye. Baku staggers backward. Boomer pulls his shoulder off of the spike and approaches. The blinded orc is shaking his head and mumbling. Boomer marches forward and raises a fist in the air like a hammer. The monster's words become clear: "Confirm purchase." Baku smiles. "Confirm purchase: One broken leg." Boomer stops. A sound of rushing wind. Boomer's left leg snaps. He howls and collapses to the ground.

Cal steps onto the platform at the crest of the iron bell. Janey is on the other side. Above her is the short ladder up the steeple. Soon Janey will have nowhere else to go. Cal circles the top of the bell and says, "I mean, yes, *I've* killed lots of people. But that's just me, not Hello Corp. It's important to see the distinction. I could be a janitor somewhere and still find a way to air out a few meatbags here and there. It's more of a hobby at this point."

"You killed Father Canseco . . . and Tyler," says Janey, shaking with the books in her arms.

"And Father Clay, and *lots* of other people. See, now you're getting it."

"You're a murderer."

"Yes, but my company gives money to sick people."

* * *

Baku must have paid for a gun. Boomer uses his good arm to drag himself away from the monster. Baku blows a hole through Boomer's right thigh. Boomer flops on the ground like a fish and chokes on a scream.

Cal is getting annoyed. "What're you gonna do with that book, any-way—post it online? Call my news companies? I literally *bought* every spectrum in the air. I've been God for years now, and no one even understood how."

"I don't believe you."

"You know what? This just got boring." Cal snaps his fingers. Janey's eyes grow wide. She grabs her chest, over her heart, and looks at Cal. She coughs out a sound that isn't a word and falls to the ground.

Baku watches Boomer writhe on the ground. Baku aims the gun at Boomer's head.

Cal leans down and pries the two books from Janey's hands. He stands in the spotlight from the opening in the church steeple and flips through a few of the pages. At his feet, the dead body of the girl turns instantly gray—as if it was only a quest villain. Cal only notices when it turns to powder and sieves through the grates in the platform, onto the iron bell.

"Hey."

Cal looks up the steeple. Janey and Boomer are leaning over the edge. Janey says, "Spent my whole piggy bank on those two."

Boomer says, "Sweet AI tho, right?"

Cal flies toward the opening, but Janey presses the panic button to the NoFi chamber just in time. The roof of the steeple flips shut.

Panic sequence initiated. Reverting to default chamber contents. Please stand clear of air lock during the purging process, as it may be hazardous to individuals above and below the height of five feet. Standing inside the air lock during the purging process is 100% fatal and in no way a result of actions taken on the part of Hello Corporation, its signatories, or subsidiaries.

"Jane's Blog"

I STILL CAN'T believe my plan worked. I lured him right into the air lock (villains win!). I'll write the whole thing later. Boomer fixed the car (had to buy an engine from the NoFi chamber, heh-heh). He knows a guy with a wood-house publishing machine, so we can make lots of Father Canseco's book, and people can't google and delete them as easily.

I think about Father Canseco's letter a lot. I read it out loud to Boomer, and he said, "The old man called you ugly."

And I said, "Yep," 'cause it really meant something else (like, close to the opposite, in my opinion).

Like this: If I could re-create the world, I wouldn't change a single thing about Boomer (I know, crazy). I think FC wouldn't change a thing about me, either. (That's a nice thing to have.)

FOR IMMEDIATE RELEASE

Unrelated to Cal's Mysterious Disappearance, The Hello Corporation™ Pushes "ReCreation™" Schedule to a Holiday Season TBD!

Hello there . . .

WISH
POLICE

One of the advantages of near immortality is that we can learn to accept and adapt to most anything — eventually.
— Bigby "Big Bad" Wolf, *Fables*, Bill Willingham

The Wish List

Case no. p31-6374, ICU, NYPD

Case file: What the Orphan Wished For

RANDY BIEMAN [male, Caucasian, thirteen years of age]
hated his parents so much that he wished they'd die.

So they did.

Or they would have, if the APB hadn't hit the wires in time,
rerouted through dispatch in Special Divisions, ordering homicide
detectives out to patrol the crime scene—crime to come.

More specifically, the subject had wished for his whole family to
die. He lay in bed three hours before curfew, on the night in question, the night his parents grounded him. Cause for grounding?
Punching his little sister [Clara, five years old, likes yellow, dislikes
peas]. Randy stared up at the Glo-Lite glow-in-the-dark star system
stuck to his ceiling. His dad [Neville Bieman, occupation: pharma-
ceutical scientist] had tried to teach him about astronomy back in
the fifth grade. Instead, the boy had grabbed the stickers and spelled
"Randy Rocks!" out of the stars and planets. The sun was the dot on
Randy's exclamation point.

Prior to perpetrating the murderous act, Randy was under con-
siderable mental strain. The grounding had caused him to miss
playing in an online death-match tournament in his favorite first-
person shooter. The subject became even more agitated as texts
poured in from his buddy list, labeling his rival, Jared Chen, as the

"sexy-time god of pancakes," with rocket-launching skillz described by witnesses as "wikka wild, *wikka-wikka* wild." Randy, however, was universally flamed as "teh suxor grand general."

Randy directed his hostility at his family. *I don't need them,* he thought. *No, I hate them.* He chuckled in the dark, because it was the first time he'd thought such horrible things about his parents. It would be his little secret the next morning at breakfast. When his mom asked him if he wanted another waffle, he'd say yes, but he'd be thinking, *I hate you.* And he would be the only one who knew. That made Randy feel much better and made his parents seem much smaller. With his sister, Clara, it would be no different from usual. Randy told her he hated her once a week. He also microwaved boxes of her crayons and told her she was adopted from a circus family and would never grow past three feet tall. [Bieman's list of prior crimes is available upon request; the victim: almost exclusively his sister, Clara.]

Randy shuffled under the covers. His mother [Sandra, occupation: eBay] had come in to say good night and tucked him in, even though he was too old for that. She had thrust the sheets under his mattress clear up to her elbows and then leaned over him and said, "I love you. You disappointed me today. I love you."

As soon as she left, Randy kicked at his bedding until all the sheets went sailing up and his feet were uncovered in the cold room. He turned on his side and looked out the window. Everything was black and blue, as if it had been scorched by a rocket launcher. The only stars were the ones that said Randy rocked.

Meteorological records for the evening reveal clear skies over the city at the time of Randy's premature tucking in. Bieman reportedly spotted a single speck through his window, twinkling in the night. It was as though the star was winking at him, about his secret, goading him forward. Randy thought, *They didn't even* ask *why I punched that little rat. There could have been a perfectly good reason.*

At approximately 1900 hours, Randy Bieman realized that the speck was the first star he had seen that night, and he thought, *I wish they were all dead.* [Motive, opportunity.]

At the exact moment that Randy Bieman made his wish for multiple homicide [murder weapon: starlight, star bright] not a thing happened. The speck didn't flicker out, and Randy didn't even think twice about it. Instead he yawned, rolled over, and closed his eyes to go to sleep.

CHAPTER 1

THE CITY STREET was quiet, a residential drag, cozy even from outside the brownstones. The first freeze of the year had preempted the coloring foliage. If it snowed in the early morning, the green trees would look like chumps, left holding the check for both fall and winter. A figure stood leaning on a lamppost, his face hidden by the turned-up collar of a pea coat and a pearl-knit skullcap. His three days' scruff was equal parts white and black and could sand a coffee table. His hands were bunched in front of his mouth, and when he breathed out, it looked like he was billowing a curl of Ardestani diamond dust.

A married couple had divorced each other for the rushed walk home, declining to expose their hands to the chill. After making eye contact with the dark man, they reconciled. An engine missing a filter rumbled from two blocks down. A stray tabby leaped and knocked over a trash can in an alley behind a wrought-iron fence.

A voice spoke from the man's coat pocket: "I'm telling you, Saul, she ain't coming."

The man looked at his watch. His ears were both pierced, but he didn't have any earrings in them.

"What we do now is storm the house ourselves, flash some badge, knock some teeth. Take the perp into custody, give him a room to sweat in, you know what I'm saying?"

Always, a blaring fire truck somewhere. The man had shoulders like a dresser drawer. His eyes were Persian almonds—and twelve times as black. He said, "Perp?"

The other voice from his pocket said, "Yeah, perp, the perpetrator of the crime. You outta the shop or what? The hood, the con, the mark, what's the mattah with you?"

"With me?" said the man.

"Yeah with you. I'm briefing you on location-entry tacs, running some apprehend protocols, and you're picking on my shop talk."

The man smiled to himself. Crushed a fallen acorn under his boot. He said, "Let me ask you something, Ari."

"G'head, shoot."

"How much TV you watch when I'm not around?"

"That's not called for, man. How long we been partners?"

The man rolled his eyes. "A dozen or something."

"Ten, ten centuries, Saul. We're common-law married, you and me. . . ."

His voice was drowned out by the rumble down the street. It turned up the block and accelerated toward them. A cone of light preceded it, the one center headlight of a 1950s Triumph Bonneville road bike. Saul put one hand in the pocket of his coat. "Shut up, Ari," he said.

"Don't tell me to shut up, Saul. We talked about this. You're not supposed to demean what I'm saying. You know how that makes me feel."

The man jangled his coat pocket, and Ari shouted, "Hey, hey! You of all people, Saul!"

The bike thundered up to the lamppost and screeched to a stop a few feet past it. The rider wore a visored helmet, black leather pants, and a riding jacket. Across the back of the jacket was a Celtic pattern and the words *Hogs 'n' Bogs Motorcycle Club, Loch Ness Chapter.*

The pants were so tight they could have been airbrushed on, riding low enough to expose a little tattoo on the small of the rider's back. It was a five-leaf clover. The man leaning on the lamppost said, "Whoa," under his breath.

"What?" said Ari. "What do you see? Is that her? Mmff-mmmfff!"

The man pressed down on his pocket, and Ari's voice muffled out of earshot. As the rider took her helmet off, her hair splashed into the night scene like a blood shot. It was cut at sharp jagged angles, shorter in the back and to her chin in the front. Red.

She put the helmet on the handlebars and said, "You Sulaiman al Djinn?"

"Call me Saul," said the man.

"You get my transfer sheet?"

"Yeah, McClintock, used to be detective. Didn't have a first name."

"Just Mack's fine. What's the holdup here?"

Mack dismounted the bike, unzipped her jacket, and adjusted the snaps of her double holster. Saul said, "The site's that brownstone with the red door. Bieman residence. Mom, dad, and little sister are all targets. Subject's a male Caucasian, age thirteen. Hasn't approached the scene yet."

"So. We hold our position," said Mack. She pulled out one of her handguns, a Desert Eagle, and cocked it back. Then she shoved it back into the holster and removed the other. "I was a first-grade detective, by the way."

Saul shrugged. He said, "I was a sultan's general."

Ari's voice interjected, "Yeah, well, I used to be the crown prince of Atlantis. Who friggin' cares?"

Mack looked at Saul, raised an eyebrow, then looked at his jacket pocket. "Is that your partner?"

"Yeah, sugar, I'm his partner," said Ari.

Saul breathed out a gust as he pulled his hand out of his pocket and with it a Ziploc bag full of water. Inside was a goldfish, paddling its fins in angry little swipes. It said, "You heard me. And I read your disciplinary file, don't think I didn't. You got back in somebody's good graces to get this case. But we all know about that hot water with the Major Case Squad. And you pack twin Magnums? What're you, Tomb Raider?"

When he got mad, Ari had a tendency to talk in scattershot bursts. His memory was the first thing to go when he lost his temper.

Mack made the mistake of snickering. She put her hands together and held them out to the rabid goldfish so he could cuff her.

"You think I'm funny?" said Ari.

"No," said Mack, trying to stifle her snicker now.

She looked to Saul, who mouthed, "His name is Ari."

"No, Ari," said Mack.

"Detective Ari," yelled the fish. "DT second grade, but better than getting busted down to third, huh? How did you like that?"

Mack lost her grin at the mention of her demotion to DT third grade. "I'm sorry, Ari. Have I offended you?"

"Oh, don't do that," said Ari.

"What?" said Mack.

"Sprinkle your apology over my head, demean people by snickering at them. You don't know how that makes goldfish feel. I'll fight you right now. Step in here. I'll jack you up."

Saul shook with suppressed laughter, but Ari couldn't see it. Mack clamped her lips together.

"What's the matter? You chicken?" said Ari. He swam furious circles in his bag, dodging and feinting like a prizefighter.

"I couldn't get in there with you if I wanted to, Ari. And a chicken could still probably kill you."

"Says you, babe. You look like a stripper. And don't think I can't see you, Saul. I'll drown the both of you flower pickers right here."

Saul held the bag at arm's length. Ari charged repeatedly into the plastic lining at every possible angle of attack. Finally, Saul interrupted him. "I got a visual."

Ari stopped short. He circled near the top of the bag, letting his dorsal fin break the surface with a slightly melodramatic glare. Mack was already in step with their cover, just a hog queen and big Middle Eastern guy minding their own business and talking to their fish, no big deal. Mack ran one hand through her hair and slid the other up to her piece.

*   *   *

The suspect was approaching the premises in brown sweats three sizes too small, unwashed. Dark hair. Caucasian. He was bare up to his ankles and elbows, no shoes. The cold didn't seem to bother him. If he was breathing, it didn't show. Except for a vertical scar running down his left eyebrow, he was a match.

"What's the play?" said Mack.

"You take point," said Saul, stuffing Ari back into his coat pocket. "I'll close around the side."

Mack mounted her bike, put on her helmet, and flipped up the visor. It suited her just fine to take lead, but maybe it would've been better for her to go around the back, since she had the bike. But when she turned to suggest it to Saul, he was already gone.

She put her hand to the comm unit in her ear and said, "Central post, this is DT Five-Leaf, proceeding toward suspect on vehicle. Detectives Ji-Ji and the Fisher Prince are proceeding on foot around back."

Static crackled in her ear, then the high-pitched monotone: "This is the Wishing Post. Five-Leaf, you're all clear at Central. Mission is go. Repeat. You are a go."

Mack said, "Aye-aye," and hit the light. The suspect stood on the stoop of the Bieman residence. He whipped around when the spotlight hit him. It didn't blind him—Mack could tell because he was looking right at her.

She turned the ignition. The boy nodded, then he puckered at her, a sick kiss, and a weird sneer. The boy whipped around, hurdled the iron gate, and ran out of the spotlight so fast he blurred in Mack's vision.

Mack clenched the handlebars and revved so hard the car alarms blared next to her. The suspect sprinted halfway down the block. Mack peeled out, a wake of fallen leaves trailing behind her. As she closed ground on the fleeing kid, Mack barked into her unit, "In pursuit, need backup! Saul, what is your location? I'm westbound on—"

As the kid approached the end of the block, Saul appeared ahead of him at the corner, hands still in his coat pockets. The suspect almost stumbled over his own feet, then veered off the curb. He darted between two parked cars and into the street, but Mack was right there. She slammed her forearm into the kid's rib cage and flung his body over the steering column. She pulled up to Saul at the corner. Saul got on the back of the bike, and Mack turned down the street before anyone looked out the window to see what all the rumpus was about.

"Check that backup, Angie," said Saul into his comm. "Suspect in custody. We're coming in."

Crackle. Then, "Thanks, Saul. Tell your new partner to turn the volume down next time she takes point."

"Will do, Angie."

Saul didn't need to repeat what both of them had heard in their earbuds. Mack said, "You could have told me your location. And what, you flirt up every old lady at Central Post?"

"I said I'd close around the block."

"You might not have made it—"

The static crackled in their ears again. "Ji-Ji always makes it, honey. And turn off your mike when you want to be rude."

The suspect began to stir. Mack hammered her fist across his chin and knocked him out for the rest of the ride back to the station.

"Hey, Angie, I don't like her, either," said a voice in their earbuds. It was Ari's.

Mack barreled through a stoplight and shouted back over her shoulder at Saul, "How does a carnival prize get on the comm channel?"

"See?" said Ari's voice.

The static crackled once more, Angie at the Wishing Post. "Yeah, I see. Just turn your mike off, honey."

Saul leaned on the back wall by the door of the observation room, looking at the kid through the one-way mirror. The speaker was on, but the kid was just sitting there, shivering in his torn-up sweats. You could kinda make out the sound of his teeth chattering. The interrogation room was nothing but a metal table and a couple of chairs. The floor was cement. It had a drain at the center, mostly just to freak people out.

"We should get him a hot cocoa or something," said Ari. His bag was flat on the desk but high enough so he could see into the other room.

"No," said Mack. She was leaning back on two legs of her chair, holding a cup of coffee. "He's faking it. Playing scared so we'll go easy."

"Aw, c'mon," said Ari. "He's low-level. Just look at him."

"Would have killed the whole family, cold blood," said Mack. Saul knew she still hadn't put the safety on her firearms. "You didn't see the look he gave me," she said.

Inside the interrogation room, the kid was eating the cuticles of his thumb. He'd ventured to say, "Hellooo?" and the echo from the bare walls had made him flinch.

Mack got up from the officers' desk and went over to Saul in the back of the observation room. He hadn't taken his eyes off the boy. She leaned on the wall next to him. She looked at him sidelong, then said, "I could press him. You could be Papa Bear."

Saul shook his head no.

"I'm telling you, he's hiding something. He's got more than a positive ID."

"All we *need* is a positive ID," said Saul.

Mack took a drink of coffee to stop herself from screaming at Saul. It tasted like bean juice. She said, "Fine. We get the confession and book him. Happy?"

"Not really," said Saul. He pushed off the wall and grabbed the doorknob. "I know he's hiding something. I just don't want you beating the crap out of him."

"Ha!" said Ari from his bag.

Saul opened the door for Mack and smiled at her. As she walked past him, she said, "If you're wondering about why I lost my grade, it wasn't because I roughed up a suspect."

They stepped into the hall connecting the two rooms. "I don't care," said Saul. "The file says you're a hotshot."

"Not anymore," protested Mack as they walked into the interrogation room. When he saw the detectives, the kid lifted his feet off the floor and tucked them under himself on the chair. Mack ignored the kid. She said, "Do you have any idea how awful eyelash detail can be? Had one kid plucking five of 'em and asking for Reese's Pieces to fill up his math classroom."

A rare grin from Saul. Eyelash detail was as bunk as punishments got from the higher-ups. It was running grade-school interference on wishes for extra pudding cups or for bullies to explode. The two detectives ignored the kid's sniffling. They sat down at the table, and Mack went on, "I did my time. Now I got my beat back."

Saul said, "But you don't have your rank back."

"Soon enough," said Mack. The kid gaped at them, then raised one hand in the air to ask a question.

"I just wanna be a murder cop," said Mack. She slammed her palm on the metal table right in front of the kid's face. The kid fell back in his chair.

"You Randy Bieman?" said Mack, suddenly fixing her gaze on him.

The kid whimpered and chewed on his nail. "N-no."

"You were at the Bieman residence," said Mack.

"I wanted to say hello," said the kid.

"In the middle of the night. You expect me to believe that? You're gonna stop by and say hello, middle of a freezing cold night in your pajamas?"

The boy wouldn't look up. The mention of the brown ratty pajamas seemed to embarrass him. "It's all I own," he said, fingering a hole in the sleeve.

"And when Mr. Bieman, your dad, opened the door, you were just gonna say hi and ask to play checkers?"

"I'm his son?"

Mack slammed the metal table again, hard enough to leave a print. The kid was about to bawl. "Don't play with me. Randy Bieman catches the first star, wants a triple murder. You show up at the door ten minutes later. That dad opens the door, and I say you would have put your fist through his heart. Am I right?"

"But I'm not Randy," pleaded the boy.

"I know," said Mack, "You're Randy's wish."

The boy's lips quivered; his eyes glazed. He started blubbering into his hands. "Nooo," he whined. "I don't know any Randy Freeman!"

Mack slumped back in her chair. Saul shook his head and sighed. He looked at the mirror and said, "Ari, check the APB log. Any note on the shabby jammies?"

"Hold on," said the speaker above the mirror. "Got it, no, nothing. Says the Bieman kid's pretty spoiled. Actually got a birthday wish last year for two grand worth of toys."

The boy was making indecipherable weepy noises, trying not to show his tears. He crescendoed any time Mack adjusted in her seat a little. Saul let the waterworks dry up before he said, "What's your name, kid?"

"Muh-Mustard."

"Your name is Mustard?" said Mack, already tired of softballing. The boy nodded and then got the hiccups.

"Saul, he's pretending," said Mack. "He blew a kiss at me on the scene, knew exactly what he was doing, bolted like a—" Then a question popped into her head and, turning to the boy, she said, "If you're innocent, why'd you run?"

"I was scared."

"Bull," said Mack. She wanted to go at the suspect again, but Saul wouldn't squeeze.

He put a hand on the boy's shoulder. He said, "Where do you live, Mustard?"

"At that lady Cavanaugh's foster house. They named me that 'cause I put it on my scrambled eggs."

"Mustard?" said Saul.

"Uh-huh."

Saul got up. Mustard flinched. Mack said, "Where're you going?"

"We got the wrong kid," said Saul. "Ari, get a reissue out on the APB."

"You got it," blared Ari through the speaker.

"Whoa, wait a sec." Mack followed Saul toward the door but didn't want to leave the suspect. "You just believe him?" She looked back at Mustard and asked, "Why were you sneaking around the house at night?"

Mustard opened his mouth to speak, but Saul beat him to it. "He's a runaway orphan. Let's go." Saul walked out. The boy closed his mouth. He made a wide grin. Mack, who was the only other one in the room by then, couldn't decide whether it was relief on the boy's face or contempt. She walked out into the hall and closed the door.

Saul came out of the back room with Ari's bag in his hand. She walked with him down the corridor and into the station house. On the marble floor of the vestibule was the department seal: IMAGINARY CRIMES UNIT, 31ST PRECINCT. Below it was a motto, written in plain font: *To project and to swerve.*

Saul didn't linger at the row of desks where after-hours detectives sat around, chewing the fat. The place was mostly regular, with computers three generations behind what the criminals were using, processing forms pinned to the bulletin board of the 3-1 Precinct, a few copies of the *Bestiary of Mythic Wishes,* also known as "the rap sheet."

As Saul passed through, one detective looked up and said, "Hey, Ji-Ji, that the new partner?" He looked more like a male model than a cop. His brown hair was billowy, his body willowy, as thin as a vine. He was wearing a white muscle shirt with the words CHEST HAIR printed in big and wispy black capitals. He wore iridescent glitter eye shadow. Over his back was the faint glimmer of gossamer wings.

Saul nodded and kept walking, holding Ari's bag out so the fish could see where they were going. "You pretty tall, *mami*," said the detective to Mack, leering at her legs.

"The better to kick you with," said Mack.

The detective seemed to like the back talk. "I ain't no Tink, baby. You kick all you like."

"This is Alvarez," said Ari. "You don't have to talk to him."

Alvarez batted his expensive eyelashes. "Hey, Goodie, you hear that? Fishy says she don't need to talk to us." Alvarez was talking to the old lady sitting at the desk next to his. Goodie was somebody's, maybe everybody's, grandmother. A light-blue smock and white apron, glasses on the tip of her nose, one of those cotton sleeping hats that look like shower caps. She was knitting a baby blanket, didn't look up to answer Alvarez. She said, "Now, dear, you know we don't have to be the most popular team on the force."

Alvarez nodded to his partner. The old lady added, "It's enough that we're the best. And the new tramp can talk to whomever she likes."

Alvarez tittered with snarky delight. Mack stared, unable to connect the sweet old lady with the words coming out of her mouth.

"That's Goodie," said Ari. "Don't mess with her."

"That's right, dearie," said Goodie warmly. "Or I'll cut your throat in your sleep."

Mack blinked at her. She noticed that under the cap, Goodie's ears were long enough to flop down, with warts all over.

Mack followed Saul out of the precinct, into the street, and said, "Are those two serious?"

"Oh yeah," said Ari, "they're definitely the best. Both of them are first grade. The fairy thing has him acting chippy like that. Goodie's the only person he respects. She's just an old troll, but together they bring 'em begging for prison."

"They advertise themselves well enough," said Mack.

Saul sat on the back of the bike and said, "Careful with Goodie. Internal Affairs has a file you don't want to see on her. When she was under a bridge, she used to twist people hard. Monkey's-paw kind of thing. Grant a wish, then make them sorry."

Mack got on the bike and put her helmet on. Sure she'd messed around when she was young, but nothing like that. The comm units in their ears rattled off the APB for Randy Bieman's wish at large. Mack leaned on the handle and pulled into the street. Saul's arms wrapped around her like a flak jacket.

As they rode back to the crime scene, Mack spoke through her comm unit. "If you and Ari have been in homicide so long, why didn't they offer you first grade?"

Saul's voice was so close, she almost jumped. He said, "They did."

* * *

The night was starting to freeze over. Streets were empty as a Nazarene crypt. Only the bakers had their lights on. When they pulled up in front of the brownstone, she took off her helmet and said, "You said no?"

Saul rubbed a hand over the stubble on his face, making a scratchy sound. "I said no, thanks."

CHAPTER 2

AFTER ABANDONING THE scene for so long, they couldn't risk staking out the place. For all they knew, the suspect could have arrived already and could have been one down on a two-count of B&E and three-man homicide. One . . . two . . . three, make another wish for me.

With a handkerchief, Saul lifted the latch on the iron gate. Mack followed and closed it behind her so it wouldn't clink. When she turned back to the house, Saul had already gotten the door open. She stepped silently onto the landing and whispered, "Forced entry?" Saul shook his head no.

"You picked it that fast?"

"I'm Middle Eastern," said Saul.

They entered the foyer, big enough to house a whole petting zoo. By the looks of the furniture, the Biemans weren't hurting for coin. The younger sister must have been afraid of the dark, or maybe Mr. Bieman stubbed his toes on the way to a midnight drink. Either way, the rooms each had a night-light. If you were looking to murder, they were practically a trail of bread crumbs up the stairs and into each unsuspecting bedroom.

They stood in the half-lit entry, assessing the floor plan. Saul took off his skullcap. His hair was short enough not to look messy sticking up in front. It had the same white dusting as his stubble. Mack whispered, "What does that mean, you're 'Middle Eastern'?"

Ari blared into their earbuds. "Means he's a dark male, age eighteen to thirty-four. He commits, like, eighty percent of the crimes in this country."

Saul mounted the staircase, stepping on the far edges to minimize creaking.

"Cute, but you're dodging the question," said Mack. At the top of the stairs, going left was out. One big door, snores coming from behind it. On the right, two doors. Saul paused. The night shine streamed in from a skylight above.

Mack caught his attention and said, "You know what I'm talking about. You used to be a thief or what?"

"I used to be a djinn, that's all," said Saul.

Ari laughed into the earbuds, like somebody put their foot in it at a dinner party. "Saul's quick like that. He could've picked your pocket half a dozen times already."

Mack raised an eyebrow. Twice now—including the jump on Mustard—Saul had been a Johnny-on-the-spot, and she wasn't used to runner-up.

The moonlight draped over her. She looked down at her leather pants. Saul didn't mind doing the same. She said, "I don't have any pockets to pick."

If his skin wasn't the color of burnt honey, she knew he'd be blushing.

Ari said, "What am I missing?" but Saul didn't answer. Mack walked to the second door on the right.

This time it was Saul who had to catch up. He whispered, "How do you know that's the right room?"

Mack didn't answer. She had checked the windows from outside. It was the only one with a clear sight of the murder weapon—the first star in the night sky. She decided to let him wonder how she knew.

Randy's room had two night-lights in it, as well as a bunch of glow stickers, and a screensaver brighter than a tanning bed. They slipped in like fog. Saul used the handkerchief to close the door and stood by. Mack sat down next to Randy's sleeping form on the bed. Saul flipped the light switch. Nothing. The kid slept with so much light it hardly mattered. Randy sighed in his sleep and drew the blanket up to his cheek.

"He's almost cute," said Mack. She put a hand on his shoulder and jerked him back and forth. "Hey, Randy. Randy Bieman, get up."

Randy's eyes fluttered, then focused on the stranger sitting on his bed. He tried to scream "Mom!" but Mack stuffed the sound back into his mouth with one palm. Randy kept it up under Mack's glove.

She put a finger up to her lips. "Randy, listen to me, Randy. I'm going to have to hurt you if don't stop struggling." This had the wrong effect. The kid started flailing his limbs. "Do you want that, Randy?" A hard squeeze on his cheeks, and he started to get the picture. Mack slowly removed her hand.

Randy shouted, "I'm telling my—"

Mack clamped back down on his mouth. With the other hand, she pulled a Desert Eagle from her holster and cocked it on his forehead. "You've got two angry-looking strangers in your room with full-bore semiautomatics, and you thought we were joking?"

Randy's eyes were crossed as he looked straight up at the barrel of the Magnum. He shook his head. "Then you understand?" said Mack. Randy nodded yes a half-dozen times.

"Good," said Mack, lowering the gun. "'Cause this thing doesn't need a soft spot to work, you get me?" Another hundred nods. Mack holstered the gun and sat back.

Randy's mouth hung open but not to talk. Saul reached inside his coat and flipped out a badge. "We're detectives, ICU."

"I see you, too," said Randy, still shaky.

Saul didn't bother. Ari spoke into their earbuds, "Holy jeez, we got a real honors student over here."

"What do you want? I don't steal," said Randy, sitting up in his bed.

"You probably do, but that's not the point," said Mack.

She noted that Randy wasn't wearing jammies but an oversize Dark Knight shirt.

"Did you make a wish on the first star of this evening?"

"No," said Randy.

Mack reached for her weapon.

"Yes," said Randy. "But, so?"

"So it'll come true, moron," shouted Ari in their ears.

"They come true, kid," said Saul in the monotone he used for reading people their rights. "Every wish you make comes true . . . except the ones that can't, or won't, or shouldn't."

"Really?" said Randy. His eyes widened. He was spellbound by the thought of everything he could get if all his wishes came true.

"Exactly. They become real," said Saul.

"Wait," said Randy. "I don't get it—that can't be true."

Ari sighed into their earpieces.

"Look," said Mack. "If you ask for something that *can't* happen, like you becoming king of the world, or *shouldn't* happen—"

"Like you becoming king of the world," said Ari. Mack didn't acknowledge it since Randy couldn't hear.

She went on, "And you made your wish with something effective, like the first star you see that night, or a wishing well, or whatever. That desire becomes real. It becomes a wicked idea made suddenly human."

"Wicked Idea Suddenly Human," clarified Saul. "W.I.S.H."

Mack finished her example. "It'll look just like you, and it'll try to give you exactly what you asked for, like killing all the world leaders or, in this case, your family."

"What happens if I wish for a million bucks?" asked Randy.

"Was this kid even listening?" asked Ari.

"What happens with that one," said Saul, "is that your wish goes and robs a bank, what else? You think money just appears?"

"Well, yeah."

"It doesn't. You commit three felonies, two counts of possession with intent to harm, and then maybe the wish scores a couple hundred large. But you wanted a million, so your wish keeps hitting banks. Or it runs into me."

Saul looked too big for the room. His irritated voice had a deep resonance, as though it were echoing off the walls of ancient days. Randy gulped and pulled the blanket up a little.

He ventured one last question: "What are wishes that *won't* happen?"

"Doesn't matter, kid. It gets complicated. We just catch them."

Mack put her hand on Randy's shoulder. She said, "Listen carefully, Randy. If you were going to kill your family, how would you do it? Operationally, I mean."

The idea looked new and ugly to Randy. He stammered, "I would—I would never do that. That was just a—I was just mad. They took my game."

"Well, it looks like you would," said Mack. "Actually, you already did. It just hasn't happened yet. Now we need your help to stop it."

"And we do it quiet-like," said Saul. Randy looked at the imposing detective. Saul put a finger up to his lips.

Randy thought about this for a while.

"Rocket launchers," he said.

"Did he say rocket launchers?" said Ari.

"I'd use launchers, maybe sniper rifles. Do you guys think we can stop all this *after* it gets my little sister?"

Mack turned to Saul. "The kid's useless. How do you want to do this?"

Saul went over to the dresser drawer. On top was an assortment of geode crystals, international coins, a few loose paintballs, and candy wrappers. He picked up a bank in the shape of an elephant and rubbed the side. Nothing happened. He put it back. Next to a wad of rubber bands was a pile of paper clips that Randy had bent so the two metal prongs stuck out. He used it to shoot kids on the bus with rubber bands.

When he was thinking, Saul would reach up and rub the pierced hole in his earlobe without realizing he was doing it. "Something's wrong. The kid's into tactical shooters, fine. Maybe he's taking his time. But still, they usually show up by now."

"We could get a wire up on the house," offered Mack.

"Which room? We only have one wireless mike."

"Central location, the kitchen table."

"Too much interference," said Ari through the comm unit. "Ten bucks says the dad owns a cappuccino machine."

"Fine," said Mack. "We do on-site surveillance, roll a flower truck in here, post some open-air units, tap the master bedroom."

"What're you guys talking about?" said Randy, but neither detective responded.

In their ears, Ari said, "I really hate this kid."

"Wait," said Saul. "I got an idea." He turned to Randy and said, "You or your sister have a fish tank?"

"Oh, no, no you don't, Saul," said Ari.

"Clara has a goldfish."

"Perfect," said Saul. "All we do is drop a mermaid in the sister's tank and run the singing frog bit."

"No," said Ari with the volume turned up. "I hate that bit. I'm not some cartoon pet, Saul. I'm the prince of the whole friggin' ocean."

Mack had to pull the earbud out while Ari cursed them out.

Finally, Saul took the bag out of his coat pocket. "What about me, huh? What about the fish's wishes?"

"Whoa," said Randy, getting up to get a better look. "Is that some kind of robot?"

"Yeah," said Ari, still swishing around. "I'm a robot fish. Somebody shut this kid up before I get my boots out."

Randy laughed. He definitely wanted one of those fish for Christmas.

"Let's go," said Saul. He put Ari back in his pocket, but Ari switched to the comm units and kept yelling.

Mack said, "Stay here," to Randy. "And don't make any more rotten wishes, you delinquent little creep." She followed Saul into the other room.

Clara lay asleep in a four-post bed with an American Girl doll in her arm. A dollhouse stood next to the bed, probably taller than the little girl was standing up. On the opposite wall sat a vanity with a dressing-room mirror, flanked by two columns of stage bulbs. Among the scattered makeup was a fishbowl. Inside the bowl was another dollhouse, miniature but made to look exactly like the big one. The mailbox to the underwater house said PRINCESS FASHION SHOW.

When Ari got a look at the bowl, with the ribbon around the brim and its lipstick kisses, he deserved some credit for staying on the comm channel instead of waking up the whole house. "No! No way. This is demeaning. I'm not doing this."

Saul whispered, "Sorry, buddy," as he scooped the goldfish named Princess Fashion Show from the bowl with the plastic net. Mack stayed out of the way. The old friends could handle it. As Saul opened Ari's bag, Ari dodged quickly to the side. "Don't net me! I'll go. I'll go willingly. You know how I feel about the net."

Ari let Saul pour him out into the bowl. Saul placed Princess Fashion Show in Ari's bag with the remaining water. Ari gagged like he was drowning. "You're a real piece of garbage, you know that, Saul? You promised no singing frog after the thing at the Pierpont Hotel. Remember that? How demeaning that was? Saul? Saul!"

"Good luck, partner," said Saul, patting the side of the bowl. The sound waves radiated through the bowl and sent Ari reeling into a downward spin.

"Agh!" said Ari. "You're ringin' my ears! What's the matter with you?"

As the two detectives snuck out of Clara's bedroom, Mack whispered, "What happened at the Pierpont?"

"Deaf housekeeping lady," said Saul.

"Oooh, unlucky."

They closed the front door of the brownstone just as the darkness was turning to gray. In a few minutes, the sun would slide a shank into the sky's kidney. Trash trucks would blunder down the blocks like dizzy mastodons. It was spitting now, but maybe it would rain later. Saul picked up the paper from the Biemans' front porch. Bad news. Wry comics. And then more bad news in sports. It seemed everyone considered world peace a waste of perfectly good magic.

It was too late to go to sleep.

Mack zipped up her jacket before stepping off the covered landing. Saul said, "You like waffles?"

The luncheonette on the corner avenue wasn't so flossy that you could get fresh fruit on your waffle. If you asked for strawberries, you got a ladle of Smucker's. The linoleum had so many stains, it could be modern art. The kitchen was out of sight and best not to think about. A hairy arm reached through the pick-up window and dropped the orders on a service tray, then slid the screen closed like a lady in the shower.

The only thing going for the place was that it was close enough to maintain radio contact with Ari. They sat at the counter, in front of a plastic display case of marble pound cake, a couple of stale knishes, and a croissant big enough to boomerang a kangaroo. The only other customer was the old man in the back booth, reading the early edition and gumming at a plate of feta cheese and cucumbers.

Mack sat two stools down from Saul, but he was so big, they still almost touched. To keep their holsters under cover, neither of them took their coat off. Didn't matter. The guy at the counter had them made for police officers as soon as they walked in. His tag said JON. Had a frowsy, swollen look, no chin, a greasy skirt of hair around his bald head. He said, "Officers! Cup o' soup? I get you soup. Very good soup."

"No soup, Jon," said Mack.

Jon grinned like a horse and nodded. "No problem. Two soups on the house."

"No free stuff," said Saul. "We're paying cops."

Jon didn't believe that breed existed in the wilds of the city. He winked as he placed two cups of minestrone in front of them. It had a layer of oil like vinaigrette dressing. They said thanks, and Saul slipped a ten under the saucers.

"Gimme a tea, black, in glass I can see through, no mugs," said Saul.

Jon nodded.

"And a few sugar cubes."

"No problem," said Jon. "One tea, on the house."

Mack forked the glob of jam and placed it on a stack of napkins. "We don't have any leads," she said. She filled every square of the waffle with maple syrup before taking a bite. She talked while chewing. "The wish could be anywhere, trying to find a rocket-propelled grenade launcher."

"So then he went to the Bronx," said Saul. "Should be back any minute."

Mack laughed. Some waffle made it to the coffeepot. Saul took a sugar cube and held it between his teeth. Then he drank the hot tea through the sugar.

"What part of the Middle East are you from?"

"Persia," said Saul.

"So, like, Iran?"

"Used to be Persia."

"I know."

"I'm from when it was Persia."

"Long time," said Mack, through another bite of waffle.

"Long time," said Saul, staring into his tea. A few loose leaves floated along the bottom.

"Sulaiman al Djinn," said Mack to nobody. "Solomon the Genie."

Saul took another swig of the tea.

"You were his, weren't you?" She meant Solomon the king.

"We don't have names," said Saul. "We get the master's name."

"You were Solomon's genie?"

"Didn't you know? Genies don't exist," said Saul.

"Ha! You wish," said Mack. "You think you're the only one who does his homework? Check some records. Grease a few palms. You know, detect things."

"The records should have told you that there are no records," said Saul.

"They did. That was the problem," said Mack.

Saul looked up from his tea. "You don't let up."

She shrugged and said, "I'm Irish." Then she nudged him and added, "C'mon, I'll tell you mine if you tell me yours."

Saul put another sugar cube between his teeth and took a swig. He scratched his stubble with two fingers and said, "Nothing to tell. I used to be his. A gift from the Queen of Sheba. Got passed down from king to king for a while, then stolen. I got dropped in a well during a raid in the desert. A camel driver found me; I became a padishah. . . ." Saul trailed off. He named off his old masters like a series of marriages gone sour.

Mack said, "So how'd you escape?"

Saul snapped out of the bad dream. "Escape?" he said. "Nobody escapes."

Mack pointed a finger at his head. "You don't have the earrings." The gold loops in a djinn's ear bound him, as far as Mack knew. Studying them was part of the training at the academy, under a list of lost ideas, dreamed-up stuff, notions even Wish Police didn't believe. No one had seen a djinn in a thousand years. They were the dodo of the ICU.

"No," said Saul, again. "I could never escape." He seemed like a mule rutting in a ditch. Stuck in an idea, like it had been tattooed into his heart. No one escapes.

"Once the camel driver became a shah, he had everything he wanted except some girl. I couldn't make her love him; it was a code 207 kidnapping. So he starts throwing parties, making me do stupid stuff, edible fireworks, that kind of thing. Gives it a bunch of razzle-dazzle, but she wouldn't take. Finally, she says to him in front of everybody that perhaps his djinn wishes to be free."

Mack connected the rest. "So he's grandstanding and gets called out, frees you to impress the chick. Nice."

"Not really," said Saul. He gulped the last of the tea and put a finger up for a refill.

"What, you had a cozy reading nook inside that lamp?"

"A wife and kids."

Mack put a bite of waffle back down on the plate. She said, "He forced you out?"

"Gave me my freedom, the benevolent pinhead."

"Okay," said Mack, shallow of breath. "Okay wow, you've been trying to get back to them all this time? They've been out there in . . . genie-verse, granting other people's wishes?"

"No real guidelines to it. No one had ever freed a djinn before. After the party, my old master didn't want me around anymore. I knew everything he'd ever wished for. So he put my family on one of his merchant ships. Then he had a millstone chained around my neck and dropped me in the ocean. A couple decades later, I met Ari."

Mack lost her taste for soggy waffle. The holster strap pinched her left underarm. She'd been wearing her shoes too long. She pulled the bottom napkin from under the jam and wiped her mouth with it. "What about the stories with all the genies getting freed at the end?"

"They're just stories. Nobody gives up that kind of power," said Saul. He swished around the tea leaves at the bottom of his cup. He said, "I'd appreciate it if you didn't . . ."

"I won't tell anybody," said Mack. "I mean, the other guys in the squad know. . . ."

Saul looked at her.

"They don't know," she amended. "Right."

They sat for a while, listening to the old man in the booth struggle to fold the newspaper backward over the crease. Jon brought out some more tea and went back to reading a Greek Harlequin novel. It occurred to Mack that this was the reason Saul turned down a promotion to detective first grade. If the brass had him on their radar, maybe they'd ask questions. Maybe they'd discover the first free djinn in the unknown world, right in their own rank and file. Maybe he couldn't go searching for his wife and kids with every intelligence agency prodding him like a zoo animal. As a mid-level detective second grade, he was free to keep an eye on every wish-related crime in the city. And if the weapon was ever a lady djinn . . .

In the corner of her eye, Mack saw him unconsciously rubbing the side of the pitcher of coffee creamer, like maybe it was a long-lost magic lamp.

She leaned in and said, "Wanna know why they call me Mack?"

Saul peeled his eyes off the pitcher.

"'Cause of my dad. When I was born, I was already as tall as my dad. He was so proud, he spent half his pot o' gold on cigars for everybody on the island. Said I was better luck than a four-leaf clover."

"Code name Five-Leaf," remembered Saul.

"Right. My mother wanted to name me Petunia, but my dad said I couldn't have just one name for being the tallest leprechaun of the clan, so he gave me all of them."

"All the names of your clan?" said Saul.

"All the names he could think of," said Mack. "He got the little card he looked at to remember the alphabet and gave me a name for every letter."

Saul laughed through his nose, like she was selling him the pub's license. "Go ahead, ask," said Mack. "Everybody asks."

Saul didn't want to ask. But she was actually serious. "All right," he said. He leaned back and crossed his arms.

"Aberdeen, Brigid, Caitlin, Deirdre, Ethna, Fiona, Grania, Hannah, Isolde. It keeps going. I could go on. Moira, Nessa, Orla."

"So anyone could call out any name, and they'd be talking to you," said Saul.

"I was expansive. My mom still called me Petunia. Only name that stuck was my last name, McClintock . . ." She trailed off.

"What's it like filling out government forms?" said Saul.

"Murder," said Mack, her Irish brogue seeping into her words as she reminisced. "And there was Ari last night, with all his short leprechaun jokes lined up and no one to hurl them at."

Another reason never to speak of the devil. Their comm units crackled in their ears. Ari was in place but couldn't risk speaking into the wire. He'd turned his radio on and off to signal them. The short burst of static was followed by the sound of tiny fish lips whispering, "*Glub-glub-glub.*"

The two detectives rose from their seats. Jon looked up, nodded, and said, "On the house!"

"Thanks," said Saul. He slipped another ten under his napkin. As they walked out, Mack said, "So, an ex-djinn and the world's tallest leprechaun partner up. What's the guppy's story?"

"Ari? He's just angry."

"Probably because he's named after the Little Mermaid," said Mack, sliding on her helmet.

When Clara Bieman woke up, she made a tired sigh like she was a hundred years old. She rubbed one eye with a chubby fist, then said good morning to her best friend, Felicity. She said, "How do you do?" because that's how they spoke in the olden times where Felicity lived. And to make sure her favorite doll didn't feel unwanted, she combed Felicity's long red hair four times before saying hello to each of her stuffed animals.

Wherever she went, Clara held Felicity with one arm hooked under the doll's neck. Clara had a yellow nightdress. Felicity also had a yellow nightdress.

Together they paid a visit to Princess Fashion Show. It must have been a dreadful night. The dollhouse looked like a mess, and the mailbox had snapped off and was floating at the top of the bowl. Princess Fashion Show must have hidden somewhere.

"Helloooo?" said Clara, tapping on the bowl. She put her face up to the glass. "Princess Fashion Show, would you like some dandelion tea?"

A golden flash darted across the water and pounded into the glass. She jerked back. "What, what, what? What ya want? I finally got some sleep in this friggin' sparkle palace. What? What is it?"

Clara Bieman had never heard her fish talk before. And she was pretty sure "friggin'" was a no-no word. The goldfish head-butted the glass. "Hey, what happened? Did I give you a stroke?"

Clara didn't know what a stroke was. She shook her head and held Felicity with both arms.

"Good. Listen carefully. I am an angry fish. I have large Middle Eastern friends. I don't want no dandelion tea. Now, run and tell your parents you're afraid I might gobble up your little dolly there."

Clara nodded and turned toward her door. "Whoa, hey, wait a sec!" shouted Ari

Clara stopped.

"You got any food?"

Clara nodded again. She went back to the bureau and got the food. She sprinkled it over the bowl. "Oh, yeah, that's the expensive stuff," said the fish. "It ain't like Momma's, but what're ya gonna do?"

Once Clara put the can of food down, she got a foothold on her thoughts again. She said, "Princess Fashion Show, can you talk? You're a boy?"

The fish blinked at her like she'd dropped a pair of twos against straight aces. His mouth always moved like he was chewing a cigar. "What'd you just call me?"

Clara's mouth slowly opened wider, and without taking her eyes off him, she let out a scream you kill pigeons with. She ran out of the room and down the stairs, yanking Felicity along. "Stranger danger! Daddy! A stranger fish is in my rooooooom."

Ari grumbled as he stalked around the miniature dollhouse. He knocked over the wind vane with his tail fin.

When Mr. Bieman came in the room, wearing a patterned sweater vest and owl-eyed spectacles, Ari was padding around as harmless as a piece of coral. "See, honey? Princess is right there. It was just a dream."

Mr. Bieman lifted his daughter into his arms and walked out. As she looked over his shoulder, Ari winked at her and said in a low voice only she could hear, "Yeah sure, babe, just a dream."

Clara shrieked into her daddy's ear so loud, he jerked to the side and hit his head on the door frame. Then he lost his balance and reeled in the other direction. He managed to hold her in the air as he teetered, then crashed to the ground. Clara held Felicity the same way, so she landed softest out of all of them.

Mr. Bieman hit his head on the footboard of the bed. He lay back panting and rubbing his head in two places. Clara, who had landed on his stomach, was jostled but fine. She looked up at the fishbowl. Ari gave her the stink eye. He said, "How do you do?"

Clara screamed again. Mr. Bieman started to say, "What has gotten into you?" Clara thrashed her legs and whipped her arms around, trying to get up. Her dad howled as she connected hard with an elbow to the groin. Ari laughed over Clara's screeches and Mr. Bieman's groans. She trampled on her dad's belly and sprinted out of the room. His girl had just given Mr. Bieman the worst beating he'd had since college.

Once he recovered, Mr. Bieman sent Clara and Felicity to time-out and took the fishbowl to the master bedroom. He placed it on the nightstand, as he began complaining to Mrs. Bieman about their daughter's IQ. Mrs. Bieman stood in front of a foggy bathroom mirror with a pile of black hairpins on the counter. She grabbed them three at a time and slid them into her hair at random.

Mr. Bieman sat on the bed, trying to tie his shoes. "I wish you wouldn't sit there, Neville," said Mrs. Bieman. "I just made the bed." Her words jumped from the back of her throat, like she was constantly in the middle of swallowing a burp.

Neville let his wing tip clatter on the wood floor. He snorted. "I told you, Sandra," he said, like he was accusing her of being Sandra. "Your daughter nearly crippled me with her hysterics, and now I'm late."

"Don't forget to debrief with Randy," said Sandra through her acid reflux. "The counselor said you have to tell a teenager why they were punished."

"I'll be at the lab till late. Don't leave my dinner out. I'll pick up something."

"The dishwasher is still overflowing dirty water into the sink."

"What?"

"Nothing, I'll take care of it."

Mr. Bieman grabbed his briefcase and walked into the bathroom. He leaned close to Mrs. Bieman's cheek as he put one hand under the faucet. With the wet hand he dabbed down a cowlick. Then he left.

Ari whispered into his comm unit, "Was that supposed to be them talking to each other? No wonder the Randy kid's such a puke. I feel like I'm watching my aunt's first marriage . . . minus all the broken shells and Momma pretending to have a heart attack."

Saul's voice came through from out on the sidewalk. "Just catch us a lead, sweetheart."

"I'm just bait to you," said Ari.

"Lotsa fish grow up in a two-bowl family," said Saul. He liked getting under Ari's scales.

Ari sputtered, "I hope your head gets stuck in the plastic rings from a six-pack of soda."

"You'll find your guppy love someday, Ari," said Saul. You could hear a twinkle in his usual deadpan. "And you'll break the family cycle."

Mack piped in, "Maybe you two should get the name of that couples counselor from the Biemans."

"Everybody shut up. I think I got something," said Ari. "She's checking if he's gone. Now she's getting out her phone."

Mrs. Bieman couldn't figure out what to do with her other hand while the phone rang. She jolted when it picked up on the other side. She whispered, "Hello? Yeah, can you hear me? He's gone now. You can come over in an hour." Then she hung up the phone and shoved it back into her purse. She found a few more hairpins on the bed stand and put them in as she left the room.

"Bingo," said Mack on the channel.

"Hey, I'm the one that's undercover," said Ari. "So I'm the one that gets to say bingo."

"All right, so say bingo," said Saul.

"Fuhgeddaboutit," said Ari. "She friggin' ruined it."

CHAPTER 3

MACK WOVE AROUND the early commuter traffic. The splashes of puddle water made a kilted arc every time she zigged in one direction and zagged in another. With Saul weighing down the back, the bike was riding on its rear tire the whole way. Taxis and town cars honked at them, just because it was supposed to be gridlock and she came off like a showboat. A bike messenger stared at Mack's boots, whistled, got a look at Saul towering behind her, gulped, then looked where he was going just in time to swerve away from a homeless lady's shopping cart.

They had Mrs. Bieman's secret visitor to check on and Ari to pick up. But first they had to talk to Randy again. They pulled up to Gramercy Middle School before the morning bell, when all the kids were either huddled under the front entry or across the street in the deli. A few older kids stood on the bleachers of the baseball field, shrugging off the sprinkling rain, just so they wouldn't have to hang out with the younger grades.

Wasn't hard to make out Randy Bieman's group of seventh-graders. They were standing around the baseball diamond, just within earshot of the girls sitting on the bleachers. A few of them kicked the muddy water at each other. The rest told them to quit being so immature, while glancing awkwardly at the girls. Randy wore a poncho designed like Batman's cape and cowl, completely oblivious of the situation. He chased an Asian kid, screaming, "Splash tag!" Then he reared back and booted the other kid in the shins. The kid yowled in pain and hopped on one leg while Randy smiled. He had smug, overstuffed dimples. He said, "You're It."

"I'm not even playing, Randy!" shouted the injured kid.

"No splash-backs," said Randy.

Randy noticed Mack and Saul watching from the other side of the chain-link fence behind home plate. He put his hands on his hips like a superhero. Mack motioned, "Come here," with a finger, and Randy trotted over.

"Didya see me tag Jared Chen?" said Randy.

"Saw your cheap shot," said Saul. His hands stayed in his pea coat. It was a habit to keep Ari's mouth shut.

"Yep, undefeated splash-tag champion," said Randy. "All-world, all-universe, all Randy." The kid watched too much pro wrestling. He flexed his twigs.

"Sweet," said Mack. "Listen, we need you to start telling us what you know about your parents."

"What you mean is that you guys still don't have a clue," said Randy, crossing his arms.

Out in broad daylight, with the fence between them, Randy felt much braver. Mack rolled her eyes. "Seriously, what do you know about your dad's job?"

"Nothing. It's a science institute," said Randy.

"So you wouldn't know where it was," said Saul, "say, if you wanted to go over there and tag him to death?"

"Nope," said Randy. "Somewhere uptown, I think." He wanted to go back and kick Jared some more.

Mack turned and looked up at Saul. She said, "You think the Wish would wait the whole day?"

"A one-time impulse from an ADHD kid," said Saul, shaking his head. "I had money on a breakfast shootout."

Mack turned back to Randy and said, "Man, how hard did you wish?"

Randy was watching the other kids strike up a conversation with the girls. He said, "Huh?"

"How hard did you wish that your family would die?" said Mack. "Like, with all your heart, or what?"

"You guys are terrible cops," said Randy. "You should read *The Punisher.*"

Randy walked back toward the diamond. "Wait a second," said Saul. "Come here." Randy stepped closer. Saul kneeled down so his face was level with Randy's. "You wanna see something?" Saul didn't wait for Randy to respond. He grabbed the chain link with two fingers and pinched it shut, as easy as bending a couple of Twizzlers. Then Saul whispered in a measured tone, "I want you to stop being so smart with us, okay?"

Randy stared at the twisted metal.

"I need you to say okay, Randy. So I know you're listening."

Randy nodded okay.

"Good," said Saul. "Now, I'll tell you what Detective Mack meant, and then you'll answer her question, okay?"

Randy nodded okay again.

"There are four kinds of wishes," said Saul. "By that I mean the technical term for WISH. The kind we catch and put in the brick house."

"I wish you guys would just go away," Randy whispered.

"And you'll get that wish," said Mack, "as soon as we finish cleaning up your last one."

"The first kind are your everyday wishes," said Saul, "the ideas that pop into your head."

"That's what happened to me," said Randy. "Just popped into my head."

"That's good," said Saul, encouraging the kid. "Those are night-shades, shape-changers. We call them *ghul.*"

The mention of shape-shifters got Randy's attention. "They have real superpowers?" he said.

"But they're the weakest. Wishes people make on a whim."

Randy imagined a version of himself out there, with all the abilities he had always dreamed of. In a way, it was like *he* was the one with all the powers in the comic books.

Mack added, "The harder you want something, the stronger it is."

"The second type is a *sila,*" Saul continued.

"What can they do?"

"They're fast, and some can fly."

Mack interrupted. "The question is whether yours is a sila. Frankly, it'd be disturbing if you hated your parents that much, but this wish of yours is taking its time, acting on strategy. Ghuls are typically all instinct."

Randy tried to look thoughtful. He was too busy imagining cool stuff you could do if you could run at the speed of light (steal homework, join the NFL, beat up Jared Chen). He scratched his smooth chin and said, "So what you're saying is the other me is either Beast Boy or the Flash?"

"And he's trying to kill your parents," said Mack.

"I'd rather be the Flash," said Randy.

Mack grabbed the fence and shook it. "You ever been slapped in the face, Randy?"

Randy took a step back.

"Think," said Mack. "You have to be sure. How strong was your wish?"

"Okay, okay, what's the third kind?"

"You don't need to know the third kind," said Mack.

"They're for obsessions," said Saul. He put a hand on Mack's shoulder and let the weight of it press her like a blanket. He said, "The third kind is the *ifrit*. They can bend elements. Fire ifrit, dark ifrit, that kind of thing. But that doesn't matter in this case. They're so strong, a whole town has to be wishing the same thing, like inquisitions or revolutions."

"Are they omnipotent?" said Randy, then clarified in case they didn't know. "That means all-powerful godlike status."

"Not omnipotent," said Saul, "but definitely magnipotent."

"Like you?"

"No, I'm just potent," said Saul, smiling. Mack elbowed him in his ribs.

Kids were usually beglamoured by the whole ugly idea, but Mack had seen too many wishes come true to encourage it. The worst crimes never committed. Saul said "magnipotent" with precise distinction, as though it were a job class or a power-up. Randy was probably imagining video games. Mack wanted him to imagine funerals.

"Well, have you ever beaten up an ifrit?" asked Randy.

"Not me, kid," said Saul. "Out of my pay grade."

Randy's mouth hung open. Most people who met him couldn't imagine anything stronger than Saul.

"If my wish was a sila, could you beat it up, then?" asked Randy.

"Probably not," said Saul. Randy was deflated.

"So what's it gonna be?" said Mack. "How bad did you want them dead?"

Randy dug his galoshes into the wet dirt. It's hard to weigh how badly you wanted something, especially when you don't want it anymore. It's like asking the feeling of a feeling. His secret—that he hated his parents—wasn't even true by the time his mom asked if he wanted another waffle. Randy looked up. "It was my first time. I'm sure."

Mack let go of the fence. Her arms dropped to her side. Saul looked at his watch. The morning bell rattled in its cage. Kids from all over the block pooled toward the entrance.

"Can I go now?" said Randy.

The detectives stepped off the curb and got back on the bike.

Mack said, "Thanks, Randy."

Randy called after them, "Hey, what about the strongest wishes?"

"They're the *marid*," said Saul. "Let's not talk about them."

"Are they omnipotent?"

Mack lifted the kickstand and put on her helmet. As Saul pulled down his skully, he said, "Yeah. Probably."

Unlike the regulars, ICU cops started with the criminal and worked backward to the crime. If you work the case right, then you catch the wish before it comes true. Lock it up in the brick house. Nothing happens but an evil thought. A dirty impulse. And the crook gets away with it. The guilty go free.

Maybe it was nothing but another sanitation job, thought Mack as she cornered the bike on the inside track of a delivery van. Maybe all they were doing was scurrying around the sewage mains, tightening leaky pipes full of bad dreams. But it could be only a matter of time before a flange blew, spilled over, and burst the canal. And then a whole deluge of our deepest desires would crash over us. Every appetite would be satisfied, every fancy become fact — for every itch, a long and lusty scratch. The face in the mirror would be a self we never thought possible. Next to our list of favorite movies will be our list of jealousies and insults we've hurled. A new constellation of meannesses we'll have no choice but to add to our public profiles. Our civilized postures will be laid waste. And the waste will be the biggest shame of it — waste of a pretty decent shot at getting away clean.

Maybe it was that Sludgment Day that all the Wish Police in

the ICU could see coming. Saul's shoulders were as wide as a ram's horns either *because* he was carrying the same burden or because he didn't have to. Maybe it was only Mack who felt the weight of it.

The second time they entered the Bieman residence, they knocked.

Maybe Mrs. Bieman was stepping out on her husband. Or maybe she was having his gift delivered and wanted to keep it secret till Christmas. Maybe a lot of things. None of them mattered so much to the investigation. The job was *how,* not *who.* To project and to swerve what would otherwise come to pass. What maybe may be.

Mrs. Bieman answered with one hand patting her hair, which was still battened down by enough pins to clog a toilet. Her royal-blue sweater had three red poinsettias across the front and made her look like a music teacher. She wore blush in two perfect circles, a shade of pink you only find in 1952. She had an indistinct twitchi-ness about her, like she kept realizing something was burning in the oven or, in her case, some online auction was expiring.

"Sandra Bieman?" said Mack. With her sunglasses on, she looked like highway patrol. She pressed her badge up to the screen door.

"Yes?"

"This is Detective Djinn. I'm Detective McClintock. Can we come in, ma'am?"

Both Saul and Mack noticed Mrs. Bieman's glance outside as they walked in. The visitor hadn't arrived yet. The house was just as classy in the daylight. Nothing prefab, a TV you could pull off the wall and sleep on. Neither the front door nor the screen outside made a squeak on its hinges. Anyone could sneak in without stirring a louse. Saul didn't step farther than the foyer. Mrs. Bieman shut the door and scooted around him.

Saul said, "Should we take off our shoes, ma'am?"

"Oh," said Mrs. Bieman. "Uh, don't worry about it."

Mack looked back at Saul. "Wood flooring," she said.

"We could scuff, and there're nice carpets." Saul went ahead and pulled off his size-fourteen shoes and propped them up on the front door, leaning on the jam so they'd plop over if the door moved. "It's polite," he said.

"You really don't have to," said Mrs. Bieman.

"It's no trouble, ma'am."

Mack waited, bemused, as Saul also took off each sock and wadded it up into his coat pockets. His feet were the size of barbari bread, the same brown color, with a ridge of black hair instead of black sesame. Mack kept her boots on. She said, "Hey, Emily Post, you ready?"

They followed Mrs. Bieman past the staircase they had snuck up last night and into the kitchen. Clara was seated at the round table with Felicity in the seat next to her. "This is my daughter, Clara."

"I don't have to go to school today. Are you here to arrest my brother?" said Clara. She couldn't decide which one of them to stare at. The policeman was much bigger than her dad and had hair on his face, even though her dad said that kind of hair was for "jobless illiterates." The girl was unlike any girl Clara had ever seen. Her hair was redder than Felicity's and jagged and short. She didn't look like she'd be scared of Randy.

"Are you in kindergarten?" said Mack, extending her hand. Clara shook it.

"Yeah, but I got scareded of my goldfish," said Clara, as she chewed a piece of pumpernickel toast, "and I might be exhibiting abnormal psycho behavior."

Her mother said, "Close your mouth, dear."

Mrs. Bieman stood by the sink, pretending to wash out coffee grinds from the espresso scoop. She had checked her watch three times already. Mack took her glasses off. "Ma'am, do you have any reason to believe you're in danger?"

Mrs. Bieman sprang an arm's length away from the sink and repressed a burp of acid reflux. She had all the poise of a hamster. "What? What do you mean, danger?"

"You seem anxious. Are you waiting for someone?"

"No. Not at all."

"For example, you haven't asked us what this is all about."

Mrs. Bieman dried her hands on a dish towel, then pinched the bridge of her nose to stave off a migraine. "Okay, what is this about?"

"We're with ICU, ma'am."

"Intensive Care Unit?"

"Imaginary Crime Unit," said Mack.

"I've never heard of that," said Mrs. Bieman.

"Let's stay on task, ma'am." Mack had a small beauty mark up and to the right of her lips, and when she smirked, it pushed up to the crown of her cheek. She smirked when she was getting a kick out of being a hard case. "Is there any way you can think of that your son"—she looked at her notepad just for the effect—"one, Randy L. Bieman, could get access to a gun?"

"Oh, my — a what?"

"Calm down, ma'am."

Clara was riveted by her mother's agitation until Saul hunkered into the seat next to her. "Is that black tea?" he said, picking up the demitasse in front of the doll. "I didn't know Felicity drank black tea."

Clara turned to him, toast and marmalade jam still in her mouth, agape. "How did you know her name?"

"Felicity?" said Saul. He took a sip of the tea. It was cold. He winced. "Why wouldn't I know her name?"

Clara didn't have an answer for this. She closed her mouth to think better. "It's rude not to introduce yourself to a lady in the room," expounded Saul, scratching his stubble. He leaned over and whispered, "I have two daughters."

Clara couldn't have friends over because of Randy. "Do they like American Girl dolls?" she asked.

"I don't know," said Saul. "But I keep up, just in case. Do you guys have any sugar cubes?"

Clara shook her head. "We only brew tea for Felicity."

"Makes sense," said Saul. He picked up the mini ceramic teapot and lifted the lid. Dregs. He rubbed the side of the pot. Nothing. He poured the dregs into a used mug on the table.

They all heard the unmistakable clomp of Saul's size-fourteens falling to the wood floor. They fell silent. Someone had entered the house.

Mack pulled her firearm and took two long steps to the kitchen door. Mrs. Bieman suppressed her astonishment with the dish towel.

Clara hadn't blinked since they'd arrived. Mack winked at her. Saul put his mug down and rose from the table. He pushed open the kitchen door, and Mack slipped under his arm to cover the hallway. Slowly, she reached with her thumb and pulled back the hammer of her firearm. In tight quarters like this, she could have blown a slug through the Sheetrock two rooms over. Barefoot, Saul jogged down the corridor as quietly as if his lower half was nothing but smoke. He hugged the corner and waited for Mack to sneak up.

She could hear the clumsy sounds of a thirteen-year-old, the inadvertent tics of having too much sugar in your system . . . and maybe a Bronx-made rocket launcher. Mack butted up next to Saul. He reached into his pea coat and pulled out a gun roughly the size of a cigarette lighter. It had embroidered lettering along the barrel that said *Sweetheart*. Mack raised an eyebrow at Saul. She mouthed, "A BB gun? Are you serious?" Saul blew on the barrel of his BB gun like a Bond girl, only more stubbly. Mack rolled her eyes and counted a silent "one, two, three." Both detectives turned the corner and yelled, "Hands up, Randy."

Except it wasn't Randy. Or Randy's wish—they usually responded to the same name. It was Mustard, bent over on the landing, trying to prop up Saul's shoes. He still had on the hand-me-down pajamas and the hangdog droop of his lower lip. Just as pathetic were the half-dozen corner-deli roses, the kind they dye blue with food coloring for no reason at all. Both the roses and the boy looked like they'd wilt if you gave them a nice hard glare.

When the two DTs bore down on the kid with the business ends of their firearms, he shrieked and threw the roses up in panic. They poofed into a saggy cloud of petals. Mustard fluttered his empty hands like he'd burned himself. Mack grimaced. She holstered her Magnum.

"What're you doing here, Mustard?"

"The question is: What are *you* doing here, Detective?"

It was Mrs. Bieman. She rushed over to the boy and held him by the shoulders. "Could have been an intruder, ma'am, intending deadly harm," said Mack.

"Well, it wasn't," said Mrs. Bieman, with all the indignation she could muster over a burp. "It's a young boy."

"Same as our perpetrator, ma'am," said Mack. She peered deep into Mustard's eyes, trying to see if he was a ghul. Not that she could tell. But maybe there was something, some glint of newborn evil. But Mrs. Bieman seemed to know the kid from before Randy's crime.

"Look what you did to his flowers," said Mrs. Bieman.

"I got them for you, Mrs. Bieman," said Mustard. A real Oliver Twist routine, forlorn and dirty. You just wanted to feed him soup.

Clara ran from the hallway. "Muth-toad!" She hugged his knees; he patted her head.

"You said you weren't expecting a visitor," said Mack. Mrs. Bieman checked to make sure the hairpins were still jammed into place. She lifted her chin so she could talk down her nose at the bungling investigators, but a gassy buildup made her press it down into her neck again. "My husband wouldn't approve, all right? He thinks Clara will catch something."

"You help orphans when he's not home?" said Saul. She seemed like an unlikely candidate for Mother Teresa of Gramercy Park.

"Mustard showed up at our door a few weeks ago, and I just give him breakfast sometimes," said Mrs. Bieman. "Is that against the law? He's freezing in the clothes they give him in the foster home."

"Can't argue with that," said Mack.

"He's far nicer to Clara than her own brother, and I don't see a problem with it."

"I do chores," offered Mustard.

That was the end of it. It was time to go. They were shaking down a depressed housewife, an orphan, and a little girl scared of her goldfish. May as well clap the irons on a diabetic nana.

Mack pulled out her sunglasses. As Saul put on his socks and shoes, she said, "Just one more question. What does your husband do?"

Mrs. Bieman snorted, then let a burp escape. "Who knows," she said. "Is thinking too highly of yourself a job?"

"Only in Washington," said Mack.

"He's head of research at Sun Chemical, but mostly he swans around taking credit for the work his assistants do."

"So you didn't meet him in biology class?"

Mrs. Bieman blorted again. She seemed like a miracle of science herself. "I met him at a dinner party a few years ago for a do-nothing friend of mine on the Upper East Side. He was her husband's college roommate, and I was bored, so, you know, we got together."

Saul got up and opened the door. Mack smiled at Clara. "Oh, right," said Mack. "Do you keep any fish on the premises?"

"I have an angry goldfish," said Clara.

"Is this some kind of joke?" said Mrs. Bieman.

"We'll be the one asking the questions, ma'am."

They retrieved Ari and put back Princess Fashion Show. Nobody said anything until the three detectives got outside to the bike. Mrs. Bieman was holy pissed and promised to call their "manager." A sunny winter day. The breeze felt like a hug from Caesar's friends. Then Ari said, "You tell anyone about that tiara, and I'll finish the both of youse. In your sleep. Demean me again like that—the Talking Frog bit? The fishes you'll be sleeping with . . . Why does your pocket smell like feet?"

CHAPTER 4

"AM I THE only one who thinks the orphan is playing us?" said Mack.

"Yeah," said Ari. "He's a friggin' poster child for the Make-A-Wish Foundation."

"My point exactly," said Mack as they walked up to Sun Chemical Labs, a corporate warehouse on the West Side piers. Next to the ranch-style complex was a storehouse for the hard-drive farm and a backup generator large enough to run Atlantic City for a few nights.

"Maybe he's running a scam," said Mack. "He was snooping around the house last night."

They opened frosted glass doors. Everything in the lobby was ergonomic and shades of white. You got the feeling the place could double as a nightclub or the staff lounge of the SS *Enterprise.* The receptionist sat behind an egg-shaped desk, listening to music on his headphones. His gray gingham tie ended in a square line, like he thought office work was ironic.

Saul put a finger to his ear. "Central, this is Ji-Ji. Do you copy?" They heard the cackling sound and then, "Go ahead, Ji-Ji. This is Central."

"Angie? Is that you?"

Maybe a flirty giggle or just static. "Yep, still at the desk. Maria's kid is sick."

"Angie, you overworked darling, could you run a search on a Sandra Bieman, *B* as in 'broke-down'? See if she has any priors. And one on the name Mustard, as in French's yellow . . ."

"Sure," said Angie. "But that second one might take a while without a real name."

"No problem," said Saul. "Thanks."

Another burst of static. Either the electronics in the lab were breaking up the signal or that Angie had a thing for tall, dark, and married. Not that she would know.

Mack tapped on the plastic desk. The receptionist bobbed his head, jiggered his eyebrows to say, "Go ahead," but didn't bother to pull out an earphone.

Mack said, "Dr. Bieman." Then she raised her voice. "Here to see Dr. Bieman!"

"Yeah, I got it," said the receptionist. His hair was greasy and seemed insincere. The collar of his shirt was stained with last night's alcohol sweating out. Mack leaned on the desk.

Saul said, "All we know is the orphan isn't Randy's wish. The mom has known him for weeks. But I'll give you the weird stuff."

"Kids are just weird," said Ari over the comm channel. "My sister had a kid who dried the bed till he turned fifteen."

"Yeah, but this is really . . . fishy," said Mack. As soon as it

· 265 ·

came out, she tried to suck it back through her teeth, but it was too late.

"Now, why would you say something like that?" said Ari. "You think my people don't have enough trouble?"

Mack's hands made a strangling motion at Saul's coat pocket. Everything was something with Ari. "I was just saying," said Mack. "Don't spin it that way."

"What way? Fishes are dishonest? They are imbued with certain immoral tendencies? What, what?"

"Sometimes they smell funny is all," said Mack, wondering if the hipster was ever going to give them directions to Bieman's office. He didn't seem to do anything in the way of paging Dr. Bieman. She knocked again on the desk, but he was too cool to do anything twice.

"Oh, so that's it! Saul, are you *hearing* this bigot?"

Saul answered in a neutral drone, "You have to admit, some of your people smell bad after three days in a barrel on Mott Street."

A long pause.

Ari was boiling himself into a bouillabaisse. "All these years," he said finally, "and now it comes out. My best friend thinks I'm *fishy.* Fine. Whatevuh."

"You're a fish," Saul protested.

"I want out of this pocket, you—you gorilla. What do you think of that, Middle East? You are hairy like a baboon. I choke on the hairballs from your jungle-man body. This *whole* case stinks like a friggin' ape!"

Saul shut off his comm unit and pressed his pocket closed. More race-related insults continued to muffle out like an ostrich scream-ing in a snowbank. Mack finally reached over the desk and palmed the hipster receptionist's face like a basketball. He jerked, but she held on. "WTF," said the receptionist through Mack's fingers, pulling out his earphones. "What're you doing?" She'd smudged his thin layer of eyeliner.

Mack leaned over the desk, nose to nose. "I. Need. To. See. Dr. Bieman. Now," she said. "Do you understand?"

"Gaw," said the hipster. "I did that already. You can go up whenever."

"Where is he?" said Mack.

"Hello? Third floor?" he said.

Mack stood back and pointed at her own cheek. "You got a little schmutz there." They went to the elevator and pushed three.

On the way up, Mack twiddled the snap on her holster. "And the mother," she said. "Claims she met the dad *a few years ago.* What do you think?"

"You think he's Randy's stepdad?" said Saul.

"I mean, how long is a *few* years? The kid's what, thirteen years old?"

The doors opened on the third floor.

"Maybe Randy's wish is off blasting a biological dad somewhere in his mom's past," said Mack. "Maybe his dad is the milkman."

"Let's ask," said Saul.

Dr. Bieman stood in the hall outside his office in his white lab coat, looking over the test results of a junior researcher. He nodded and signed. The junior scuttled off with the clipboard. The doctor peered over his bifocals at the two visitors. A six-foot churlish mesomorph, either a cop or a sailor, and a biker in black leather, with hair thermometer red. The other doctors were no doubt already constructing plausible scenarios for comedy. Dr. Bieman wasn't fascinated with comedy.

He forced a rectangular smile and approached with his hand out. Saul would have shaken the hand, but it went limp in his grip. *A dead fish,* thought Saul, grinning to himself. "Dr. Bieman, thank you for meeting us," said Saul. "Do you know if you are Randy's real father or if your wife slept around behind your back?"

The doctor swiped his hand back and put it in his lab coat. "Who are you?"

"Sorry about my partner," said Mack, showing the police ID. "What he means is, how many years ago did you meet your wife at the dinner party of your college buddy and his do-nothing lady?"

"Follow me, if you *don't mind.*"

The doctor turned on his heel and clipped back to his office. He preferred the authority his desk provided, looking down on slightly lowered chairs. Mack and Saul followed. His glass office overlooked the main laboratory, where half a dozen scientists were working at various experiment stations. Mack took a seat. Saul leaned on the door frame, out of earshot—Ari was still foaming.

"The answer to your question is fourteen years. But I assure you, I am Randy's real father. He was, how would you say, the motivation for our marriage."

"But you don't know for sure," said Saul.

"I know," said Dr. Bieman.

"You ran a test?" said Mack.

"Look around you, officers. I can run a paternity test as easily as you can use a microwave."

"So you're a science guy," said Saul.

"Yes," said Dr. Bieman, all condescension around the beak and peepers, "I am a *science guy*. I am also very busy and very law-abiding, so I'll need to know what this is about immediately. Where are you from?"

"Me?" said Mack. "New York, born and raised." She said *Nu Yowk* like Brooklyn *coiffee*. Saul tilted his chin. At the luncheonette her story had been Ireland with a brogue.

Dr. Bieman sighed at the boobery he was forced to deal with. "I meant your police division. I will also need your badge numbers and your precinct boss."

"No need to play it that way," said Saul.

"And what way is that, officer?" said Dr. Bieman, folding his hands.

"Like the snippety *science guy*. We're here because we have reason to believe you and your family are in danger."

"By the way," said Mack, "we're not officers; we're detectives. We tell the officers what to do."

Bieman's lips pursed. His balding forehead was corrugated like the knobs of a burette clamp.

"What does that mean?" he said, squinting over his specs. Mack could see why the assistants acted like simpering domestics.

"Means we did better in cop school," said Mack.

"It means you need to answer some questions," said Saul.

"Why would anyone want to hurt my family?"

"You'd be surprised all the things people want," said Mack. She put her boots up on the corner of Bieman's desk.

"Is this about my research?"

"What's your research?" said Mack.

"The biochemical response patterns of—"

"No."

A few rounds of silence. The doc racked his over-applauded brain for answers to his own self-centered questions. Must have been a vicious know-it-all when he was little. He was Randy's dad, all right. That's all they needed for now. Mack dropped her boots from the desk and took out a permanent marker from her jacket. "Well," she said, grabbing the beaker mug on Bieman's desk. "Call us if anything weird happens." She wrote the number on the side of the glass.

"Wait," said the doctor. "We didn't solve anything. What about assigning some kind of protection?"

"We've already solved all kinds of things," said Mack, getting up to leave. "Found out you're Randy's family. The sign outside says kids aren't allowed in the lab area. And you're having the kind of marital troubles that keep you here at the office all night."

Mack explained the last part with a nod at the metal locker in the corner. "You keep clothes and toiletries here, maybe a grad student to keep you company?"

The doctor went radioactive. He spurted a bunch of fallout sounds. "How dare you . . . *himminy, himminy, himminy* . . . Just what do you . . ." His acidic tone would have burned through a submarine hull. He stood, pressed his palms flat on the desk, and leaned forward. "You're implying I cheat on my wife."

"Do you?" said Mack.

"Get out of my lab," hissed the doctor.

"Why so defensive, Doc?" said Mack.

Bieman compressed a response into a furious squeeze of his

eyelids. Mack walked past Saul out into the hallway. The doctor stared at Saul. When the detective didn't scram, he began to fidget. Bieman plopped back into his chair and put his hands between his knees.

"What do you know about a kid named Mustard?" Saul asked.

The doctor had burned up all his fission and sat. "He's a strange little urchin who skulks around our home. I've told my wife to call the police the next time she sees him."

"Doesn't seem to be much of a home these days," said Saul.

Bieman looked adrift behind his bifocals. "You've made fun of me enough, Detective. I made my mistakes in the past, like everyone. But I'm not cheating on my wife. It's not much of a home, fine. Say what you like. But I'd still rather not have old lady Cavanaugh's foster children hanging around it."

Saul hooked a thumb under the band of his skullcap and said, "Apologies, Dr. Bieman." Saul turned to leave.

"Close the door behind you," said Bieman.

Saul turned back. "So you know Cavanaugh?" he said.

"Huh? What?" said the doc.

"Mustard's foster care. You know where he lives and that Ms. Cavanaugh is old. You've met her."

The doctor jerked his head up, then thought better of saying anything. Saul bowed again and smiled. "Don't bother," he said, "The truth might spill out. Best wishes, Doctor."

Saul stepped into the hall and closed the door on Bieman. The man seemed like nothing more than a barrel of green chemical guilt, eating holes in itself somewhere on the dark floor of the ocean.

*   *   *

On the way to Mrs. Cavanaugh's, Saul chewed on the mystery of his new partner's fake accents. She was lying about something. Maybe she was Internal Affairs, mixing up her phony backstory. Maybe the brass knew he was a djinn and had sent her to investigate. After all these years, maybe it was time to move on again, leave the policing to pigs like Alvarez and wolves like Goodie.

Now Saul had two cases to solve. On top of the Bieman murders, he'd have to dig the dirt on his new partner. And the thing about digging dirt is that it has a way of turning into a grave.

Angie interrupted his thoughts. She came over the line and called them back to the 3-1. "Reroute to headquarters, Ji-Ji. Request of the chief of detectives."

"I'm here, too," said Mack.

"That's great, honey."

The early lunch crowd was tapping a foot at the pizza counters or customizing their own salads. The smell of halal chicken and turmeric sizzled off the street-side carts. Nothing said New York like the immigrant guy screaming, "New York!" and selling *I ♥ NY* shirts from the back of his cousin's van—Jersey license plate. The traffic on Second Avenue was a heart surgeon's meal ticket.

Mack popped the curb in front of the precinct and parked next to the main entry. Inside was the same. Same stale coffee smell. Same cold cement floor. The sergeant at the front desk was as still as a gargoyle with the pallor to match.

Alvarez was still at his desk, feet up, reading page six. Goodie was still knitting in her housedress and slumber cap. Mack noticed that Goodie's fingers were monstrous and so knobby you could barely see the needles. Good for wielding a battle-ax or strangling livestock. She had a to-go platter of hot pastrami, prosciutto, and other deli meats on her desk. No bread, no silverware. Just a pile of red meat and a jug of vino to wash it down. Alvarez had four Pixy Stix, acacia honey, and a Diet Coke.

When he saw Mack and Saul walk in, Alvarez folded his paper and said, "Hey, Saul, says here a cabbie crashed into City Hall. Friend of yours?" Instead of laughing at his own jokes, Alvarez had a habit of puckering his lips and nodding his head in affirmation.

"I think I read that one," said Saul. "It said your fairy godmother was the one who crashed into City Hall."

Alvarez stopped puckering.

"That's true," added Mack. "I read that article, too."

"Don't talk 'bout my godmutha like that," warned Alvarez, kicking his legs off the desk. He crumpled up the newspaper and looked like he would have lunged at them if Goodie hadn't distracted him.

"Tell the maggots about our case, dearie," she said, not looking up. Mack noticed that the pile of meat had gotten smaller, but she hadn't seen Goodie put down the knitting.

Alvarez said, "We gotta case."

"Yeah, we heard that already," said Mack.

"Murder one," said Alvarez. "Brother wants brother out of the way. Big one too. *Sila* maybe."

Saul opened the door to the captain's office. "So go work the case," he said.

"When we're ready," said Alvarez. "Just thought to tell ya so you'd eat some when we close our case before you close yours."

Mack walked into the office. Ari spoke over the comm unit, "Hey, Tinker Bell called, said she wants her wings back—" Saul shut the door before Alvarez could scream curses at him.

Cap looked more like a tax man—khakis, loafers, the urge to call him grandpa—than a chief of Ds. He was about the size of Saul's left leg, with a slouch he got from riding a desk too long. His office was no bigger than a falafel stand, but it was orderly. The files hung in perfect rows under block-lettered tabs. The routing slips were stacked as neatly as printer paper. The pens in the pen holder stood in color-coded divisions—subdivided by type, ballpoint, fountain, retractable. His hand trembled as he wrote something on his desktop calendar. He was bent over so close to the page that his glasses almost touched the paper.

The captain didn't look up as he said, "Hello, Saul. How're you doing? Good?" His lower lip was sucked in a little, like his dentures didn't quite fit. When he finished saying anything, he'd mush to a slow stop. His glasses magnified his eyes.

Saul stood at attention. "Yes, sir. Can't complain."

"Did you see the new coffee creamers we have?"

"Yes, sir. Hazelnut, sir."

"You enjoy that," said the captain. "That's there for you to enjoy." He was still writing on the calendar.

"I will, sir."

The captain looked up. "And you, Detective, how's your first case back from lash detail?"

Mack straightened under the gentle glare of the captain's attention. "Um, yes, sir. Enjoying it very much."

"Are you making progress?"

"Good progress, sir. We think the boy's wish will attack the family around dinnertime. We'll be there to apprehend."

"And why is that?" said the captain.

"What?"

"Why do you think it'll attack at dinnertime?"

"Well, sir . . ." said Mack.

The captain threaded his fingers together and put them on the desktop calendar. He said, "Why don't I let Ari debrief me on this."

Saul pulled the plastic bag out of his pocket and placed it on the mouth of an empty mug. "We got nuthin', Cap," said Ari. He took a quick lap around the cone-shaped space to get his bearings. "We're lost at sea over here. The brat says his wish was a one-off, should have been a quick lookup and lockup, na-mean?"

"I know what you mean," said the captain.

"Right, but there's no sign of the ghul anywhere. Meanwhile, we got another kid, a little older, orphan, who's playing all nice-nice with the family."

The captain nodded. "The kid you brought in last night."

"The one," said Ari. "Mack and the big guy gave him the hard sell, but he ain't buyin'."

Mack coughed into her fist. The captain raised an eyebrow. "You don't agree with the assessment, Detective?"

"No, sir," said Mack. "I think the orphan knows more than he's letting on. More than the Muppet show he gave us, anyway."

"Fine," said Ari. He puffed a few bubbles. "May it represent on the record that DT Mack over here believes our Little Orphan Annie is secretly a sila, a friggin' sila, for God's sake."

"Noted," said the captain. "Go on, Ari."

"That's just it, Cap. No place to go. The mom's life is cornflakes. The dad might have something on the side, but a guy like that, he's already having the affair with his job. We could tail him if you want."

"No point in it," said the captain.

"Cornflakes," said Ari, "bland as brunch."

"We do have one lead," said Saul. "Old lady Cavanaugh, the foster mother."

"That ain't a lead," said Ari. "That's a shred of a hunch. It's fish food." Then Ari swam over to Mack's corner of the bag and said, "See how that works? I can say stuff like that 'cause they're *my* people."

"Do whatever you want," said Mack, arms crossed. "I think fish food is great. Had a salmon steak last Thursday."

"I loathe you," said Ari, a quiver rolling over his iridescent scales.

The captain frowned. He didn't frown often. The grooves of his old age had given him a permanent wistful look.

"I've been getting calls all morning about two detectives flashing badges all over town," said the captain. Ari swam to attention. Mack straightened up. "The scientist called in, got the brass worried about exposure."

"Sorry, sir," said Saul.

"We'll keep a lower profile," said Ari.

"You should do that," agreed the captain. "Act like the regulars unless you have to."

The comm channel crackled in their earbuds. Voice of Angie. "Ji-Ji, this is Central, do you copy?"

"Ten-four, Central," said Saul. "But I'm a little—"

"I got the information you asked for," said Angie.

Saul put two fingers up to his ear and looked at the captain. "Go on," said the captain. "And be more neighborly. And try the hazelnut."

Saul nodded, grabbed Ari's bag, and walked out. "I'm in the building, Angie. Be there in a second." Angie didn't turn off her mike in time to cut her swoony exhale.

When Saul closed the door, the captain said to Mack, "How are you really?"

Mack didn't know how to answer. She railed the zipper of her jacket up and down. "Good," she said. She hadn't figured out old man Magoo just yet. The whole squad respected him, even Alvarez. Her last captain was a megaton of slobbery abuse who tooted more than a steam train and smeared beef grease on every report he pawed at. This guy had on a cardigan and probably took his grandkids to the shore.

"Your previous issue . . ." said the captain.

"Won't be a problem again, Captain. My word on that."

The captain smiled at her, which pushed the wrinkles up his cheeks and closed his eyes. He mushed invisible creamed corn and looked sleepy.

"Thank you for the opportunity."

"Don't thank me," said the captain. "Saul was the one who requested you. Otherwise, he and Ari work alone."

Mack walked out of the captain's office, back into the sleepy detectives' bureau. Saul was gone.

"Hey, Alvarez," she said. He was still reading the paper. A Pixy Stix dangled from his mouth. "Saul never had a partner but me?"

"Man," said Alvarez, making a *snikt* sound through his teeth. "Punk ain't even really Wish Police."

"Captain says he's even better than the first-grade detectives."

"That's 'cause regulars keep it tight like that. If it wasn't for the goldfish, Saul wouldn't even be ICU."

Goodie clarified, "The ape is the minnow's chauffeur, dearie."

"You're on the donkey ride, Mami," said Alvarez, laughing. "And Saul is the donkey."

"Wait. Wait, you guys think Saul's a regular? A regular regular. Like, just a regular schmo carting the magic fish around?"

Alvarez and Goodie just smirked.

"But his last name is Djinn," said Mack.

"Don't be stupid, dearie. No one's a djinn."

Mack skipped the comeback. Nobody would believe Saul was the only free genie in the unknown world. And maybe he wasn't. What proof did she have? Just the guy's word. Worse yet, the whole squad thought he was Ari's goon. But then, if they had all the angles covered, why had Saul requested a discipline case like her?

"So the captain is a regular, too?" said Mack. Alvarez snapped the paper in half and looked at Mack like she was pudding thick.

"Did you see pixie wings on him? Last name Rumpelstiltskin, hawkin' magic beans on the corner? No? Just an old white guy in power? That's that, whatevuh bein' whatevuh. I mean, he's captain. Believe that. But he don't do wishes."

Goodie said, "He is very organized, though."

That was the first nice thing out of the old troll. Mack noticed that her meat platter had been licked clean. Mack couldn't decide if a compliment from Goodie meant you were starlight . . . or scum chunks.

Saul walked back from the Wishing Post Central Dispatch. Mack was waiting outside on her bike. Saul saw her through the double doors and stopped short. Before he opened the doors, he switched to the private channel and said, "Hey, Angie? I forgot one thing."

Angie rolled a salacious "Hmmm?" over her tongue, like maybe he'd forgotten to ask for her house key.

"Do me a favor and run a background check on Mack?"

"She's a pub wench, and her voice sounds like she's got too much makeup on."

"C'mon," said Saul.

"Fine," said Angie. "Slow night, anyway. Lot of wishes but none of them are biting."

"Maybe the goodness thing is taking off. You know. Bibles on Broadway."

Angie scoffed over the channel. Saul did the same. Maybe bad dreams were going out of style. Sure. Maybe a lot of things.

Saul pushed open the double doors. Mack tossed a helmet his way and said, "What'd you get?"

Saul saddled the bike and talked as Mack raced a Chinese deliveryman downtown.

"Turns out Mother Bieman's about as bland as Tabasco on tobacco. She used to be a hand model by the name of Sandy Pumpkin, then danced at a knockoff Alvin Ailey for a while, played in a few indie films. All the while she was going through more men than an X-ray. The only problem was she got wrinkles. Nobody wanted to see her frolicking in the Lincoln Square fountain anymore. Became a theater instructor."

"It was midnight and the Pumpkin turned into a stagecoach," said Mack, through the comm unit.

"Yeah. So she met Dr. Bieman, who'd already played Prince Charming to a couple wives. Left his third wife to marry Sandy. Their first kid was already on the way."

"Scandal in a lab coat," said Mack.

"Guess that's why they named him Randy," said Ari.

"So where does that get us?" said Mack. They came up to the Brooklyn Bridge in the early autumn sunlight.

"Nowhere," said Saul. "The birth records panned out. Randy's their kid. He wants them dead. We have no idea where the wish is."

The towers of the bridge brooded over them like a colossus straddling the gates of an eternally lost city. Its waist disappeared above the ceiling of the clouds. But the people had gone and leashed the giant with a thousand steel cables, thought Sulaiman al Djinn. Without reason, maybe fear, they'd chained their own guard. Made him stay put. Made the protector a prisoner.

And like a free genie, the colossus wasn't a colossus anymore. It was the dead hulking towers of a bridge gone sad. Rocks inanimate. Rocks regular. The foot stones would only move with the shifting silt on the river floor. No one would ever see the eyes of the gentle giant again. The bridge would only ever get you to Brooklyn.

* * *

Mack drove like she'd left her pot of gold someplace. The East River lapped at the piers of the Navy Yard and smelled like the ocean's infected eardrum.

The houses on Ocean Parkway didn't look out on the ocean. The view was an interstate highway clogged with white vans delivering cold merch to the city. All the businesses in the outer borough—carpeting, studio space, restaurant equipment—existed to service the great floating island of Manhattan. Every single block of the crystal city needed ten blocks in the outer boroughs for glass warehouses, cleaning supplies, and a little casa for the window washers to sleep in.

The whole neighborhood felt like it was a low-res version of another neighborhood, surviving on the hopeless idea that they'd get a turn on the swings someday if they pushed long enough, if they stuck with their lives of propping up other people's lives.

Lady Cavanaugh's house sat on the corner of a block of houses as mismatched as a box of crayons. Periwinkle eaves hung over the wraparound porch like an afterthought. The siding was sea-foam green. The front door used to be red. Every other piece of the house looked like donated material and fit together like Frankenstein's quilt.

When Mack knocked on the screen door, it dropped off the hinge and made a divot in the porch. Kids were laughing in the back. Mack knocked again.

"Awright, awright! Gimme a second, will ya?"

The woman who yanked open the door wasn't quite so big as an ice-cream truck, but she could probably pack as many Klondikes. She had a hairnet on a wispy scalp and the gaunt twitchy eyes of either a pill popper or a mother of ten. She said, "Who're you two?" The detectives heard a sudden shriek come from inside the house. Lady Cavanaugh looked back in the hallway and screamed, "Carissa! Get that cat out the washin' machine!"

"Just your regular old NYPD," said Mack. "Here to talk to you about one of your kids."

"They ain't *my* kids," said the lady. "Most these brats ain't even orphans yet. Bunch of rat parents leaving their weasel kids for others to take care of. Carissa! I know you heard me the first time, now you get that cat out the rinse cycle or God-help-me I'll slap you into yer twenties."

"Nana? Is that you?" said Ari on the comm unit.

Lady Cavanaugh stared down the hallway, brandishing the back of her hand in some kind of standoff. Carissa must have relented; a mewling sound came from a drenched cat, and Cavanaugh huffed, "Gaw, I wish to high heaven some of these kids would—"

"Whoa, whoa there, lady," said Mack.

"Can we come in, ma'am?" asked Saul.

The lumpy lady didn't have space on either side to let the detectives through. She wiggled backward into the hall like a catfish. Before Mack followed, she unzipped her jacket and felt the twin Desert Eagles dislodge from the grooves they'd dug in her rib cage. She glanced up at Saul, whose hands were still in his pea coat, and wondered if he even carried a firearm other than the BB shooter. She stepped inside the house first, just in case he was stupid enough not to.

Lady Cavanaugh barreled through the house toward the kitchen, smacking random kids and shouting threats, but otherwise resigned to living with a tangle of unwashed gremlins. The walls of the foster home had running tracks of Magic Markers, crayons, and the treads of toy cars. Saul counted at least seven different kinds of cereal scattered on the carpet. Two boys were wrestling on a second-floor landing, one of them squishing a Jell-O pudding cup in the other's hair. A little girl in an oversize shirt, Carissa most likely, ran across Mack's path dragging a run-down cat by the neck. The sharp sounds of toys with ratchets inside, a game of shriek tag, and blaring TV commercials paired nicely with the dull smells of moldering dishes, dried slobber, and dusty windowsills.

Mack stepped around a girl with a Mets cap who was spray-painting a boy's name on the drapes.

Everything in the kitchen was broken in some way. The glass doors leading to the backyard were splattered with grease from a fry-o-lator by the stove.

Lady Cavanaugh turned and said, "Well, which one do you want?"

"Kid named Mustard," said Saul.

"Runt of the litter," said the lady.

"We just left him on the island," said Saul. "Seems he's picked up a day job doing chores for a Bieman family."

"Wanted to talk to you 'bout him," said Mack.

Lady Cavanaugh crossed her arms and rested them on her countertop chest. "I don't know no Biemans, but Mustard sure don't have no day job."

"We *just* spoke to him, ma'am," said Mack.

"Well, you *just* got yourself dizzy, 'cause you didn't 'spoke' to no Mustard."

From Saul's pocket, Ari said into the comm channel, "Man, she has got to be my nana. Saul. Hey, Saul, ask her if she ever used to be a snaggly old catfish. Or no, better not take the chance—just shoot her now."

Old Lady Cavanaugh did resemble a catfish. Her bottom teeth were as jagged as the city skyline. Mack missed something the lady said because of Ari yapping. She put her chin in her shoulder and said, "Shhh."

"Don't shush me, missy," said Lady Cavanaugh.

"I wasn't—"

Lady Cavanaugh interrupted, "I *said* you bunch of tick-tack po-leese can't even shake down a ten-years-old boy for his name? And now you waste *my* day, tell *me* I got a kid runnin' around half-cocked on the island when I *know*—"

Ari couldn't take it anymore. "I'm telling you, Saul," he shouted into the comm channel. "Shoot her. Shoot her. Take a gun, and put a bullet in her."

"Sorry, buddy, don't carry a gun," whispered Saul.

But Lady Cavanaugh had a librarian's ears. She cocked her head back. The steam coming out of her ears would probably smell like French fries. "Boy, you *didn't* just say that," she said. "You don't carry a gun? What's that supposed to mean? You threatening me?"

"Shoot her, Saul. Knock her out with BBs if you have to. Do it."

"You don't carry a gun," scoffed the lady. "You don't carry your daggum right mind, either."

"I would kill her," said Ari. "Or at least wound her. I would. I'd take the departmental heat, shuffle the paperwork, but I'd put her down. I'd do it."

Mack had to shout over Lady Cavanaugh's tongue lashes and Ari's tirade in their ears to say, "Can you tell us anything about Mustard?"

Lady Cavanaugh stopped. "No," she spat. "Nothing he couldn't tell you himself."

Mack slouched against the fridge. She was tired of coming up short. This was the first chance to do real police work since the disciplinary committee had busted her down the ranks. And now they'd have to drive all the way back to the Bieman residence with no more leads than when they left a few hours ago. Then Lady Cavanaugh grumbled, "See for yourself. He's been out there all morning, making a rocket or something."

"Huh? What'd she just say?" said Ari.

Both Saul and Mack looked at the sliding-glass door to the backyard. Then they looked at each other. Mack put a finger in the air and said, "Wait. Mustard and Randy look practically the same, except Mustard has a scar over his eyebrow. And we saw the scar on the kid hanging around the Biemans' place. Randy's at school, so . . ."

"That leaves the kid out there making a rocket launcher," said Saul.

"Either it's Randy's wish," said Ari, "or the orphan had himself a wicked idea, too."

Mack drew her twin Desert Eagles. Saul drew Sweetheart, and the two bounded toward the sliding door and into the backyard.

CHAPTER 5

FOR THE THIRD time that day, Detectives Mack and Saul, code-named Five-Leaf and Ji-Ji, part of the classified Imaginary Crimes Unit, jumped out with guns blazing and scared the living bejeebuz out of an orphan who answered to the name Mustard. The startled boy yowled and let go of one of the rockets he was working on. The plastic rocket screamed toward Mack's head, spiraling like a sidewinder missile.

In one blurry motion—so quick that Saul wondered if it was humanly possible—Mack managed to turn her shoulder just in time to let the missile graze past, then brought up her Magnum and blasted the other rocket Mustard was holding. Smithereens of plastic and cardboard flew in all directions. Mustard flinched, then sat shivering with the blown-up remains of his rocket still in his hand.

The whole yard was a rectangular patch of grass the size of an end zone, with an eight-foot wooden fence to cordon it off. Saul walked over and stood over the kid. "Howsit going?" he said.

The boy looked and acted just like the one they had interrogated early that morning, measly. "I knew it," said Mack. "So, *you're* Mustard."

"It's, it's 'cause I put it on my chicken wings," said the kid, still quivering in his undersize brown sweats.

"What did he say, chicken wings?" said Ari. "That don't match the record, Saul."

"Last time you told us you put it on your eggs," said Saul.

Mustard dropped the broken rocket and put both palms up to his face. He sobbed, "I put mustard on my eggs, too!"

Mack kneeled down next to the watery Mustard and put her hand on his shoulder. "Hey, it's okay, little man. Putting mustard on things isn't a crime."

"It's not?" said the boy, peeking out from behind his wet palms. Mack smiled and shook her head no. "Then why are you shooting me?"

"Lemme talk to him," said Ari.

Mack sighed. "Honestly, Mustard, we don't have time to tell you why."

An aborted pause. "That's okay," said Mustard. He seemed used to the idea of people not having time for him, maybe more comfortable with it than anything else. Pieces of the fuselage were scattered on the dirt launchpad he'd created. Mustard picked up a lacerated plastic hunk and tried to fit it, like a jigsaw puzzle, among the scraps of wreckage in his hand. Saul picked up the red plastic tip of the rocket and held it out to the kid. Mustard looked up. He reached into Saul's wide brown hand and took it. A sweet grin. Honey Mustard. The kid had a scar over his eyebrow, just like the one they had brought in that morning (not to mention the same brown jammies). They had let the wish go, 'cause he obviously didn't want to kill the Biemans. But Mack had been right. It was still a Wicked Idea made Suddenly Human. It just hadn't been Randy's idea.

Now all they needed to know was what impossible thing Mustard wished for.

"What were you working on?" asked Saul, squatting down next to him but clear of the launchpad and any tiny invisible ground crew.

"I mean, there were lots of phases," said Mustard, bashful but proud. "Phase one was my surface-to-air missile silo. Then I was gonna make a mounted warhead with the wood over there"— he pointed to a moldy wine crate in the corner of the yard. If not for the liddle lithp, or maybe because of it, he sounded like a NASA engineer. Even a deadbeat dad would have had the decency to get him out of those jammies and into a science camp.

"A rocket launcher," said Mack.

"Uh-huh," said Mustard.

"For the love of Aquaman," said Ari, "why is it every kid we meet is a munitions expert?"

"Do you like war games?" said Saul.

Mustard shrugged. "Not really."

Saul glanced at Mack. She shook her head. They didn't need a debrief to tell them they weren't getting anywhere. And now they had two wishes on the lam, en route to crimes that ought not to be. There wasn't any time to explain to the kid, as they'd done for Randy, and the captain had pinched them already about talking too much. Then Mack said, "Hey, Mustard, let's play a game."

The kid put down the pieces of the rocket. "Okay."

"It's a quiz game," said Mack. "Like, if you were an animal, what kind of animal would you be?"

"Donkey Kong," said Mustard. He turned to Saul.

"My turn?" said Saul. Mustard nodded. "I'd be a goldfish."

Ari spoke into their earbuds, "You're a good man, Sulaiman al Djinn."

"What about you?" said Mustard, looking up at the female detective.

Mack put a finger to her lips to think. "I would be a seagull, or a heron, or one of those bears that eat salmon from the river."

"You are a stone-face gargoyle," said Ari. "You're a fugly sea cow."

Mack grinned at Saul. Then she said, "Okay, let's say it was your birthday—"

"It was my birthday," said Mustard.

"Really? When?"

"A few weeks ago."

"Perfect, what did you wish for?"

The kid clammed up. "I dunno," he said. Maybe he was ashamed of it. Or maybe he still wanted it to come true. Everybody knows you can't tell people what you wished for. Dreams, like crimes, are better kept in the dark.

"Well, I'll tell you what I would wish for," said Mack, trying to jump start the kid, "I'd wish for . . ."

The detective stopped short, sucker-punched by her own question. Her mouth was still open, waiting on a thought; then it closed. Nothing. You would have thought she had nothing to wish for. Saul wondered what kind of story Angie was gonna dig up in the Wishing Post archives. *What was Mack hiding?*

"You know," said Saul resting his hand, heavy as a family quilt, on Mustard's shoulder, "I lost my family a long time ago. If I had a birthday, I'd wish to see them again."

Mustard's eyes grew wide to take in the entire king-size detective at once. They could see what he was wondering. Maybe if he got shoulders so broad, he could bear not having a family, too.

"Is that what you asked for?" said Saul.

Mustard nodded. "I wished my parents would want me back," he said. Then he picked his nose and added, "I'm not an orphan, you know. My parents just aren't around."

Mack sucked the air through her teeth and rose to her feet. Saul's knees both groaned as he got up. They'd rather the kid had wished for an undead army, a skeletal warhorse, and the cursed ice-blade of the Lich King to go rampaging up through the Brooklyn petting zoo. At least Mack could pistol-whip the wicked idea of murdering a bunch of llamas and reanimating them into a zombie herd.

But this was one of those cases that made police work stink like a witch's chimney.

"I need some chai," said Saul.

"It's chilly out here," said Mack. "Maybe you should come inside." Mustard was too busy sorting the pieces of his rocket and the fallen leaves.

Maybe there wasn't anything wrong with wanting your parents to love you.

Of the wishes that *can't, won't, or shouldn't happen,* maybe this was one of those wishes that just wouldn't happen. It could, and it should, but it just wouldn't.

The wish would become one of those pitiful creations they'd

pick up now and then. No resisting arrest, just a hangdog apparition, roaming around, waiting to come true, but unable for some reason nobody could guess. Mustard's parents were never going to want him.

In the brick house they had a minimum-security wing for them—because they never lasted long. They'd walk the prison yard with their hands in their pockets, wondering why they were in prison for a crime that didn't seem a crime.

First thing to go was their shape. The lines that made them up would look wobbly, like they were just heat rising from the pavement. Then their color would fade like an old Polaroid. Then the wicked ideas—that no one could tell you why they were wicked— would become the night's shade, the musty air.

"Doesn't matter," said Saul as they walked back into the kitchen.

"What doesn't matter?" said Mack.

"That he only wants Doc Bieman to love him again," said Saul. "His wish is with Clara right now, trying to act lovable. That thing's a weapon, don't care how pitiful."

"So we all agree that Mustard is the doc's first son, right?" said Ari. "Got a grad student pregnant or something. And left the baby at the orphanage so he could get with Randy's mom . . . before she was a mom? Right? That's what we all think?"

In the kitchen, Lady Cavanaugh was eating cashews from a plastic bag. "Ma'am," said Mack, "what can you tell us about Mustard's parents?"

"Some egghead dropped him off, says he sent his mama back to Russia or something when her visa ran out. And he'd got another woman to marry, so this kid was old baggage. He pays the rent, and we keep the kid."

"What's Mustard's real name?"

"Neville Jr. or somethin'."

Mack put a finger to her comm unit and said, "Yep, that's what we think."

As they walked out, the boy with the Yankees cap was still in the hallway, spray-painting the drapes. As Saul stepped around him, he said, "Hey, kid, what's your name?"

The boy had a familiar sneer. "I got lots of names, mister," he said. "What's it to ya?" Then he added, "Got one for every letter."

Saul stopped. Mack came up short behind him. "What?" she said when he whipped around and looked at the dirty carpet where the boy used to be.

"He's gone," said Saul. "And he used to be a Mets fan."

Mack's expression was blank.

"You really didn't notice anything weird about the boy?" said Saul, trying to catch a twitch, a shift, any recognition that she'd used the same line on him back at the diner, that she had every name in the alphabet too.

"He's got a bunch of aliases," said Mack, "and you keep calling him a boy when I'm pretty sure it was a girl, but other than that, no."

One of those pauses where everybody's too tired to change the channel.

Saul rolled his eyes, exhaled, and said, "Randy." Then he walked through the kitchen to the backyard and found Randy's wish with its hands around Mustard's neck.

* * *

The ghul looked exactly like Randy Bieman. It slackened its grip on Mustard's throat, but the orphan's body hung limp in the wish's arms.

Saul put his hand on the comm unit and said, "Central, I got visual on the wish. Looks like a G—as in ghul—class. Confirmed shape-shifter. Repeat: G-class shape-shifter, copy?"

A crackle, a nasal reply, "Ten-four, Ji-Ji. Proceed to apprehend. Standing by."

Randy's wish held Mustard up to a standing position with one hand clutching the orphan's neck. The other hand hovered over Mustard's exposed throat. Saul moved his hand up to his holster. The wish growled. Two of the fingers on its hand elongated, then sharpened into straight razors. A wicked idea. Mustard's head was slung backward and his mouth was open. As a warning, the wish tapped its morphed fingers on Mustard's teeth.

The sharp clicks made Saul pause. Randy's wish leaned forward on the balls of its feet and arched its hackles like a wolf curling over the orphan boy—Randy's half-brother. Its teeth grew outside the curtains of its lips.

Ari said, "You gotta take him now, big guy. None of that nicey-nice."

"Shhh," whispered Saul.

"Don't shush me, Saul. Not in front of the perps."

Mack's voice cut in on the comm channel. "The house is secure. I'm joining your position."

Over his shoulder, the ex-genie saw his new partner approach from the kitchen, baring the twin Magnums. "Drop him," said Mack.

The wish panicked at the sight of Mack. It dropped Mustard's unconscious body on the grass and darted. To Saul, it looked like the wish was scared of his partner, not her guns.

Mack sent a volley of rounds, each one exploding out of the barrel with a cone of fire, toward Randy. The wish took the shape of a squirrel, bouncing across the yard, then an ocelot. The .38-caliber bullets splintered the moldy wine crates and shattered a hanging pot of azaleas.

The ocelot's legs stretched as its body expanded into a cheetah. It sprinted and leaped toward the fence. When it hit the wooden surface, it turned and launched itself off the fence, flying back toward them like a swimmer in a pool. As it lanced through the air, the wish's face thinned into the prong of a swordfish.

Saul and Mack lunged in opposite directions to dodge the attack, but the blade bone cut Saul across the temple as it sliced past. When it landed, the wish was a monkey, hopping around the yard, hurling rocks.

"Now!" said Ari. "Snuff the punk."

"All right, all right," said Saul. "Quit screaming."

Saul pulled Sweetheart from the holster and ran toward the monkey. He sighted the BB gun and sent three pellets whistling through the air.

Tack, tack, tack. The monkey squealed at the stinging shots and dropped the stone in its paw. The outline of its body rippled with pain.

Just as the ghul turned back into its original shape, Saul came barreling down on him and smashed his right fist into Randy's face.

"Ha-ha!" shouted Ari over the unconscious ghul—shaped like a kid with a shiner and a broken jaw. "Ha. Howsit feel now, Ran-dee?

Guess every wish comes true, and dreams are songs our hearts sing . . . except ones that try to kill family and get beat like a friggin' rug, you little urinal cake!"

Saul cuffed Randy's wish and carried it through the house. Mack stopped in the kitchen, where Lady Cavanaugh was leaning on the counter, eating cashews.

"Ma'am, you should probably check on the boy," said Mack.

Lady Cavanaugh looked out the glass doors. Mustard was sprawled out like a starfish. "Wish his papa would wise up." She sighed. She didn't even ask whom Saul was carrying. "But you know what they say," she said. "If wishes were horses, even beggars would ride."

"Oh, they're not horses," said Mack.

Back at the 3-1, Alvarez and Goodie were still lounging around the DT bureau, the captain was still counting case files at his desk, and the seal on the floor still read, "To project and to swerve."

The first star of that night would still be a deadly weapon for someone else. And Angie was probably still at the Wishing Post—a lambent halo sitting on her hair like a tiara, wondering how an angel ever ended up in a dispatch office.

The fact was they had all been wish-makers of some kind—the angel, the fisher prince, leprechaun, pixie, troll, and genie. All except the captain—he was just an old man. They knew the job. Some of them even liked the job. Most of them, it was all they had.

The badge set them apart, made them outsiders among their own kind. Alvarez talked like he was a Don Juan of the pixies—Ari like he vacationed with mermaids. The truth was they were nothing but

Wish Police. But that was a choice they'd all made. No point crying about it now.

When Mack slammed the door, dragging Randy Bieman's wish behind her, Alvarez took his feet off the desk and said, "Wokay, you got some cholita in you, Mami."

Mack shoved the kid into the metal seat across from Alvarez and cuffed him to the armrest. "Don't call me mommy," she said. Mack looked at the comic books on his desk, then at Goodie, still knitting a shawl. "We take a case off the board, and you guys haven't even started?" said Mack.

Alvarez shrugged. Mack took off her leather jacket and dropped it on her desk. She filled a paper cone at the water cooler. As she drank, Randy's wish squinted at Alvarez and said, "Why are you wearing makeup?" Alvarez leaned forward over his desk, a comic book in his hand crumpled into a ball.

"Whatchu say?"

"I think she's making it up," said Angie. Saul stood in the tiny dispatch office. Angie sat at the switchboard. A touch screen showed a map of the city with dotted lights representing the imaginary crime activity for that night. The room was dark. The city looked like a Christmas tree. It even had Angie and her shining halo to look over it. "I couldn't find any records on Mack before three years ago, when she joined the force. Before that, she could have been anywhere."

Saul didn't tell Angie about the ghul getting spooked at the sight of his partner or the fact that her stories didn't match up. Angie was a good girl—by definition she was—but she had a lot of time on her hands, and gossip was her stock in trade. Those morsels would have tempted even a cherub. Besides, Saul was the last person to give up somebody else's secrets.

"Thanks, Angie," said Saul. "I owe you."

"Wait, what happened with your case?"

She wanted him stay, maybe cook her a nice penne with grigio for dinner. She'd told Alvarez once, at the Christmas party, that she liked Saul 'cause he was so . . . normal. She just wanted a regular guy.

"I got this one, Saul," said Ari. "Truth is, Angie, we got a seawall of paperwork. Turns out we had two kids get their wishes crossed. Rich kid wanted his family dead, so we stake the place. Orphan's wish shows up instead and plays like a pound puppy. So at first, we lost the scent."

"Oh, my," said Angie, her eyes admiring Saul.

"But then we finally track the real orphan to his foster home, and he turns out to be richie's half-brother. Then Randy's death wish shows up, and we grab it before it starts popping family members— guess he started with the furthest one out."

"What about the orphan's wish?" said Angie.

"Seems to be harmless, a *hopeless cause* kind of thing. The dad just doesn't want him. So he's hanging around the stepmom trying to be useful."

"We'll pick him up after we book this one," said Saul.

"But—" said Angie.

"Darling, we really gotta go," said Ari.

"But what if the orphan's wish is the big case we just put out?"

"Goodie and Alvarez are on that," said Ari.

"But that's a murder case," said Angie. "A big one, second tier, sila. They could all be dead already—"

"You're wearing makeup around your eyes, like a girl," said Randy's wish, a bratty sneer on his face just like Randy himself. "And you have fairy wings. And your ears look like Tinker Bell's."

Goodie didn't look up from her knitting. She said under her breath, "Tranquilo, baby. Don't let the—"

Alvarez lunged over the desk at the kid and shouted, "I ain't no Tink! Say it, say it, 'fore I put holes in you. Say I ain't no Tink."

Faster than a speeding Mexican pixie, Mack uncuffed Randy from the chair and scooped him away from Alvarez. Goodie looked up from her knitting for the first time since Mack had arrived at the 3-1. Maybe leprechauns could move like that—maybe, but she doubted it. Mack moved as smoothly as liquid fire—and even quicker than bad news. She nodded to Alvarez to sit back down. "Oh, that was *very* good, baby, very good," she said. Alvarez relaxed a little. "You just found us a real case," said Goodie.

Mack yanked Randy's wish down the hall by his ear, swung open a holding cell, and tossed him inside. "Jeez," she said, "if I had one like you, I'd get my tubes tied."

When she turned around, Saul was standing in the jail cell door. He held her riding jacket.

"We gotta go," he said.

CHAPTER 6

THE SUN'S YOLK had broken on the sharp edge of the city and flowed down into another evening. The autumn was giving up, letting the bully winter take more months than it deserved. Some brothers just don't know how to treat each other.

When the lamppost flickered on in the residential block, it revealed the same dark figure as the night before. The tall man in a pea coat — and a skullcap his wife might have made for him centuries ago. When he breathed out, it looked like the stirring of a galaxy.

The man reached back and rubbed the side of the lamp, but there was no magic in it and no home for a genie to find.

Nothing had changed. The brownstones still huddled together and looked down their noses at the walkabouts. The tabby cat knocked over another garbage can leaping over the wrought-iron fence. Maybe that was the hard rub. If the Wish Police did their jobs right, nothing would change. It chafed.

*   *   *

"Saul. Ay, Saul, listen, man, we break down the door right now, and I bet we catch Mustard's wish playing Jenga or something with the little girl."

"No," said Saul.

Mack's voice crackled over the comm unit. "I knew it," she said. "I knew there was something off about the kid when he blew me the kiss and took off running the first time." Saul and Ari didn't need the comm units to hear Mack grinding the engine at the end of the block. She added, "And then later I thought if I had a kid like Randy, I'd never want another boy."

"So when Mustard's wish figured it out, badda bing badda boom, new objective. Gotta shiv the kid before the Biemans would ever adopt another one," said Ari. "But Randy ain't home, so the wish is prolly playing UNO with Clara right now, while we freeze our fins off."

"Everybody holds position until Clara is secure," warned Saul.

"You spoil children, you know that, Saul? You spoil 'em. So what, she's an unwitting hostage of a murderous ultra-powerful sila, and suddenly you want to play it safe? I say you take that big boot of yours . . ."

Saul slipped his hand from the butt of his BB gun down to his coat pocket. With two fingers he pinched the opening . . .

"Hey! All right, all right, ease up, will ya? Don't forget that sweet little girl in there almost boiled me alive."

"I hear Princess Fashion Show *likes* chamomile tea," said Saul. He felt Ari ramming him in the stomach, but it hurt about as much as a goldfish's head butt.

*   *   *

Even in dog years, the temperature wouldn't have amounted to the driving age. The night was all anticipation. Maybe it would snow. Maybe the sun would never come back around.

It felt like a theater hall, when the houselights have gone dark but the stage curtain hasn't moved. An in-between and in-betwixt time, when maybe you'll get what you want, or maybe what you want will get you. The folks in the seats are scared to check their watches. It might not be the classy thing to do. They're holding their breath without knowing it.

Mack whispered over the line, "Spotted the mark, heading east from my position."

Saul squinted down the sidewalk—it was Randy, all right, walking home two hours late. His hoodie obscured his face but also kept him from noticing Saul. Randy jumped onto the stoop of his house and pounded on the door. "Mom! I'm home from detention. MOM! Lemme in, I forgot my keys."

His fist got tired, so he turned around and mule-kicked with his heel. The decorative glass panes rattled in the loose joints. When the door swung open midway through a kick, Randy almost did the splits but caught himself on the frame.

"What're you doing? I almost fell—"

Randy didn't finish yelling, because it was Mustard standing in the foyer, not Mrs. Bieman.

"Go, go, go!" whispered Saul, as he moved to approach from the blind side.

"Who the heck are you?" said Randy.

Face-to-face, it was easy to tell the boys shared a father. Mustard was a little taller, since he was older by about eighteen months. Randy had his mother's jaw.

"I'm their new son," said Mustard. "They don't want you anymore."

When Mustard's wish swung his hand at Randy's neck, it was a karate chop, and it was moving faster than an impulse. At that speed it would have lopped Randy's head right off. But the sila's hand slashed across something much tougher than a seventh-grader's neck.

Mustard's hand had cut through Saul's pea coat and sliced into his shoulder. Saul gritted his teeth as he reached out and pulled Randy down the porch steps, to the sidewalk below. Saul huddled over the shell-shocked boy, covering him until backup could arrive.

The sila was made from a whole decade of birthday candles and Christmas lists. It was faster than a speeding hero. For ten everlasting seconds, Mustard's wish was a blurry barrage. It jackhammered on Saul's back, elbowed his ribs, and knuckled his shoulders.

Saul's spine cracked like a rusted bike chain. Under his eyelids, white bursts of light popped in a quick scattershot.

It was only ten seconds. But it was a whole city of time for Mustard's wish. Randy shivered in a rain puddle. Saul covered him, like the heavy comforter his mom tucked him into every night. In the insulated space, the fight only sounded like a distant drumming. Saul let out a groan. Randy jolted at the noise. The sila had found the bleeding cut on Saul's shoulder and focused its attention. A thousand and one punches in a thousandth of a second—and a good chunk of the shoulder bone had crumbled into powder. Randy felt Saul's weight getting heavier on top of him. From somewhere under the detective's body, Randy could hear a voice screaming. "Angie! Angela, come in, for heaven's sake," shouted Ari. "This can't be happening. We got an officer down."

The sila was the size and shape of a fourteen-year-old, but it lifted Saul's limp body like a sleeping bag draped over Randy. Randy's hair was wet with the gray muck that the city's newspapers made with rainwater. He said, "I can give you money. M-m-my dad's rich."

Mustard's wish said, "So's mine."

It reached for Randy when the familiar growl of a '57 Triumph Bonneville interrupted. Mustard's wish looked up.

"You didn't think I'd back up my partner?" said Mack as she drove toward them on the sidewalk. "What're you, simple?"

The monster Mustard twitched when it saw Mack. And just like the night before, it hid the fear under a grin, a cocky pucker, and a nod.

But this time when the wish darted over the wrought-iron fence, it didn't have to keep up appearances. It hurdled the fence and rocketed past Mack in an instantaneous flash. A half a blink later, when the wish had really gotten itself up to a sprint, Mack felt a sonic boom slap her in the face and crack the center headlight of her bike. It had broken the sound barrier.

The sila was three blocks away in a fraction of a second. It looked back over its shoulder as it ran. A mistake. It's always a mistake. When it looked ahead again, Mack stood in front of him, her arm extended like a clothesline.

It was too late to stop. Mustard's wish clipped the arm at mach speed, upended, and hit the ground. Its head slammed into the pavement. The cracks that webbed out in the sidewalk would have broken every back in the PTA.

"You're under arrest," said Mack, turning the sila over and cuffing its wrists. "And you owe me money for my bike."

In the distance, the sirens of half a dozen squad cars hiccuped toward the scene. Saul's bleary voice came over the communication channel. "Did you get him?"

Mack lifted the sila by the handcuffs and said, "Go back to sleep, tough guy."

A light snow began to fall, the first of the season. The Biemans' house shimmered with cop lights. Neighbors peeped from their windows. Goodie stretched caution tape from a tree to a lamppost to cordon off the area. Alvarez got aggressive telling a civilian that he couldn't get back to his house after walking his dog.

Saul held his shoulder as he got up. Randy was tending a scrape on his knee. "You okay, kid?" Saul said.

"Randy!" shouted Mrs. Bieman. She ran down the steps to cradle her son. Dr. Bieman wasn't home yet. As usual, it was his family that had to clean up his mess. "What happened?" asked Mrs. Bieman. "Why are you shaking? What in the world happened?"

Randy glanced up, his eyes begging Saul not to say anything. The brat knew how much of this had been his fault. And that maybe, if he'd gotten his way, his mom would be dead right then instead of coddling him. Saul didn't say a word.

Clara appeared in the doorway in her pink nightgown. She held her doll, Felicity, who sported a brand-new hairstyle. Clara had cut it just like Mack's—short in the back, sharply getting longer as it came forward. And red, her mother's lipstick red.

Clara's doey eyes stared first at her brother—whimpering on the ground, wet and muddy—then at Saul, then at Randy again. She smiled, real big, and she said, "Are they gonna arrest him now?"

Saul shook his head. "No, doll, we aren't."

"But you will if he punches my head again?"

Saul had to turn away. Clara was the same age as his daughter, all those millennia ago. If Saul didn't turn away, he might have broken up worse than his shoulder. As he left he said, "Yeah, sweetheart, we'll put him away for good if he does that again."

Clara waved good-bye and helped Felicity wave good-bye, too. The detective slumped past the beat cops, under the cordon, and into the snowy evening. "Jeez," said Ari on a private line to Saul. "Sorry, big guy, it's a shabby thing."

CHAPTER 7

BACK AT THE luncheonette, the dinner rush was a young couple nursing one order of home fries and the old gander in the back, reading the *Times.* Jon poured another round of chai for Saul. "How about some cream of turkey? On the house, eh!"

Saul and Mack pushed the soups back across the counter. Ari swam manic circles in the water pitcher, to keep in fighting shape after being cooped up in the plastic bag all day. "I'm tired, Saul," said Ari. "I'm dogfish tired, after stayin' up all night. I might even be so tired I won't be able to fall asleep, if you know what I'm sayin'. But two busts in one night and making Alvarez and Goodie look like chumps. Made them our algae eaters, if you know what I'm sayin'."

"I know what you're saying," said Saul, talking a drink of hot tea. His shoulder was getting stiff under all the bandages the med guys had wrapped it in.

Mack swiveled around on her bar stool and leaned back on the counter. "Not bad for a new detail. They'll have to let me stay in homicide."

"Heck, Captain'll make us detectives first grade," said Ari, jumping like a dolphin into the air.

"No promotions," said Saul. It wouldn't be a promotion for Mack, just a reinstatement of her old rank. She didn't mention it.

"I know," said Ari, "but a fish can dream, can't he? All my life my nana tells me I won't amount to a coral junkie, and this DT first-grade badge, I could shove that in the old nag's face. But no, I got a best buddy who refuses to get promoted. Doesn't ask me how I feel about it. But hey, it's cool. I'll keep his identity secret. I'll go belly-up someday, a lowly second-grade DT, but it's cool. What're pals for? No problem. It's cool."

Saul nodded at Jon, who was watching the Greek soccer team play in a snowstorm during an earthquake—or maybe it was the TV. Jon reached into the pastry display and sprinkled some crumbs over Ari's pitcher.

"Is this . . . croissants, Jon?" said Ari as he pecked at the surface of the water. "Mmm, oh yeah, that's definitely fresh baked. It's all about how flaky it is with croissants. This is good."

Saul hid a grin by taking another drink of tea. Mack said, "For what it's worth, Alvarez is sure you're a regular. You and the captain."

"The pixie's half right," said Ari. "Mmm, this is a good pastry. This one's nicely done."

Saul had a look in his eye as far away as a sultan's dinner party. He blew a typhoon over the surface of his tea and said, "I asked Cap about that once. He looked at me and said, 'If I was regular, I wouldn't be eating so many fiber bars all the time.'"

Mack drained her chai and set it back down like a shot glass. She pushed off the counter and stood up. "I should get some sleep," she said, zipping her riding jacket.

"Hold on a minute," said Saul. He poured some more tea into her cup. "Something I don't get."

Mack slid some cash under the saucer. She put an elbow on the counter and waited. Saul traced a finger along the teapot. "I get how Randy wished his family would die. And Mustard had been wishing his parents would want him back. I get how the wishes crossed, and Randy goes to kill his half-brother, while Mustard figures his parents won't ever want another son as long as Randy is around. I get all that. I even get why Mustard's wish was sila—after all the kid's been through, he wants it pretty bad. Fine. I get that . . ."

Saul picked up the top of the teapot and looked inside. Nothing but dank tea leaves. The ex-genie closed one eye. Maybe he could read some kind of future in the shapes they made. Maybe he could see shadows of people he used to know. "But the thing I don't get is how you managed to drop a wish that strong."

"You saw that? I thought your eyes were swollen shut," said Mack, suddenly fascinated with a smudge on her shoe.

"Honey, half the block saw that and decided to lay off the sleepin' pills," said Ari. "The biggest bust the precinct has seen in years."

Saul said, "You outran a sila. Took it straight on and went muscle for muscle. Him and the ghul panicked every time they saw you. All day you've been telling me you're a gigantic leprechaun, but you can't decide if you're from Ireland or Brooklyn. You say you got more names than a directory, but Randy's wish used the same line at Lady Cavanaugh's place. And you couldn't think of a wish to tell Mustard. On top of that, Angie says she can't find so much as a magazine subscription on you before you joined the force."

"Your story's bogus, lady. Strictly fiction," added Ari.

Mack scraped the smudge on top of one shoe with the heel of the other. She made a *tsk* sound when it smeared and said, "What, is Angie scared 'cause I don't run around with a pet and shoot a BB gun?"

"Save it, lady. We know you're a wish," said Ari. "Nothing else is that strong."

"I've heard djinns are that strong," said Mack.

Saul didn't take the bait. He said, "If you're stronger than a sila, you're either an ifrit or a marid."

A muted gasp. Ari held his breath. Nobody ever imagined a marid would come around in their lifetime. Crimes so rotten, they were black plagues of the imagination. "I'm not that," said Mack, forgetting the shoe. She sat back down. "I think I'm an ifrit. I don't really know. I don't know what I'm supposed to do, either."

She wouldn't look up. The shame hung around her neck like a millstone. Somebody somewhere had wanted something they wouldn't, or couldn't, or shouldn't have. And that was her. A hopeless or hapless or hateful idea. Except she didn't know which one. Or wouldn't say. She couldn't be trusted anymore.

If he were smart, Saul would book her right then. So maybe he wasn't smart.

They sat on the gibbous bar stools and listened to exclamations of a Greek sportscaster and the sizzle of the fry-o-lator in the back kitchen. It was cooking lost potato chips, dregs of batter, and crumbs from a chicken patty.

Then Ari said, "Well, if nobody's gonna ask, I will. What can you do? My guess is you're an ice ifrit, what with yer demeanor and how bad you are with kids. But you could also be fire 'cause of how hot-headed you are. That could also be 'cause you're a woman. I dunno. Is *bad attitude* an element ifrits can control, Saul? Maybe she's a snark ifrit."

Mack was smiling again, if only because she imagined dropping a few Alka-Seltzer tablets into Ari's bag and swinging it around her head. "I like to ride. Maybe I'm a bike ifrit," she said, then added, "I dunno. I never figured it out. I'm a good swimmer . . ."

"No. No way," said Ari. "That's my thing. Don't take my thing."

"I assumed you were a fire ifrit," said Saul. "'Cause of the red hair."

"No, I think I'm still Irish."

Or, as they both knew, the duplicate of someone Irish. At some point, she was going to commit a terrible crime. It had to happen. And Saul would have to bring her down. Lock her up in the brick house till she was forgotten.

For now, he nodded for Jon to bring hot water and said, "Have some more chai." Maybe it wasn't such a bad thing. Each of them had a secret—heck, everybody does. They could hide each other.

Maybe there were more reasons for things than the ones they knew. Or maybe not. Maybe they could be friends for a while, anyway.

The whole city had a thousand and one possibilities that night, and the moon was the best seat in the house. Jon came by with another teapot, and Saul rubbed the side of it, just to make sure.

"Hey," he said, nodding at the digital clock radio in the corner. "It's eleven eleven. Make a wish."

Mack laughed 'cause it was a little sad. And maybe worth a try. She looked up. It was eleven twelve.

DOOM
with a
VIEW

"Okay, you axed for it, Piggie." Wolfie is huffing —
huff, huff. And Wolfie is puffing — puff, puff, poof.
Badda boom! Nothing. This is a brick house;
they do not blow over so easy. So Wolfie gets himself
a ladder, climbs up onto the roof. Piggie sees him
climb onto the roof. Wolfie makes for the chimney.
Piggie lights a fire in the grate. Wolfie goes down
the chimney; he burns. Wolfie burns. Wolfie
burns and Piggie lives. Happily ever after.

— Christopher Walken, *Saturday Zoo* (1993)

Chapter 1

I Swear I Be Not Proud

I KNOW IT'S only self-centered wieners who say stuff like, "You don't *know* me." But it's true. You don't know me. You may think you do. But you don't. Most people think I'm some cosmic bogeyman here to rain down God's holy judgment on the heads of mankind. That is completely untrue and, honestly, a little hurtful. I have feelings, you know. I have a sense of humor. I *hunger and thirst*. Well, actually I don't really hunger or thirst, but I have it on good faith that I'm moderately funny.

And don't tell me the problem isn't all the stereotypical depictions of me on television, because it is. We all know TV is turning our brains into yogurt, but we don't care 'cause the screen people are so shiny. Harlequin novels aren't helping, either. They all describe me as a tall, dark hunk with undulating loins. That's nice, but it sets people up for a letdown.

I'd say I look more like Matt Damon than Skeletor. Okay, maybe not *Matt Damon*, but you know, that look. That healthy corn-fed look.

So let's just get it all straightened out right now. Nothing on me heaves or undulates—I live alone actually. And I don't judge anybody—except for people on TV.

All the judging's from the main office. I just take people individually, when I get a Recovery Notice in my in-box. That's it. In that way I'm closer to a cabbie than what you'd call a harbinger of darkness. I mean, *harbinger?* When you actually see me, you'll realize you're only embarrassing yourselves with stuff like "harbinger."

I'm even courteous most times and tell people what finally did it. I don't have to do that, you know. I could just point at them with an icy finger and let them whimper all the way to the waiting room upstairs. But instead, I'm indulging their endless questions about all the damage cheezy poofs did to their livers.

And here's what I get for the trouble: a reputation as the ultimate bad guy.

I mean, the Ghost of Christmas Future? Come on. A black cloak? A skeletal hand? A sickle? That's just libelous. I'm a vegetarian, since it's your business. I take pictures of my bunny sleeping in my house slippers. I collect Precious Moments dinnerware. I mean, really, I'm bleeding here. You cut me.

And if you thought this was gonna be another war scroll or my tell-all of every famous person that begged for mercy, then you're wrong again. This is a love story, punk. A certifiable, irrevocable, maybe sometimes metaphysical *romance.* It began a long time ago, in Old Timey Europe, as a lot of love stories do, with two people hating each other. . . .

Oh, and also, they all croak by the end of this story. Just letting you know now . . .

Chapter 2

Better Bred
Than Wed

BABBO GIOVANNI WAS the don of the Chianti family in
Cortona. Pierre le Seigneur was head of the Vouvray family in the
Loire Valley. Simply put: Giovanni Chianti did not like Seigneur
Vouvray. With names like Chianti and Vouvray, you might think the
trouble was over wine. It'd be easy to imagine wealthy old men, yelling at each other from the grand porches of their vineyard estates,
arguing over reds and whites, and whose country tortured witches
better, and whose Riviera had less tourists. But no, Giovanni and
Pierre weren't winemakers, although they did despise each other
because of their livelihoods. It wasn't in the common trades like
bookbinding or carpentry that Pierre and Giovanni competed for
acclaim. It was mid-market home decorative products. Well, really
just one particular product, made of their two arts.

Pierre was a flower quilter. He hand-sewed silk sunflowers, velvet violets, and poplin poppies with such delicate digits that his
fellow Frenchmen came up with an idiom: "He's Vouvrayed it." Like
if a peasant managed to harvest ten acres of flax in one day—that

would be some genius-level toiling—and everybody would say, "He Vouvrayed that pitch." Unfortunately, the Academy of French Language killed the new idiom before it hit the dictionaries. I couldn't do anything but watch, then gather the remains as if it were Latin or the phrase "cool beans."

Nonetheless, when Pierre Vouvray hung his trifocals on the hook of his long and knobby nose, the entire village knew that he needed perfect silence. As he hemmed his denim daisies, millers brought their grist wheels to a complete stop. Ducks wouldn't quack. Children would halt their school-yard games to sit under the shade of trees and calmly play games like "silent reflection" and "sitting on your hands." Mimes pretty much continued as they were, but every-one else in the entire Loire Valley held their breath so that nothing would disturb Pierre le Seigneur.

Everyone, that is, but Chloe, his daughter, whose humming was the only noise Pierre approved of while he worked. And truth be told, he secretly cherished it more than even the work itself. Pierre's flowers may have brightened up millions of bank lobbies around the world, and he may have been the "Prized Genius of the Valley," but it was Chloe that he prized above all else.

Babbo Giovanni, back in Cortona, worked in a completely different style. He was a marble painter, which is just as intricate a job as flower quilting, as any marble painter will tell you. Babbo painted the colorful patterns inside of toy marbles better than anybody. This was before marble making became the exact science that it is today. They didn't have temperature-controlled kilns, prefabricated glass rods, or any of that fancy stuff the celebrity marble craftsmen are using nowadays. Babbo Giovanni had to develop all his own techniques. At first people thought he was an evil alchemist harvesting the essences of rainbows and women's cosmetics.

First, he painstakingly cut Murano glass beads in half with a hair from the chest of the monster, Bernardo the Hammer which could cut through anything, even the scales of a thousand-year dragon in the middle of true love. Bernardo the Hammer was such an evil, irritating man that his heart became black and bilious (we didn't talk much on the way down). It was like a poisoned well inside his chest, and the hairs sprouted without anything but the two Primal Sins, pride and fear, to nourish them. Anything that touched one of Bernardo's hairs immediately drowned in despair. Every cell they touched would wallow in its own semi-permeable misery. And so each hair could cut through anything, like tiny medieval lightsabers, ripping cell walls with no other Force than sheer cruelty.

How Giovanni came to possess a Bernardo chest hair is a story so mortifying that I can only tell it when the birth rate in the world is high enough and a few extra fatalities by extreme shock and uncontrollable laughter won't shake things up. Suffice it to say that Giovanni had plucked the rare item and could now snack on coconuts with ease.

Giovanni had carefully wrapped the curly hair around the only two tines of an old (even for back then) olive fork. With such a powerful device, he had to be ever vigilant. If a townsman came to his workshop and thought it was a dental floss holder, the poor guy would probably prevent gingivitis all the way up to his brain. I've never seen one of those, but I taxi about six kids a year who have managed to wrap the floss around their necks and somehow gotten the other end tied to the leg of a stampeding zoo animal. So . . . yeah, now you know, and knowing is pretty unsettling if you ask me.

After cutting the marbles, Giovanni sat at his easel with each clamped under a microscope lens. He'd sing an operetta and let his mind wander. Then, to the rhythm of the music, he would brandish his brush, which had exactly three fine bristles, plucked from the tail of the family mule, Santa Maria. And then Babbo would paint. Every once in a while, his son, Giacomo, would bring him a basil-and-tomato sandwich. Babbo would take a break, declare, "Let's see the French seamstress do that!" and run outside to chase pheasants with his son, whom he loved.

Who's to say which is more difficult, hand-sewing a flower so perfect that nature itself would be fooled or painting the swirls of a thousand tiny universes inside the center of crystalline globes? No one alive these days, that's for sure. Frankly, the crafts have been entombed for centuries. I have them inside an oak duvet chest at the foot of my bed, along with pickling pigs' feet and full-contact hopscotch.

Unlike Pierre, Giovanni painted his colorful constellations by committee. He'd mosey through the stone streets of Cortona with a leather purse filled with tiny planets, and each time he passed someone, he stopped to get their advice. The traveling medicine show gave him the idea to create a miniature starscape by sprinkling paint onto the glass with a toothbrush. A roving puppy made him think of dragging a wet towel over a painted surface to make speckled streaks. Even Nonna Brava—the old lady who sat by the second-story window of her home, yelling at pushcarts to slow down and eavesdropping on the conversations of young lovers—had an idea for Giovanni. "Stupido Gio," she spat, "you need a real job one of these days." Admittedly, Gio was just about to think of heating the paint for a tie-dyed effect before Nonna started yelling, but Gio gave her credit, anyway.

Of course, the reason Babbo and Pierre became such bitter rivals should be obvious by now. Everybody knows, marbles and fake flowers are the principal components of those decorative vases that are filled with marbles and fake flowers. They have entire aisles of them these days at the mega-marts, with all different shaped vases. The marbles hold the flowers in place and resemble water if you're real forgiving. The flowers never wilt, which makes them perfect for offices and lazy people.

The marbles are sometimes river stones and the flowers are sometimes candles, but more often than not, it's the balls and bulbs in a glass vase for $27.99.

They're not exactly my cup of tea. But hey, to each his own, as they say. That is, until they bite the big one, then, to each *my* own.

In Old Timey Europe, around the time chubby German kids were getting eaten by witches in gingerbread houses and all the hot chicks had to be chained to a tower, the vases were *huge*. Every season you'd see unscrupulous peddlers toting around a pile of them to sell at ridiculous prices, because everyone had to have them. And I can tell you it wasn't just a fad, because it hasn't vanished since. Old couples, kitsch collectors, single dads trying to spice up a living room—they all go straight for the faux foliage in marble arrangements.

Pierre and Giovanni were the only two grand masters in the art of vase filling. And so naturally, friendship and professional courtesy were out of the question. They hadn't ever met, mind you. There were no trade shows back then. Giovanni and Pierre disliked each other by reputation alone. When Pierre presented his finest creation at the court of King Louis, the king actually removed a perfect fountain branch of linen lilies in order to paw at the toy balls underneath. And when Giovanni was commissioned to decorate the summer villa of the Duchess of Como, the tasteless cow walked through the halls and ordered more fabric flowers. "Flowers?" said Giovanni, pacing his workshop afterward. His son, Giacomo, sat on a nearby counter, dangling his legs. "Flowers!" Giovanni never returned to Lake Como. When Pierre heard of the episode, he sent a nice thank-you card.

And so, by the time Pierre and Giovanni assumed the mantles of the world's undisputed best, their animosity by proxy had ballooned to a full-scale hate by mail. It seemed that no one could reconcile the two geniuses of the craft. The rivalry of their houses would last until Chinese manufacturing.

Chapter 3

I Don't Smile on Them *All*

BUT NOTHING — and I mean nothing people come up with, whether civilizations or cities or feuds — lasts very long on the eternal scale. If anyone can attest to this, it's me. From high enough in the exosphere, a nuclear blast looks like a bursting pimple. A tsunami kinda resembles a landmass tucking itself into bed. A massive earthquake just looks like the earth is getting goose bumps. Those things that send shock waves through the populace, the ones so catastrophic that the rich start giving to the poor, they don't even blow stardust across the wind chimes on my porch. So, to be honest, you're not even dust in the wind.

What can I say; my graveside manner has withered.

The point is if we're talking big picture, everything made gets unmade eventually. It all just sputters out after the time is up. Trust me, I've seen more contraptions that have passed for ladies' undergarments over the years than is probably appropriate. A bright idea for a new pyramid scheme, the memory of killing a hundred insects, even the reason you hate that one Indian restaurant, they'll all fade on you.

And for the most part, it's best to let 'em RIP. Just pray I don't take them in bulk.

Like all those other things, the rancor of Giovanni and Pierre had to expire eventually. But let's not jump to postmortem theoreticals just yet. There's a lot of story in between angels and autopsy.

As I said before, Giovanni had a fifteen-year-old son, Giacomo, whom I knew very well. He was barely knee-high when we met, during a plague they called "The Great Mortality." When the pandemic hit their village for three long weeks, I brushed past him over and over again to ferry his friends and neighbors. The shopkeeper who snuck him a caramel every time he came in with his father. The dog from the alley behind the inn. The distant cousin for whom he was intended. All of them I visited. The town was emptied. I even took the rats.

Until one morning, I came for Giacomo's mother. By then, the boy knew who I was, even though he was just a pup. He'd seen the leather dry up as I walked past the tannery. He'd heard the bells toll, as they say. So when he saw me that sunny Thursday in June, as she lay on the straw bed with a wet towel on her forehead, he knew I wasn't the milkman. (The real milkman had curdled a few days previous, actually. I mean the *proverbial* milkman.)

Young Giacomo eyed me with a shy disquiet. He had been playing marbles at the foot of his mother's bed. He rose to his feet. I stood in the doorway, not wanting to seem callous. The fact is, however, that I'm rarely welcomed in, so at some point duty has to win out.

He stared at me. I wasn't even sure if the kid was old enough to form sentences.

When I crossed the threshold, the boy ran at me. I don't usually fear anything that can decompose, but I was startled. I paused.

I had expected him to smash into me, hit me with his baby fists. Instead, he hugged me. He could barely wrap his arms around one of my legs, and I'm not all that big. I'm about the size of your average rock star, shorter than you'd expect, but with a large presence. His two little hands grabbed at the back of my knee and clutch my jeans as hard as they could. I thought maybe he'd mistaken me for his dad at first, but then I spied some of the young boy's drawings nailed above the hearth. They were charcoal on onionskin, but even so, the father looked like a king-size gingerbread man with fur.

The boy didn't say anything. At that age you can never tell if that blank look is a profound sadness for being stuck here on earth or if they've just junked in their underpants. But with baby Giacomo, I knew immediately. I had broken that brand-new heart. And the look on his face wasn't profound meditation or spaced-out mesmer. It was more hurt than the kid knew what to do with.

I tried to lift the leg he was hugging. He let out a whimper and held tighter. His mother had long ago passed the throes and groans. The struggle was over. Now she lay still on the straw bed, the cold sweat drying in lonely beads on her collarbone. She was down to a last fading ember—the only person that could have noticed a difference between her and a corpse was me. Me and Giacomo.

Those are the moments you really hate the job, think about retiring by a river and carving ducks out of soap. I pried him off my leg and kneeled down to look him in the eye. I shouldn't have done that, but I had been working doubles in those days—I think I already said that—and I needed an explanation, I think, as much as he did.

When we looked at each other, I'm a little ashamed to say, I was the one who wept. I thought, it's a stupid thing, being so fragile, expiring. It's a stupid idea, a rampant disease every person contracts at some point, a cosmically gross afterbirth of after birth. I wanted to tell him that I wasn't taking his mom on purpose, but I was. I wanted to assure him that she wasn't leaving him, but she was. I suppose I just wanted him to know I hated this as much as he did.

Maybe that's how repo men feel. Maybe I'm the galactic hand of repossession—just another kind of Wish Police. Maybe I'll retire after all—you never know.

Anyway, that was when I broke the number-one rule of my job. I told Giacomo I owed him a favor, and that I wouldn't forget him. Then I took his mother. Her body stayed on the bed, of course, but the important parts. You get the idea. I noticed she had that same look to her eyes, far-off and dreamlike. I promised her the same thing, that I'd protect her son.

After losing everything they ever loved, Giacomo and his father, Giovanni, moved away from their decimated village, burdened with grief as heavy as the Mediterranean. They settled in Cortona.

At that same time, Pierre Vouvray had already lost his wife and was raising a little girl all by himself. But his loss didn't involve my services directly.

When Chloe was born, the housemaid washed her in a basin and wrapped her in a towel, because her mother, Lady Delice de Bourgogne, was too tired to do it. But even after a long nap, the maid brought the sleeping girl to the lady to hold, and the new mother was uninterested. She was the rare woman who could actually be insulted by a baby's need for attention. The housemaid took the baby to the kitchen, where the iron hearth was warm like a belly.

Chloe's eyes were closed when she met the stove, but when she felt its warmth, she gave out a long sigh. The maid could tell it would be a lasting friendship. She leaned down and kissed the tiny nub of Chloe's nose. The baby nuzzled the maid's lips, and then Chloe sneezed. This sent the maid reeling with adoration. The way Chloe had scrunched her eyes. The imperceptible sputter from her lips. The deep breath after such a taxing ordeal.

The cuteness of the newborn baby—wrapped in a towel, sleeping on an iron stove—was, in a word, lethal.

The housemaid put her hand to her heart. Her apathy toward her job, her resignation to a low embittered life, even the bacterial infection on her lower back—all gave up the ghost, right then and there. The baby was simply *too* cute. And so I was on hand for the little girl's birth, to collect all the deceased unhappiness she caused. Monsieur Vouvray was so proud of his baby girl that the week before her birth, he had sewn pansies, hundreds and thousands of them. Then, on the big day, he took them to the bell tower and poured them over the town square.

But only a few days after she was born, her mother, the Lady Delice, gathered her silks in a handbag and declared the rest of her belongings as "moldy rinds unfit for bovine society." As she left, she announced that she would move to Paris, to pursue a career in the picture business. She would be featured in crowd scenes of biblical stories on stained-glass windows, paintings of coronation ceremonies, and, if she made the right connections, a starring role on a clamshell. As she tromped to her carriage, she said she planned to never return.

When Monsieur Vouvray asked her to think of the well-being of their newborn daughter, the lady flushed, walked from the carriage back to Monsieur Vouvray, at the door, and slapped him across the chin. Then she whirled on her heel, whipping him with her tresses, and melodramatically mounted the carriage once again. As the coachman gathered his harnesses, she allowed one delicate tear to roll down her profile. And with a soliloquacious flounce, she said, "Of course, *you* wouldn't understand, Pierre. I'm doing this for Chloe *most* of all." True to her word, she never returned.

From then on, young Chloe was the lady of the house. That is, until the next time I saw her at the age of seventeen. I'll get to that in a minute.

Chapter 4

Because She Couldn't Stop for Me

UNABLE TO REMEMBER her mother at all, Vouvray's daughter, Chloe, had never tasted the bitter draught of mourning. Everyone she knew was healthy. Even her goldfish had miraculously survived for some five years now. She was at that age when they wear sundresses and run around hillsides making things out of wildflowers. She was as blithe as a bee, as bonny as a bunny.

She made Pierre sit cross-legged on the lawn for all to see, at the tree stump, which served as the mademoiselle's parlor table. And on Saturday evenings, the resident genius of France could be found in the glen just behind his house, employing his vast talent with a sewing needle to making dandelion tiaras for his daughter and her favorite goose.

Meanwhile, at the age of three, Giacomo did nothing but climb the tallest trees he could find, sit in the highest branches, and weep.

*   *   *

Chloe and Giacomo, of course, barely knew the other existed. Sure, Pierre would refer to "Giovanni and that illiterate whelp," and Giovanni would mention, "That poor, poor little girl, whose only crime is in her blood," but that's not much to go on.

To be honest, even I didn't know they would become, you know, "star-crossed," as they say—struck by love's killing shot. By the time they were teenagers, anyone would have assumed they were just plain incompatible.

Giacomo slowly recovered from that day I met him, and he became a little rowdy at the age of fifteen, a classic Cortonan. His father and he lived like boars. If they wanted to eat nothing but panforte and prosciutto for dinner, they would. If the inspiration struck, they would paint at four in the morning. The old women of the town treated them like free labor, calling them over to mend chicken coops, set the stone wheels of the olive presses into their nocks. They were paid, anyway, in cookies and jam. They were the brother and uncle every little girl needed in order to feel safe walking in the woods. His father had wild tufts of hair on his back, and someday so would Giacomo. They laughed in the cathedral and startled the gargoyles off their slumbering haunches. They weren't ashamed to weep like babies at the playhouse tragedies, holding on to each other and blubbering louder than the chorus. Each thought he could outrun the other.

Chloe certainly wasn't rowdy. If I had one word, I'd say she had the tendency to be a little cloudy. Opaque. Hard to tell what she was thinking behind that sweet smile. And you know, she never once mentioned how she felt about her mom leaving. That was sort of odd. It goes without saying that a young girl abandoned by her mother bore some immeasurable sadness. But wherever it was, growing inside young Chloe over the years, it was not in her smile.

Each year she was the lady beside her father at the winter ballet, at first in a little velvet coat, reaching up to hold his hand, then later in a long white cape, reaching gracefully down to twine her arm around his. That last winter, when she was seventeen, Mademoiselle Chloe looked impossibly beautiful. Her blond hair, like safflowers, peeked from under the snowy blanket of her white hood. Her lips like red poppies, her eyes like blue bonnets, were all in perfect bloom, all flowers even the brilliant Pierre could never hope to re-create.

Pierre had his annual smile unfurled for the public as he strode into the hall in his tuxedo, an organdy oleander on his lapel, to match his daughter's coat.

So you may have already noticed a few problems with this story. First of all, Giacomo in Italy could not possibly have attended the winter ballet that year, when every man in the Loire Valley plummeted into desperate love for Chloe. Second, Giacomo was a boorish fifteen, while Chloe was a regal seventeen. If you don't know the massive difference between those two ages, then you've never been to high school. Even if he had been there, Giacomo would no doubt have irritated the entire theater, guffawing good-naturedly like any groundling at a penny-scribe comedy.

So then, what good is a love story where the star-crossed lovers aren't even in the same room? Or even in the same country? And what's more, if they actually met, they probably wouldn't even like each other? I'll tell you. But this is where it gets a little complicated, so bear with me.

The thing is, to be "star-crossed," you have to start on opposite ends of the universe. You have to give yourself up to some purposeful arc hurtling you through years of black lonely space. You have to burn with some fire that doesn't burn you up, but doesn't let you shuffle inertly along either. And when you see that other star flying at you from the other side of the sky, you have to smash into it with a violent force that absolutely disintegrates your old self and becomes some new composite, some creation the world has never seen. The incompatible parts shuffle off, like so much drifting space dust. Insecurities, overdeveloped prides and humilities, forgotten manners, they're like the pockmark craters on a meteor. And at the moment of impact, they are filled to completion with the earth of that other star, like the two of you were made to collide.

But they had to get to each other first. And this hadn't happened yet, not before the night of Chloe's seventeenth winter ballet, which, I'm sorry to say, was also the night I saw her again. Like any of them, I fell in love a little, too. So I was just as heart-struck when in the middle of the third act, she passed away.

Chapter 5

The Masque of the Red Mouse

WHEN CHLOE ENTERED that recital hall, and the pre-curtain hubbub turned to ravished silence at the sight of her, no one could have guessed that a vastly improbable clerical error would take her life before any of them left the auditorium.

I guess it was just one of those nights. Outside, flecks of snow drifted in the air like confetti, reflecting moonlight and imparting everything and everyone with the importance of slow-motion and gloss. Within, the theater's balconies were made of chestnut and brass, and its seats were red velvet. As you walked into the grand hall, it seemed like walking in from the bluish night toward a coddling fire.

That night the Saint Petersburg Dance Company was presenting its star, Maximoff Vladinsky, to all of France. His pirouettes were of such legendary beauty that Russian doctors began prescribing his performances for melancholics, impish babies, and infertile women. His body was an elfin ornament. His leaps made gazelles look clumsy. They called him Vlad the Regaler. The crowd was frothing.

But that night's performance of *The Winter Mouse* was in fact supposed to be Maximoff's last on earth. At the very climax, when the title character (played by Vlad, of course) was rescuing the Summer Mouse from the halls of the Mountain Queen, a cord was to snap high in the rafters. That fateful rope would be the one that fastened the Mountain Queen's gemstone chandelier, which the set designer had made with candles situated inside a giant mobile made of none other than Giovanni's painted marbles. The magnificent prop would fall on top of the Russian star at the crest of a spinning leap. The candle flames and Vlad's elaborate mouse costume would combust in a sudden flash and vaporize the dancer, leaving nothing but a pair of ballet shoes and the thimble and wire they had used for the nose and whiskers. It would become instant theatrical folklore. For years the term "Russian roulette" would involve dancing around a candle and spitting mouthfuls of vodka at the flame. The audience would actually give it a standing ovation, for fear of not appreciating what might have been an eccentric interpretation of the piece by the genius performer.

I reread the Recovery Notice. It said:

> Item No.: 23-*M62vtr*
>
> Modus Mori: *Lights out*
>
> Comments: *A fan favorite, center-stage beauty goes out with a flash. Could involve overtime for multiple faintings and collective loss of wills to live.*

Don't blame me. The filing department insists on coding everything. I just show up where it tells me to and wait for something to go "legs up." It ain't exactly brain surgery. Actually, sometimes it is brain surgery.

Well, I slogged my way to the theater feeling like I'd been warmed over. I got there around the end of act 2. During the intermission, I saw Chloe, who was indisputably the center of everyone's attention. The concession clerks and stagehands stared openly. The ladies of the court twittered with envious peeking. A few musketeers laughed especially loudly at all their own jokes and stole glances to see if she was paying attention to their charm. She was truly lovely. And not just lovely, but lively.

No one seemed to notice the sadness perched in Chloe's heart, singing her a low and constant song about one thing: her mother. Chloe had long since forgiven the selfish woman. But on nights like the winter ballet, when all of French society seemed to be in one building, she couldn't help but scan the mezzanine or perk up every time she heard an overplayed chortle. She was as silent about her feelings as a porcelain doll. Everyone was content to stare at her.

I can't say I did any better. Maybe it was the mulled wine (I've always been a cheap date), but I spent the entire time in the corner with a hobo from the standing room, both of us gawking at her. She had this freckle right next to her lip; it twitched like her father's mustache whenever she was annoyed.

Anyway, the bell rang. Chloe and Pierre went back to their balcony. Soon Vlad would prance out for his grand finale.

The battle of the Winter Mouse and the Mountain Queen was at its height. The oboist and the cellist were dueling in the orchestra pit to parallel the action. Even the great Maximoff seemed to feel the magic of the night. He outshone even his own reputation. He crossed the entire stage in two leaps. The Mountain Queen staggered to keep up, to dodge his whipping tail and slash him with her manicured and murderous mole claws.

As they circled around the stage, the flickering candles, shining through Babbo Giovanni's painted marbles, created a kaleidoscope of spotlights. It made the dancers look like animated stained glass, like a *cinéma fantastique.*

Overhead, a cord began fraying. In the jumble of ropes up there, I couldn't tell which of the chandeliers it was attached to, but I was expecting the marble one to smash the dude center stage, 'cause that's what the note said. I looked at it again; all it said was "Lights out." Made sense. I looked over at Chloe, leaning forward in the balcony, enthralled by the show. The cord was down to its last few strands. The oboist was red in the face, in the midst of a frantic solo. Vlad was regaling them. Another strand snapped. I almost missed the moment 'cause I was staring at the stage waiting for it. Instead, the crystal house unit all the way in the back of the ceiling lurched forward a few feet.

The Mountain Queen was the first to notice. She stopped dancing, gasped, and pointed at the chandelier. Vlad looked up too, with a choking feeling in his throat, as if he felt his time was up. The whole crowd turned to see the lighting unit swaying precariously on a final taut cord.

The only person unaware was Chloe, with her elbows on the wooden rail, a dreamy expression on her face, as though she didn't need the show to go on in order to see the rest of the story. The final strand broke, and the chandelier came swinging over the third-floor balcony like a jungle man. A musketeer screamed like a balladeer. That got Chloe's attention. She looked at the crowd. They were all staring at something behind her. She turned. The chandelier was shrieking toward her. She stood just in time.

The chandelier sent her sailing over the balcony. I swear to you, for a split second she was suspended up there on the power of everyone in the room wishing the same thing. Then she fell.

When she landed, the oboist passed out as well. In his alarm, he had held his piercing high note too long and had lost too much air.

At that very moment, thousands of miles away, young Giacomo's heart clenched so tightly that he crashed to the floor, sending a tray of tempered glass into the air. Shards rained down on him as he fell like pieces of a chandelier. In the silent theater, Pierre was crippled with an unthinkable thought. He cowered away from the balcony.

I smoothed out the notice I had crushed in my fist. Center stage? Yeah, once everyone turned around. Fan favorite? She had more suitors than Savile Row. Lights out? That's not even funny.

I walked over to her body. Everyone thought I was an usher trying to help. They crowded around. Her spirit sat up, and I introduced myself. She noticed that I wasn't wearing black. I told her pink brings out the autumn tones in my skin. No one could see her incorporeal form get up to leave with me. No one noticed me as I wove back out through the crowd.

I pretty much flubbed it from there. The elevator ride isn't all that long. And I've seen cute girls before; it wasn't just that. I couldn't figure out what to do with my hands. She was so calm, and I was so sweaty, you'd think I was the one with blunt-force trauma. I'd never met anyone so at ease. . . . I usually get people at their blathering worst. She was almost silent to a fault. She had this freckle right next to her right eye. . . .

The elevator doors finally opened on the waiting room and Eudora, who's the preternaturally chipper lady at the help desk. Dora has a cherubic face, with curly hair that looks like a baby's before its first haircut. The waiting room itself is pretty standard. You got your uncomfortable seats, pictures of Jesus, *Highlights* magazine, and Eudora at her desk, dressed in a cardigan. She also likes to keep an old typewriter around, so when people walk in, they can hear the clacking of the keys. She says it soothes them. Plus it keeps her busy.

"Dora, my dear," I said as Chloe and I walked in.

"Hieee!" said Dora, in a pitch close to dog whistle. When she looked up from typing, she gasped at the sight of Chloe in her white opera dress. "Oh, honey," she cooed. "Is that dreamy skin or what? Did you moisturize every ten minutes? What do you bathe in, Lon Lon Milk, ambergris, tears of the unicorn?" All these years and Dora can still small-talk.

"Sit down," she said. "Wait, no, is that silk? Will it wrinkle? Oh, that is just *too* stunning to wrinkle." She had her hand on her heart as she talked, deeply worried for the silk.

"Thank you," whispered Chloe. "My dad made it."

"Well, honey, your daddy is a genie," said Dora. She got up and scooted around her desk, taking Chloe by the arm like they were best friends. Dora was overjoyed to have a gal pal for a couple of minutes, before processing her ticket.

Dora took a breath. But she couldn't contain her delight and made this suppressed squealing sound. "You know what I've heard,"

she said with a conspiratorial look in either direction. "I've heard—
I know it's weird but—polenta, that's what I heard. It's all the nutrients. Midwives sell it to aristocrats now. Smoothes wrinkles, everything. Seal blubber, too. But I could never do that. That's cruel."
Chloe looked around the room, probably wondering if all of eternity
was going to be like this.

I was happy just to sit down for a couple of minutes. I don't
know how long I was out, but by the time I jolted up at the sound
of the ticker printing out my next pickup, Dora was back at her desk
and Chloe was asleep in a chair with her hair braided.

I grabbed the ticket (shipwreck, shark feast), and Dora said,
"We've got a problem."

"You ran out of scrunchies?"

She usually gives a courtesy laugh but not this time. She looked
at me, scared almost, and said, "She's a sleeper."

That's shoptalk. Being a sleeper (as in: alive) means you're a mul-
ligan, a refund. It meant I had no business picking her up instead of
Vlad. It meant she was all dressed up and no place to croak. She had
to go back, wake up, and talk about having one of *those* experiences
while everybody pawed at her to make sure she was real. It meant
she had just become a bureaucratic nightmare.

Dora was still trying to find the E-73 Return Forms, which we
only use once every thousand years. Meanwhile the tickets were
printing nonstop. Dora finally found the form and started the paperwork right away. I had to get back to work. But to Chloe's credit, she
was real nice about the mix-up. It was sort of weird, actually. She
didn't even complain. For the next several hours, I rushed in and out
with different fares. Chloe flipped through the magazines, listened

to the drowned sailors talk about mermaids, never had the kind of conniption some women have over a messed-up salad. I think she had the opposite flaw. She just took it in stride. I kept apologizing, but she didn't seem all that bothered by it. And she had this freckle right below her elbow . . . but that doesn't have anything to do with anything.

Still, you don't get a three-day turnaround on that kind of thing unless you're seriously connected. When you factor in all the forms, routing them through the proper channels, and the whole time difference, then you see why Chloe's processing took so long. To her it seemed like a week. In France it was two long, fallow years.

Chapter 6

The Big Snooze

ONCE THEY LAID Chloe's body to rest in the mausoleum, Pierre crumbled under the weight of a colossal aching. I didn't tell anyone, 'cause I didn't want it getting back to Chloe, but I had to go there to pick up the hundred pieces of Pierre's permanently broken heart. As she slept on the stone, Pierre slunk to his cottage, past the tree stump where she made him tea, past the headstone of her favorite goose, past the meadow where they picked flowers. Since he had nothing left, Pierre continued to sew. His solitary genius grew more and more legendary.

When Giovanni saw the first vase of the new year, he was actually making fun of the Frenchman at the time, at a dinner party on his veranda. "The flowers he makes, they are like garnish to my marbles, like a sprig of parsley. Little accents on the main course, yes? And who eats the garnish? Nobody. But who eats the veal parm—?"

A delivery boy brought in the new vase.

Babbo stopped.

He walked up to the vase, gauze gardenias planted in his own marbles. He lifted a finger toward the flowers, then retracted it before making contact. Everyone at the party saw a specter wash over him. Babbo's mustachioed lip quivered. Then, with a roar of grief, he wept.

Only Babbo could have seen it, the funeral in the fabric; only the eye of the great marble painter could have spotted the pain in the petals. The rest of the company, Giacomo included, stood at the dinner table dumbfounded. "What is it, Babbo Giovanni?" asked one of his patrons. "What news is this?" But Babbo could not talk. The great artist blubbered random miseries about his rival. Giacomo had to see the guests out, and Babbo sat on the ground, holding the vase like an injured child.

And so for Giovanni, too, the time of Chloe's absence became restless. Maybe under all the bluster, Babbo actually liked having Pierre's constant epistolary abuse in the margins of his invoices, the backbiting he'd pass along through their mutual vendors, the snarky asides they would volley in their separate interviews with kings. Maybe Babbo had grown old into one of those mischievous geezers who picked fights to keep the blood flowing.

But Babbo never let on that he cared for Pierre. And then Pierre simply disappeared behind the doors of his house, slouching through the halls like a tired skeleton. Both the great craftsmen of the age were adrift, one a sorrow-drowned tailor with a mermaid he swore he saw everyplace he looked, and another who missed his friend—well, maybe not his friend, but something close to it. Slowly, slowly, each man began to neglect his craft.

*　*　*

In those two years, the homes of Old Timey Europe became drastically less well decorated. People started buying kitsch items like bones of the saints and fuzzy-colored reproductions of a sparkly cottage in the woods. Hideous, just awful stuff.

Most people blamed the subsequent downturn in society on broken families. Ugly homes breed ugly lives. Incidentally, this was when killing became popular. So that was kind of a big deal. Another thing that happened was that Giacomo had to become a man during that time.

With Babbo Giovanni doing nothing but moping over the worktable, Giacomo was left to run the house. He only knew how to make *pasta e fagioli,* but each day he would replace a new bowl by his father's desk. Babbo never ate. He just sucked up tears from his thick beard. He had given up all his jovial songs and silently painted lonely stars into the heavenly spheres. Until one day, that spark in him, the sprezzatura, the fat frolicky horseplay, withered in my hands. The potbelly remained, but the spirit of the potbelly was gone.

Meanwhile, Giacomo traded heavy lifting with the butcher and baker for wild boar and semolina bread. He drove Santa Maria, their mule, to deliver the marbles to the wholesalers. On his day off, he helped the old widow of Venice stanch her basement when the water levels rose too high or her home sunk too low — no one could tell which. He knew the time for play and the time for work. His shoulders were broad enough to carry burdens when others couldn't, or thought they couldn't. In short, he'd become a man.

*　*　*

And finally, finally, the processing forms cleared Accounts Payable. And just in time, before Chloe started fermenting into a gorgeous French zombie (the way she would have purred, "Le brains!" while shambling in that white dress — don't get me started).

Two years after she had taken her exquisite flight from the balcony of the theater, in the early morning of a Wednesday, the wrought-iron gate of the Vouvray mausoleum squealed on its ancient hinges. The morning birds had just begun to warm up their love songs and alibis. Chloe, in her ball gown, rubbed her eyes, yawned and shivered and stretched and sighed all at once. Then she simply walked home as though it had been nothing more than a weeklong nap.

That morning, when old Pierre walked downstairs, he found his daughter standing in front of the kitchen sink trimming the stems of freshly picked flowers. She looked just as she had two years ago. He said, "Oh, thank God I didn't jump from the bell tower," and fainted to the ground.

Chapter 7

The Land of Little to No Return

WHEN OLD TIMEY Europe heard of the sleeping beauty rising up from her stone bed in the woods, it caused such a stir that writers immediately began plagiarizing the story for themselves. The idea was too enticing. A babe in a slinky outfit, breathing softly from lips imperceptibly open—who *wouldn't* write himself into the story as a dutiful prince, there to kiss her awake? Over time the details got butchered, but they kept the sewing theme, and the evil witch became real instead of a staged ballet, and the prince must have come from some collective wishful thinking. But hey, historians, what are you gonna do? Mostly lonesome types.

The story was an overnight bestseller. Once it got around, along with an engraving of Chloe, I had something close to twelve cases of village bachelors getting fatally sick from making out with corpses. But you should have seen that engraving.

Even the people in Chloe's village bought it. And like all the big stories, it felt instantly classic, new but with the sense of ancient truths. The anecdote became a good yarn. The yarn a legend. Till finally the legend became myth, mixed up in the cultural ether, a branch of the eternal redemption story.

In just a few weeks, no one would believe that their own village beauty was the source of the story. Their memories started blurring. That Vouvray girl must have just gotten up after her fall from the balcony. It couldn't possibly kill someone to fall from that height. She dusted herself off and ran away, mortified with embarrassment.

She had probably been keeping a low profile for the two years. Maybe she'd given birth to an imp in secret. Some people could have sworn they had seen her around town. None of them could recall what they wore to the funeral.

Suddenly, Chloe had always been there, and the Sleeping Beauty was a fairy tale everyone had loved as a kid. You people really are sheep sometimes.

Pierre was in and out of consciousness during the days immediately after Chloe's return. He would see her, faint, wake up, faint. It was kind of cute. Slowly, between fits of passing out, Pierre began to accept the impossibly merciful reality that his daughter was alive. And very slowly, after more paperwork for Dora, Pierre's heart rekindled, too. His flowers, so to speak, began again to bloom.

And of course it was only proper that the first bouquet be sent to his arch-rival, his once-again enemy: Giovanni di Cortona. Babbo received the bouquet with a note: "These tulips have never seen dirt. Kindly prevent your recently amateurish gewgaws from making it seem as though they have."

Babbo read the note in front of Giacomo. Giacomo, who had

already read it, expected an outburst. There was definitely an out-burst. Babbo Giovanni laughed aloud and grabbed Giacomo in a bear hug, saying, "That snobby garden wench, he's back!"

Babbo set himself to painting all day, sniggering under his beard. Giacomo went out to look for their mule, Santa Maria. He found her by the barn, grazing on wild rosemary, and took her to the hill in front of their house. Santa Maria liked a good stretch before bearing the bridle for a long journey. Giacomo had the return of his father to celebrate. So together they rolled on their backs and kicked their legs at the clouds.

That evening Giovanni, Giacomo, and Santa Maria set off for the Alps with a cart full of their finest work—aggies and opals, a cat's-eye marble that winked when spun, tinted crystals you call "princess," ones with a drop of crimson called oxblood, and round galaxies that twinkled and breathed like real galaxies. Along the way, each village turned up at the side of the road to see them through. Babbo tossed marbles painted in patterns of corkscrews and bumblebees and turtle shells to the kids who ran alongside the cart.

Every village had heard that Babbo was coming. They lined up in the byways, threw their goats to the bridge trolls to clear the paths, and young heralds-in-training blasted cacophonous toots from their brass horns. It was as if the little cart was an army going to war.

Actually, the war was more of a crafts fair, the first crafts fair put on by the royal family of Bavaria, by invitation only, for the grand-masters of crochet, mosaics of macaroni or sea glass, outdoor play-houses, and pretty much all things découpage. Two weeks earlier and Babbo would never have made it. Now he was ready to take his rightful place beside his rival, billed together as co–guests of honor in the brochures (try to guess whether that ticked them off).

The rivals would finally meet. Promoters were billing it as "The Rumble by the Jungle Gyms." Never mind that comparing the two was like comparing gorillas and chinchillas, vanilla with manila, but whatever; it sold news parchments.

The Black Forest of Bavaria was a dangerous place in those days, lots of baby stealing going on. If you were in the peppermint bricklaying or gingerbread siding business, you'd be making a killing. It was a good time to be a lumberjack, a terrible time to disobey your parents. Cats did well, mice not so much. Stepchildren could go either way.

And unless you had an invitation with the seal of the House of the Royal Family of Bavaria, you and I would be sharing a cab out of the forest. This was especially true when Prince Dimple Pimple turned eighteen and took over as Kaiser for his senile uncle Gustav, who would arrange flotillas of paper ships in the royal fountain and tromp in the water in full regalia shouting, "People of foldy town, the tax is axes on your axis!" I know it doesn't make sense. That's because he was senile.

The prince had a regular name, by the way; I just don't really care what it is. I'll give him one thing: he had spectacular dimples. He wore only white tapered shirts with overlong sleeves and red leather pants. His dirty blond hair had more highlights than a Rembrandt and spiked out like a palm tree or fell in his face like moody curtains.

As he swaggered through the halls of his castle, a troupe of musicians followed to provide a "hella-cool" soundtrack. When he'd enter a room, he'd stop and pose, first one profile, then the other. With each profile, a drummer and trumpeter would bang a sonic exclamation point, one for each of his dreamy dimples.

The guy could charm the scales off a gorgon. Also, he might have killed his parents.

Chapter 8

His Good Side
Is Patricide

YOU'D THINK OF all people, I could tell you if Dimple Pimple's parents were murdered. I should know these things, right? Why would I have anything better to remember than when and why that random old couple from someplaceville shoved off, right around the same time a billion others did it?

Why, for example, do I spend my evenings cutting up bok choy and placing bite-size pieces in a trail for my bunny to follow around the house, when I *could* be cataloging every sun that flickers out, every virus you ever fought off, every birch that slumps in a field somewhere under the gentle crush of snowfall?

I'll tell you why. It's a grave world, full of last rites, and ghosts are what we breathe. And at least for me, sometimes you feel like a Tut; sometimes you don't. It gets tiring. Sometimes you do your job, and sometimes you hunt for nom-nom treasure with Mr. Bunnersworth.

I have no idea what happened to the king and queen of Bavaria. The prince showed up to his eighteenth birthday party by himself, and when people asked, he said, "My good father and mother have passed on, terribly, with a lot of screaming involved. Is this cake lemon?"

He was immediately made Prince Kaiser, no questions asked. The whispers at court were that the king's and queen's cessation of breaths was the work of Dimple Pimple's second-in-command and bodyguard, Brutessa, the dwarf general always by his side.

They called her Brutessa the Brutest. She was captain of a gang of land pirates, who roamed the forest and pillaged travelers. I got to see a lot of their work firsthand. The thing about land pirates is that even though they don't get as much media coverage as the seafaring variety, they're much more . . . well, brutal. The most the two types have in common is that they both run the Jolly Roger, the black flag with that skull everyone says is my head (gives me the hibbly-jibblies).

Land pirates travel on carts that have been cobbled together from the pieces of other carts, pulled by wolves and wild dogs. They can gain on a four-horse carriage at full gallop. And instead of sending a boarding crew, they have keelhaulers, who're basically dwarves who went crazy in the coal mines. They stand on the running dogs, and when they pull alongside a speeding carriage, they'll curl themselves up into a ball and jump into the spokes. The wheels crunch on the dwarf, and wood goes splintering in every direction. The carriage goes flying over its own startled horses, all to the tune of the keelhauler going, "tee-hee" somewhere in the middle of the whirling smashup. They're lunatics. Like, howl-at-moon, smoke-dirt-in-their-pipes, cartilage-eating types.

Land pirates think of sea pirates as the spoiled upper class, what with their "code," and their noses not falling off, and all that sea water for their bubble baths.

Think about that. To the land pirates, Blackbeard was too pro-fessorial. One-Eyed Jane was a yacht-club princess to these people. You really have to have made a few wrong decisions along the way if you've gotten to a place where you're thinking the infamous marauders of the Barbary Coast are *too* civilized.

The way Brutessa met Dimple Pimple is predictable enough. He was joyriding through the forest with half the tavern wenches in Bavaria, just about to start a bodice-ripping edition of the Alphabet Game, when all of a sudden his carriage went flying in the air and landed upside down in a ditch.

Fortunately for him, Dimple Pimple had just bought a vowel, if you know what I mean (like, you know, you *know*). It's best to leave the details alone. He climbed over the dazed tavern babes and found himself face-to-face with Brutessa. He was still standing in the ditch, so the height thing worked out.

Dimple Pimple immediately recognized the pirate queen, and, like most greedy rich kids, he wanted her in his collection. He would need a pet assassin for his future plans, someone with both ears to the ground. Meanwhile, Brutessa had a sharp eye and immediately realized she had hit the mother lode. She had ambitions of her own and needed a corrupt princeling to manipulate.

And a few years after that, Babbo Giovanni and Giacomo came down the same road toward the crafts fair. The land pirates had changed career paths by then, to royal guards—well, a grubbier, less-regimented version, anyway, involving a lot more exposed innards than seems usual.

Chapter 9

It Was a Good Day to Sigh

I KNOW WHAT YOU'RE thinking. You're thinking this is a terrible love story, on account of the fact that the two lovers haven't even met. Plus when Chloe took the terminal plunge, Giacomo didn't even know about it. Maybe his own spirit—which had been fused to hers—should have been ripped from his chest and left nothing but human post-consumption waste, a love-shorn collection of bio-organic watch parts, a homunculus.

After all, that's what *should* happen when our love leaves us. We turn into those secret experiments of alchemy.

Fair enough. Maybe a love story should have the lovers within a hundred-mile radius of each other at the beginning. But in my experience, it's not so much the beginning as the ending that matters for most people. And endings are kinda my specialty. I mean, you can start anywhere if you think about it, but you're gonna end up like everybody else someday, listening to Dora clacking on her type-writer till your name comes up next on her clipboard.

And the whole point is who you were up until then, what justifies you. What reason you got for door number one or door number two. I mean this seriously. There are only two doors in the room, and Dora keeps great files.

And I'll tell you a secret about the two doors. You always get the one you walked in from. So really, every story's different, and every story is the exact same.

As for Chloe and Giacomo, they finally met on the first day of the crafts fair. Around lunchtime they both wandered away from their father's booths to peruse the tchotchke shops. In between the dreamcatchers and the infused oils, merchants of mixed reputation sold turkey legs, mead, fried boar, grog, wine, cupcakes, and ale. The crowd was half fairyland, half anonymous alcoholics.

I will admit I was tempted by the bulletin board made out of wine corks arranged in a frame, with all the stamps of the different chateaux and vineyards on them. Classy, functional, would have looked great in a den, home office, or kitchen. Kicked myself that I didn't have my wallet.

Anyway, like most instances of love, it was just an accident that Chloe and Giacomo ran into each other in the middle of the raucous crowd, with a loud Spanish baker yelling, "Churros! Get your churros. Hot churro. Not burro. They're sticks you can eat!"

As Chloe and Giacomo strode through the medieval festival, they were unaware that their stars had almost completed the long and winding course across eons and would come crashing into each other right then, as they turned a corner. Chloe and Giacomo barely knocked into each other. The baker didn't even notice as he peddled his pastries. But high above them, where no one could see it, two space rocks rammed into one another, tiny stars that simply refused to pass each other by.

Bam! Thunderclap! "All right, how about some funnel cake instead?" Love!

As a result of the slightest change in lunar gravity caused by the comets' crash, a wave off the coast of Pago Pago poured over a thousand newborn tortoises and enfolded them back into the warm sea. A rock was wrested from its position by the faint concussive force and tumbled into a creek in the Americas, minutely altering the course of the stream, which poured over a slowly eroding cliff. A gentleman astronomer of Arabia saw the blast of two young stars in his telescope and fell from his stool backward, knocking his head, then called his assistants to his aid, including the assistant whose job it was to turn the dial each calendar day.

You might consider what I'm saying a bunch of overwrought lovey-dovey talk. You might think I'm being a sentimentalist, schmaltzy, or "grazing corn." Yeah, yeah, you're saying, that's a story for moms to forward a dozen times on e-mail. Sell it to Hallmark, buddy. That kind of thing.

And you might be right, but then I'd say don't push me, punk. I like this part, and I can schmaltz your face off. And more important, it's not corny when it's true. To some of you, it may be corny *because* it's true, and that puts you beyond my help.

For the rest of us, I will say that when Chloe and Giacomo bumped into each other in the middle of the crowded fair, their sudden love set off fireworks in space. It ushered in life and the tide. It was earth-shattering. And in a way, even time stopped for a while (the assistant finally remembered around midnight and snuck back into the madrassa in his nightclothes to set the calendar right).

Chloe blushed. Giacomo smiled like a doofus. Her eyes had seen the tops of clouds and were blue. His neck could pull a plow through parched clay. She opened her lips and said, *"Pardonnez-moi, monsieur."*

He looked at her and said, "Huh? . . . Mi dispiace—non capisco."

And thus came to light a slightly important detail: Giacomo couldn't speak French, and Chloe didn't have a lick of Italian.

At that same instant, both Babbo and Pierre spied their son and daughter fraternizing with exactly the last person on the planet they should be fraternizing with. The two of them interrupted their admirers and rushed toward the new lovers.

Also at that same moment, from his seat on the elevated stage, Prince Dimple Pimple noticed Chloe. He noted her darling freckles but didn't fall in love. At any given time he had two dozen chicks on speed-beckon. He was constantly in that greedy state of wanting the next thing, so he thought of women like a spice rack—each one was good for a single flavor. Chloe was the darling freckle flavor.

I hope I'm not the first person to tell you that beauty is a little more complicated than the box-of-crayons approach.

Well, the Dimple Pimple didn't know that, and he wasn't in any kind of position to recognize that Chloe—just another hottie by his standards—was in fact the most beautiful woman alive. Too soft-spoken, perhaps, but a heart as shiny as the diamond as big as the Ritz. Real beauty is important in my industry, so I'm using the word as a technical term. She was actually the most interesting person to watch among you people. Best alive. My professional opinion.

So on the plus side, there was no sleazebag prince butting his head to steal our heroine away. But, on the other hand, Brutessa, who lurked behind the prince's throne, had seen Giacomo, promptly developing her first-ever crush (which at first expressed itself as a gassy buildup and then a toady belch).

This all happened at the same time—love, hate, indifference, and burps that smell like burro. The old red hound asleep on a sunny patch of cobblestones perked an ear, then woofed under his breath. The lovers realized that language is almost completely useless, anyway. Brutessa was already clubbing Giacomo in her mind and dragging him back to her hovel of love. All in a few seconds, just like that. And just like that the easy ending—the *happily ever after*—wheezed its last breath in my arms.

By that I mean it got complicated.

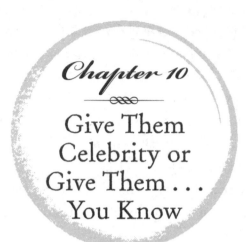

Chapter 10

Give Them Celebrity or Give Them . . . You Know

NOT TWO SECONDS after Chloe and Giacomo exchanged their first few pleasantries in languages the other couldn't understand, their dads keelhauled the whole pretty picture.

Pierre squinted so hard that his eyes couldn't be seen behind the glare of sunlight on his spectacles. He took his daughter by the elbow and said to Giacomo in almost perfect Italian, "You? You? I'd rather she marry a beast or someone in advertising. Or become an au pair for the orcish horde. Or . . ."

Then Babbo came up behind Giacomo, grabbed him in a headlock, and turned back toward his booth, dragging his son behind him. He said over his shoulder, in almost perfect French, "Shut up."

As she was being pulled away, Chloe watched her love, Giacomo, hunched over, bucking to free his head from Babbo's grip. He looked like a spaniel in a banister. Undeterred, Chloe sent swooning missives with her eyes to Giacomo's preoccupied rump.

Babbo didn't pay attention to Giacomo's kicking as he strolled through the fair. For a marble painter, Babbo was abnormally beefy.

He looked like he smelled like cedar and old spice. If there was an adjective for lumberjack—lumberjacked, maybe—he'd be that. He strolled with Giacomo's neck under one arm, eating a rainbow sno-cone and slurping the excess from his beard.

Back at the flower-quilting booth, Pierre ruffled a display of gingham geraniums just to keep his hands busy.

"Oh, stop googing at that boy already," he said. The comment was pretty harsh in person. I'm bad at describing it, but it had that dismissive quality that makes your biggest feelings seem stupid all of a sudden.

"I'm not *googing* at him, Daddy. I . . ." Chloe trailed off. It was "I love him" that she had stopped herself from saying. Pierre knew it, and it wrinkled the crap out of him. But worse was that she hadn't said it. As if he would overreact—which he probably would— but he didn't want his little girl to *think* that he was the kind of person who would. And that wrinkled him, too.

Chloe was still staring in the direction of Babbo's booth, which was a few rows away but sporadically visible through the clutter of other stations. Pierre watched her watching. Already, she seemed lost to the old man. Pierre's tongue could be as sharp as his pins and needles, but he hadn't pricked his daughter since she'd returned to life. He regretted it, and regretted that he wasn't the man who could make everything better anymore.

At the marble booth, Babbo had let Giacomo go from his headlock but refused to explain himself. He just went back to licking his sno-cone. Giacomo, who was a grown man now, or at least a young man, demanded to know why his father had interfered.

Nothing from Babbo. Then a loud slurp.

Giacomo said, "And another thing. How in the name of Peter's Papal Pardon did you know French and her dad know Italian?"

Babbo Giovanni said, "See? You're still too young to understand. I've been writing letters to that fop since you were this big." He held up a marble the size of a ball bearing and continued. "I had to learn French because I ran out of dirty words in Italian. I even learned calligraphy just to add curlicues for emphasis. And you, you want me to send my *son* to grovel for his daughter? You think I'm nuts? You think I'm some kind of nincompoop? You'd be his stable boy. And he'd mail me oven mitts or hot pads or some sewn thing with pictures of his cottage on it and a nice newly painted barn with a little silhouette of a strapping young boy, *my* boy, painting. The master you could become, painting *a barn*. And no one would believe me, when I show them, because that gerbil of a man would sew it so it looked like a shadow. But *I'd* know. I'd know it was my boy sweating his life away. I'm telling you, he'd do it. It'd be you on the oven mitt, Giacomo, the damned bucolic *oven mitt*."

And Giacomo simply wasn't prepared to counter an argument that crazy. Obviously, Babbo had marinated for years on just such a nightmare scenario. It didn't even make sense. Pierre would never stoop to making oven mitts.

It didn't matter to Babbo. He kept going, "And for what? For *him*. And some girl—okay, she's beautiful, I'll say that much, Giac-Giac, cute as every button in the old man's caboodle. But you just have to find someone else."

That was what tipped it over for Giacomo, who'd been playing with a purple teardrop launcher—a half-pounder. The idea that he would have to find anyone other than Chloe. Giacomo flung the marble at the back of Babbo's head. It smacked Babbo in the neck and sprayed a cloud of sno-cone mist from his beard.

Babbo turned around, slowly. Giacomo wasn't sure whether to run. He was smart enough to grab a few more marbles, though. Babbo chuckled. A stray dream-catcher rolled behind him like a tumbleweed.

Ten seconds later, both men were hopping around the booth, pelting each other with marbles. Priceless spheres of every color whistled through the air. They ducked and yelped and screamed at each other, "Stop! I'm serious—just stop, seriously." But neither would stop first. They started to throw fistfuls at a time. They stood on either side of the booth with both arms swinging, while leaning back, trying to keep their faces out of the line of fire.

One-inch welts popped up all over them. Finally Babbo ran around and caught Giacomo in a bear hug. It only deteriorated from there into Giacomo elbowing his dad in the belly, and his dad giving him noogies.

By the time they hit the dirt, they were both bruised, panting, and slumped with their backs to the booth.

Babbo caught his breath and said, "That bad, huh?"

And Giacomo said, "I love her, Pop."

And Babbo laughed, then groaned and touched his swollen jaw. "You coulda just said that."

They got up and started gathering the marbles. After a little while, Babbo said, "You know he'll never—"

"Yeah, I know," said Giacomo.

More talk would have killed the solemnity of Giacomo's trouble.

Their marbles were scattered all around, so they hunched over the dirt in silence as the sun sank into the horizon like a marble they could never retrieve.

Night was falling on the fair, and shadows of the surrounding forest began to extend branched hands farther and farther into the great glade.

A few people began to notice that there were no lampposts at this fair. They had all admired the ribbons drawn across the tops of the trees, girded with honeysuckle vines that hung down every few feet, creating aromatic curtains above their heads. But now the fear of night obscured even the flowers' scent. And the glass baubles that hung between each flower curtain, what good were they, people whispered, if they weren't lamps or candelabras?

A worried murmur began to rise among the row of blacksmiths, big dudes who were getting skittish. They grumbled that they never would have put out their smelting fires if they'd known it'd be pitch-black. A few of them scuttled over to the lady who made night-lights out of glow-in-the-dark seashells.

Personally, I like the dark. But then, I guess deep down you guys aren't really afraid of the dark, so much as meeting me somewhere in it. Thanks for that, by the way. Real good for my ego.

I said that to a guy I knew once, and he goes, "I'm not afraid of meeting you in the dark. I am afraid of being left alive after getting mutilated by a bear." That was nice of him to say.

*   *   *

So the last sliver of sunlight faded out in the fairground. The black-smiths made a collective whimpering sound. It was so dark, you could only make out the eyes of a thousand different were-creatures, watching from the surrounding edge of the Black Forest.

When some poor girl in a corner booth got her ankle nipped by a were-mole, her scream sent fear through the crowd. If you ever want to see true chaos, get a bunch of artists in an enclosed space and threaten their work. It gets ugly. They're like monkeys in a fire.

In that second before someone screamed bloody artwork, a dozen drums pounded a single beat, and the stage at the head of the fairground suddenly lit up with a single flash. Then the darkness descended again, but everyone turned toward the stage. Another drumbeat, another flash.

A few people thought they could make out the outline of an extremely hot guy. The drums thumped a third time. The light flashed again. By this time everyone could see one very stylish person, obviously Prince Kaiser Dimple Pimple, standing in the middle of the stage. It was obvious because a huge backdrop behind him said his name in shiny ten-foot sequined letters that lit up with every flash.

The prince was standing with his hands crossed in front of his crotch and his head down. The light and the drums slowly sped up the beat.

As their eyes got used to the bursts of light, the audience rec-ognized the source. Every land pirate in Bavaria stood around the stage and held an outrageously long fishing pole. At the end of the fishing lines dangled paper stars. Candles flickered inside the spiky white lanterns, and when all the pirates strained to cantilever the long poles out over the stage at the same time, it made a sudden synchronous flare. The bulbs of celebrity. The light of awesome.

It must have taken weeks to choreograph the land pirates. In perfect unison, they bowed the stars before Prince Kaiser and lifted them to create a strobe effect.

The drums and stars pulsed, and every heartbeat ramped up, until suddenly, with a surge of radiant sex appeal, the prince looked up. The stars flew up and away. The drums abruptly halted in the dark.

A beat.

The crowd vibrated and possibly wet its pants.

With a blast of starlight, a thunder of drums, the prince is back. He looks left. The dimple is honestly stunning. Another blast, and he looks right. The other dimple is, impossibly, even better. His cheeks must have been worked on. They're just too perfect. A final blast, and he does a little chin flick and walks toward the crowd. They're freaking out, screaming like banshees on vacation. A few jewelers have already gasped and given up consciousness.

The land pirates stake the fishing poles into the ground, creating ambient starlight for the stage. The drummers go silent.

Prince Kaiser sashays his pretty self to center stage and says, "—."

It doesn't really matter what he said. The guy talked too much. He welcomed a few dignitaries from a craft factory in Manchester and some muckety-mucks who appeared onstage for a few seconds before getting rushed off to restore the prince's limelight, and then he says, "—."

It was nothing special, actually; he just introduced the two great grandmasters among them, the flower quilter, Pierre Vouvray, and the marble painter, Giovanni Chianti. The crowd went insane. The blacksmiths couldn't stop clapping. Dimple Pimple basked in the glory.

After the crowd settled, the prince casually mentioned that the crafts fair had all been a trap, they were all his prisoners, and anyone who tried to escape through the forest would be keelhauled and promptly eaten. Turns out land pirates are cannibals. Who knew?

Chapter 11

The Naked and The Bread

WELL, IT'S NOT technically cannibalism, because dwarves aren't people. I mean, *little people* are obviously people. But I'm talking about Old Timey Europe dwarves. Which are like elves, which aren't human. So the fact that land pirates happened to be dwarves means that when they eat people, it's not exactly cannibalism. It's just super gross is all.

But that wasn't the point. We're not getting started talking about all the things land pirates eat. That's a car game that'd keep your kids preoccupied till you hit the ocean.

The point is that after all the showboating, his royal good-lookingness was holding the entire fair hostage. It was brilliant really. Lure all the greatest artists in the land with the promise of adulation and sales potential. And they swarmed to it like flies to roadkill.

A riptide of terror overcame the artists as they realized that, yes, in fact, this had all been a ruse, and no one would be appreciating their art after all. They began to replay, hungrily, every comment they had received from every customer. They finally understood why they had all been so carefully thought out, expressed as though in a writing workshop, and perhaps tinged with a little jealousy. "These macaroons are sentimentally interesting. I feel like I'm consuming childhood as well as marzipan." "Are these wreaths made of wagon wheels? Heavy, aren't they. And wrought with meaning." "I like that it's a sundial *and* a wind vane, but what would it be if it weren't either one?"

Only artists had been invited to the fair. Every customer had a booth of his or her own somewhere. Dear God, they had been selling to other artists!

Other artists didn't count as true fans. They bought art out of professional obligation, or competitor research, or the raccoony obsession to own shiny things. Think about it. No one is impressed with the Girl Scout who has twelve rich fat uncles.

Suddenly a wave of nausea, worse even than knowing they were slaves of a ruthless dictator, crashed upon the crowd. They had not, in fact, helped the uncultured swine of the world better themselves with threaded candy-corn necklaces. The unwashed masses would stay unwashed, even though scented soaps and body scrubs took up an entire aisle. The churlish "left brain" types would go on with their usury, the clacking of the abacus their only music, the blood of artsy children their only wine.

Most of the crowd curled into the fetal position, rocking themselves and humming tunes by their favorite singer-songwriter before the prince could finish his announcement.

Giacomo, however, was already sneaking through the hedgerows of angsty creatives to find Chloe. As the prince trumpeted on about his elaborate trap, and the fact that the head of every artisans' guild was here somewhere, and that everyone would be put to work on a project so ambitious it might stop the wind, all Giacomo could think was, *What do you suppose would make Chloe happy?*

As the prince instructed the crowd that they'd be grouped in pairs and imprisoned in different wings of his castle in order to work on his project, Giacomo thought, *I know. Flowers.* She seemed to be into flowers, what with her dad and all. But then again, maybe she wouldn't want flowers because she always had them. But maybe she couldn't get enough flowers. What would Chloe say about all this? Chloe would have the answer. She seemed clever. And cute. Chloe was the cutest. . . . Maybe she'd like perfume. . . .

It just went on like that. Over and over about everything to do with Chloe. Like some penny rolling around a sink, his mind just kept coming back to how cute and clever and pretty she was. I don't want to embarrass the guy, but I definitely heard the phrase "cutie patootie" under his breath more than once.

It was all too obvious by the time he found Chloe—and the sparklers above her made her eyes shine—that the penny of Giacomo's mind had rolled around and around and finally fallen, fallen forever down the sinkhole. And what was that sinkhole? That sinkhole was lunacy.

Anyway, at the same time, Prince Kaiser was about to unveil his grand plan: "—."

Okay fine, the sinkhole was also love. Are you happy? It's not like we didn't know that already. Their stars almost knocked the earth off its axis. Time-space had to reboot itself around the enchanted moment. They had so much chemistry, the pH balance of the ocean flipped, and all the leftover dinosaurs started feeling headachy. Let's just move on.

The Prince Kaiser had taken them all hostage for one reason: he wanted them to make something so beautiful that it would give life to the lifeless. Essentially, the rich little snot was trying to put me out of work.

The idea was that if something, anything in this world—say, a painting, or a poem, or a really fancy egg holder—was actually more beautiful than any other place I could take you, well, it would uproot the whole soular system.

After all, everybody wants a far, far better place to go. What the prince wanted was something so mind-boggling marvelous, so unimaginably stunning, so good, so *very* good, that it would be the greatest place—only to be in front of it. Just gawking at it would mean glorious release from all suffering. Your soul would demand that you stay, instead of shuffling off to the great beyond.

You starting to get the picture? He wanted a towel set that could replace the hope of an afterlife. He wanted embroidered napkins that could become as gods! Bum, bum, BUM!

Chapter 12

God Is Thread

IT WAS A common misconception in Old Timey Europe, where smooches were all you needed to jump out of your grave, that I was kind of a chump. Laughable, I know, but it's true.

Everybody assumed I was some ninety-pound wuss who'd get punked any time an old crone cooked up some chicken feet. Or a fisherman caught a talking trout. Or genies crossed their arms. People, please . . . who do you think smacked them upside the head and shoved them in a lamp in the first place?

For having more bodies to my credit than communism, you'd think I'd have more street cred. Right now I feel like all I get is sixth-graders drawing my name on their Trapper Keepers so their divorcing parents freak out and pay them some attention.

That's not respect. That's not even bad poetry. And another thing, rappers, you gotta stop calling yourselves "Killa MC." You're not fooling anybody when your manager's looking for endorsement deals on soft-serve ice cream. If you're on a major record label, the closest you come to killing people is the slow painful demise of your publicity team's self-respect.

But me? I put down the Monkey King and Mickey Rooney's sunny disposition. I dropped Atlantis, and I had mono at the time. I even got Rasputin, eventually. If that's not gangsta, you haven't been paying attention. You ever see a long-tailed antarctica hamster? You ever hear Pachelbel's harmonica suite? You ever take the bullet train out of Newark, New Jersey? No, you haven't. Extinct. Forgotten. Lost in appropriations committee. That's me, baby. How do you like me now? I'd say, "If you don't know, you better ask somebody," but you'd need *Stargate* technology and a burning bush just to get high-enough clearance.

And yet somehow, *somehow*, princelings like Dimple Pimple used to walk around Old Timey Europe thinking they could publicly fire me. I think it's because I like to wear khakis, I really do. But I'll tell you something: I have a dream, a dream that someday a man will be judged by the number of galaxies he's snuffed out of existence, rather than the number of holiday costumes he's made for his bunny.

That's what I was stewing on, as I zipped back and forth to the fair. (A hurricane in the Indian Ocean, a marriage in Russia, a really annoying phoenix that just couldn't make up its mind.) As the prince wrapped up his speech, he unveiled the name of the life-giving creation, whatever form it might take. I forget what exactly, but he said something to the effect of: "And it shall be totally Most High, for it shall be called the Objet d'Awesome!" (Exclamation mandatory.) Sadly enough, I think it kinda made sense. If it ever got made, it would be certifiably awesome. Maybe even "Awesome!"

As soon as he said the name "Objet d'Awesome!" a dozen drums hammered on the exclamation point, the sparkling stars overhead converged into a climactic glow, and everyone gasped at the biggest surprise of the night.

Let me explain. The stage management had been orchestrated to cast the most dynamic light on Dimple Pimple. So the darkest shadows were directly behind the stage wall. That's why Brutessa could stand behind him onstage, using the residual shine from the prince's spotlight to make shadow puppets on the stage wall, and not be noticed by the crowd. She had two cudgels for hands, so all she could make was the moon falling on a baby octopus.

It's also why Giacomo and Chloe snuck behind the wall to have their conversation.

A lot of people wouldn't call it a conversation per se. There was some miming, some sign language, a little "me Jane, you Tarzan," a lot of unnecessary touching of the other one's arm, that sort of thing.

Giacomo presented the one orange gerber daisy he'd found. Chloe touched her heart with one hand as she took it. Then she put it up to her nose, though she knew full well that daisies don't smell like anything. Then she looked up with the flower still at her nose. You know what I'm talking about. That demure look girls do. Innocent and vampy at the same time. Posed and spontaneous. Not exactly a look that could kill, but it could definitely maim. It's how Cortés conquistadored the Aztecs. He just sent his smoldering mistress into the jungle, doing that look from behind a folding fan. A whole civilization, teased, tamed, and twitterpated.

Giacomo barely survived the look. And after that, they mostly just stood together, with moony expressions, enjoying the company. In terms of nonverbal, they were chatting like squirrels in springtime.

In terms of verbal, they just said each other's name in baby talk over and over. Chloe started it, by calling Giacomo "Co-Co," which, coming from those puckered lips, with that little French accent as if she was flicking the words with the tip of her tongue, and the freckles right on the pucker's edge . . .

Too much.

Giacomo responded with his own pet name, "Clo-Clo." He actually said that. Clo-Clo. This before they exchanged a single coherent sentence. Chloe crept up and nuzzled under Co-Co's chin. And Co-Co ran his finger down Clo-Clo's nape. And they both shivered together and said "Co-Co" and "Clo-Clo" a hundred more times.

They were tooth-achingly cute. Like those pictures of kittens exploring an empty carton of French fries. I once took a shot of Mr. Bunnersworth licking a lettuce magnet on my fridge. I had to delete it. It was so sweet, I almost got adult-onset diabetes.

You probably know what was coming. The two lovers stood behind the stage wall snuggling. Brutessa had discovered she could also make a shadow puppet of a cheese wheel rolling up a staircase.

Then the prince christened his ambition the Objet d'Awesome! And the logical thing would have been for everyone to cut up laughing at the absurd name. But instead the drums roared, like a knell for all things good and holy. The dwarves lowered the star lamps and lit up the entire glade. The prince had his arms out and his head back, as he basked in the radiant overflow. Except now after the stage had been backlit, everybody could see Co-Co and Clo-Clo back there touching their noses together.

The prince expected adulation. Instead, he got a synchronized

"Baroo?" He blinked, then looked up. The crowd stared past him, so he whipped around to see Brutessa two knuckles deep after a booger. But even more interesting was a ten-foot-tall projection of a young couple, casting its shadow on the backdrop of the stage. He was holding her in his arms. She was looking up and nuzzling into his neck. A picture of love that stole the show.

Pierre and Babbo immediately recognized the silhouettes and shouted in unison, "Ah jeez, that's exactly what I told you NOT to do!"

Chapter 13

Evil Head . . . of State

THIS IS THE part where things got crazy. The prince was so angry at being upstaged that he started shrieking a bunch of stuff in German. The land pirates didn't understand German, but they knew shrieking really well, so they charged into the crowd, beating everybody up. People scattered. The Hand-Painting Society couldn't decide whether to run into the woods or stay with their custom T-shirts and tablecloths. They ended up sprinting circles around their booth, making gobbling sounds, with shirts flapping behind them like tail feathers.

The pirates pillaged every peck of pickled peppers at the fair. Clouds of cotton candy, handmade paper, and loose straw stuffing billowed into the night air as the dwarves pounded everything in sight. At first they employed an overhand smash technique with their clubs, then they ran around for a while biting and spitting, and after that they grabbed the wooden beams of the booths and lifted them into the air like a caber toss. By that point they were just breaking stuff for all the funny sounds it makes. Only Babbo and Pierre were spared from the indiscriminate drubbings. Even land pirates decorate the mantels in their hovels—they loved fake flower marble vases as much as anybody.

Meanwhile, Brutessa tore through the stage wall and grabbed Giacomo by his belt loop and Chloe by her skirt strap. You could tell Brutessa was in a state she didn't recognize, the way she kept turning in circles, wheeling the two around her, looking for something in the chaotic scene to give her a clue. It was rejection or, more specifically, the ipecac feeling of being rejected by her first crush, Giacomo. Brutessa would have slobber-knocked any pirate who said so, but she was experiencing her second emotion. She didn't like it. After all, *her thoroughly silted-over heart had to make room for a jilted part.*

Poor Chloe got the worst of it. She was getting yanked around like a Beanie Baby on a metronome. But before Brutessa could fight off the befuddling feeling of feeling and get her bearings enough to break Chloe's femur, she fell off the stage and began pummeling the first thing that got in her way. It was a booth of potpourri sachets. She slammed into it and thrashed around so wildly that a miasma of fragrant dust flew into the air. Suddenly, the already-hysterical craftsmen all stopped and screamed in pain, "Agh, my eyes! I might never collage again!" The frenzied pirates didn't know what to do, other than try to punch the pain out of their own heads. Pulverized anise, orange peel, and lavender may sound nice, but they kick the crud out of your sinuses.

After that, everyone needed to sit down for a while. Prince Kaiser took the opportunity to pull a knife on Chloe and Giacomo. He brandished the short ivory dagger at both of them and motioned them to walk backstage, into the Black Forest.

When they reached a safe distance away from the fairgrounds and entered the royal hazelnut orchard outside the castle, Chloe ventured a question. "Did you really kill an entire elephant for that letter opener?"

The prince responded in French and said it was hippo. Baby hippo, actually. Said the ivory is whiter before they spend all that time in swamp water. (I end up feeding the little guys wheatgrass smoothies from a straw.)

Giacomo said, "I don't know what you just said, but is that real ivory? Really? Is that necessary?"

The prince said it was, in Italian this time, and followed up by threatening to have both of them executed on his castle lawn if they ever upstaged him again. Giacomo and Chloe stopped walking at the same time and said in their own languages, "Wait a minute. You speak Italian?" ". . . French?"

The prince nodded *sí* and *oui.*

Then the two together again: "Can you tell her I think she's the cutie-patootiest?" ". . . he's the bubby-wubbiest?"

The prince's dimples filled with displeasure. He knew he was hopelessly outmatched by a force of unimaginably destructive power: puppy wuv.

He had no choice but to stand there, while they sent each other butterfly kisses, translating their sweet nothings. "Okay, now tell her I love the way she does her hair."

Strawberry blond and dazzling, in case you were wondering.

When he finally got fed up with it, the prince prodded them on, and they walked again, through the brambles of the Black Forest, to the castle of the Bavarian royal family. It seemed to settle on everyone involved that a life-altering event had happened. The prince was on the path of an international hostage crisis and a coup to give him power over mortality. In its course, many innocent human beings with a lifelong passion for scrapbooking could have been murdered. Giacomo and Chloe both knew their fathers were somewhere back at the fairgrounds. They themselves were also prisoners, but their young love made them feel invincible.

As they walked under the portcullis, into the grand entryway, Chloe said, "Why don't you just hire Vlad the Regaler? I've seen him dance a breathtaking ballet. Maybe he could perform it in reverse."

The prince gave her the news—what happened to Vlad, the once most beautiful legs in all the world. When Chloe took that fall from the balcony, Vlad, like all of us that night, was struck with horror. But for Vlad, it became a crippling obsession.

Deep down, he knew that the chandelier had been meant for him. He knew I was there to get his autograph. And where anyone else would have been relieved to be passed up, Vlad was overburdened with the injustice that someone as innocent as Chloe had taken his place.

Vlad quit the Saint Petersburg Dance Company mid-tour and hired a carriage to Moscow. He refused to come out at the inns along the way but suffered alone in his little cage for months. The racking guilt broke him slowly over the course of the trip. At first his confidence, his performative energy, the desire to please, all dissipated into nothing. Then gradually his hamstrings began to atrophy, his elegant posture drooped, and his taut stomach became a belly from compulsive overeating. Every once in a while, I'd visit and take a few things. It felt like I was robbing the same house over and over.

By the time the carriage arrived in Moscow, the world's premier dancer emerged an ugly, ill-kempt slob. No one knew this but the royals of Europe, who required an excuse as to why Vlad would not be dancing at their courts. Everyone else was told the dancer was on vacation, indefinitely, and that all physical trainers with strong backs and minimal gag reflex should inquire for employment.

Chloe wept when she heard this, and Giacomo held her as she did. Then he looked over her shoulder at the prince and whispered, "I heard a lot of Vlad's name in your talking. You gonna hire him or what?"

Chapter 14

House of the Well Fed

THE NEXT DAY opened on a grim reality. Prisoners were paired with a collaborative partner and housed in lavish rooms all throughout the castle. A full English breakfast was served to them as they lay in their four-post beds. Slices of cantaloupe were provided, as well as granola yogurt parfaits, for any captives who preferred lighter fare. A page boy was assigned to every room, and dry-cleaning services were available upon request. In the evening, hostages would endure turndown service, which came with chocolates, optional tuck-in, and a few chapters of their favorite storybook.

Oh yeah, it was a real Día de los Cuervos.

The problems arose if you decided to leave your room—a dwarf would yank your head backward until it touched your ankles. Or if you tried to go on a hunger strike—a dwarf would pretzel you like before and feed you scones like a mother eagle. Or, worst of all, if you decided not to do your art—a dwarf would inspire you, which involved a pile of how-to art books, a two-ton wench, and a size-zero French maid outfit. Don't ask. Just feel bad. Those how-tos are brutal. Aside from the disemboweling and all. Even back then, those who could did, and those who couldn't sold short cuts.

Speaking of which, three things happened at this time that not only set the stage, but escalated the tension, for the climax that would follow. Then the dénouement. Me. The first thing was that Babbo and Pierre were partnered together in the north tower. Their fates were entwined from then on. Either the two geniuses would work together or they'd become unfortunate founding fathers in the sport of BASE jumping. And if everyone was facing facts, they'd admit that these two were the prince's only hope for an Objet worthy of d'Awesome!

Could anyone realistically expect the team-up of the doily twins and the funnel-cake guy to come up with something prettier than heaven? Really? The découpage gal took a fatal dose of glue when she found out her life was in the hands of an urban renewal artist. And frankly, I thanked her. Saved me time later on.

An old widower came close with a pipe-cleaner exhibit that incorporated his roommate's balloon animals, but even that fell just short of eternity's holy light. Close, though. I shook the man's hand after Dimple Pimple fed him bleach and fast-tracked the paperwork to see his wife.

The rest of the craftsmen were playing against the clock. They had to stall their executions by pretending their work wasn't finished and wait for Pierre and Babbo to bail them all out.

Obviously, that plan didn't work out for a lot of folks. The prince was arrogant, but he wasn't an idiot. He was a vain, irreverent, entitled puke stain on human history, with an upper-class sleaziness that no amount of hot tubs or sponge baths could wash off. He had that frat-kid, lad-mag, guy-guy misogyny about him. He thought he could dance. I hated his penmanship, I really did. And his red leather pants. He used to say he *loved* women, like, *all* women, womankind, the female form, and there was nothing wrong with that. He thought that was intelligent discourse. (It isn't, and there *is* something wrong with that, you chlamydia-ridden mule.)

Okay I've lost my place.

. . . But he wasn't a complete idiot. Stalling didn't work for the imprisoned artists. Each morning he and Brutessa took the horse-drawn cart through the massive halls of the castle, evaluating progress. The complex was so gargantuan that it took most of the day. The castle was as large as a city. The halls were more like indoor highways, four lanes, sidewalk, and billboards that told you which exit to take for the southwest stables. If you were traveling by foot between kitchens, it was best to pack salt tablets to stave off dehydration.

And now, for this, the Prince Kaiser's greatest ambition, every single room in every wing was occupied by a pair of artists. Bards played lyres to the interpretive dancing of their partners. Potters spun their wheels, and muralists tried to paint the creations as they spun. A sausage maker and a pickler made a discovery the world wouldn't soon forget. The hairstylists worked themselves into a corner real quick, except for the one who was paired with the doll maker, and the one with the juggling bear.

It was pretty much a mad soup. The prince was throwing in every ingredient he could think of, figuring he'd hit the right combination eventually. And until that happened, it was awfully fun seeing how many times Brutessa could fold a person in half.

★   ★   ★

As I said, everyone knew that the only conceivable chance of success was in the creation of a vase full of quilted flowers and painted marbles—a pairing so sublime that every tomb in Old Timey Europe would be left empty. The perished would rise, for heaven's advantage would be no more, brought low by the hands of two men—great and mighty in craft.

Except the problem was that the two buzzards were quibbling the whole time about which one of their kids seduced the other one and ruined the chances of a classy wedding.

The next thing that happened was that Chloe escaped the castle and Giacomo got his skull cracked by Brutessa and fell into what they used to call "a mortal sweat."

Chapter 15

The Funeral Plot Thickens

WHEN GIACOMO AND Chloe were imprisoned, Prince Kaiser Dimple Pimple forgot to have them separated. Not for propriety, mind you. This was the same prince, after all, who kept mermaids in his bathtub. He should have separated them because of Brutessa.

He just assumed that the pirate queen would forget all about Giacomo as soon as he was out of her sight. So he'd locked them both in the northeast wing, which technically wasn't a wing so much as a buttressed outcrop on the cliff side of the castle. It had been boarded up ever since the suspicious passing of Dimple Pimple's parents. The secret wing was where the prince grew up, a lonely brat with room after room dedicated to building blocks, trampolines, and merry-go-rounds. Now the abandoned dark halls felt like a haunted *carnevale*.

But the prince had underestimated the strength of Brutessa's first emotion. She had become a broken-down machine. A killing machine, but still. Among the land pirates, the rumor was going around that she had lost her edge. But it wasn't that. She'd just changed her focus. She was still the pirate queen, but now she wanted Giacomo as her king.

And so Brutessa boiled the thought of killing Chloe in her stomach, until finally she decided to act. Brutessa drove a cart at full gallop to the northeast wing and sent a giggly keelhauler crashing through the boarded-up double doors.

A mile farther up the grand corridor, past the hall of naked bathtub portraits from the prince's childhood, and then she reached Chloe's room. When she bashed open the door, she saw Giacomo, wrapped in Chloe's arms, drawing a plan for escape. Brutessa would have been horrified, but she'd never been horrified before, so she just let out a gurgly hiccup. In the silent second before Brutessa went manic, Giacomo whispered one of the only French words he had learned into Chloe's ear. "Sugarlips," he said, but Chloe knew it meant, "Run."

The emotions were coming three at a time now for Brutessa. Envy. Insecurity. Panic. The desire to read more fashion magazines and learn 57 seduction secrets. She swung her arms in no discernible rhythm or direction, punching herself as often as not, charging around the room.

I got a rush call to the scene. I expected one or all three of them to be breathless by the time I got there. But no, I arrived as Giacomo covered Chloe with his body and Brutessa ran around hiccuping and sending shards of anything that got in her way into the air. I wasn't there long before one of her wild swings connected with Giacomo's head and sent him flying into a dresser. His body landed with a toothy clack on the floorboards.

Both Chloe and Brutessa froze. I was already walking up to him to say hello when his back heaved a few unexpected breaths.

Brutessa expressed her first grief by rushing up to the body of Giacomo and wailing like an orca. She alternately beat her own head and nibbled on the unconscious man's toes. Chloe had the intuition that Brutessa wouldn't hurt him. She would be of better use if she escaped. She edged toward the door, slowly, in between the phlegmy sobs of the pirate queen. Meanwhile, messengers had been dispatched across the palace to inform the prince that his war general had gone insane . . . more insane.

Chloe slipped across the hall, into a broom closet, just as the prince arrived at full gallop. Prince Dimple Pimple slid off his horse and tied the reins on the doorknob of the broom closet. Chloe held her breath. The prince marched into the room to see Brutessa weeping and Giacomo unconscious.

Thankfully, a violist in the prince's soundtrack entourage had some medical training. From what he could tell, the knock had jostled Giacomo's brain loose. He'd make it but barely, and only if he didn't suffer another concussion for a while. Even a strong shake would push him over the brink.

At this point I had to leave. The prince was the first to notice that Chloe was gone. The kazooist in his entourage performed a cartoon surprise noise. Then Brutessa made him eat the kazoo. I rushed the musician to Dora. When she asked him his name, he did a disappointed *wah-wah-waaaah.* Then I returned to the castle and found Chloe.

The reason I had to stay with her is obvious, or it should be, if you've ever been in love. Giacomo could have shoved off at any minute, stepped through my door, answered the eternal footman, yours truly. But if he did, the part I was interested in wasn't with him in that bed. He'd already given it away. So when I came to collect for one Mr. Giacomo "Co-Co" Chianti, good servant, novice marble painter, a guide on the most excellent way, well, I wouldn't find it lying there with him. I'd have to find Chloe first.

And I'd honestly hate to, but I'd have to take it from her.

Chapter 16

Till I Did
Them Part

WHILE GIACOMO WAS ailing in his delirious half-sleep, Chloe snuck through the northeast wing. I kept back, out of sight. Poor girl had already met me once. When the prince noticed her gone, he ordered a search party to find her and put Brutessa in the group, which implied biting her face off when they did. Then he ordered his carriage to the north tower.

In the meantime, Babbo stood at Pierre's sewing station and held up a swatch of fabric as though it was a dirty tissue. "You know what makes me think your job is useless, Pierre?" said Babbo. "It's that you essentially make a replica of nature. It's like tracing someone else's paintings."

Pierre sat in Babbo's chair, with his feet propped on the marble-painting table. The glass rods were piled by an unused burner. Paints sat in clean tubs in manufactured rows. Neither of the men had moved a single ingredient from its position. Pierre responded,

"You wouldn't know craftsmanship if it was on a dinner menu, you boar. You make toys for children. Choke hazards at that."

"You realize that I can grow more flowers on a compost heap than you could make in a lifetime?"

"I gag just looking at them."

They heard the carriage wheels careen around the tower and the prince's high-heeled boots on the stone. The door slammed open, but the old rivals were far too busy to acknowledge Dimple Pimple.

"What would you do without a *real* flower to copy?"

"What would you do without the money-rich and taste-poor middle class?"

The prince cleared his throat. His trumpeter and his bass drummer remixed a few beats. But Babbo and Pierre had decades of snipes saved up. They shouted over the intro music.

"I always knew you flower quilters were sycophants to actual florists. It's obvious the vases would be better with my painted marbles and a few votives to accent the light."

Pierre's mustache twitched. "You, you . . . hairy man! You've got those glassblowers of Murano over-blowing vases into every fat shape so they need filler. And that's what you make, decorative packing peanuts!"

The prince shouted "—!" The men didn't notice.

"You make forgeries of true beauty."

"You wouldn't know beauty if it was on a dinner menu."

"See? You said that already. You've begun copying *yourself.*"

"Your work looks like deer pellets."

"That's good. I could spread the pellets in my garden and grow flowers for you to steal."

The prince had his trumpets blast the two men into silence. They looked irritated.

"What?" said the two men.

The prince asked if they were ever going to get to work. Pierre answered, "Of course not."

Babbo added, "I'd like brioche toast with my omelet tomorrow."

"That does sound nice. I'd like some, too," said Pierre. Then he turned to Babbo and said, "What do you think, a sweet Italian sausage inside?"

"Yes, with basil and *fleur de sel*," added Babbo, "and cracked pepper on the side."

"Perfect," said Pierre.

The two legends of house decoratives looked at Prince Kaiser with "That will be all" eyebrows. Prince Kaiser Dimple Pimple considered shoving both of them out of the tower window. Then he considered the diplomatic unrest of killing two national treasures. And the expense alone of cleaning the memorial tribute that fans would build around his castle. All those stuffed bears and tacky painted signs. And gum, why do people think prayer walls need gum to be effective?

The prince ground his heel into the stone as he turned. It scraped like a mortar and pestle. As he strutted out, he told them to keep an eye on the courtyard below their tower. The men didn't ask why, but he answered, anyway. Because that's where he'd execute Chloe and Giacomo.

A few minutes later, Babbo and Pierre could make out the figures of their two children trudging across the courtyard with hoods over their heads.

Babbo and Pierre were fear-stricken and held hands as they watched from the tower high above the scaffold. The two young lovers also held hands so that Chloe could support Giacomo in his wobbly half-conscious state. They ascended the stairs toward a portly middle-aged executioner in traditional costume (no shirt, black hood). He had a berserker sword twice the size of his body, used for breaking a cavalry or crushing a boulder. He leaned on it as though it didn't weigh anything.

Giacomo and Chloe looked up beseechingly at their fathers. One could just imagine their horrified expression under the black hoods they wore. Then they kneeled on the block, forsaken.

Babbo chewed on his own mustache. The executioner sighed and raised his sword. Pierre pulled at the remnants of his hair and said, "Tell him we'll do what he says. Tell him—" Babbo inflated his lungs to shout into the courtyard. "WAIT!"

But it was too late. The executioner had made his swing. The massive sword lopped off both the prisoners' heads. They bounced.

Babbo beat his chest. Pierre's heart shattered again along the same cracks as the first time. Chloe walked up behind them and leaned her chin on Pierre's shoulder. "What're you watching?" she said.

Babbo and Pierre whipped around. They bellowed their joy, hugged Chloe, and wept some more. Chloe never got the answer to her question, which would have been something like, "An elaborate staged execution of you and your boyfriend." When the prince looked up from the edge of the courtyard and didn't see the faces of the two craftsmen dotting the window frame, he was again furious.

The prince had dragged Vlad the Regaler from his loft in Moscow and even let him direct, as well as star, in the charade. Vlad had played the executioner, a silent yet emotionally complex role.

The victims were actually cantaloupes inside the hoods. The two supporting actors ducked their heads into their collars and let the melons fall. I was there by sheer coincidence. A pigeon flying overhead got a bug in its throat, choked, and crashed onto the courtyard stones not ten seconds later.

Prince Kaiser stormed off, ordered the doctors out of Giacomo's room, and almost killed him when he grabbed Giacomo by the hair and said in his ear, "—."

It was pretty standard evil-guy stuff. Something like: "As soon as this is over, I will butcher you personally. I'll give your body to Brutessa for dinner, and I'll bronze Chloe into a naked statue on my front lawn."

Okay, maybe not so standard.

In the tower, Chloe explained everything to the dads. Her plan, for now, was to nurse Giacomo back to health. After that, escape. She would sneak around the castle in search of food and medicine. There were plenty of empty rooms to hide in now that so many artists had been murdered. But more than anything, she needed Babbo and Pierre to quit angering the prince. They would have to work together. Pierre took off his glasses and cleaned them on his sleeve. Babbo looked off into the far corner of the ceiling. "Isn't their some *other* way?" said Pierre.

"Yeah," said Babbo. "Couldn't we just stop throwing things at each other?"

"We're geniuses, you know," said Pierre.

"We have genius ways," added Babbo.

"No," said Chloe. Pierre's mustache twitched. Chloe's freckle above her lip twitched even more. "I love him," said Chloe, "and I love you. Now, sit." After all her years of acquiescence, Chloe had finally stood up for herself. Nobody could refuse her, especially not those two. Giovanni Babbo Chianti and Pierre Vouvray finally had to agree on something.

As she left, she leaned up and kissed Babbo on the cheek. Then she hugged her father and kissed him twice. "Please be good, Daddy."

"Be safe," he said.

"Don't worry," she said. "You forget I've wilted once already. Fate must have a different plan for me than simply getting beheaded and dropped in a ditch."

This happens a lot with people who refer to me as Fate. But as I said, I don't do any of the planning. And I've found plenty of people lying in ditches. I have a huge tramp collection. But it was nice of her to comfort Pierre.

She rushed out. Babbo was still blushing, with a hand on his cheek. He jostled Pierre with a pat on the back and said, "She's wonderful."

"I know," said Pierre. "It's yours that's the problem."

"Nope," said Babbo. "They'll have fat and talented babies."

Prince Kaiser and Chloe almost passed each other in the hall. As she ran down the grand stairway, Chloe heard the thunder of hoof-beats and raced back up the stairs. She stayed barely in front of the horses as she circled the massive tower. Finally, she reached the landing and flattened herself to the wall on the left. Prince Kaiser's horse galloped up the stairs and went right. Chloe snuck back down as Prince Kaiser dismounted the horse, kicked open the door, and blitzed into the room. The prince was so enraged that he was willing to wreck his own plans and kill both of the old artists. Instead, he found Babbo and Pierre bent over their tables, working in silence. They looked quite similar, actually, in their finely tuned focus. The prince opened his mouth to shout, rethought the idea, and closed it again. Babbo's precision, as he cut a marble in half with the Hair from the Chest of the Monster Bernardo the Hammer, was not something to interrupt. Likewise, Pierre was stitching the stamens on a posy of baby's breath—a process so delicate it required even the baby to stop breathing. The prince didn't have anything to do but wheel back around a second time and leave.

Chapter 17

∞

The Dawn of
The Dads

TO DESCRIBE THE work of Babbo and Pierre, as they combined their craftsmanship for the sake of their kids' lives, is a job I'm not up for. The thing is, I'm what you might call a closer, a cleaner, a last-call kind of guy. I'm not a morning person. The glass is all empty and has shattered on the floor. Feel me? I watch stuff break. The great and terrible ballet of destruction.

So if I see Chloe, and I tell you her lips were nova, her smile was supernova, it's because I've seen about a million stars explode with a brilliant but terminal glow. I know Giacomo is a good guy 'cause I've seen him cradling his piglet as it bled out a wolf bite. I know Brutessa and Dimple Pimple, because their insides have extensive rot.

But what the dads were doing in that tower, that's about as far from my expertise as eons are from ions. They were creating something. Giving it life, in its own way. Making the new. I wouldn't know what that looks like. I'll tell you, though; I bet it's wonderful.

*   *   *

Inside the city limits of the castle, everyone was silent under penalty of dwarf. Word had spread that the masters were finally working together. As the cooks made cold, quiet meals of bologna and coleslaw, they snuck glances out their windows of the north tower. It seemed like a constant trail of colored smoke flowed from Babbo's annealing oven.

The surviving artists considered themselves saved. The prince's attention was entirely on the tower. He listened at the door for hours at a time, but all he could hear was Babbo as he hummed, then whistled, sang a few bars, then asked something like, "What do you think, Vouvray, magenta?"

Pierre responded with a grunt. Babbo considered it, then said, "You're right. I didn't even think of that. But what do I do with all this magenta I already mixed?"

By the end of the third straight day, the north tower had washes of every color streaking down its side.

During this time, it was Chloe who had it hardest. She had to evade Brutessa's murderous hunt but also tend to Giacomo, since the doctors had been ordered away. She spent the three days running through the castle, stealing towels and soup in a locked-down complex full of guards, servants, and land pirates.

She almost collapsed from exhaustion. When she stole into Giacomo's room that third day, Giacomo stirred in his semi-conscious state and groaned something indecipherable. He seemed to be recovering. For the first time in three days, Chloe smiled. The curtains had been pulled back, and the light seemed to admire her with its shine. Anyone could fall in love with Chloe.

Except for Brutessa, who tore out from behind the curtain in a simple rage. The pirate queen lunged at Chloe, let loose a war cry, and swung her arms like wagon wheels.

Chloe managed to sidestep the dwarf's first pass. A bust of Dimple Pimple at the age of five was not so lucky. Chloe scrambled to the other side of the room, behind Giacomo's bed, hoping Brutessa would slow down rather than hurt her jealously guarded prize. She was wrong. Brutessa ripped the footboard off the bed frame with one hand. The bed jerked. Giacomo groaned. Chloe darted from behind the bed, so that the enraged land pirate wouldn't trample over Giacomo's sternum.

Brutessa gave chase. She rounded the corners of Chloe's path, in order to make up for her own shorter stride. The result was that they ran in circles, with Chloe just out of reach, Brutessa crashing down behind her, and a wake of shattered things trailing them both.

At some point, the Prince Kaiser made his entrance, but Chloe couldn't hear anything other than banging and war cries. The prince had to shout to tell Chloe that it was over for her—no one could keep Brutessa from mauling her—but if she wanted to save Giacomo, she'd at least tell him what the dads were up to. In turn, the prince would keep Giacomo safe from marriage to Brutessa.

The prince never got an answer, because Brutessa managed a glancing blow across Chloe's shoulder blade. Chloe yowled in pain as she slammed into the wall and fell to the ground. Brutessa rushed forward to stomp Chloe's head through the wooden floor, when suddenly the door swung open and a blinding light filled the room.

Chapter 18
The End of Ends

BABBO AND PIERRE had created a vase of marbles and fake flowers so perfect that it seemed to cast its own light. This was the *magnum opus* of all mankind, beauty that was Truth, a piece of home furnishing that could, in fact, refurnish the empty halls of our sin-addled souls.

When the two men entered the room, the light from the window hit the vase and was reflected and refracted a thousand times in the prism of every marble, a glare bright enough to halt even Brutessa's charge.

Prince Kaiser Dimple Pimple marveled at the vase. It was exactly what he wanted. The men had built him the morning sun. He ran up and grabbed the Objet. Then Brutessa ran up and grabbed it from him. The tentative partnership they had developed all that time ago in the ditch, next to the prince's wrecked carriage, was dissolved. All Brutessa cared about was winning Giacomo—the Objet was just another weapon to her.

She ran to Chloe, who was leaning against the wall, and held up the vase in front of her. "Ooohh," said Chloe, immediately mesmerized. Brutessa moved the Objet to the left. Chloe's head followed. The Objet went to the right. Chloe turned to the right. With her target fully transfixed, Brutessa wound up and let fly a punch toward Chloe's head that could have dropped a rhino. Chloe didn't even flinch. She was staring at the vase. Pierre screamed, *"Non!"*

Bone crunched as Brutessa's fist pounded into a jaw. But it wasn't Chloe's. It was Giacomo's face that she battered. He had wrested himself from the bed and stumbled into the way of Brutessa's kill shot just in time. Even healthy, it wouldn't have mattered.

Giacomo slumped to the floor, lifeless at Chloe's feet. Brutessa's arm was still extended in disbelief.

It was Babbo's turn to scream in pain. He ran to Giacomo and crouched over his son. The old man wept into his boy's chest. The once-broad shoulders of Babbo Giovanni broke. I let him have a moment. Chloe kneeled down and put a hand on Babbo's shoulder. It was so delicate and small, I can't imagine he felt any of the consolation.

When it dawned on Brutessa what she had done, she put back her head and howled like a beast. Then she ran to the window of the cliffside northeast wing and plunged out. I knew I'd have to go get her next.

But first, I had to put my hand on Babbo, to let him know it was time. He didn't let go of his son, and I became distracted, anyway, by the sound of someone laughing.

It was Dimple Pimple. He'd picked up the Objet, and he was looking at me. He said something like: Welcome.

I usually keep a low profile, so I didn't say anything. The prince said all this stuff about his plan going perfectly, even down to the dwarf offing herself. That was when I got the feeling something was wrong. I couldn't figure it out, but I knew there was something.

The prince said something along the lines of: Now that you're here, you should know, I've been wanting to meet you for years. I said something like: That could have easily been arranged, and he laughed at me like I was so naive.

I cut the crap. "What do you want?" I said. And he said he wanted my job. Can you believe that? The kid wanted my job. Man, don't tempt me. Like I'm loving this beat or something.

Anyway, Prince Kaiser said that's what the Objet was for. His real plan was to kill me and take my place. Immortality, ultimate power, and all that. Didn't even realize I'm just a gopher. He wanted it.

He raised the vase over his head, and that was when I realized what was wrong with the scene. I said, "Hey, Pimple, hold on."

He didn't hold on—he smashed the vase over my head. I blacked out for a second on the way to one knee. Marbles rolled down my shirt and into my pants. I tried to shake the dizziness out of my head, but the only thing that shook off was a nosegay of lilies. The prince didn't waste time. He came over and kicked me right in the gut.

I took it and stumbled back. As he came up to hit me again, I said, "How do you think you're talking to me?"

He put a left hook right into my eye socket, harder than you'd expect, and said he'd been waiting to kill Giacomo for that exact reason. And now he'd jumped me when I came for him.

I stumbled back, and he kept coming. He uppercut, then grabbed my shoulders and put his knee right into my chest. I felt three ribs crack inside me as I doubled over and tried to catch my breath. I saw he'd gotten a jagged chunk of the vase in his fist, and he was about to cut me open when I said, "Yeah, I get the plan, but why do you think *you* can see me?"

He stopped. He hadn't thought of that. I stood up straight and said, "Huh?" He didn't have anything, just mumbled something about the Objet d'Awesome! And I said, "You thought a vase full of fake flowers and some marbles would make you a god? The glass is made of sand. Who do you think invented sand?"

I couldn't tell you if the Big Guy was laughing up there. I figure not. But I was definitely enjoying myself. Prince Kaiser did the "But . . . but . . . but" routine.

I told him, "You can see me 'cause you had an aneurysm back there. You know that tingly feeling? It wasn't deity. It was a vein in your head bursting from all the stress you've been putting on yourself. You really should have tried some hot tea. It's good for you."

The prince glazed over. The piece of glass clattered to the ground. He followed it down.

I fast-tracked him and then Brutessa. Then I came back for Giacomo.

Chapter 19

The Dirt Snap

THERE'S THIS JOKE Dora tells that I really like. It goes: A group of scientists come together for a convention, or symposium, or whatever. And they say, "You know, we've got all kinds of stuff figured out, what with nano-machines, and genomes, and cloning and everything. I bet if we put our heads together, we could build a human being better than God."

So they go up to God, and they say, "God, you did pretty well with making us, but we think we've got you beat."

And God thinks about it for a bit, and then He says, "All right, why don't we have a contest. We'll each make a man and see whose is better. But let's do it the old way, Adam style, with nothing but dirt."

The scientists say they'll take the challenge, so they huddle together and start fiddling in the dirt, taking samples to see how they can genetically recombine it into a human, when God says, "Whoa, whoa there. What do you think you're doing? Make your own dirt."

That makes me laugh every time. And I suppose you could take out scientists and insert spoiled princes with mass-market home accessories, albeit the best art man has ever seen.

When I came back for Babbo's son, I knew I'd have to take Babbo's heart, too. I tried to get his attention, but the mountainous man was still sobbing. What was I supposed to do? I started to leave with what I had come for, when I heard him say in between sobs, "You can't. You owe him." I knew he was talking to me, and he could see me just fine.

It was a weird thing to say, though, until I remembered. I did owe him. All those years back, when I took his mother, I had promised Giacomo a favor. Serves me right.

I remember thinking: *Dora is going to be so ticked at this paperwork.*

A part of me didn't want to return Giacomo. As I stood there, looking at Chloe, the only thing I wanted was for the prince to have been right. Maybe if he could have killed me, I'd end up here, next to her. And maybe I could have a life. I'll admit I wanted that.

But I never wanted to see her crying the way she was. And who knows? Maybe I wouldn't be her type, anyway.

I turned and walked out.

I got this shivering feeling as I left. Like seeing the Objet for the first time. But not a regular shiver. Anyone can get a shiver up their spine: just get out of a swimming pool. This is on the *inside* of your spine. Try to imagine it. Inside, behind your stomach. Right there in the middle of you. Felt good.

Giacomo gasped and said, "Get off me," in a weak voice. Babbo jumped up. Pierre hugged Babbo—Babbo hugged Pierre. They hugged and jumped while Chloe leaned over Giacomo and purred, "Co-Co," as she kissed him. I didn't have any reason to watch the rest. In fact, I didn't have a reason to visit Co-Co and Clo-Clo for decades.

There. Happily ever after. Finally.

Chapter 20

The Jolly
Codger

BUT MAYBE YOU'D like to know how they went out. In the end, I mean, since all my stories end with everybody interred. It might seem like a gyp if I didn't at least mention it.

Well, Pierre and Babbo became inseparable once they realized how much Pierre loved Italian food and Babbo loved French food. It doesn't take much sometimes. They continued to work together in a shared work space, with Babbo talking nonstop and Pierre grunting a reply now and then.

As grandpas, they were doters. They spent so much time talking and thinking about the babies that they even changed their business. Instead of quilted flowers and painted marbles in vases, Babbo and Pierre teamed up to make the first mobiles Old Timey Europe had ever seen. Plush dolls, shiny painted beads—it made sense.

In addition, Babbo was expert in horsey and piggyback rides, while Pierre handled all the questions about why some rocks look like clouds and some clouds look like castles in the sky.

*　*　*

When I found Pierre in his study, still holding the quilted carnation his granddaughter had given him that night—her first ever—he saw me and sighed. "That was something. Did you see that? That was *really* something."

Babbo picked me up in a bear hug when I came back for him a few months later. It was in the middle of a song, in the middle of dinner. He plopped me down and said, "Now, let's go catch up with that French prune or he'll think he's beaten me."

As for Chloe and Giacomo, they fell, too. You all do, eventually. And I guess what I've been saying is it doesn't have to be so bad. You shake my hand. We talk. Dora gives you candy, and then you get what you came for.

I think the hope is that somewhere along the way, you craft yourself some love. Some of that thing you can only say what it is with laughing. And then you're really sharing your life. So then you croak. So what?

Like Co-Co and Clo-Clo. They were old and holding hands— went together, if you'll believe it. I still didn't have any words for her, so she came up and kissed me on the cheek. She always had a way about that. And then she turned and said, "Hey, Co-Co, what did you have for lunch?"

And he said, "A Doom sandwich!"

Then the two idiots squish me in between them.

The End.